# THE DEEP™

kaboom!™

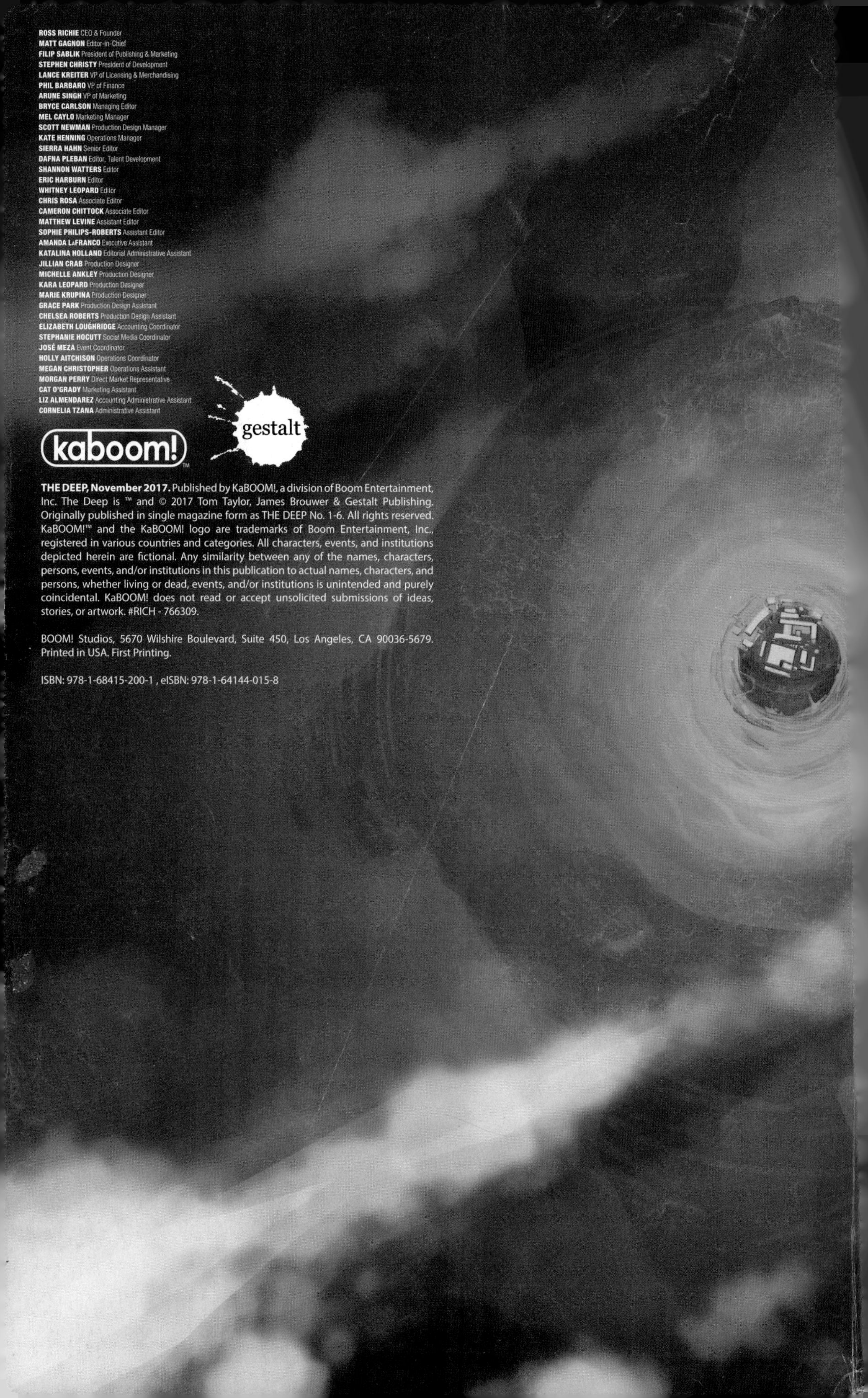



kaboom!™ gestalt

**THE DEEP, November 2017.** Published by KaBOOM!, a division of Boom Entertainment, Inc. 

BOOM! Studios, 5670 Wilshire Boulevard, Suite 450, Los Angeles, CA 90036-5679. Printed in USA. First Printing.

ISBN: 978-1-68415-200-1 , eISBN: 978-1-64144-015-8

# THE DEEP

Created by
**Tom Taylor & James Brouwer**

Written by
**Tom Taylor**

Illustrated by
**James Brouwer**

Lettered by
**Wolfgang Bylsma**

Cover by
**James Brouwer**

Logo Design and
Original Art Director
**Skye Ogden**

Original Assistant Editor
**Gary Edwards**

Original Editor
**Wolfgang Bylsma**

Designer
**Kara Leopard**

BOOM! Studios Editors
**Dafna Pleban**
**Jasmine Amiri**

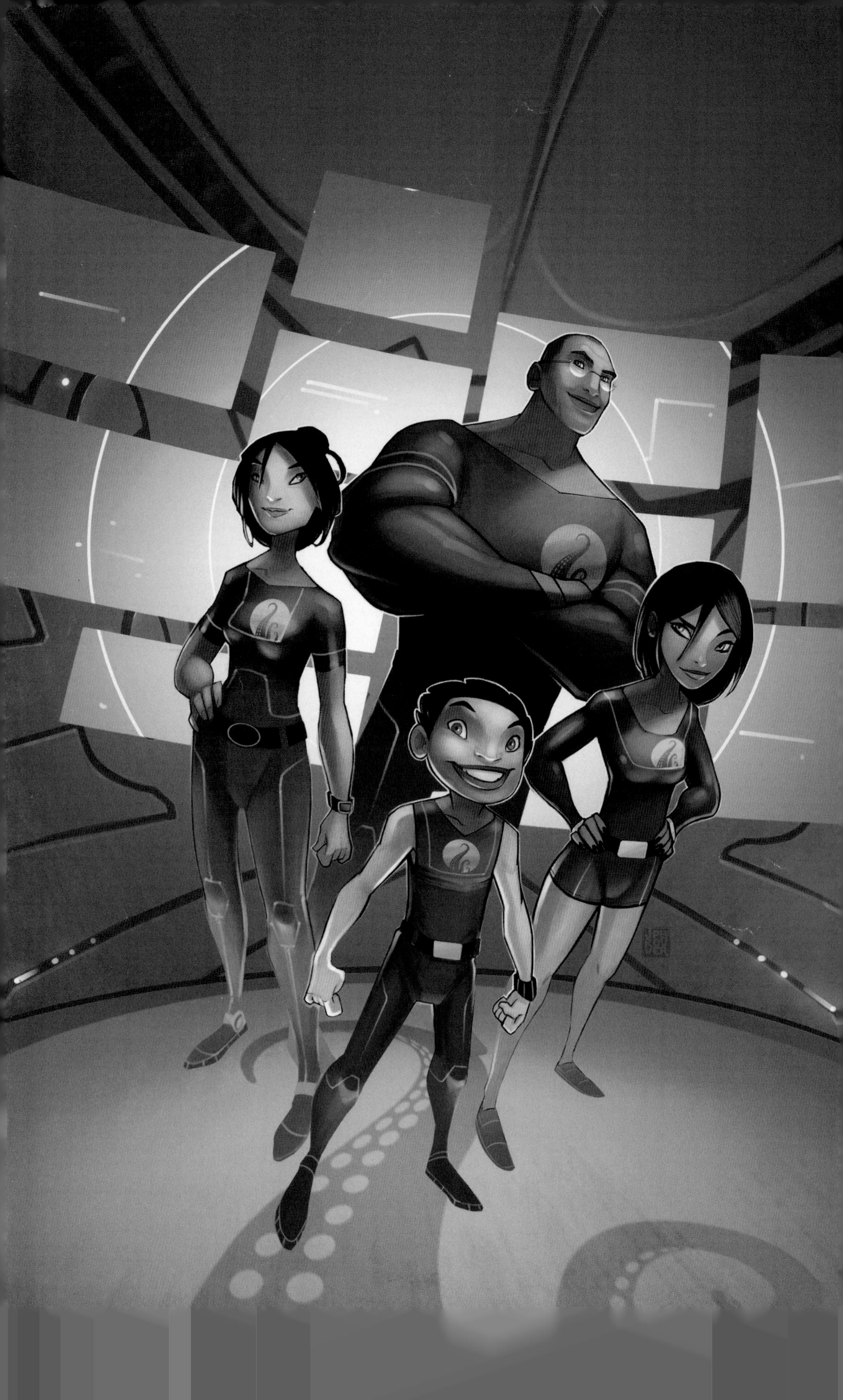

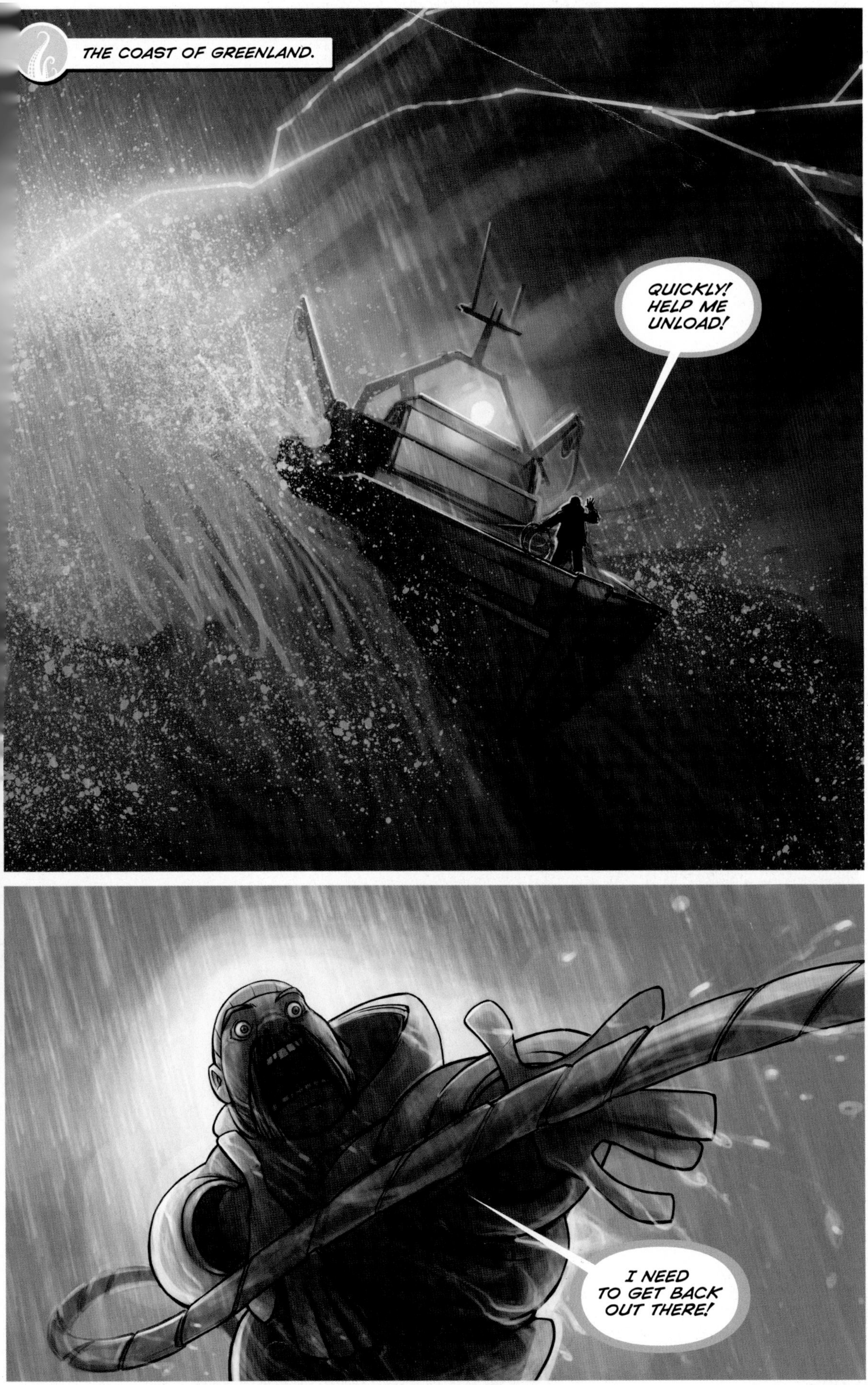
THE COAST OF GREENLAND.
QUICKLY! HELP ME UNLOAD!
I NEED TO GET BACK OUT THERE!

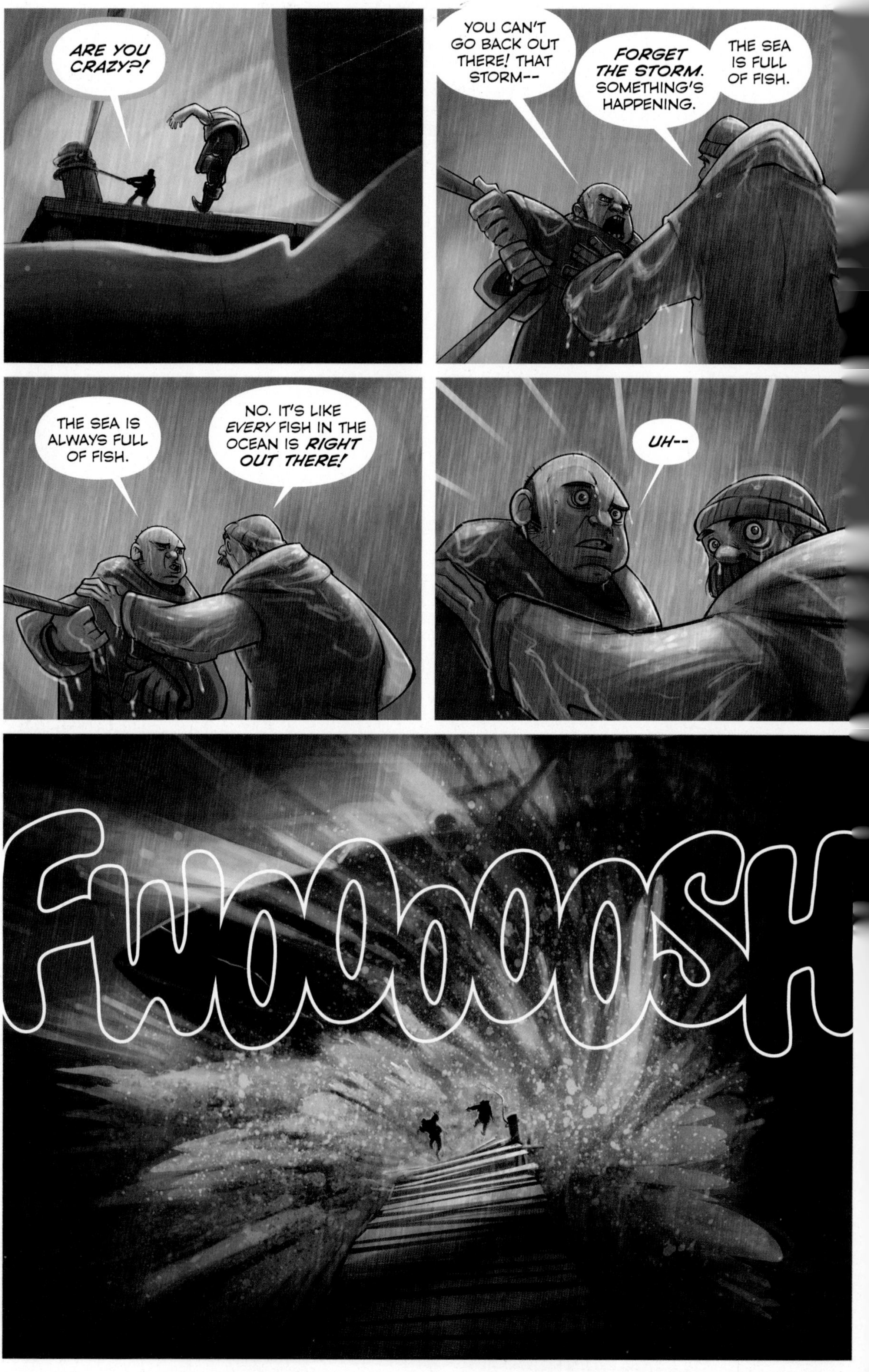
ARE YOU CRAZY?!
YOU CAN'T GO BACK OUT THERE! THAT STORM--
FORGET THE STORM. SOMETHING'S HAPPENING.
THE SEA IS FULL OF FISH.
THE SEA IS ALWAYS FULL OF FISH.
NO. IT'S LIKE EVERY FISH IN THE OCEAN IS RIGHT OUT THERE!
UH--
FWOOOOOSH

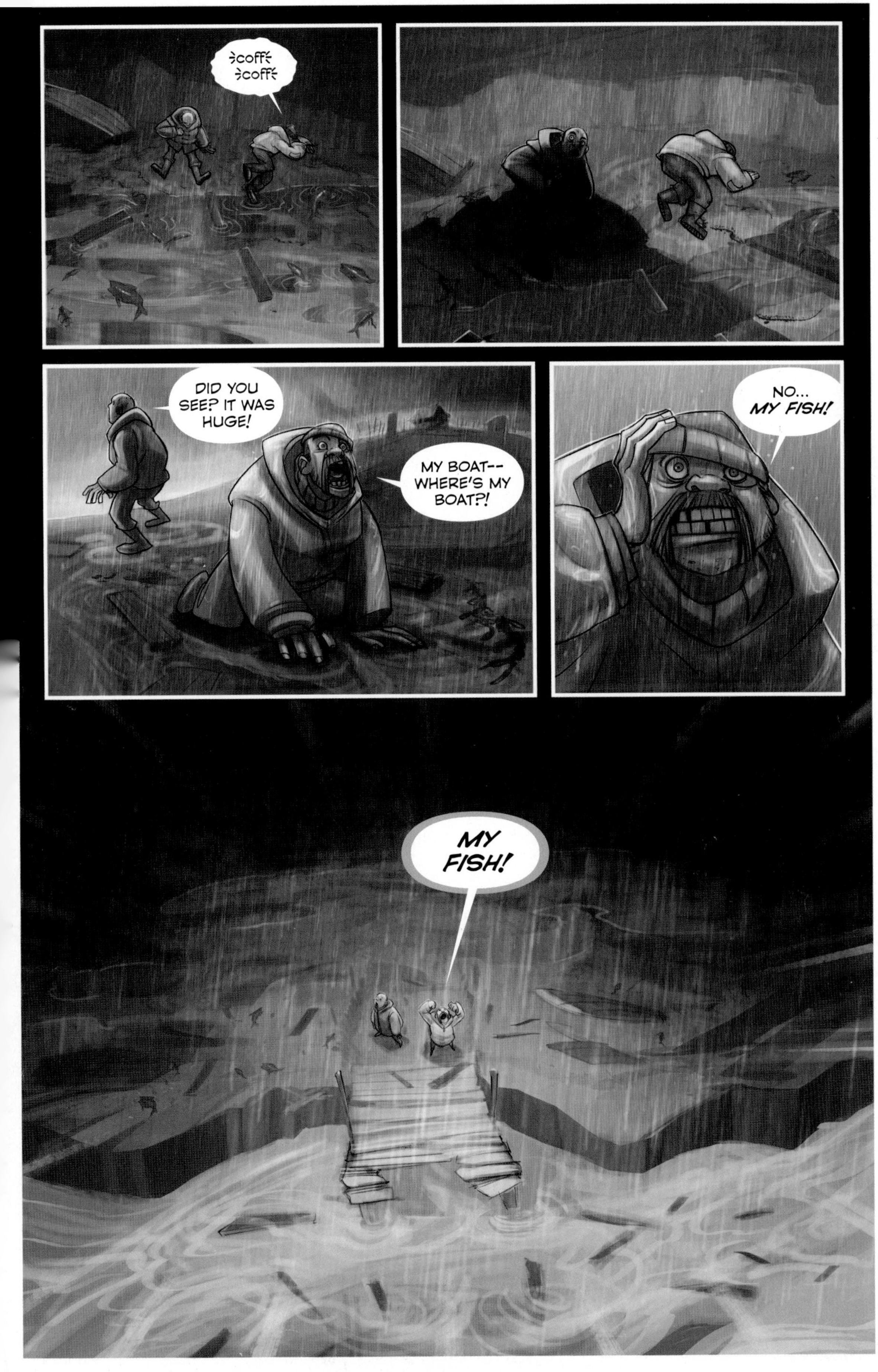
coff
coff
DID YOU SEE? IT WAS HUGE!
MY BOAT-- WHERE'S MY BOAT?!
NO... *MY FISH!*
*MY FISH!*

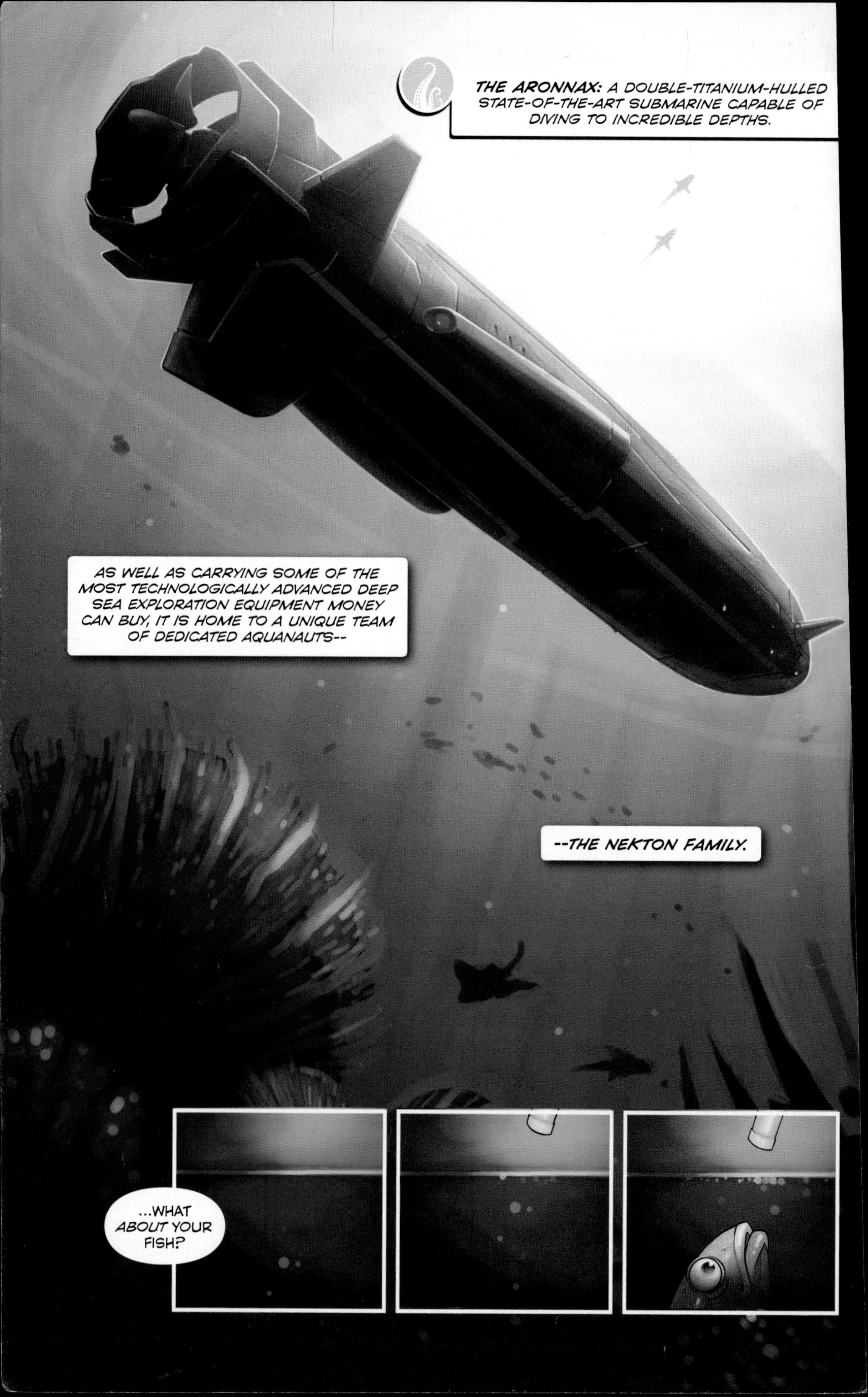
THE ARONNAX: A DOUBLE-TITANIUM-HULLED STATE-OF-THE-ART SUBMARINE CAPABLE OF DIVING TO INCREDIBLE DEPTHS.
AS WELL AS CARRYING SOME OF THE MOST TECHNOLOGICALLY ADVANCED DEEP SEA EXPLORATION EQUIPMENT MONEY CAN BUY, IT IS HOME TO A UNIQUE TEAM OF DEDICATED AQUANAUTS--
--THE NEKTON FAMILY.
...WHAT ABOUT YOUR FISH?

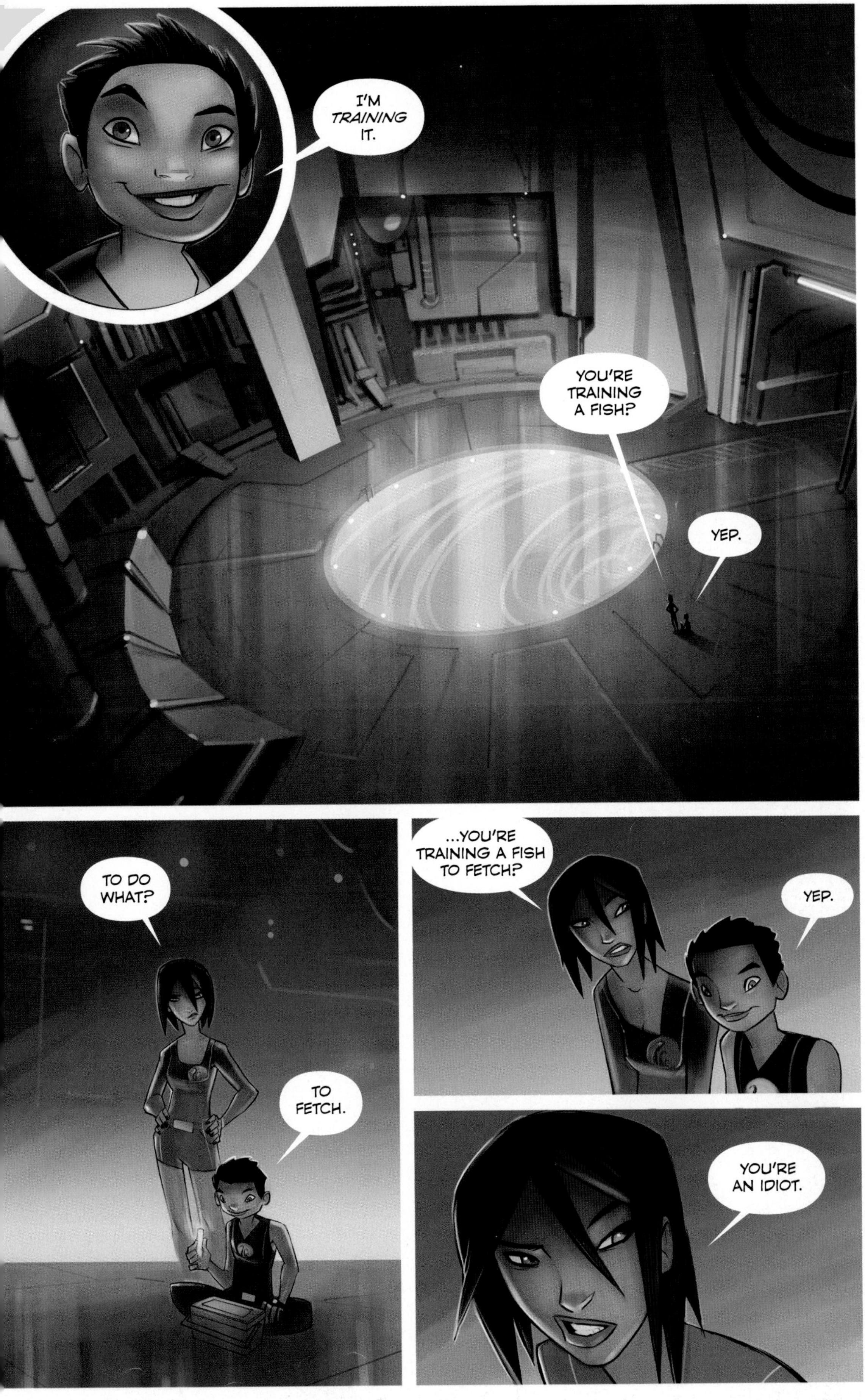
I'M *TRAINING* IT.
YOU'RE TRAINING A FISH?
YEP.
TO DO WHAT?
TO FETCH.
...YOU'RE TRAINING A FISH TO FETCH?
YEP.
YOU'RE AN IDIOT.

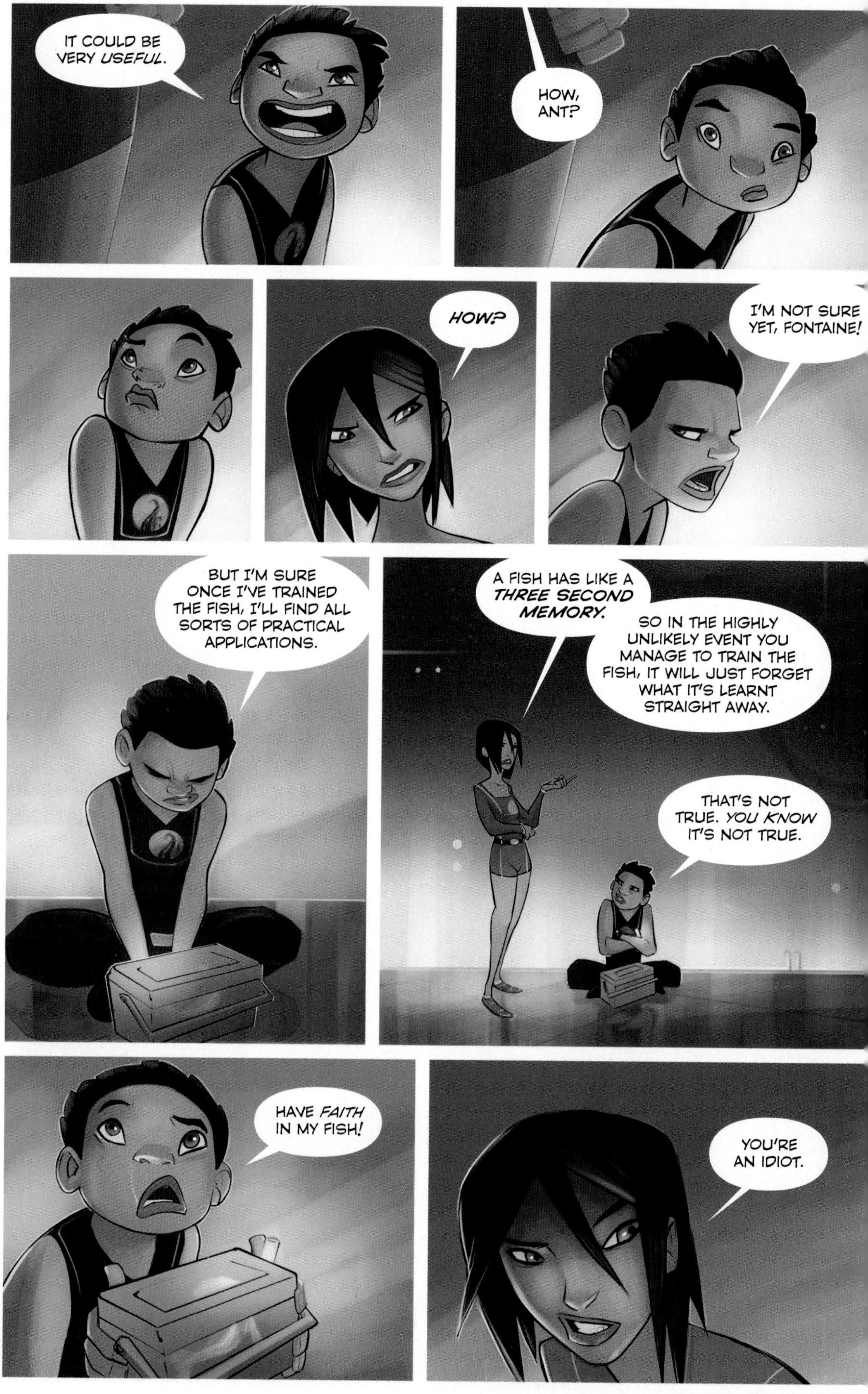
IT COULD BE VERY *USEFUL*.
HOW, ANT?
*HOW?*
I'M NOT SURE YET, FONTAINE!
BUT I'M SURE ONCE I'VE TRAINED THE FISH, I'LL FIND ALL SORTS OF PRACTICAL APPLICATIONS.
A FISH HAS LIKE A ***THREE SECOND MEMORY.***
SO IN THE HIGHLY UNLIKELY EVENT YOU MANAGE TO TRAIN THE FISH, IT WILL JUST FORGET WHAT IT'S LEARNT STRAIGHT AWAY.
THAT'S NOT TRUE. *YOU KNOW* IT'S NOT TRUE.
HAVE *FAITH* IN MY FISH!
YOU'RE AN IDIOT.

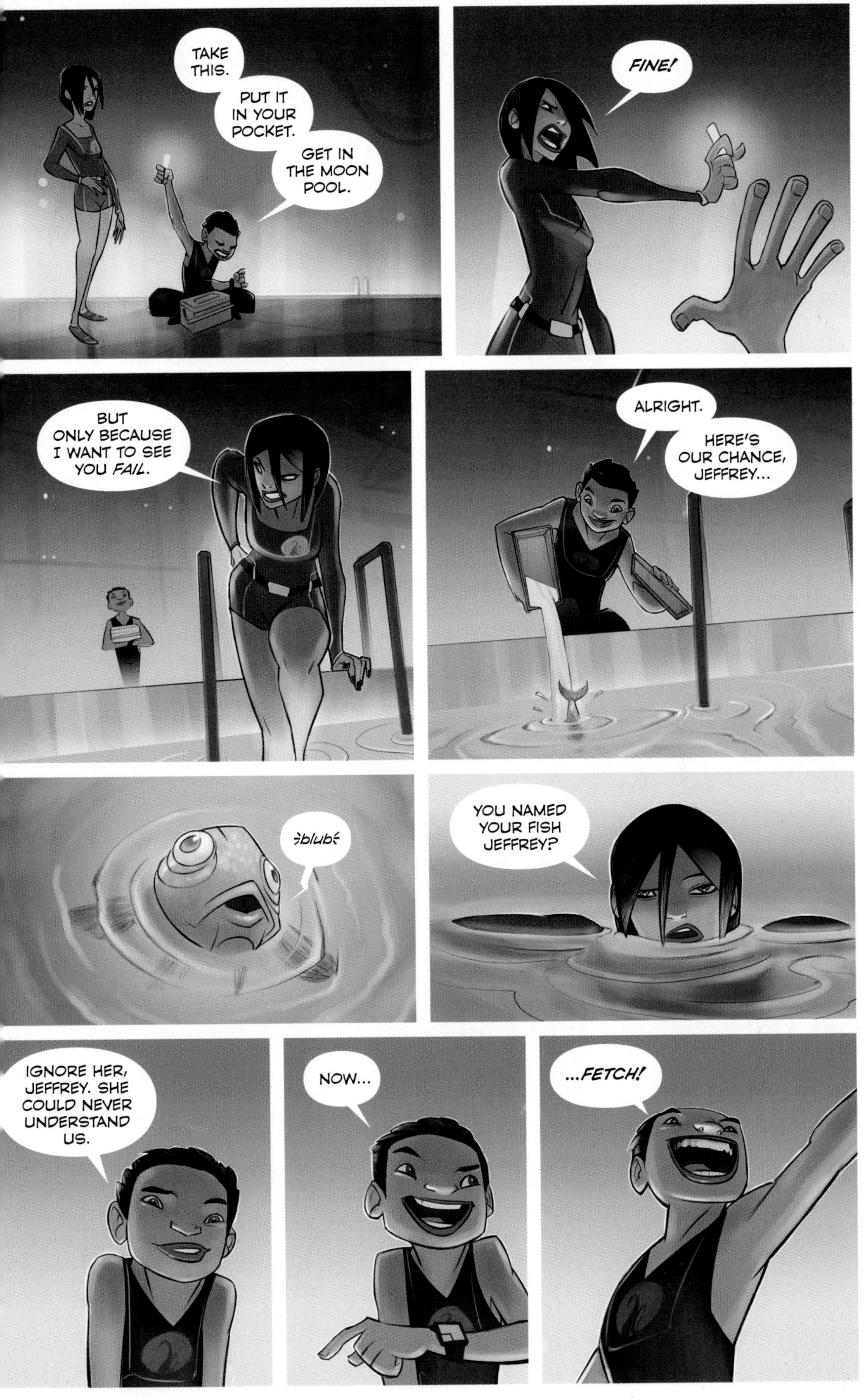
TAKE THIS.
PUT IT IN YOUR POCKET.
GET IN THE MOON POOL.
FINE!
BUT ONLY BECAUSE I WANT TO SEE YOU FAIL.
ALRIGHT.
HERE'S OUR CHANCE, JEFFREY...
blub
YOU NAMED YOUR FISH JEFFREY?
IGNORE HER, JEFFREY. SHE COULD NEVER UNDERSTAND US.
NOW...
...FETCH!

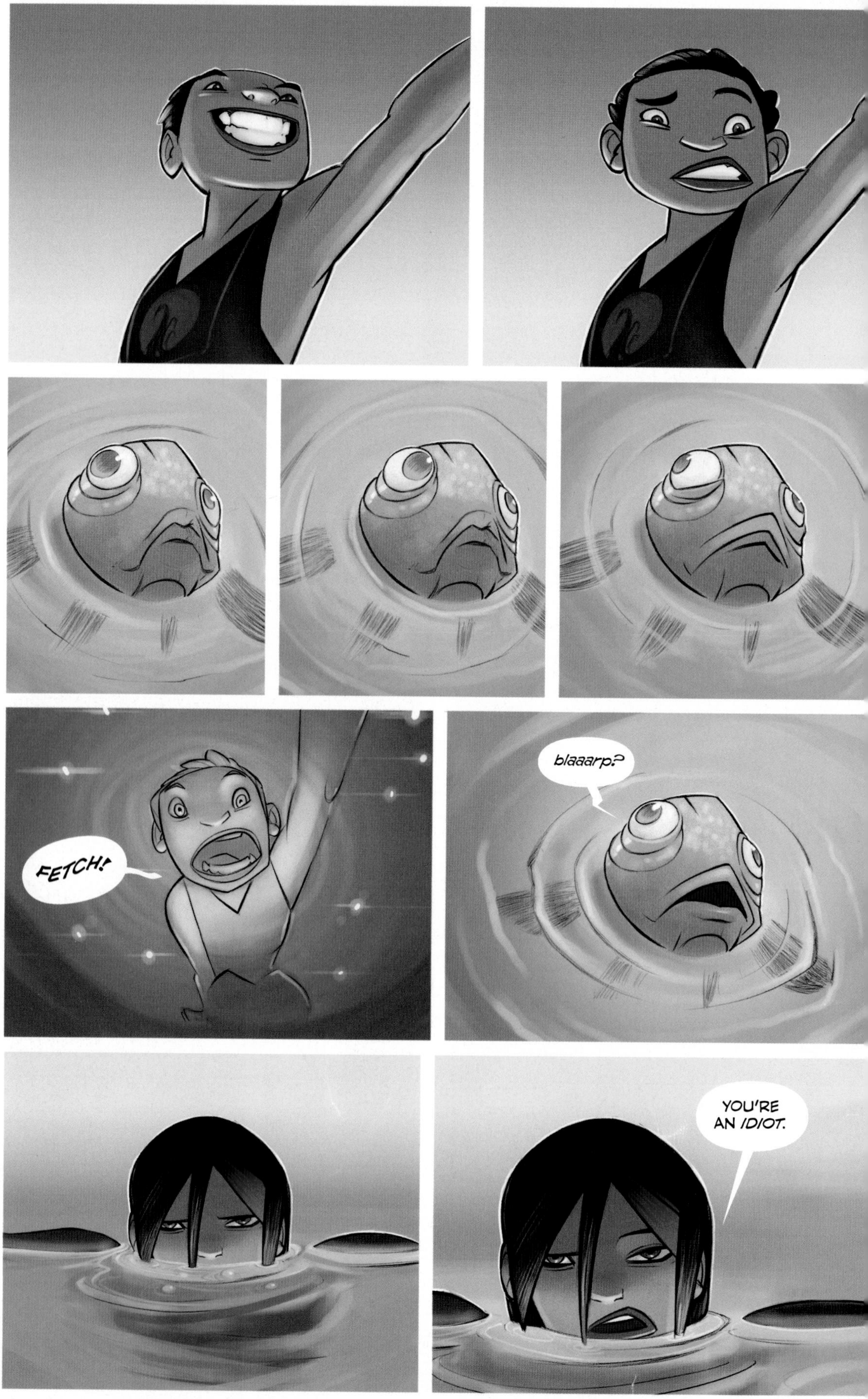
FETCH!
blaaarp?
YOU'RE AN *IDIOT*.

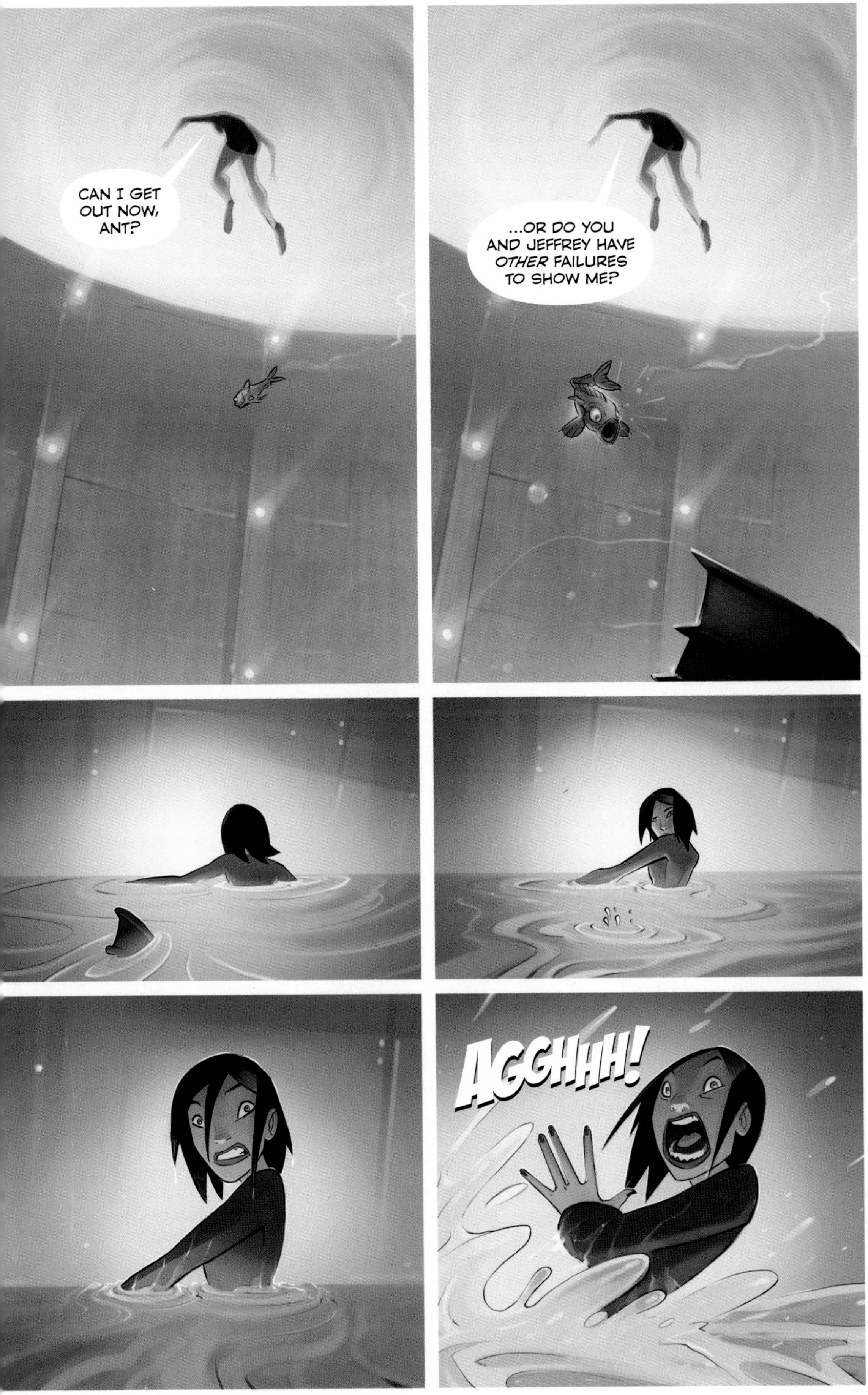
CAN I GET OUT NOW, ANT?
...OR DO YOU AND JEFFREY HAVE *OTHER* FAILURES TO SHOW ME?
AGGHHH!

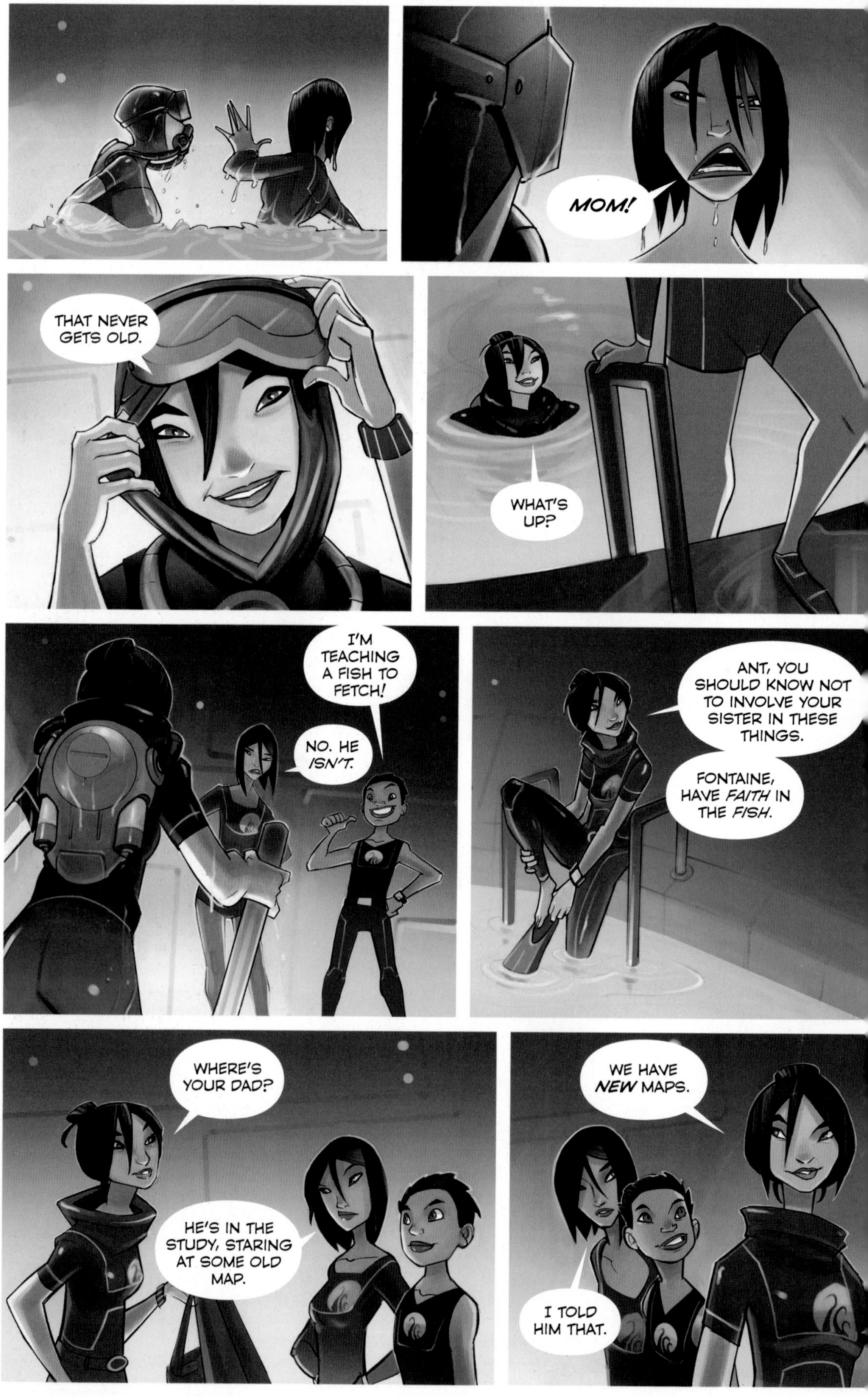
MOM!
THAT NEVER GETS OLD.
WHAT'S UP?
I'M TEACHING A FISH TO FETCH!
NO. HE ISN'T.
ANT, YOU SHOULD KNOW NOT TO INVOLVE YOUR SISTER IN THESE THINGS.
FONTAINE, HAVE FAITH IN THE FISH.
WHERE'S YOUR DAD?
HE'S IN THE STUDY, STARING AT SOME OLD MAP.
WE HAVE NEW MAPS.
I TOLD HIM THAT.

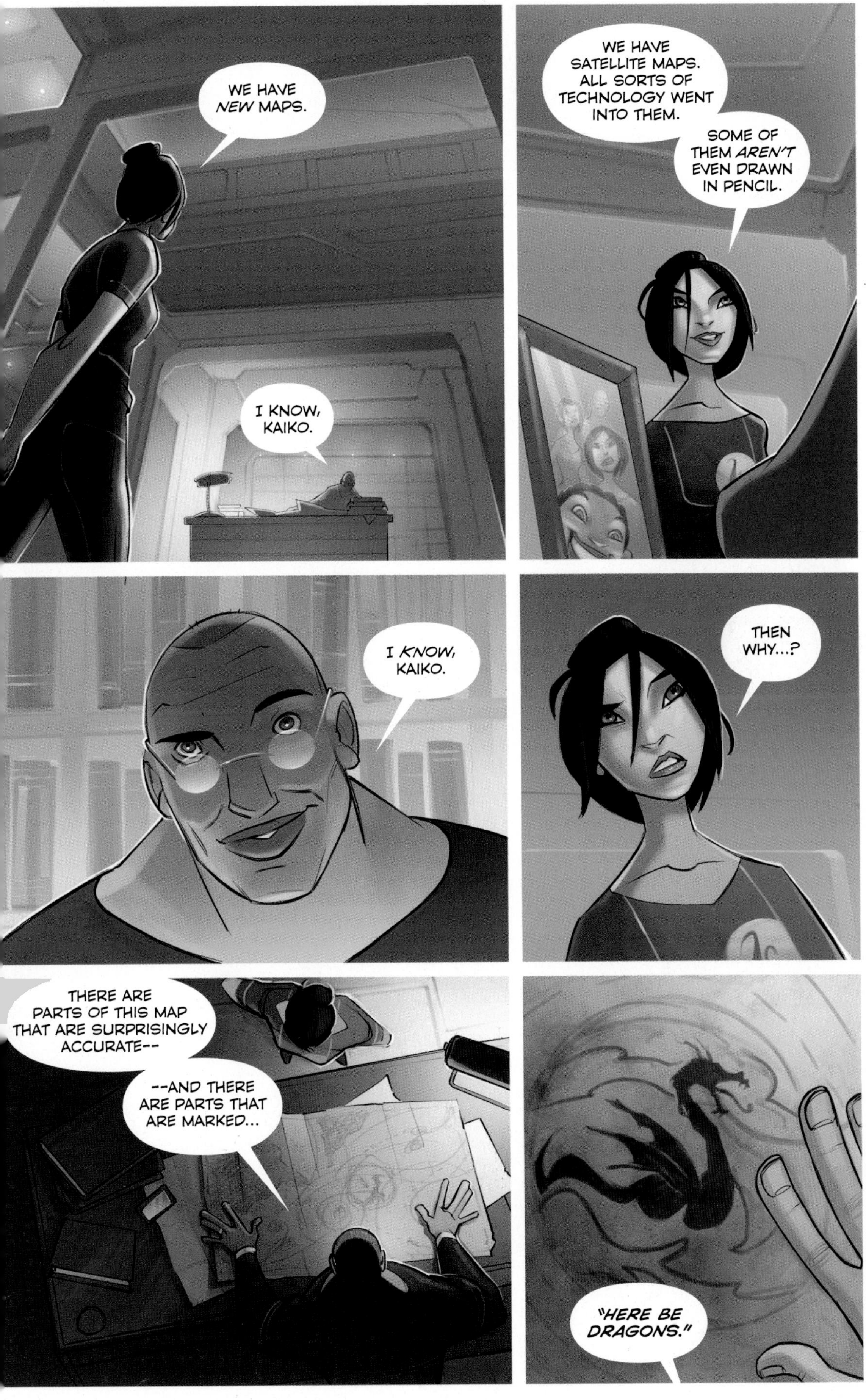
WE HAVE *NEW* MAPS.
I KNOW, KAIKO.
WE HAVE SATELLITE MAPS. ALL SORTS OF TECHNOLOGY WENT INTO THEM.
SOME OF THEM *AREN'T* EVEN DRAWN IN PENCIL.
I *KNOW*, KAIKO.
THEN WHY...?
THERE ARE PARTS OF THIS MAP THAT ARE SURPRISINGLY ACCURATE--
--AND THERE ARE PARTS THAT ARE MARKED...
*"HERE BE DRAGONS."*

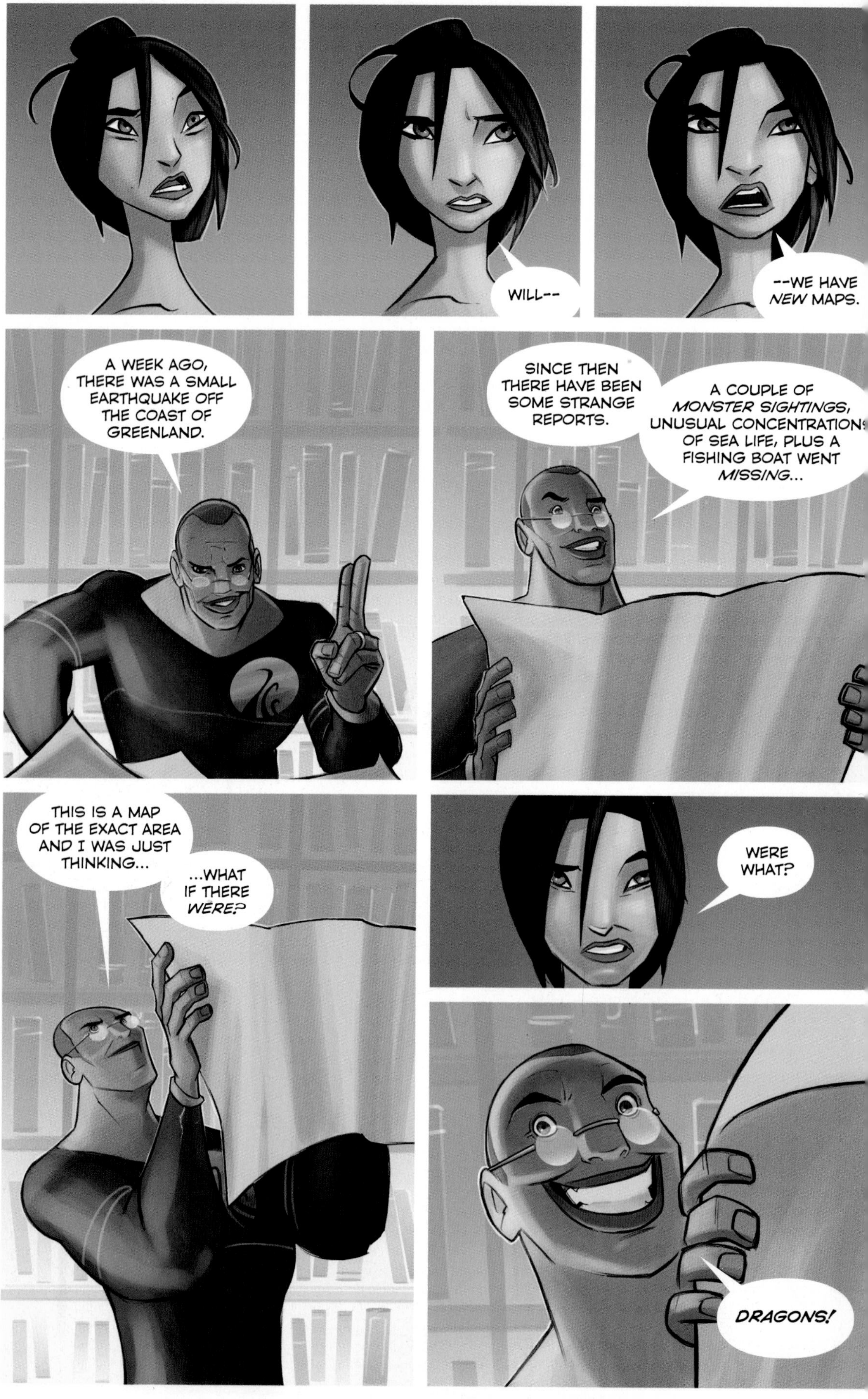
WILL--
--WE HAVE NEW MAPS.
A WEEK AGO, THERE WAS A SMALL EARTHQUAKE OFF THE COAST OF GREENLAND.
SINCE THEN THERE HAVE BEEN SOME STRANGE REPORTS.
A COUPLE OF MONSTER SIGHTINGS, UNUSUAL CONCENTRATIONS OF SEA LIFE, PLUS A FISHING BOAT WENT MISSING...
THIS IS A MAP OF THE EXACT AREA AND I WAS JUST THINKING...
...WHAT IF THERE WERE?
WERE WHAT?
DRAGONS!

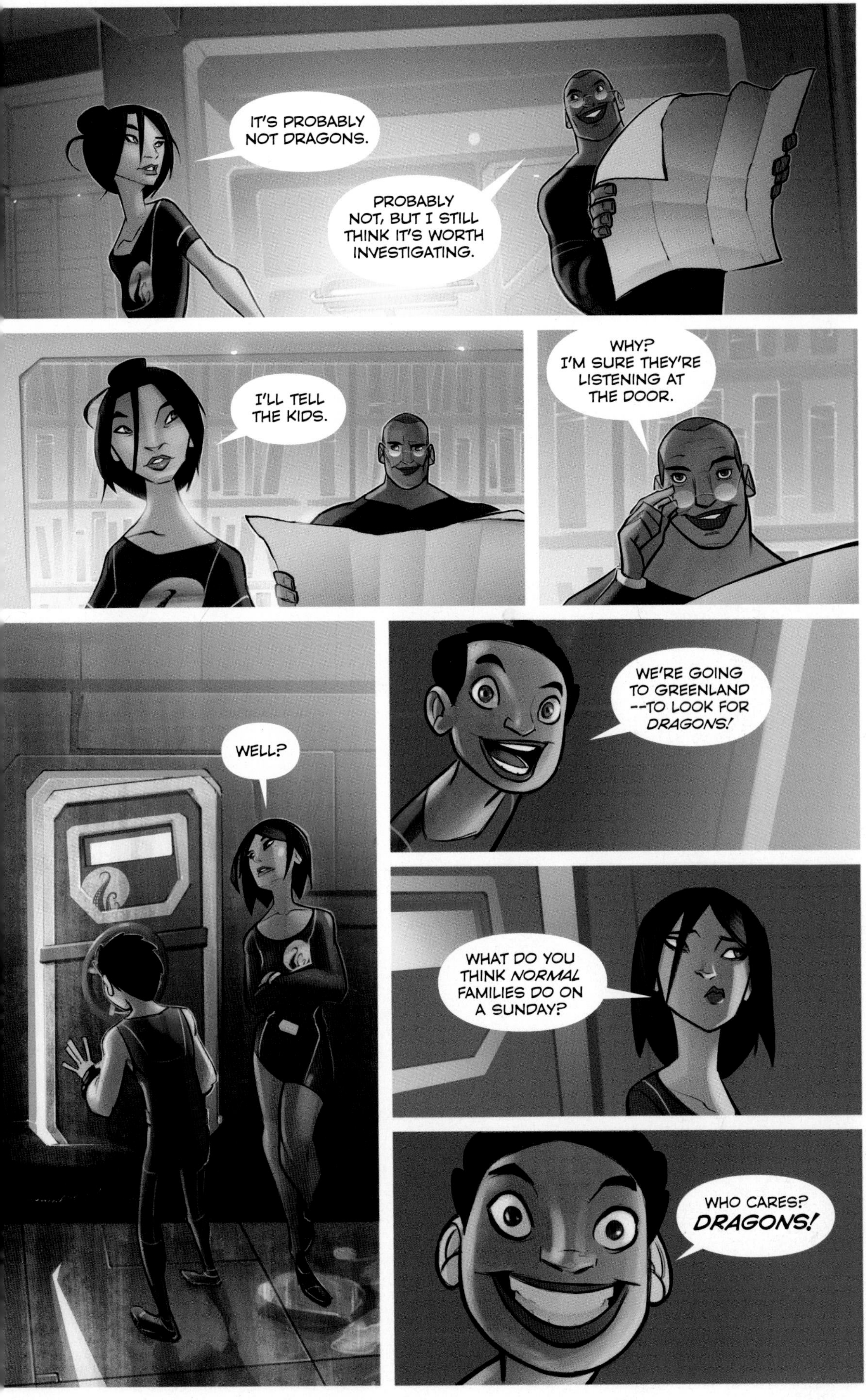
IT'S PROBABLY NOT DRAGONS.
PROBABLY NOT, BUT I STILL THINK IT'S WORTH INVESTIGATING.
I'LL TELL THE KIDS.
WHY? I'M SURE THEY'RE LISTENING AT THE DOOR.
WELL?
WE'RE GOING TO GREENLAND --TO LOOK FOR *DRAGONS!*
WHAT DO YOU THINK *NORMAL* FAMILIES DO ON A SUNDAY?
WHO CARES? ***DRAGONS!***

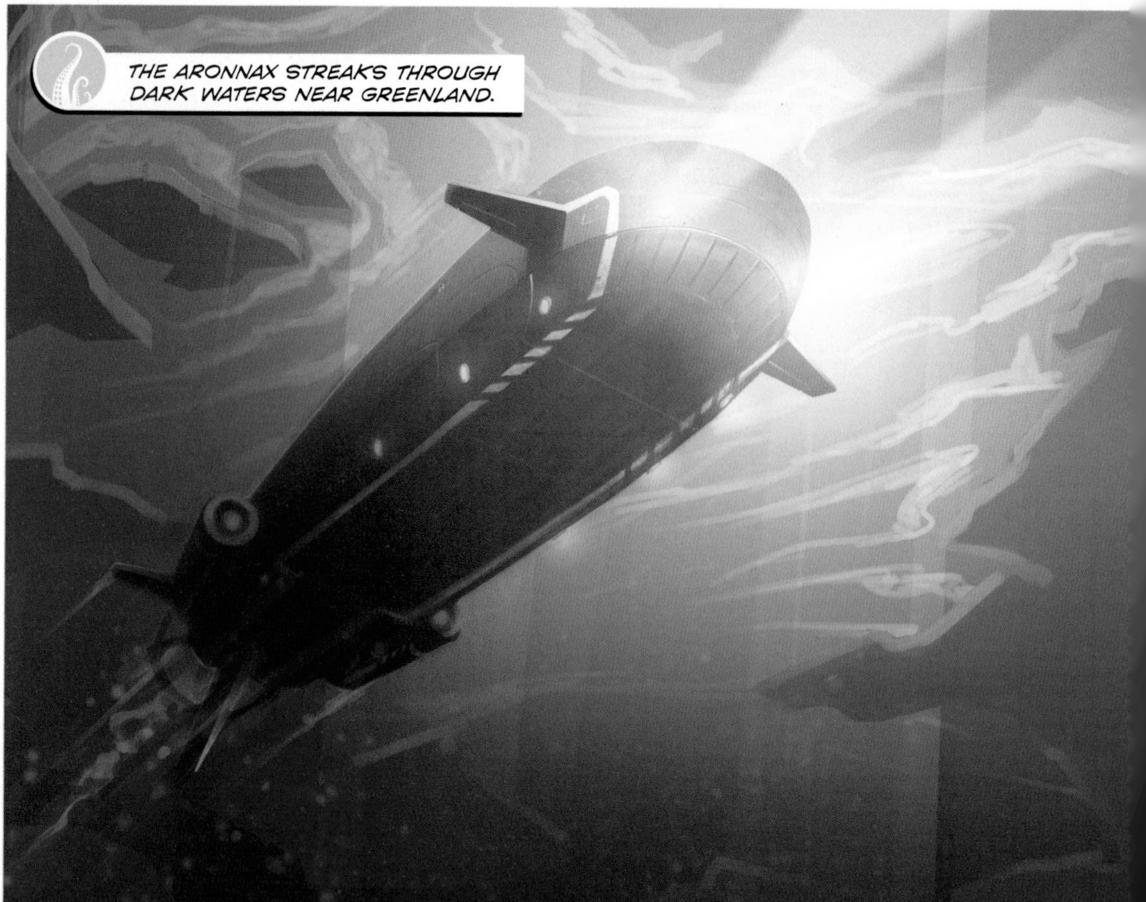
THE ARONNAX STREAKS THROUGH DARK WATERS NEAR GREENLAND.

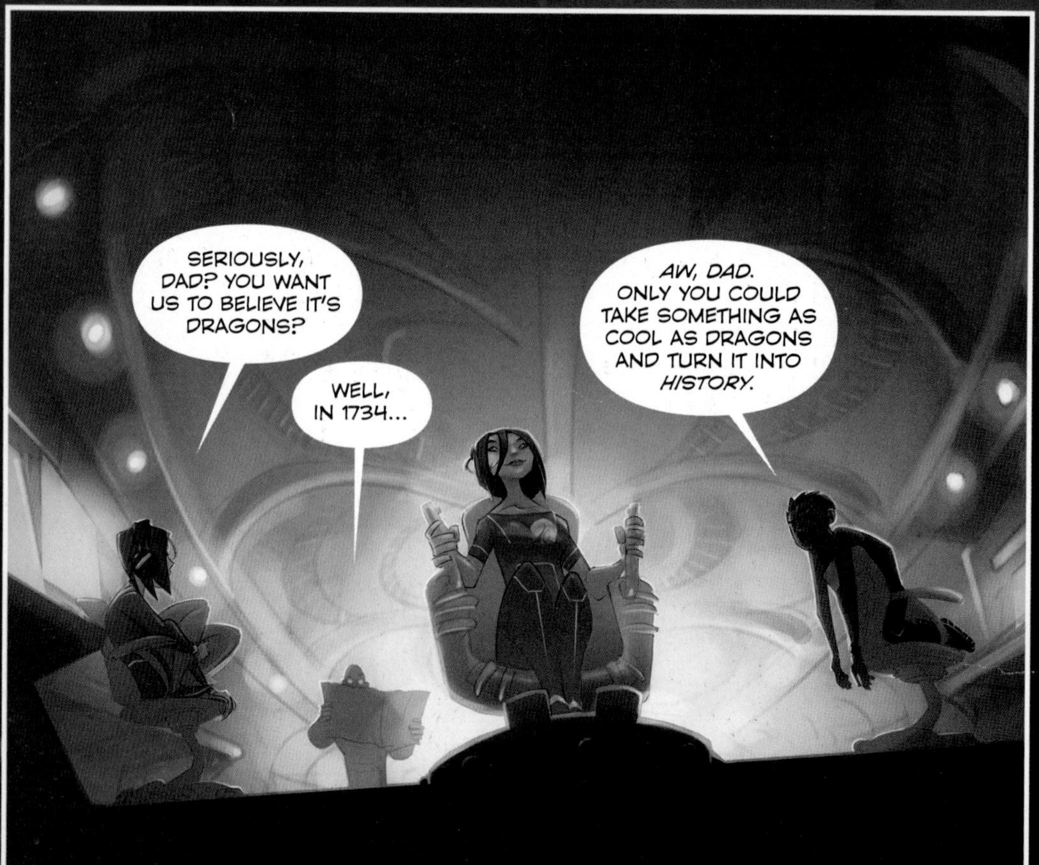
SERIOUSLY, DAD? YOU WANT US TO BELIEVE IT'S DRAGONS?
WELL, IN 1734...
AW, DAD. ONLY YOU COULD TAKE SOMETHING AS COOL AS DRAGONS AND TURN IT INTO HISTORY.

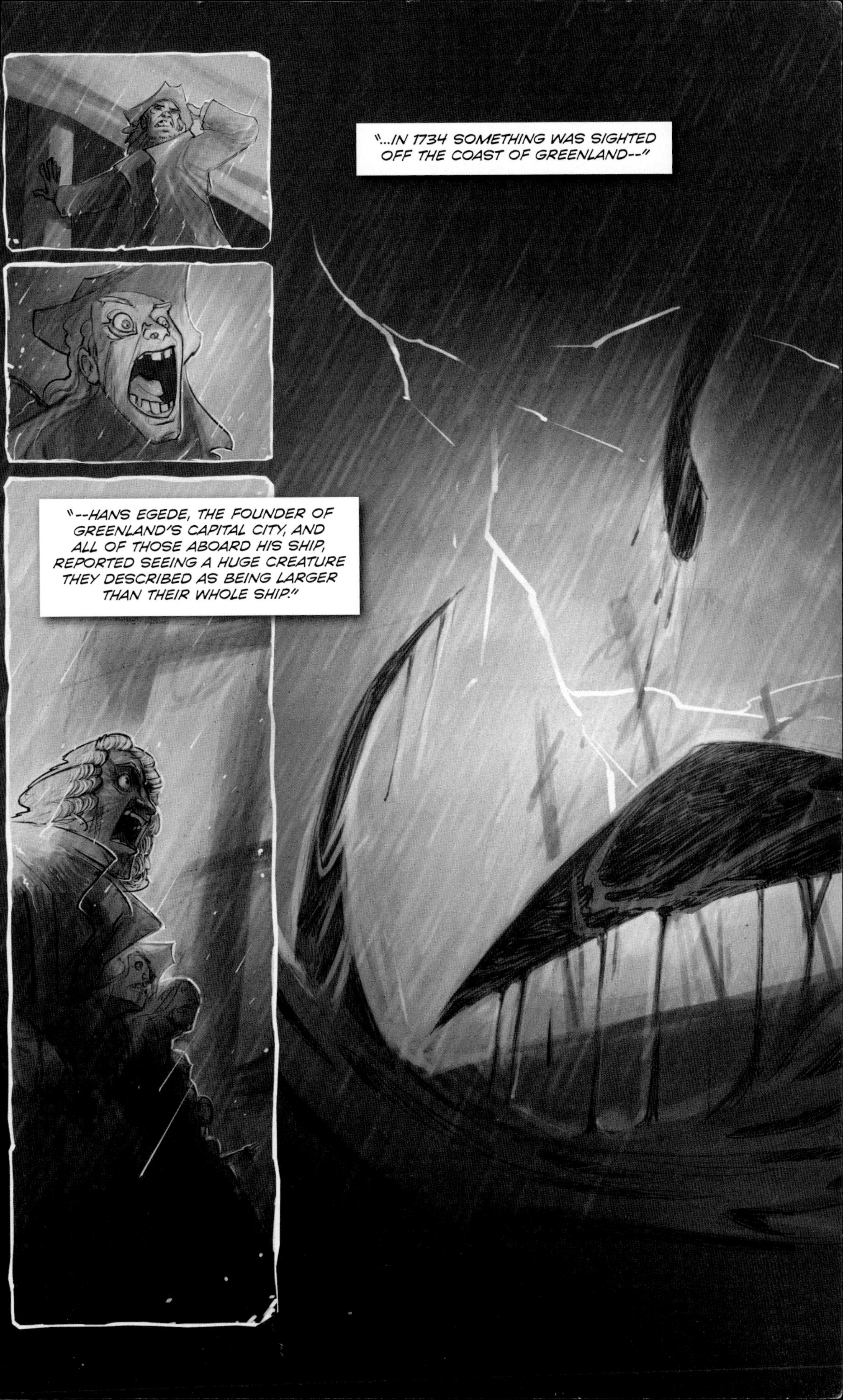
"...IN 1734 SOMETHING WAS SIGHTED OFF THE COAST OF GREENLAND--"
"--HANS EGEDE, THE FOUNDER OF GREENLAND'S CAPITAL CITY, AND ALL OF THOSE ABOARD HIS SHIP, REPORTED SEEING A HUGE CREATURE THEY DESCRIBED AS BEING LARGER THAN THEIR WHOLE SHIP."

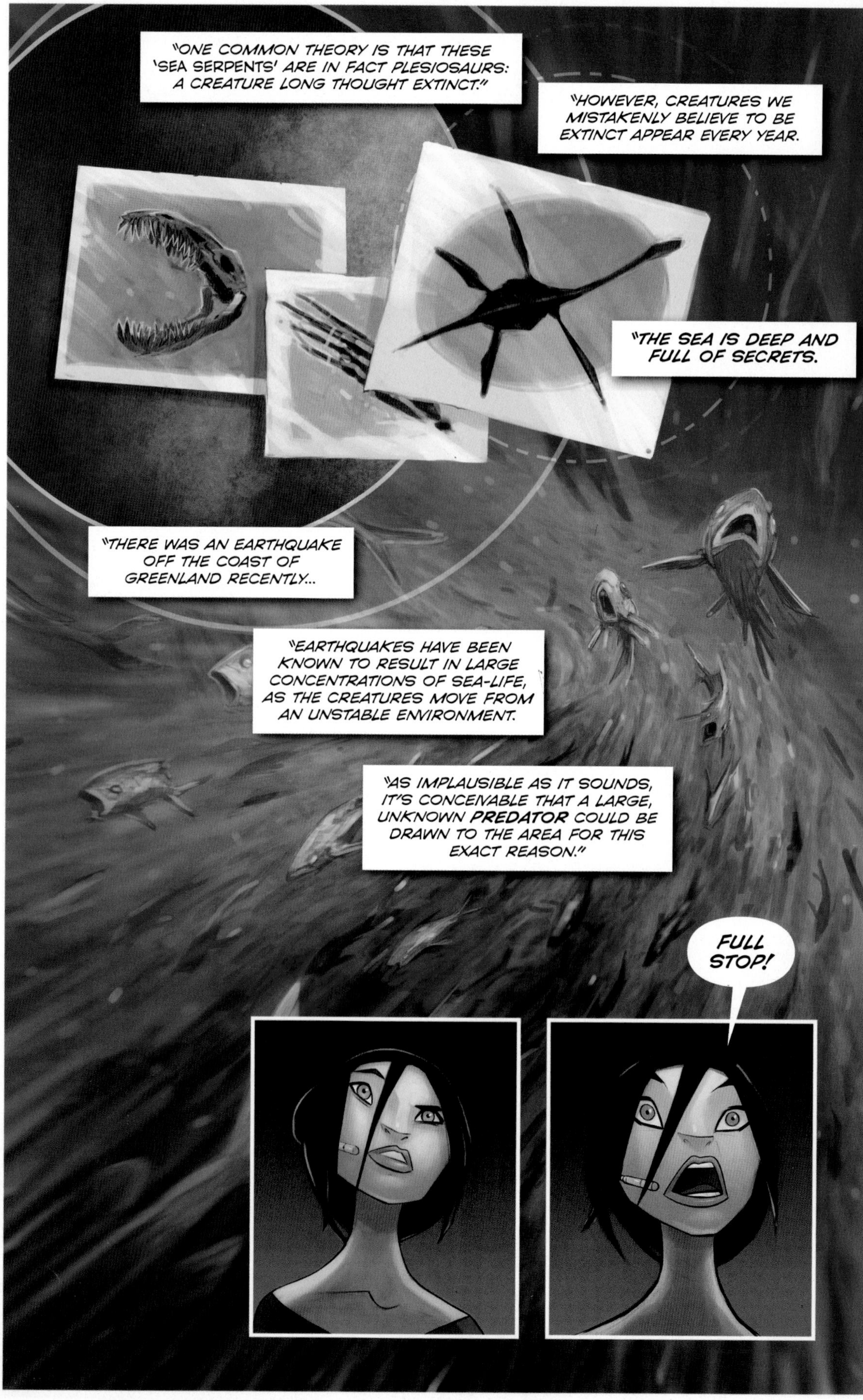
"ONE COMMON THEORY IS THAT THESE 'SEA SERPENTS' ARE IN FACT PLESIOSAURS: A CREATURE LONG THOUGHT EXTINCT."
"HOWEVER, CREATURES WE MISTAKENLY BELIEVE TO BE EXTINCT APPEAR EVERY YEAR.
"THE SEA IS DEEP AND FULL OF SECRETS.
"THERE WAS AN EARTHQUAKE OFF THE COAST OF GREENLAND RECENTLY...
"EARTHQUAKES HAVE BEEN KNOWN TO RESULT IN LARGE CONCENTRATIONS OF SEA-LIFE, AS THE CREATURES MOVE FROM AN UNSTABLE ENVIRONMENT.
"AS IMPLAUSIBLE AS IT SOUNDS, IT'S CONCEIVABLE THAT A LARGE, UNKNOWN PREDATOR COULD BE DRAWN TO THE AREA FOR THIS EXACT REASON."
FULL STOP!

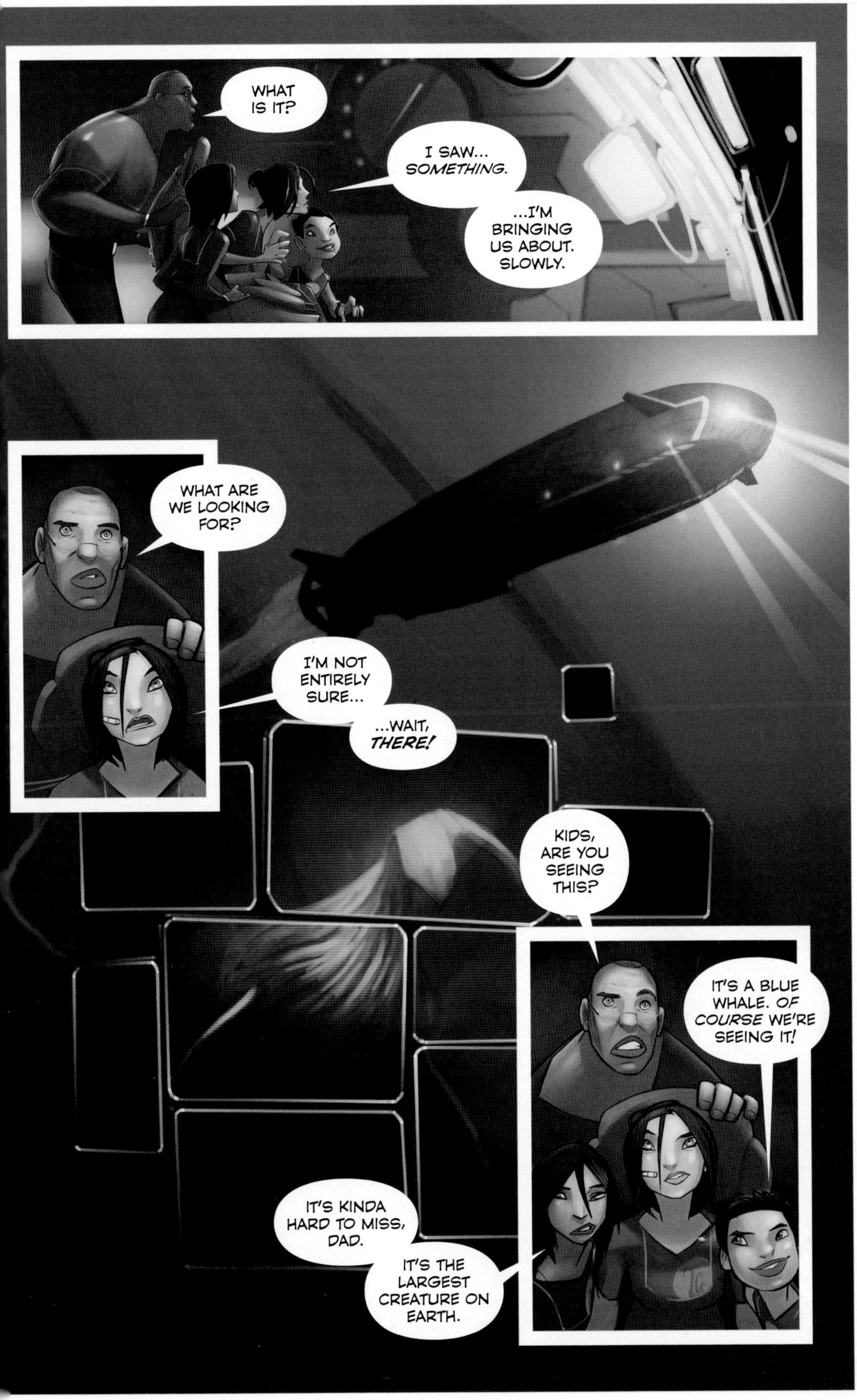
WHAT IS IT?
I SAW... *SOMETHING.*
...I'M BRINGING US ABOUT. SLOWLY.
WHAT ARE WE LOOKING FOR?
I'M NOT ENTIRELY SURE...
...WAIT, *THERE!*
KIDS, ARE YOU SEEING THIS?
IT'S A BLUE WHALE. *OF COURSE* WE'RE SEEING IT!
IT'S KINDA HARD TO MISS, DAD.
IT'S THE LARGEST CREATURE ON EARTH.

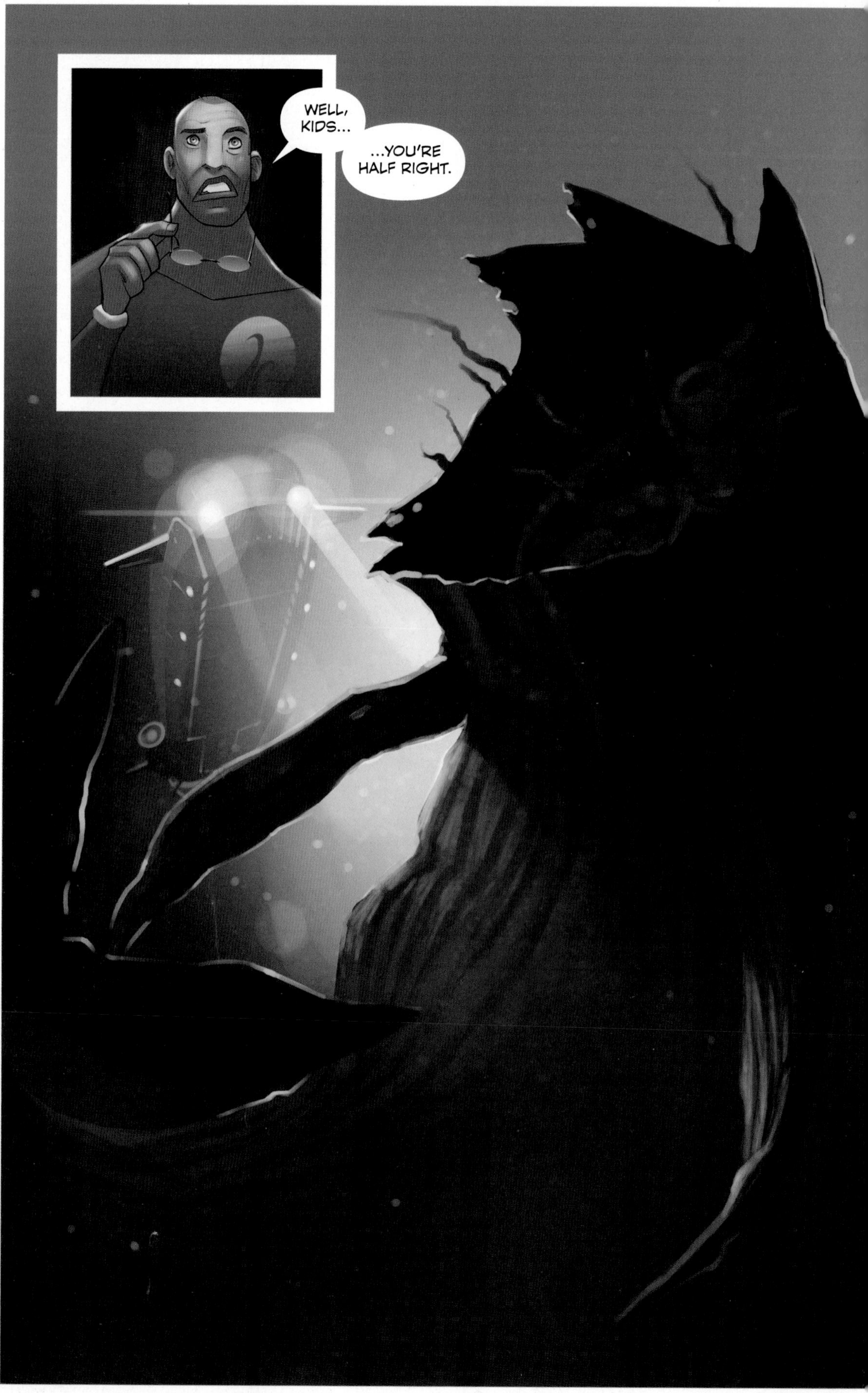
WELL, KIDS...
...YOU'RE HALF RIGHT.

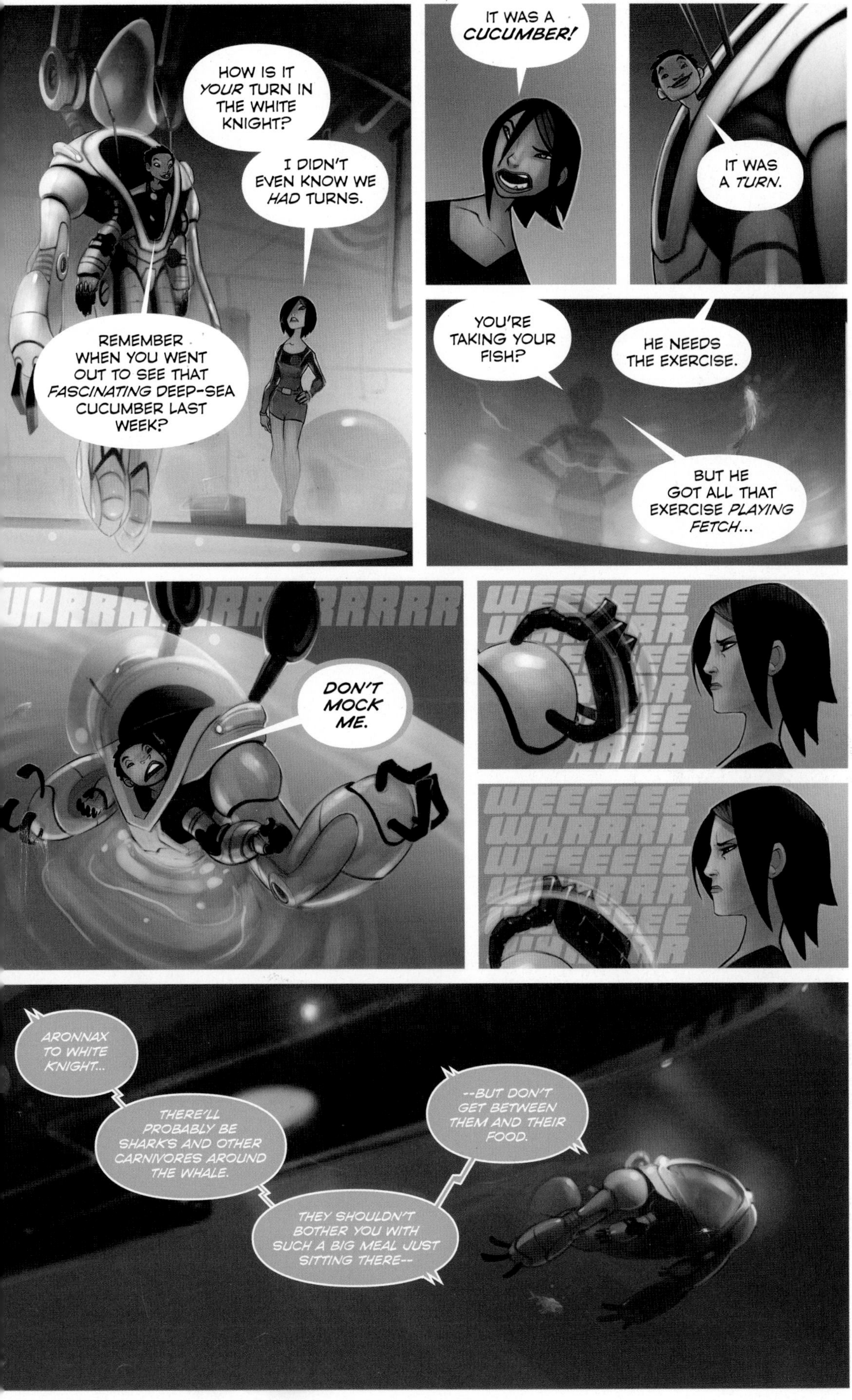
HOW IS IT *YOUR* TURN IN THE WHITE KNIGHT?
I DIDN'T EVEN KNOW WE *HAD* TURNS.
REMEMBER WHEN YOU WENT OUT TO SEE THAT *FASCINATING* DEEP-SEA CUCUMBER LAST WEEK?
IT WAS A *CUCUMBER!*
IT WAS A *TURN.*
YOU'RE TAKING YOUR FISH?
HE NEEDS THE EXERCISE.
BUT HE GOT ALL THAT EXERCISE *PLAYING FETCH...*
WHRRR
*DON'T MOCK ME.*
WEEEEEE
WEEEEEE
WHRRRR
WEEEEEE
ARONNAX TO WHITE KNIGHT...
THERE'LL PROBABLY BE SHARKS AND OTHER CARNIVORES AROUND THE WHALE.
THEY SHOULDN'T BOTHER YOU WITH SUCH A BIG MEAL JUST SITTING THERE--
--BUT DON'T GET BETWEEN THEM AND THEIR FOOD.

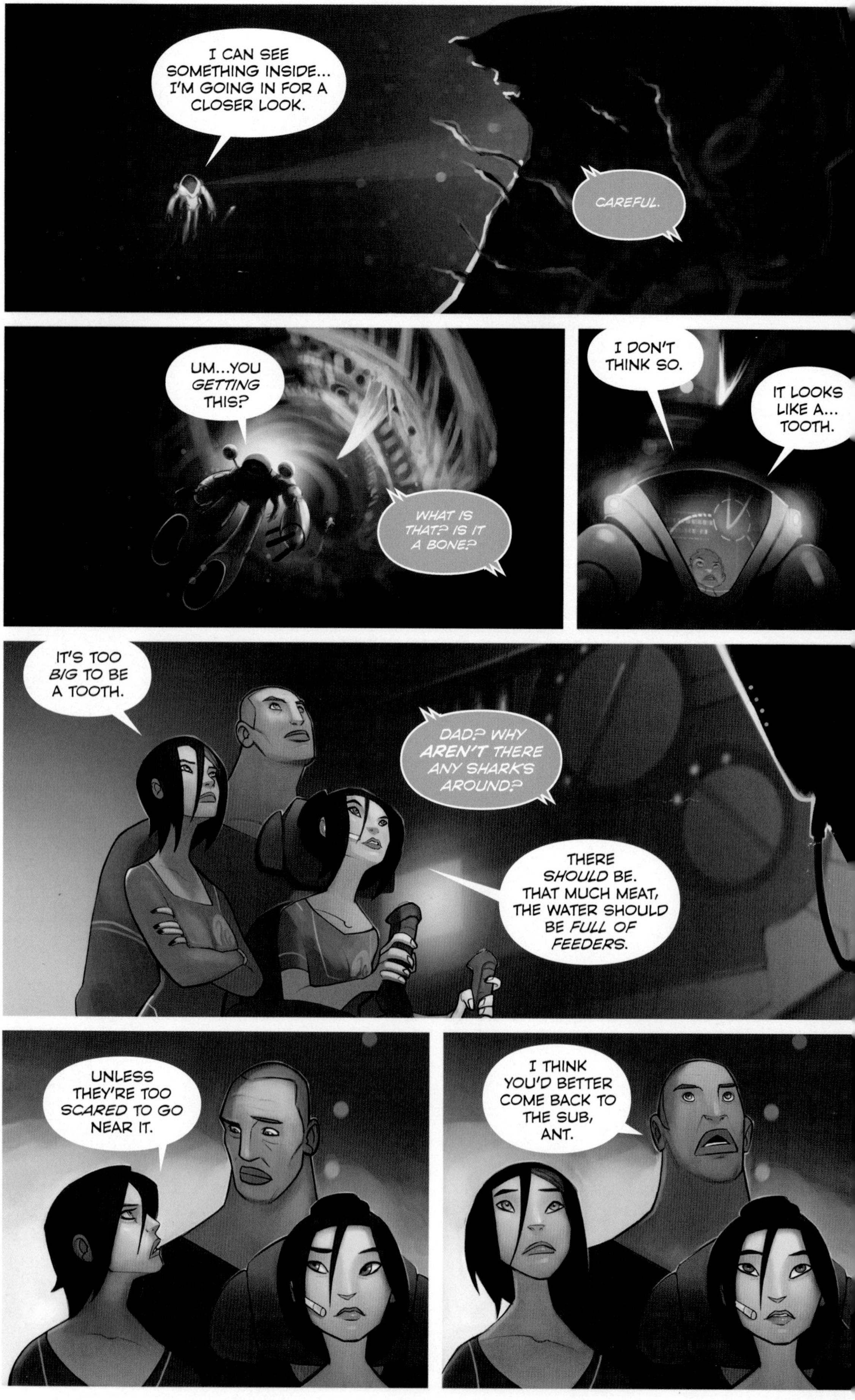

I CAN SEE SOMETHING INSIDE... I'M GOING IN FOR A CLOSER LOOK.
CAREFUL.
UM...YOU *GETTING* THIS?
WHAT IS THAT? IS IT A BONE?
I DON'T THINK SO.
IT LOOKS LIKE A... TOOTH.
IT'S TOO *BIG* TO BE A TOOTH.
DAD? WHY **AREN'T** THERE ANY SHARKS AROUND?
THERE *SHOULD* BE. THAT MUCH MEAT, THE WATER SHOULD BE *FULL OF FEEDERS*.
UNLESS THEY'RE TOO *SCARED* TO GO NEAR IT.
I THINK YOU'D BETTER COME BACK TO THE SUB, ANT.

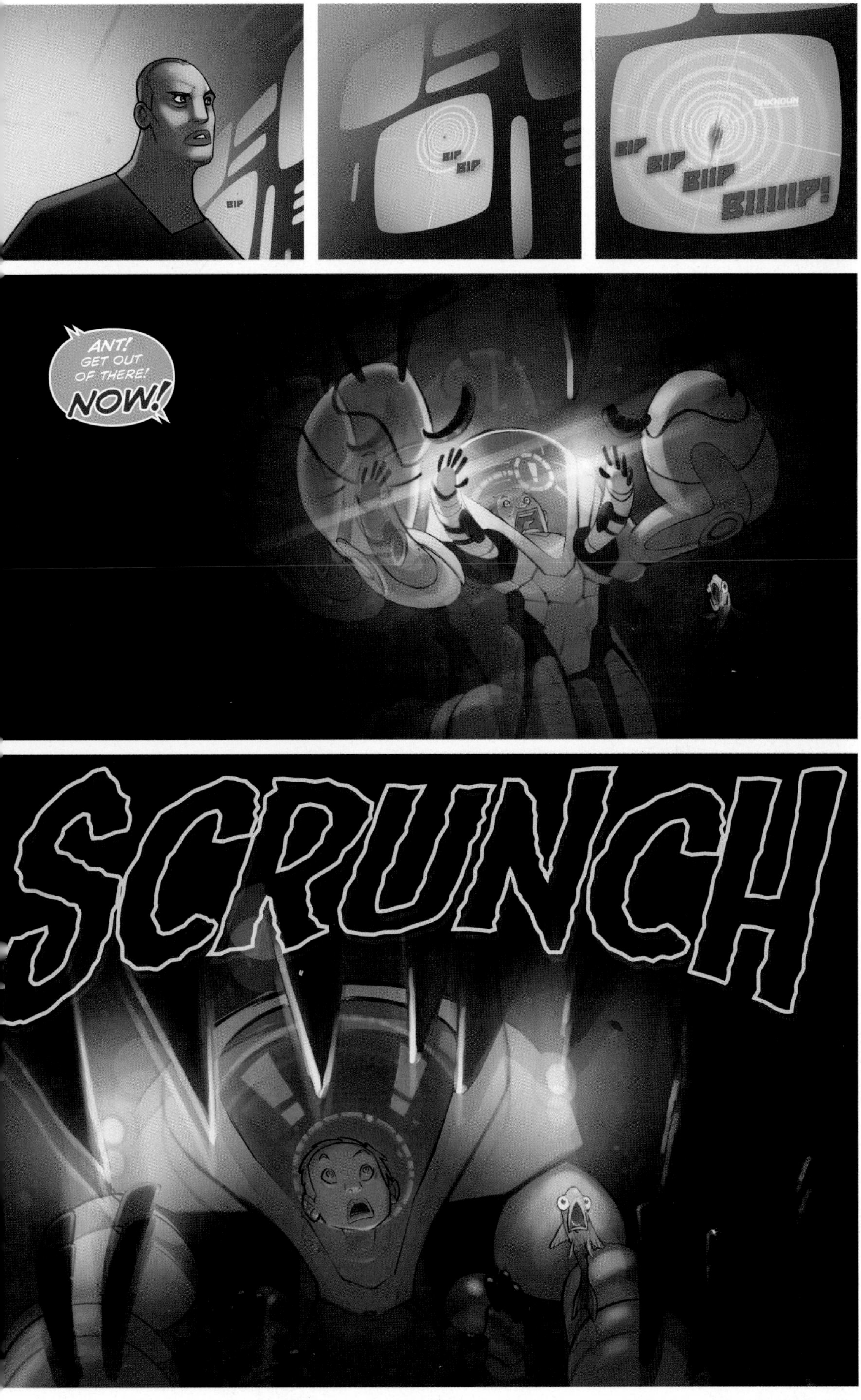
BIP
BIP BIP
UNKNOWN
BIP BIIP BIIP BIIIIIP!
ANT! GET OUT OF THERE! NOW!
SCRUNCH

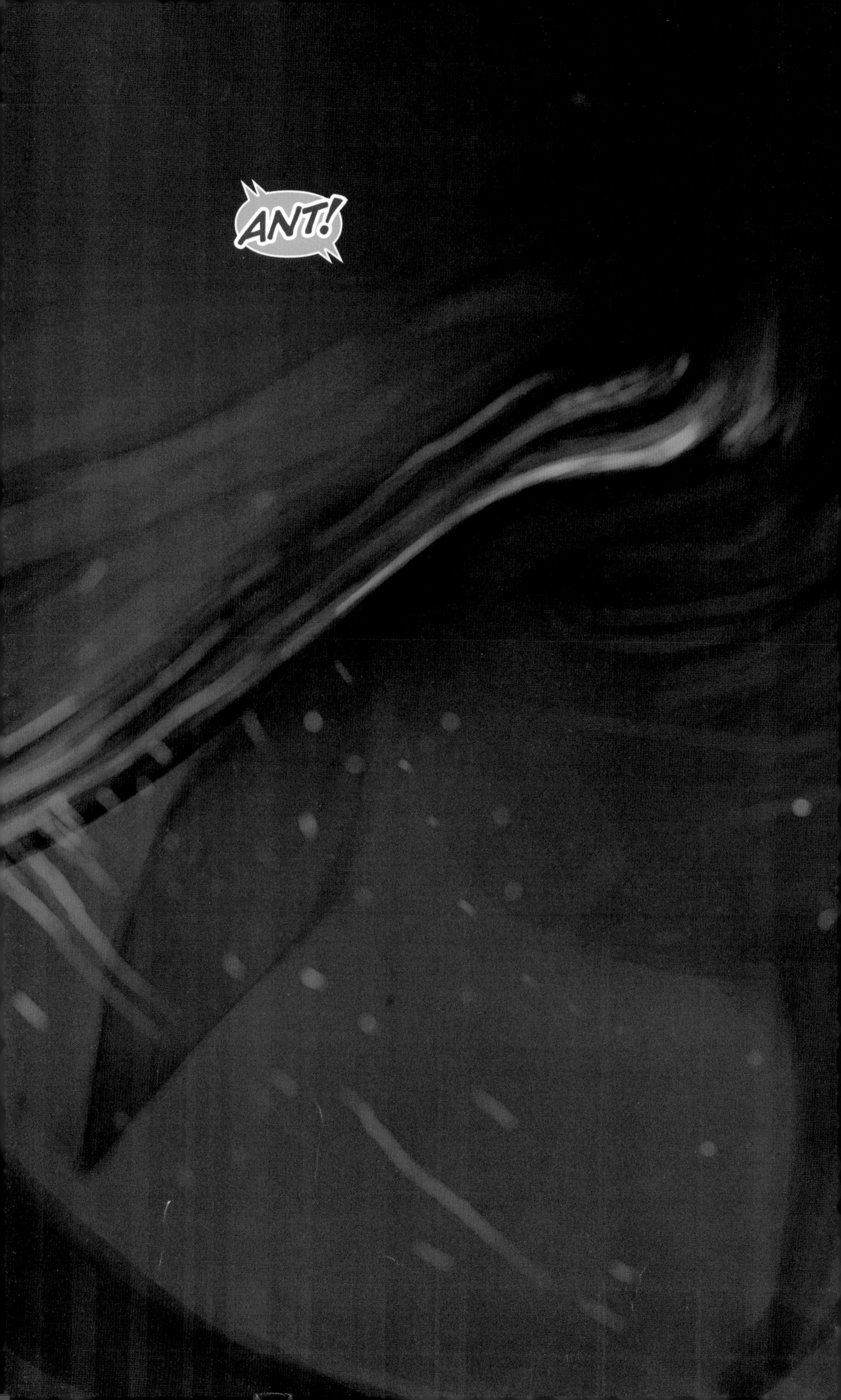
ANT!

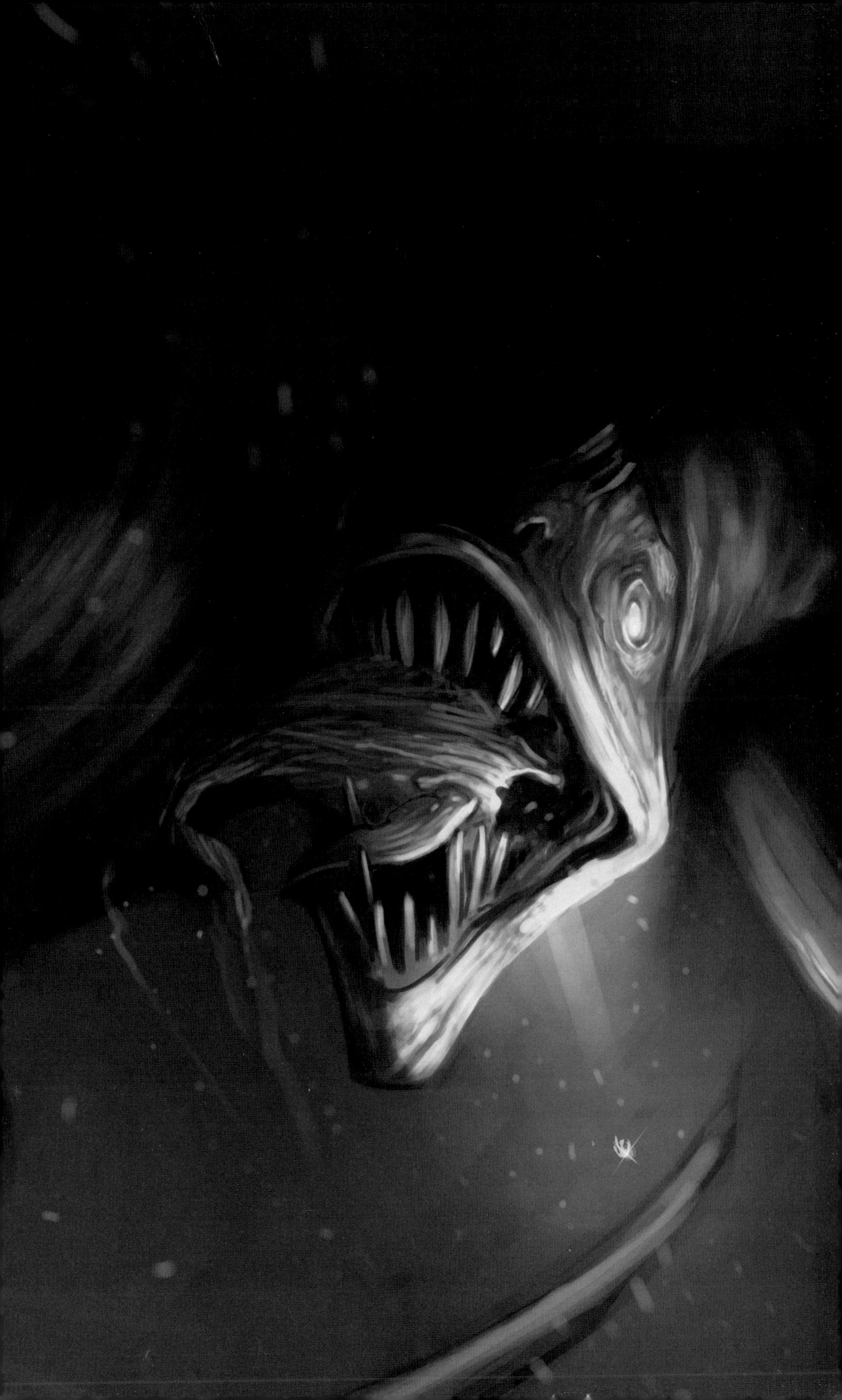

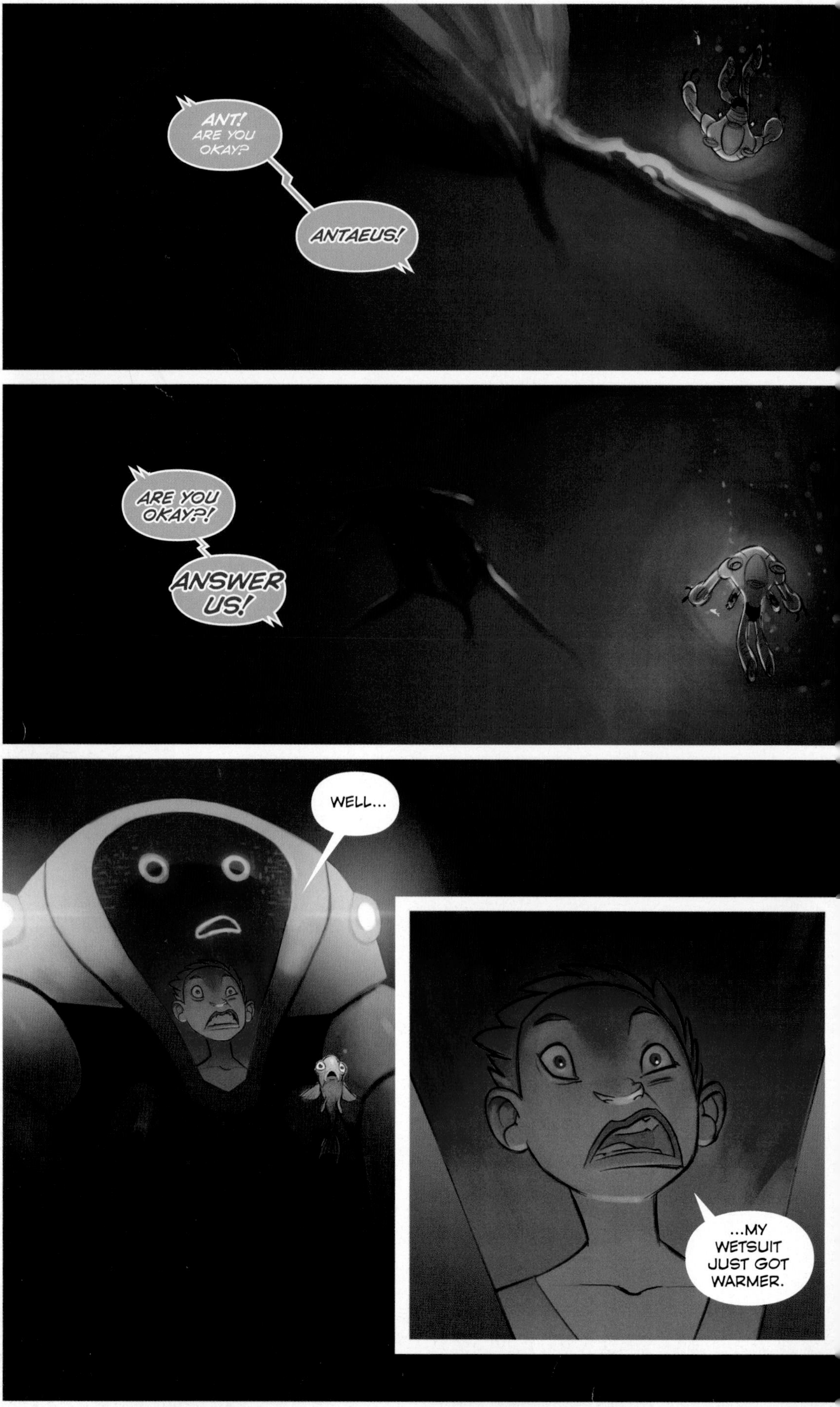
ANT! ARE YOU OKAY?
ANTAEUS!
ARE YOU OKAY?!
ANSWER US!
WELL...
...MY WETSUIT JUST GOT WARMER.

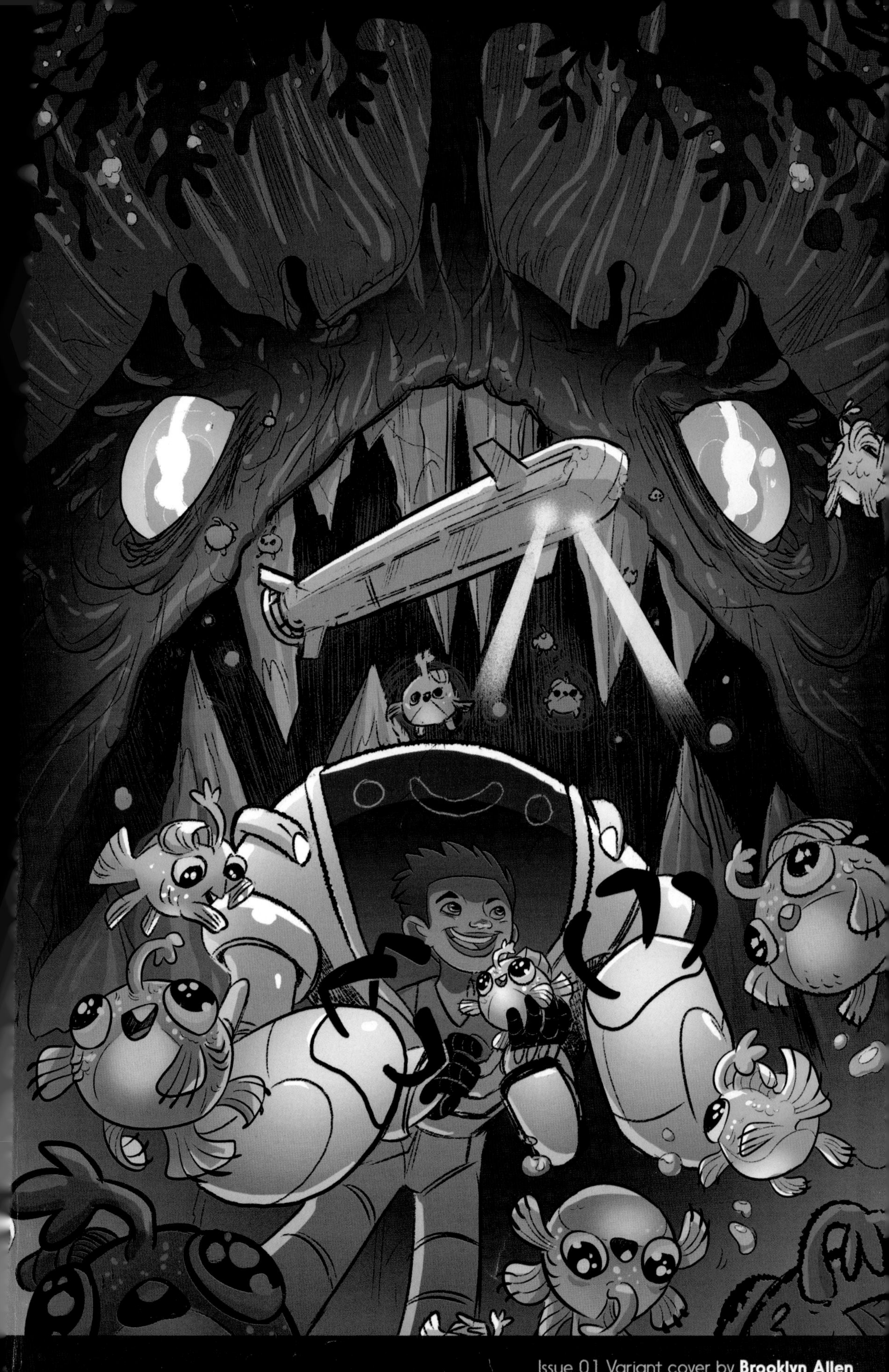

Issue 01 Variant cover by **Brooklyn Allen**
with colors by **Joana Lafuente**

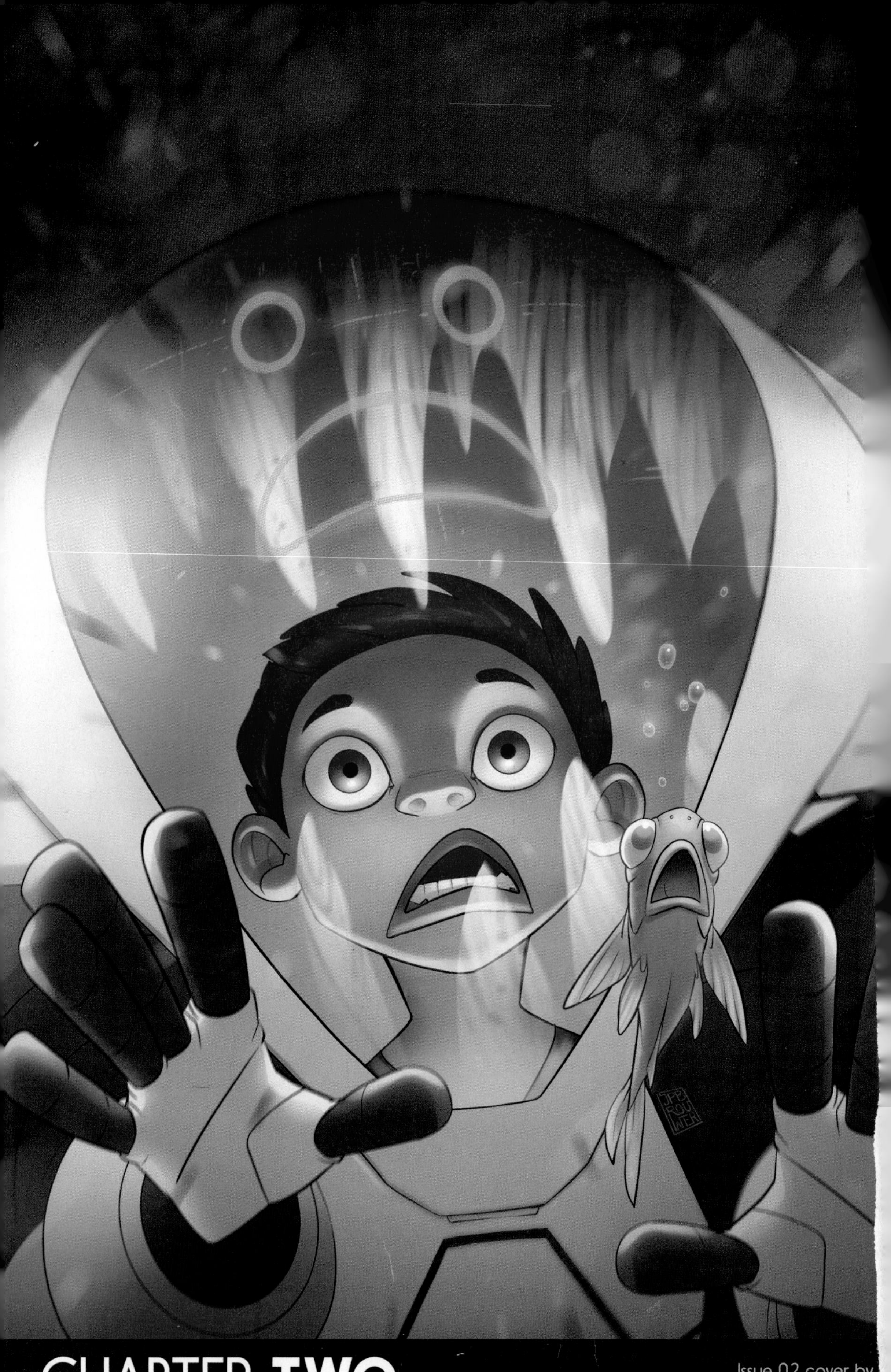

# CHAPTER **TWO**

Issue 02 cover by
**James Brouwer**

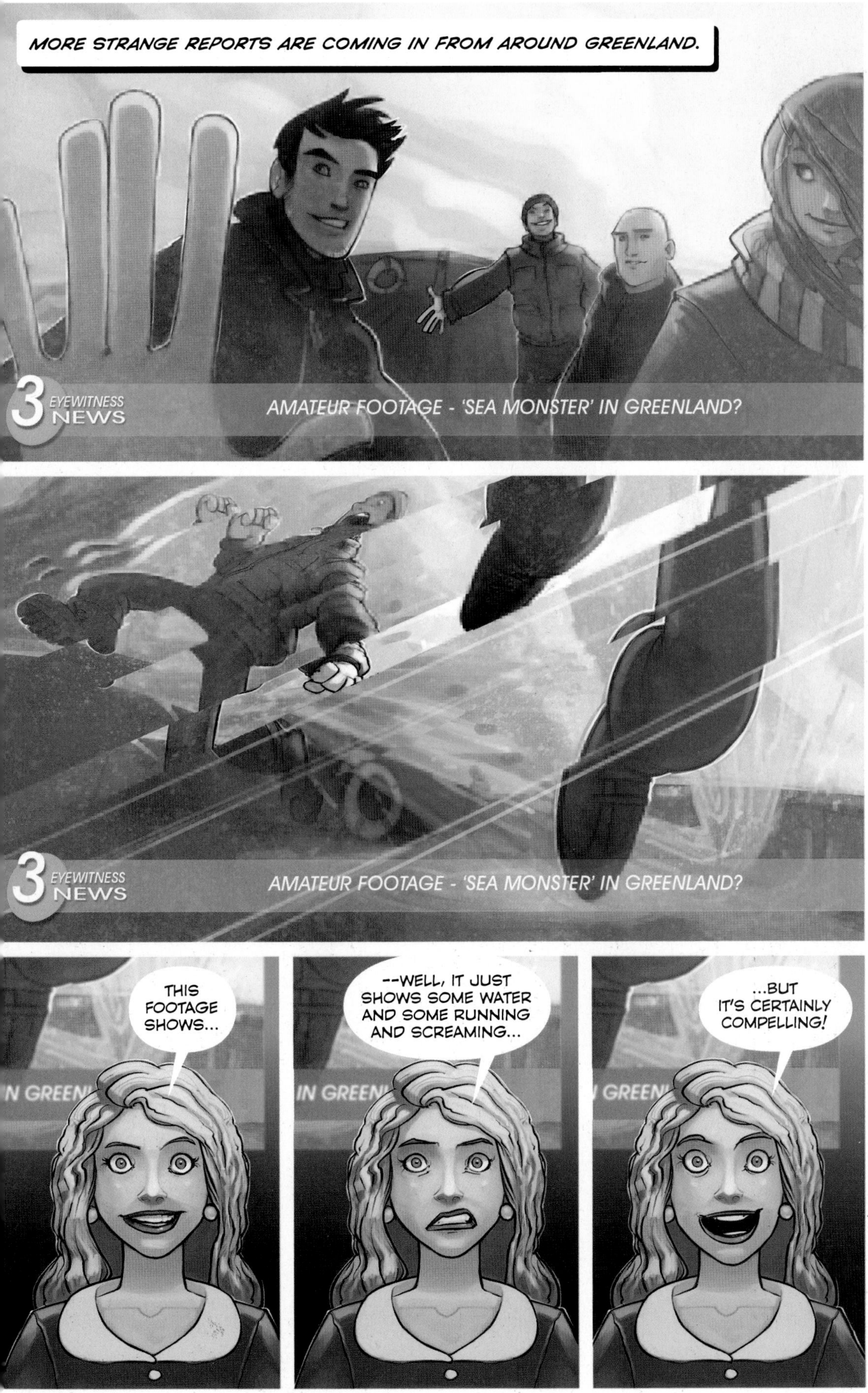
MORE STRANGE REPORTS ARE COMING IN FROM AROUND GREENLAND.
3 EYEWITNESS NEWS
AMATEUR FOOTAGE - 'SEA MONSTER' IN GREENLAND?
3 EYEWITNESS NEWS
AMATEUR FOOTAGE - 'SEA MONSTER' IN GREENLAND?
THIS FOOTAGE SHOWS...
--WELL, IT JUST SHOWS SOME WATER AND SOME RUNNING AND SCREAMING...
...BUT IT'S CERTAINLY COMPELLING!

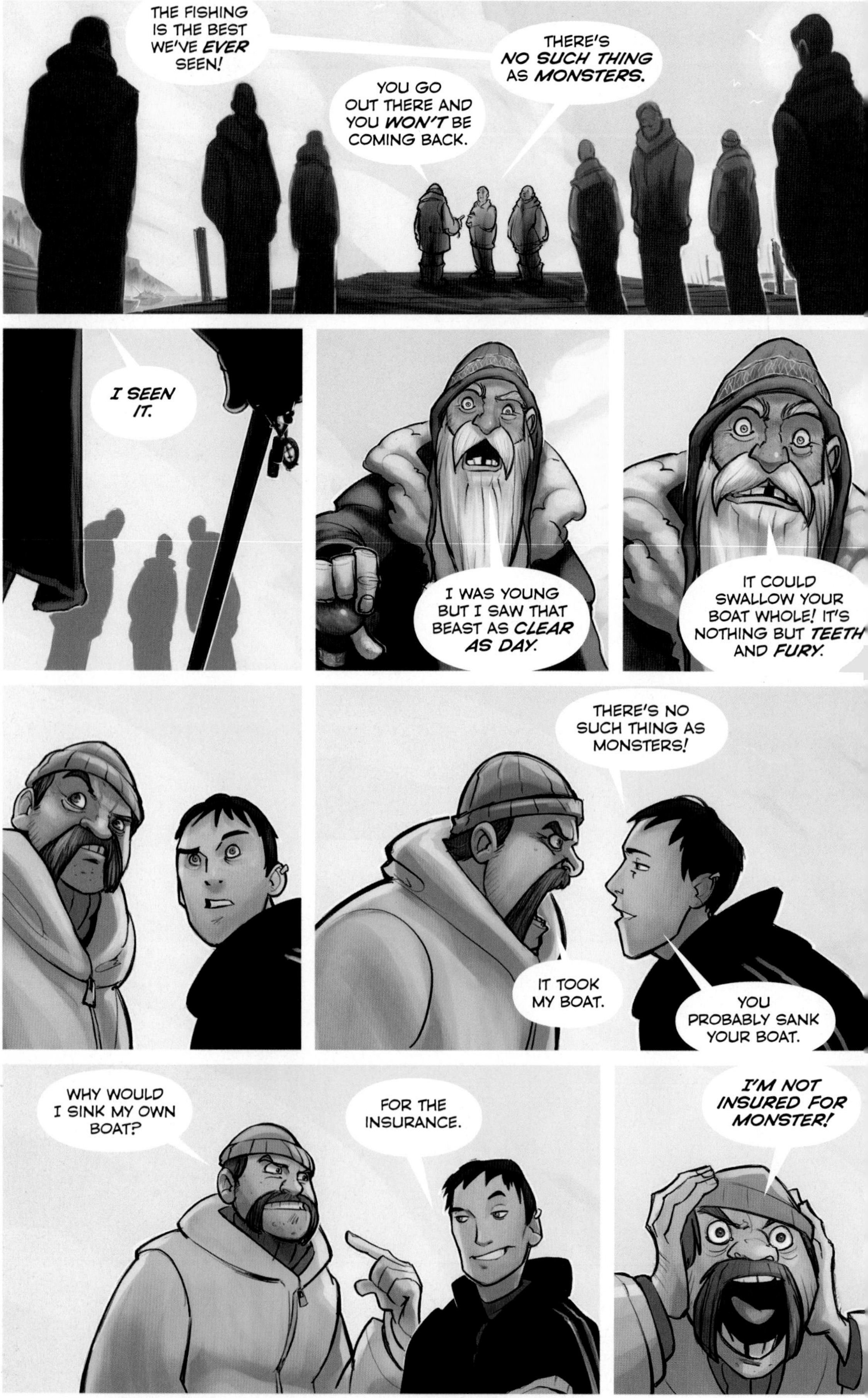
THE FISHING IS THE BEST WE'VE EVER SEEN!
YOU GO OUT THERE AND YOU WON'T BE COMING BACK.
THERE'S NO SUCH THING AS MONSTERS.
I SEEN IT.
I WAS YOUNG BUT I SAW THAT BEAST AS CLEAR AS DAY.
IT COULD SWALLOW YOUR BOAT WHOLE! IT'S NOTHING BUT TEETH AND FURY.
THERE'S NO SUCH THING AS MONSTERS!
IT TOOK MY BOAT.
YOU PROBABLY SANK YOUR BOAT.
WHY WOULD I SINK MY OWN BOAT?
FOR THE INSURANCE.
I'M NOT INSURED FOR MONSTER!

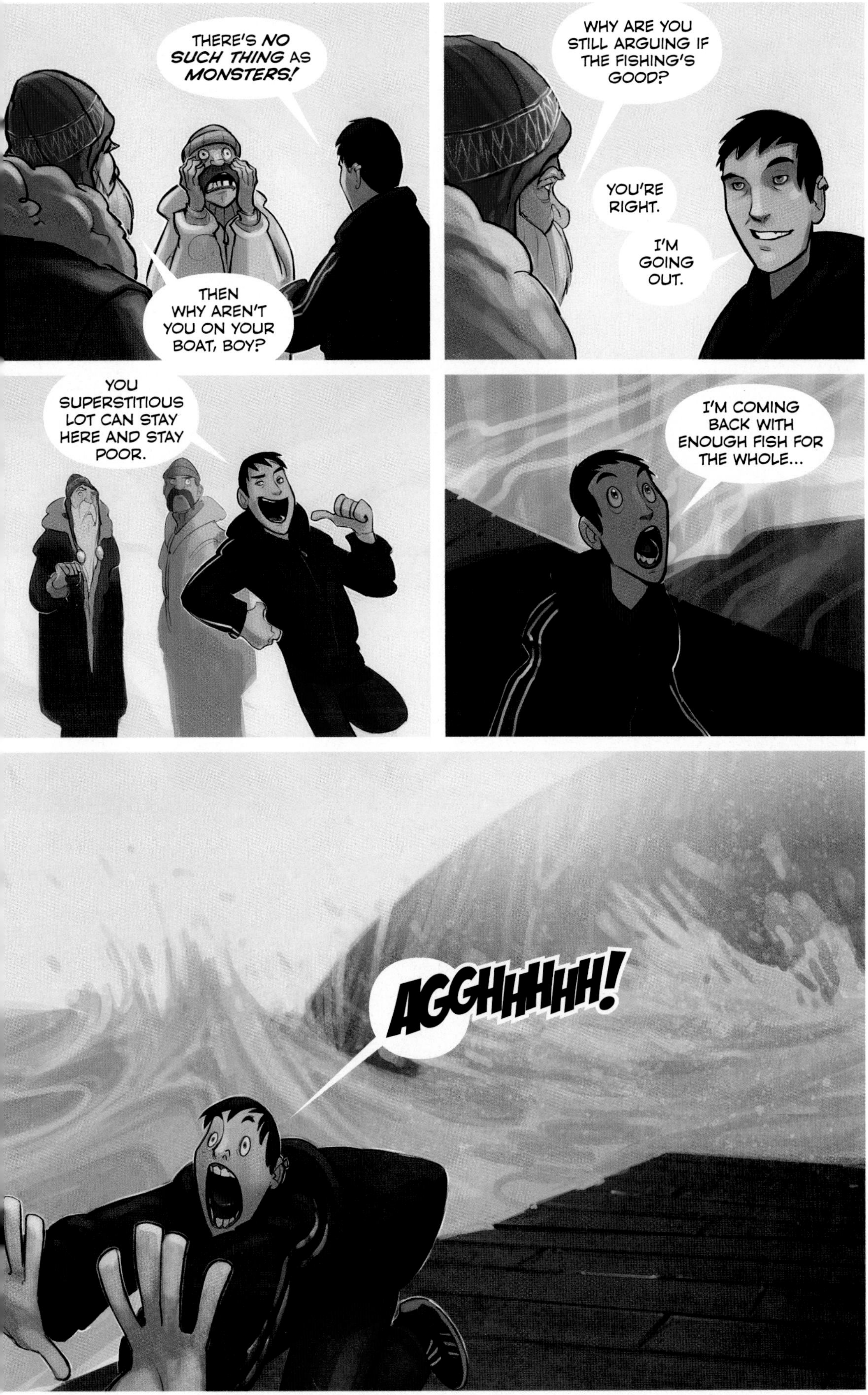
THERE'S NO SUCH THING AS MONSTERS!
THEN WHY AREN'T YOU ON YOUR BOAT, BOY?
WHY ARE YOU STILL ARGUING IF THE FISHING'S GOOD?
YOU'RE RIGHT.
I'M GOING OUT.
YOU SUPERSTITIOUS LOT CAN STAY HERE AND STAY POOR.
I'M COMING BACK WITH ENOUGH FISH FOR THE WHOLE...
AGGHHHHH!

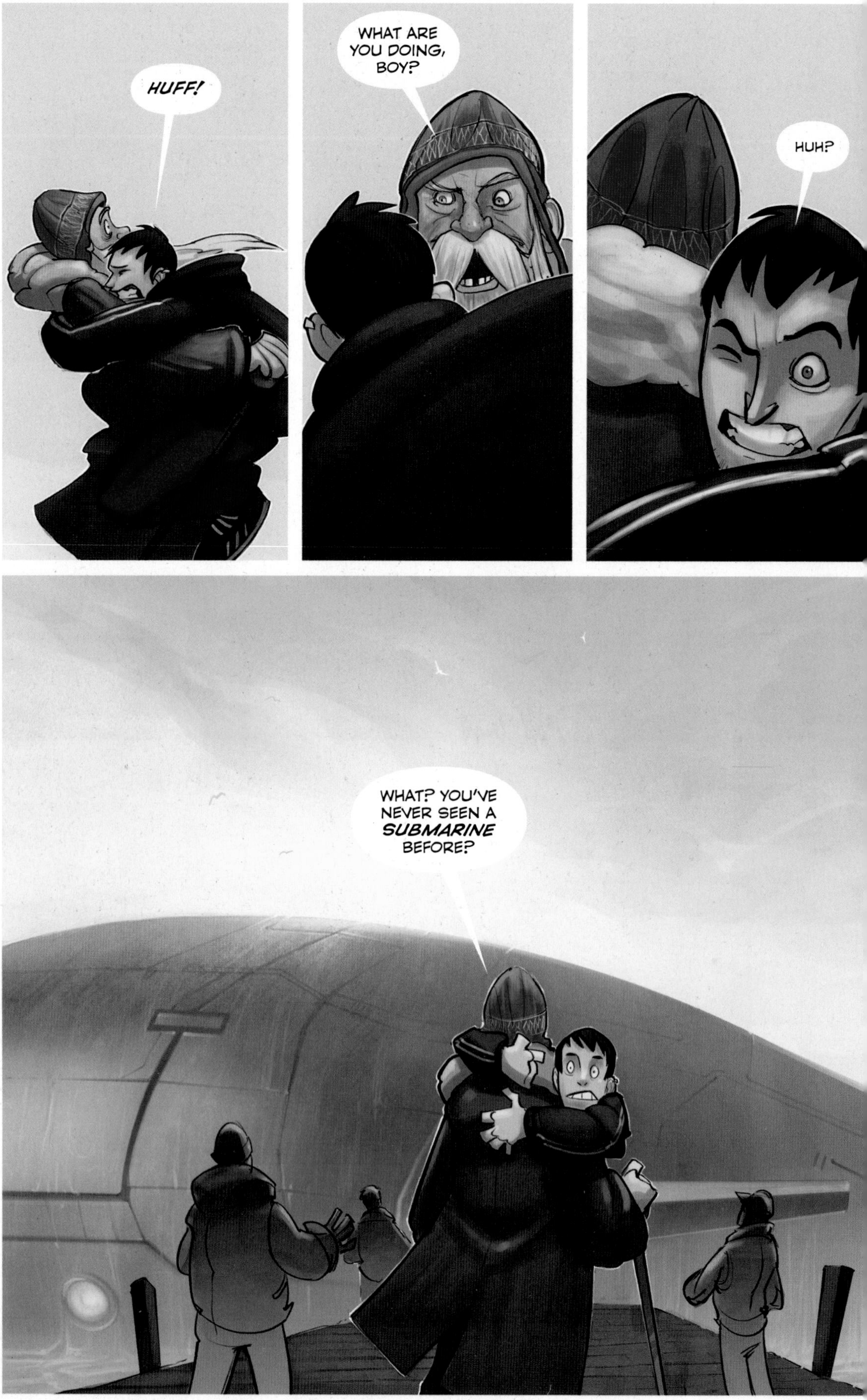
HUFF!
WHAT ARE YOU DOING, BOY?
HUH?
WHAT? YOU'VE NEVER SEEN A SUBMARINE BEFORE?

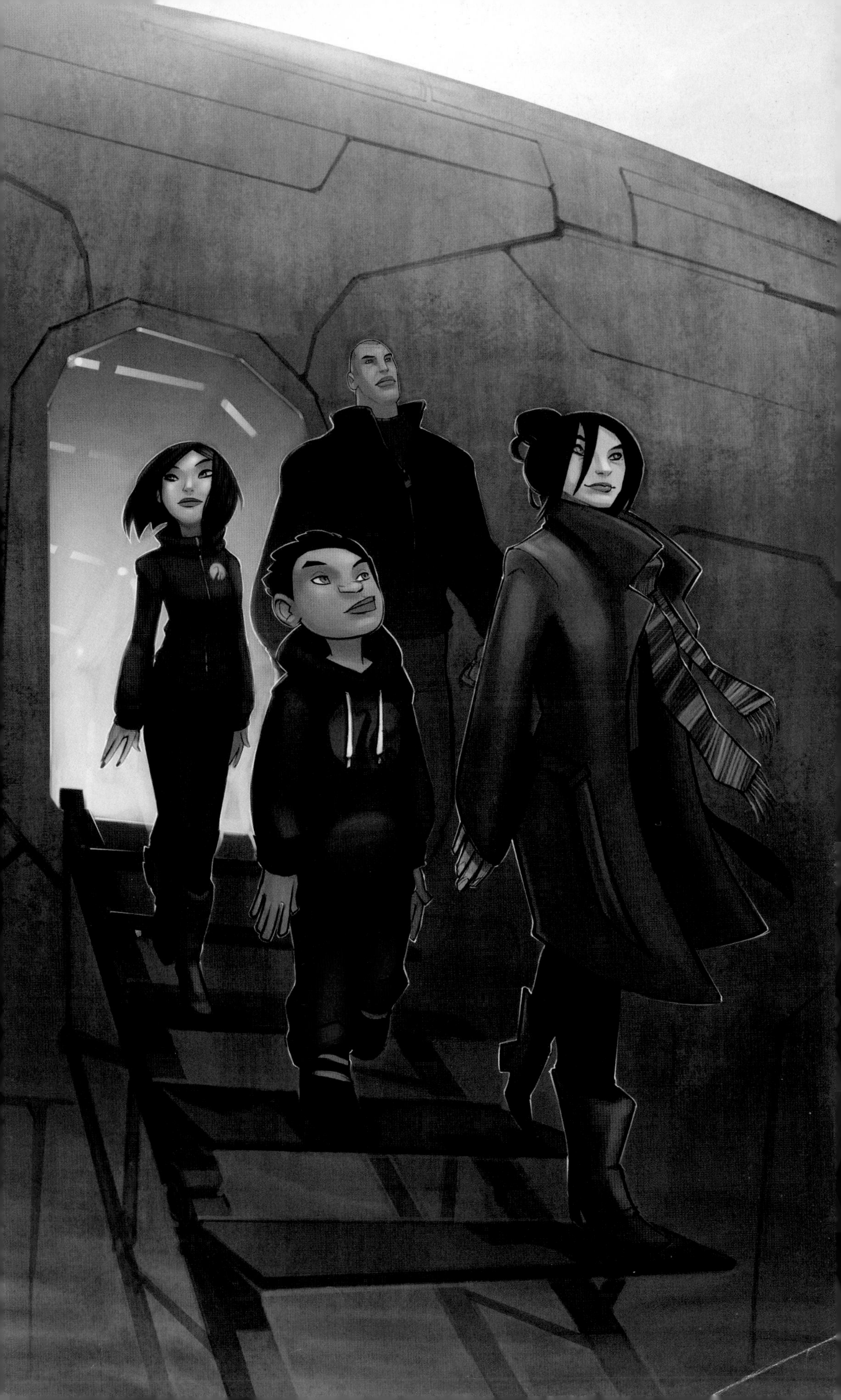

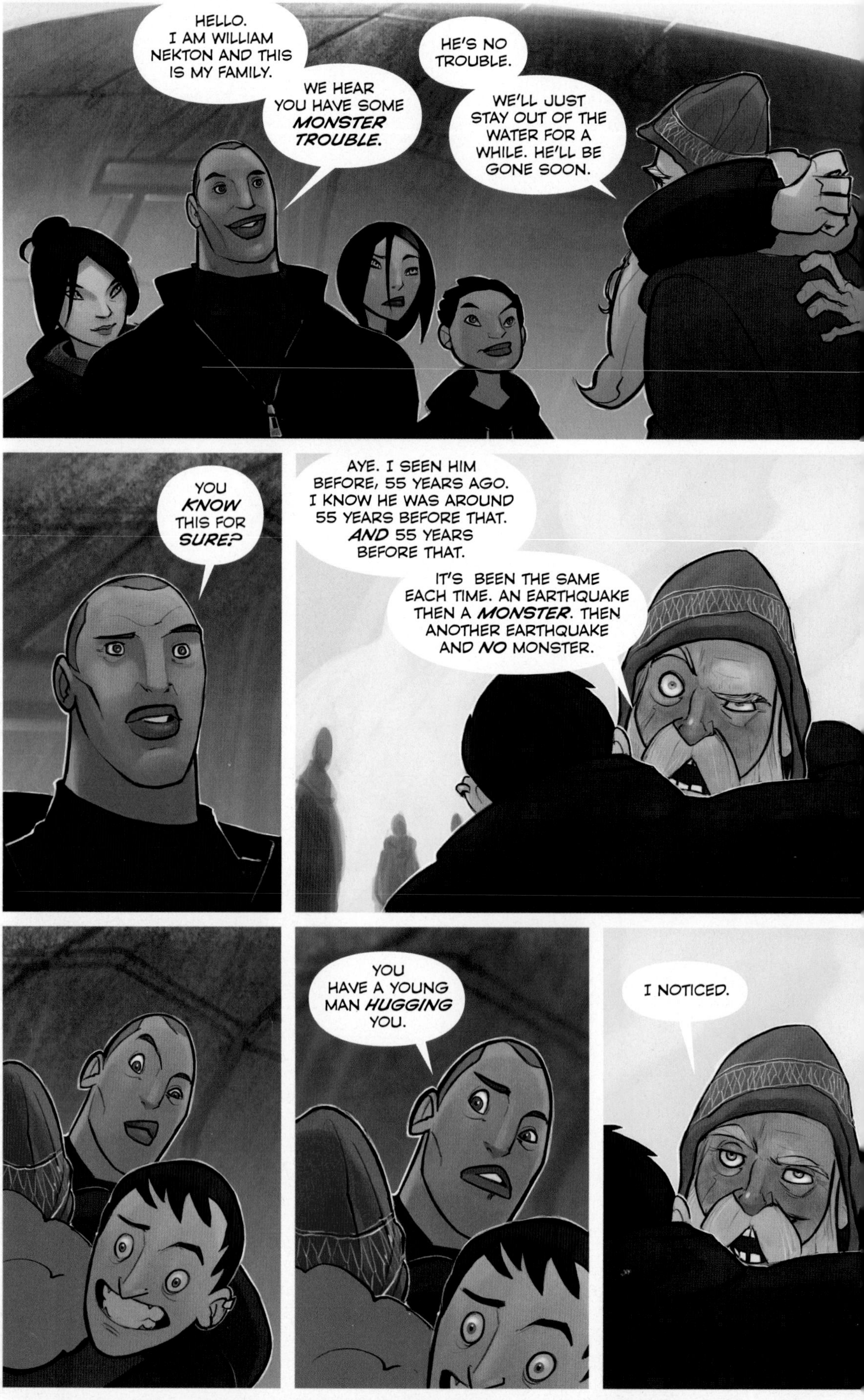
HELLO. I AM WILLIAM NEKTON AND THIS IS MY FAMILY.
WE HEAR YOU HAVE SOME *MONSTER TROUBLE.*
HE'S NO TROUBLE.
WE'LL JUST STAY OUT OF THE WATER FOR A WHILE. HE'LL BE GONE SOON.
YOU *KNOW* THIS FOR *SURE?*
AYE. I SEEN HIM BEFORE, 55 YEARS AGO. I KNOW HE WAS AROUND 55 YEARS BEFORE THAT. *AND* 55 YEARS BEFORE THAT.
IT'S BEEN THE SAME EACH TIME. AN EARTHQUAKE THEN A *MONSTER*. THEN ANOTHER EARTHQUAKE AND *NO* MONSTER.
YOU HAVE A YOUNG MAN *HUGGING* YOU.
I NOTICED.

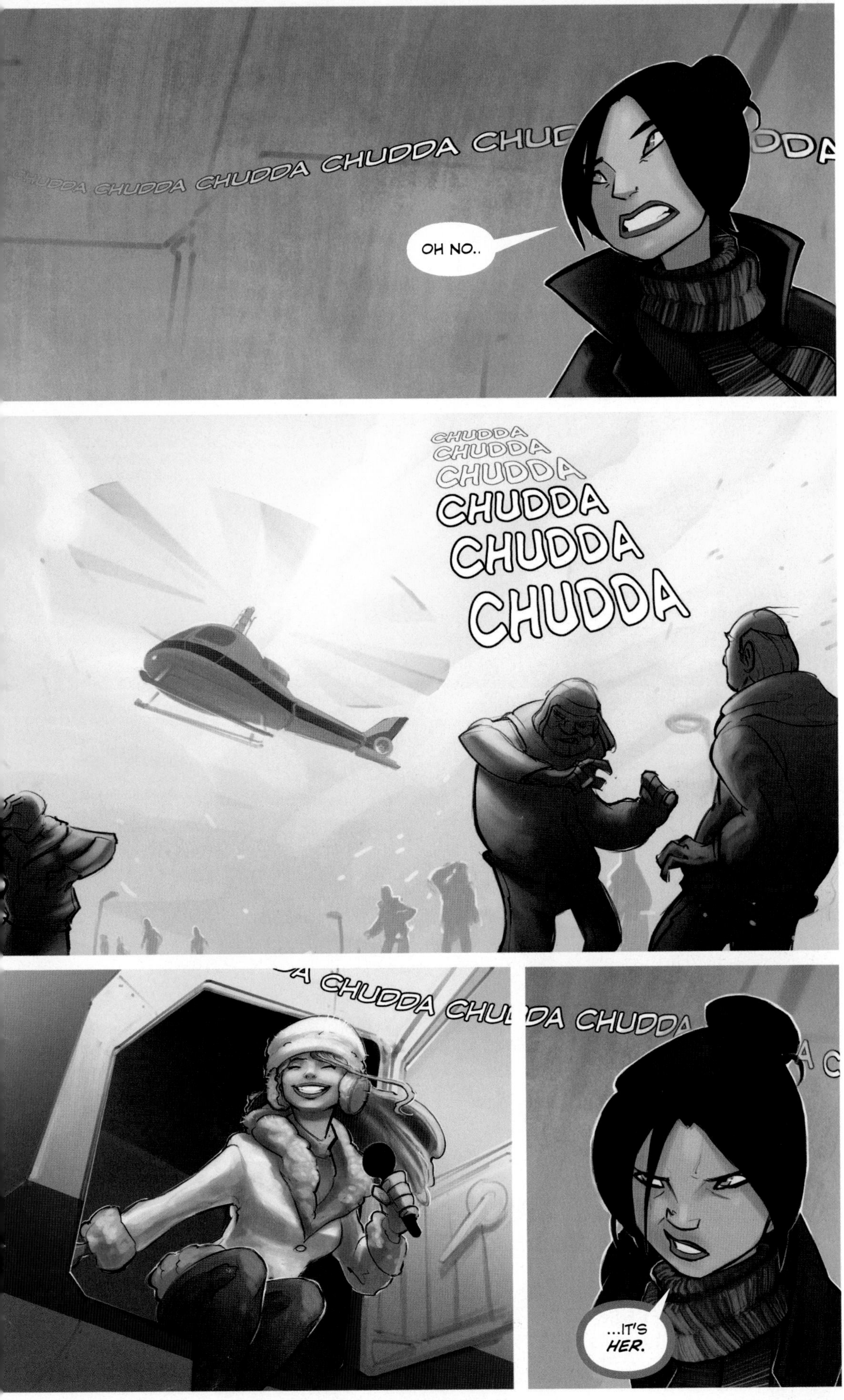
CHUDDA CHUDDA CHUDDA CHUDDA
OH NO..
CHUDDA
CHUDDA
CHUDDA
CHUDDA
CHUDDA
CHUDDA
CHUDDA CHUDDA
...IT'S HER.

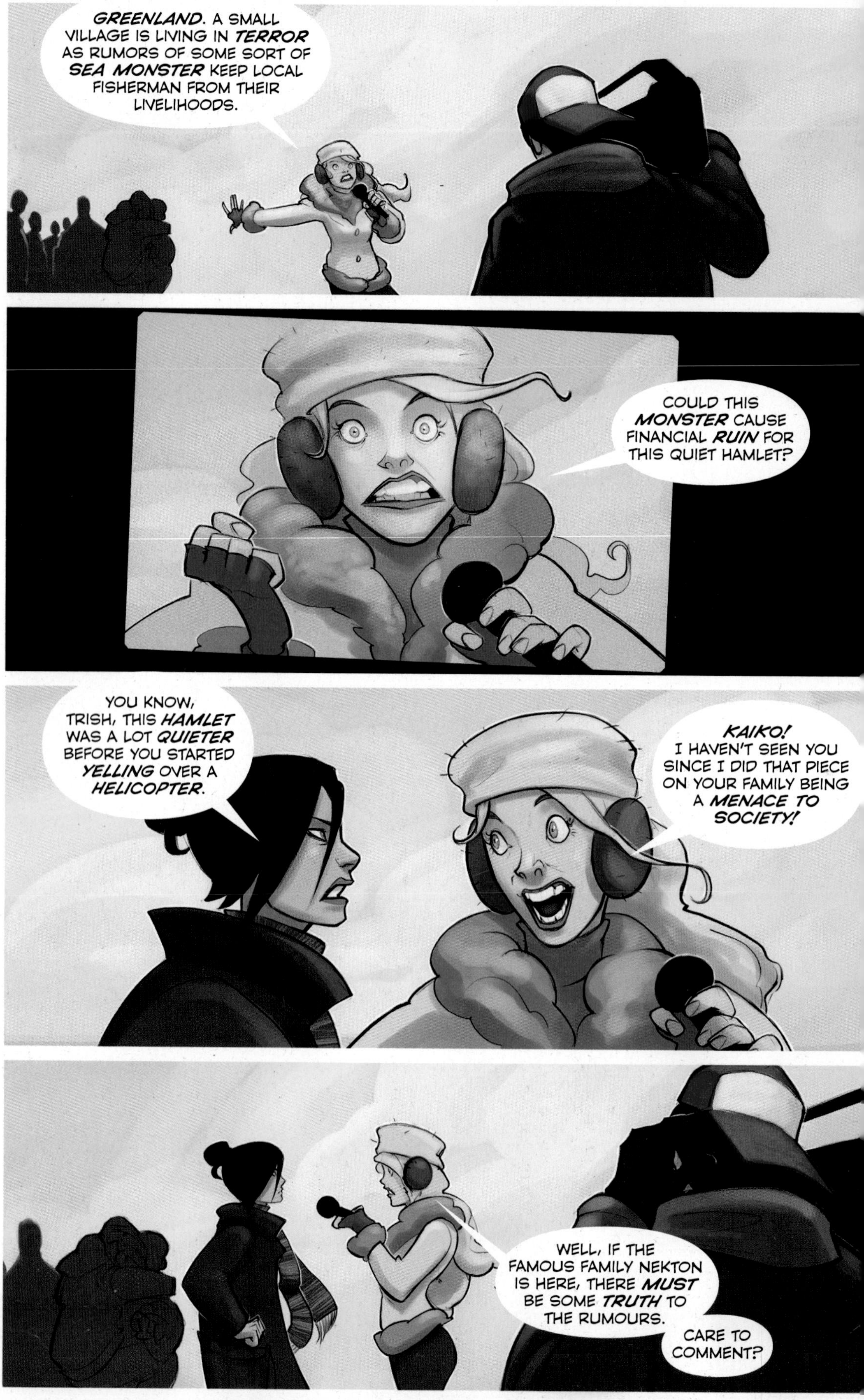
GREENLAND. A SMALL VILLAGE IS LIVING IN TERROR AS RUMORS OF SOME SORT OF SEA MONSTER KEEP LOCAL FISHERMAN FROM THEIR LIVELIHOODS.
COULD THIS MONSTER CAUSE FINANCIAL RUIN FOR THIS QUIET HAMLET?
YOU KNOW, TRISH, THIS HAMLET WAS A LOT QUIETER BEFORE YOU STARTED YELLING OVER A HELICOPTER.
KAIKO! I HAVEN'T SEEN YOU SINCE I DID THAT PIECE ON YOUR FAMILY BEING A MENACE TO SOCIETY!
WELL, IF THE FAMOUS FAMILY NEKTON IS HERE, THERE MUST BE SOME TRUTH TO THE RUMOURS.
CARE TO COMMENT?

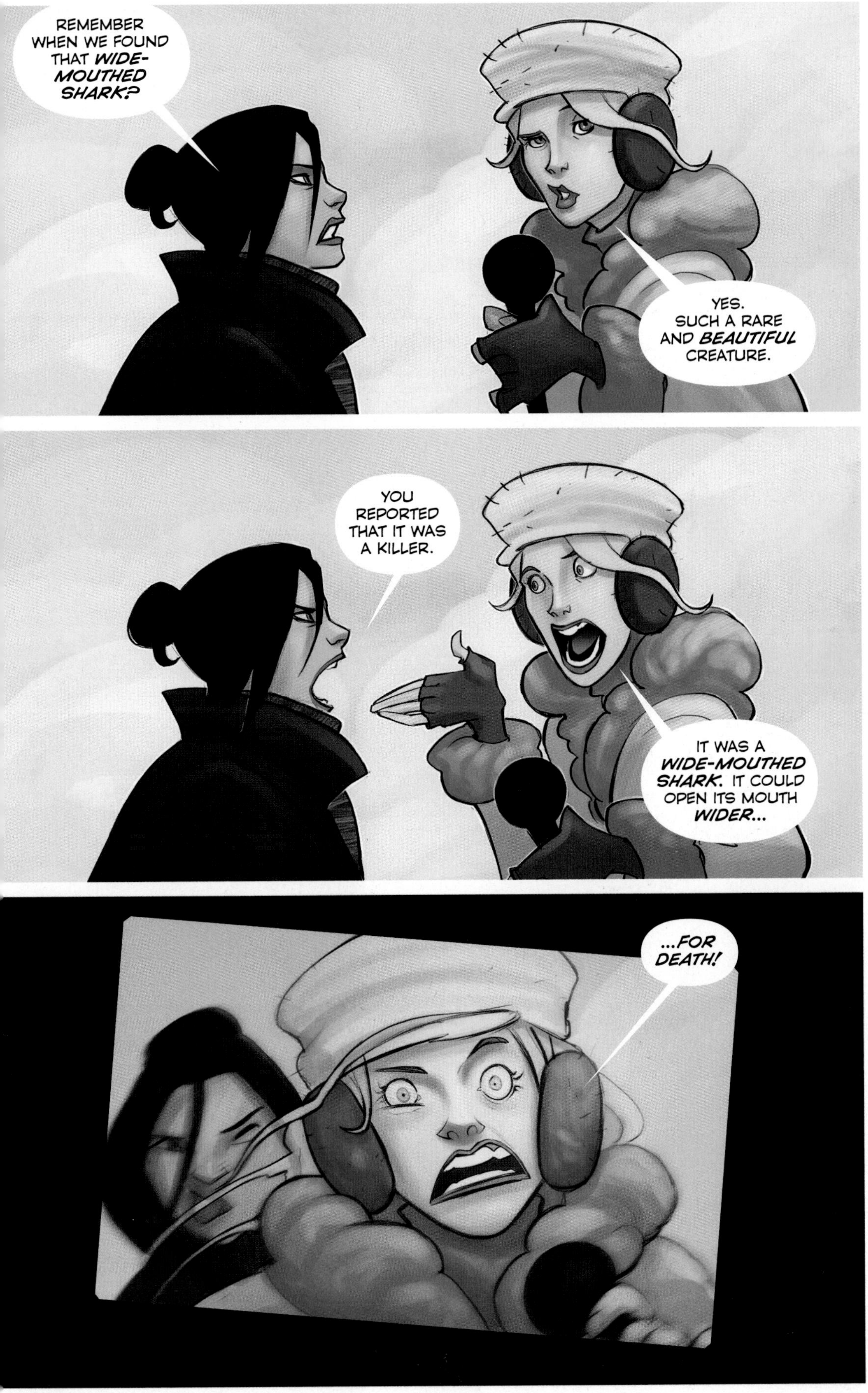
REMEMBER WHEN WE FOUND THAT *WIDE-MOUTHED SHARK?*
YES. SUCH A RARE AND *BEAUTIFUL* CREATURE.
YOU REPORTED THAT IT WAS A KILLER.
IT WAS A *WIDE-MOUTHED SHARK.* IT COULD OPEN ITS MOUTH *WIDER...*
*...FOR DEATH!*

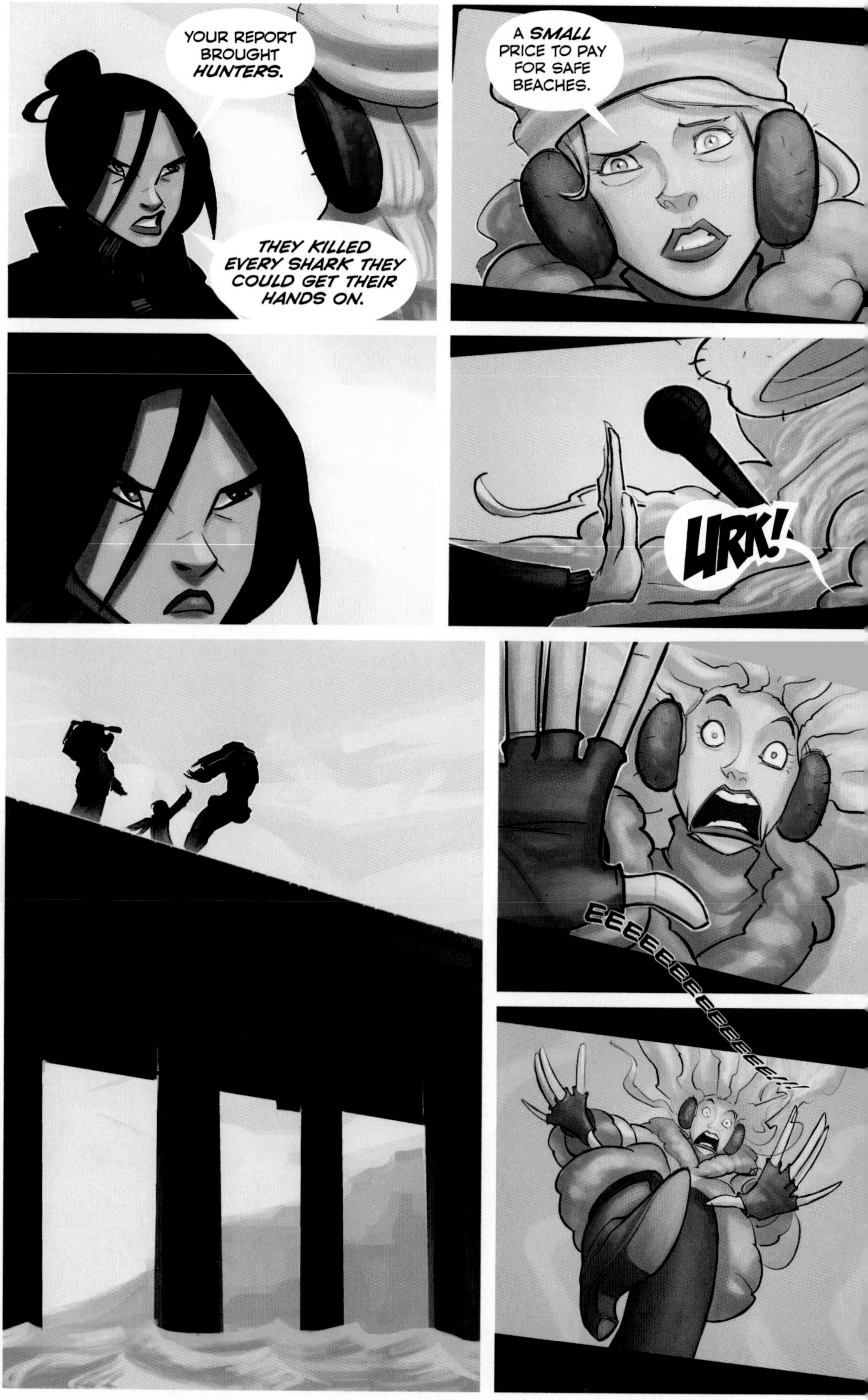

YOUR REPORT BROUGHT *HUNTERS.*
*THEY KILLED EVERY SHARK THEY COULD GET THEIR HANDS ON.*
A *SMALL* PRICE TO PAY FOR SAFE BEACHES.
URK!
EEEEEEEEEEEEEEEEEEE!!!

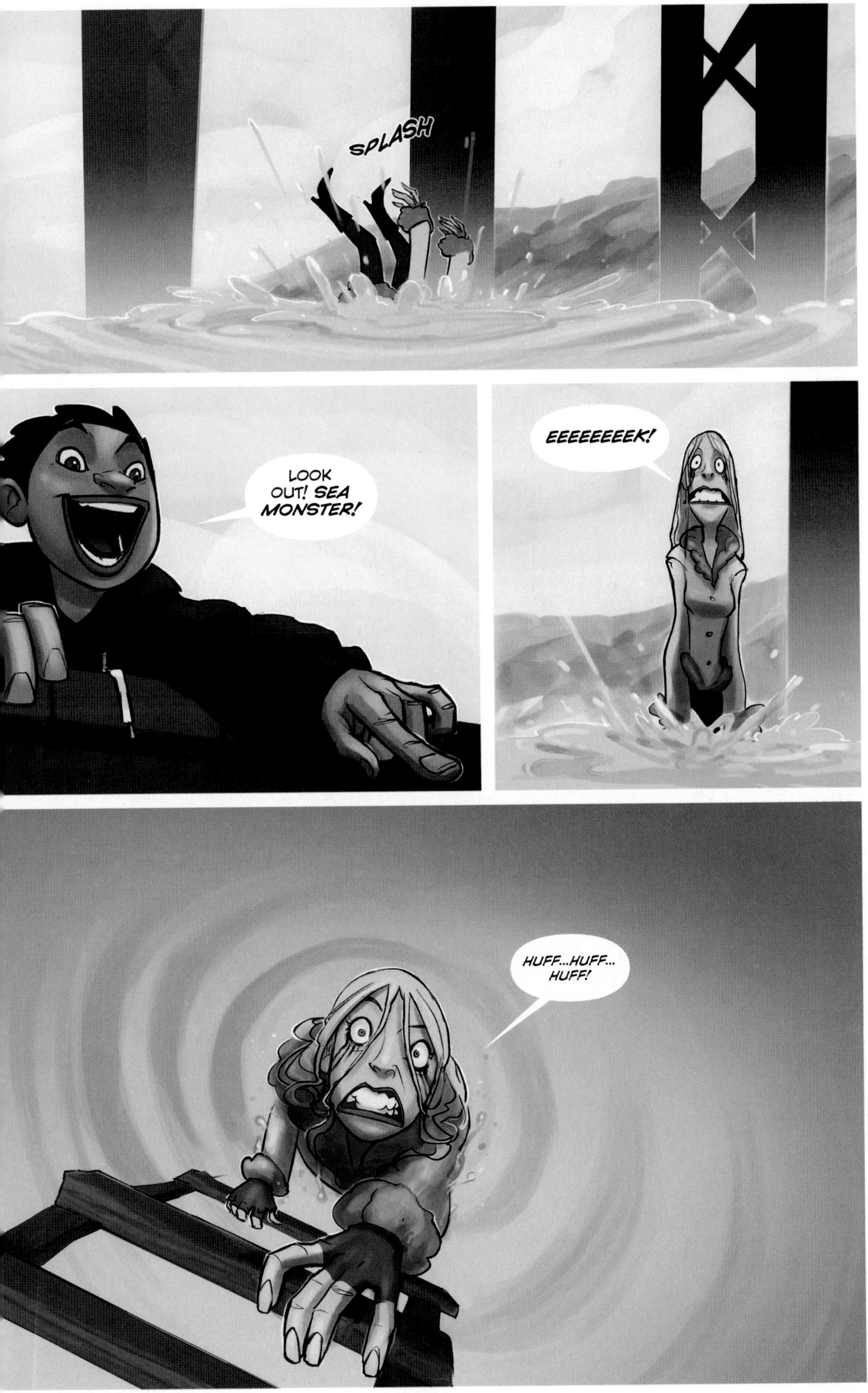
SPLASH
LOOK OUT! SEA MONSTER!
EEEEEEEEK!
HUFF...HUFF... HUFF!

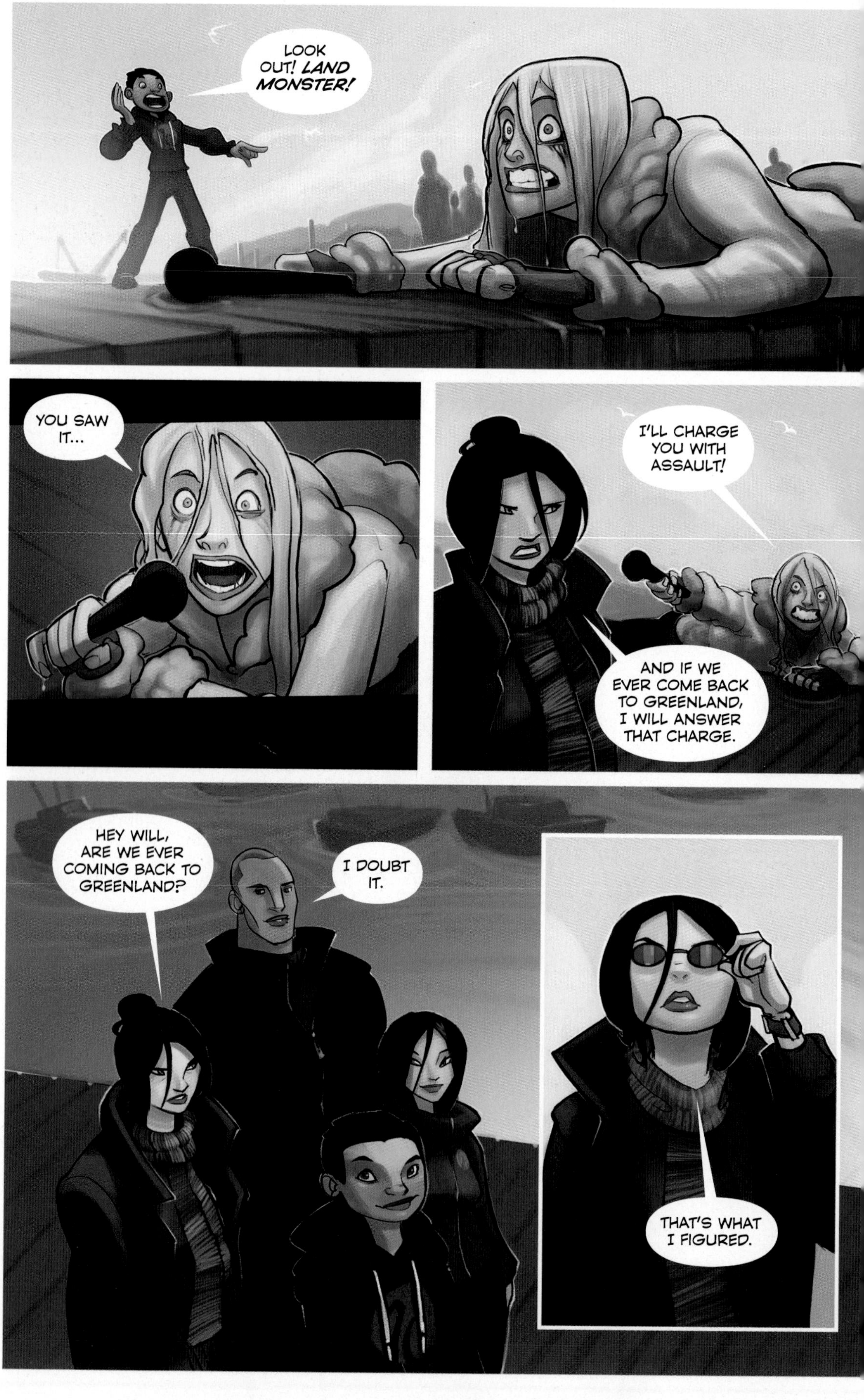
LOOK OUT! *LAND MONSTER!*
YOU SAW IT...
I'LL CHARGE YOU WITH ASSAULT!
AND IF WE EVER COME BACK TO GREENLAND, I WILL ANSWER THAT CHARGE.
HEY WILL, ARE WE EVER COMING BACK TO GREENLAND?
I DOUBT IT.
THAT'S WHAT I FIGURED.

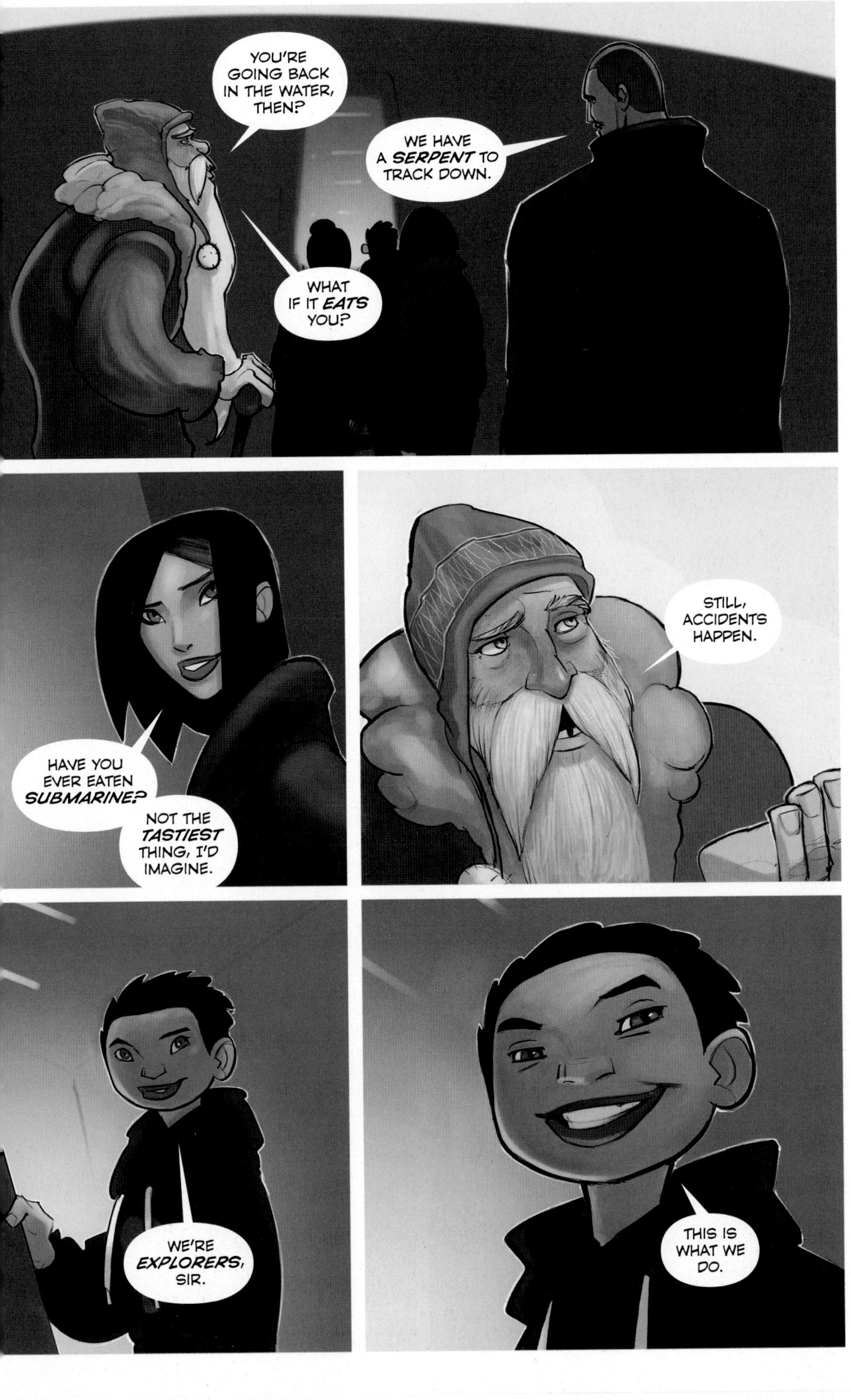

YOU'RE GOING BACK IN THE WATER, THEN?
WE HAVE A *SERPENT* TO TRACK DOWN.
WHAT IF IT *EATS* YOU?
HAVE YOU EVER EATEN *SUBMARINE?*
NOT THE *TASTIEST* THING, I'D IMAGINE.
STILL, ACCIDENTS HAPPEN.
WE'RE *EXPLORERS*, SIR.
THIS IS WHAT WE DO.

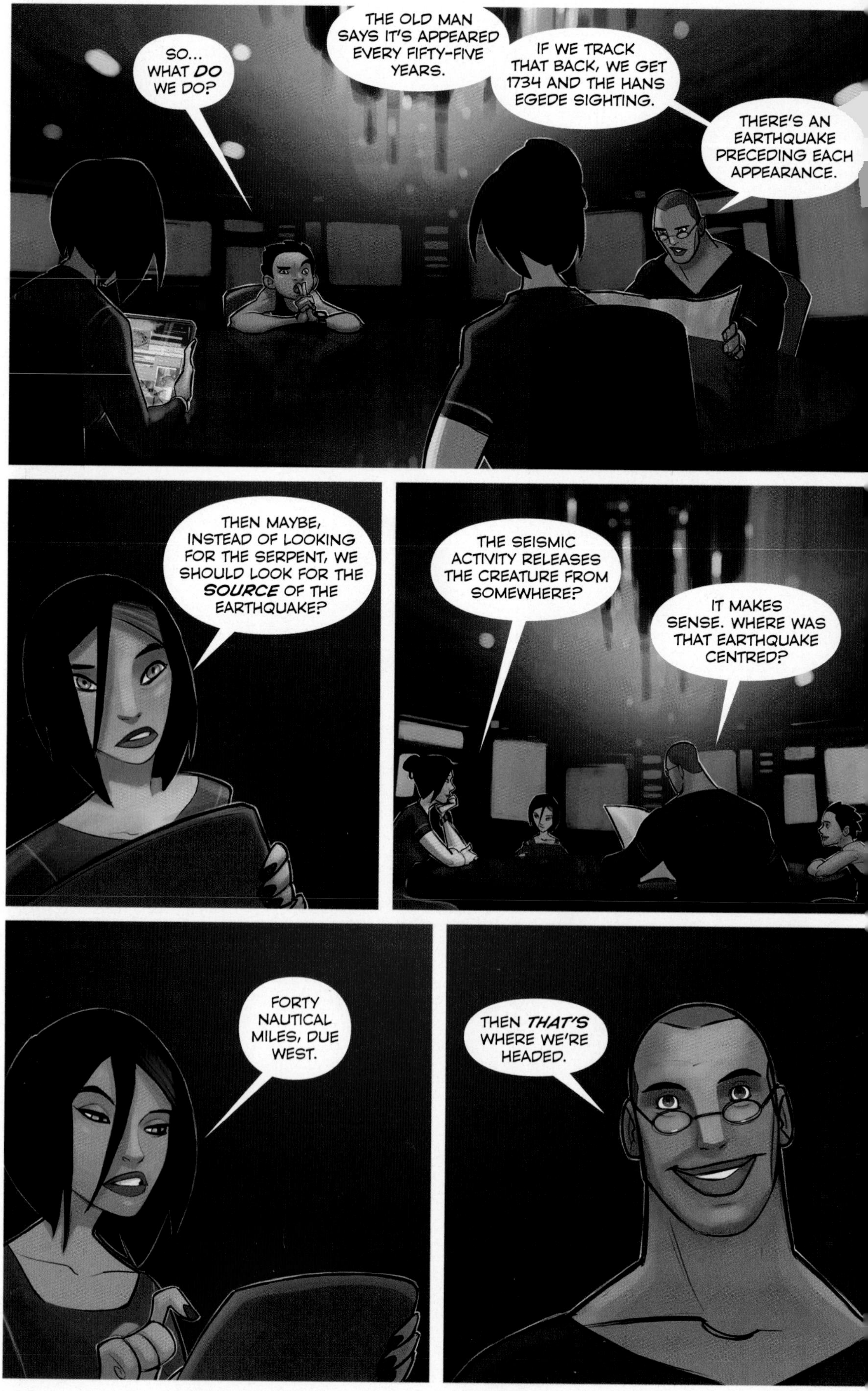
SO... WHAT DO WE DO?
THE OLD MAN SAYS IT'S APPEARED EVERY FIFTY-FIVE YEARS.
IF WE TRACK THAT BACK, WE GET 1734 AND THE HANS EGEDE SIGHTING.
THERE'S AN EARTHQUAKE PRECEDING EACH APPEARANCE.
THEN MAYBE, INSTEAD OF LOOKING FOR THE SERPENT, WE SHOULD LOOK FOR THE SOURCE OF THE EARTHQUAKE?
THE SEISMIC ACTIVITY RELEASES THE CREATURE FROM SOMEWHERE?
IT MAKES SENSE. WHERE WAS THAT EARTHQUAKE CENTRED?
FORTY NAUTICAL MILES, DUE WEST.
THEN THAT'S WHERE WE'RE HEADED.

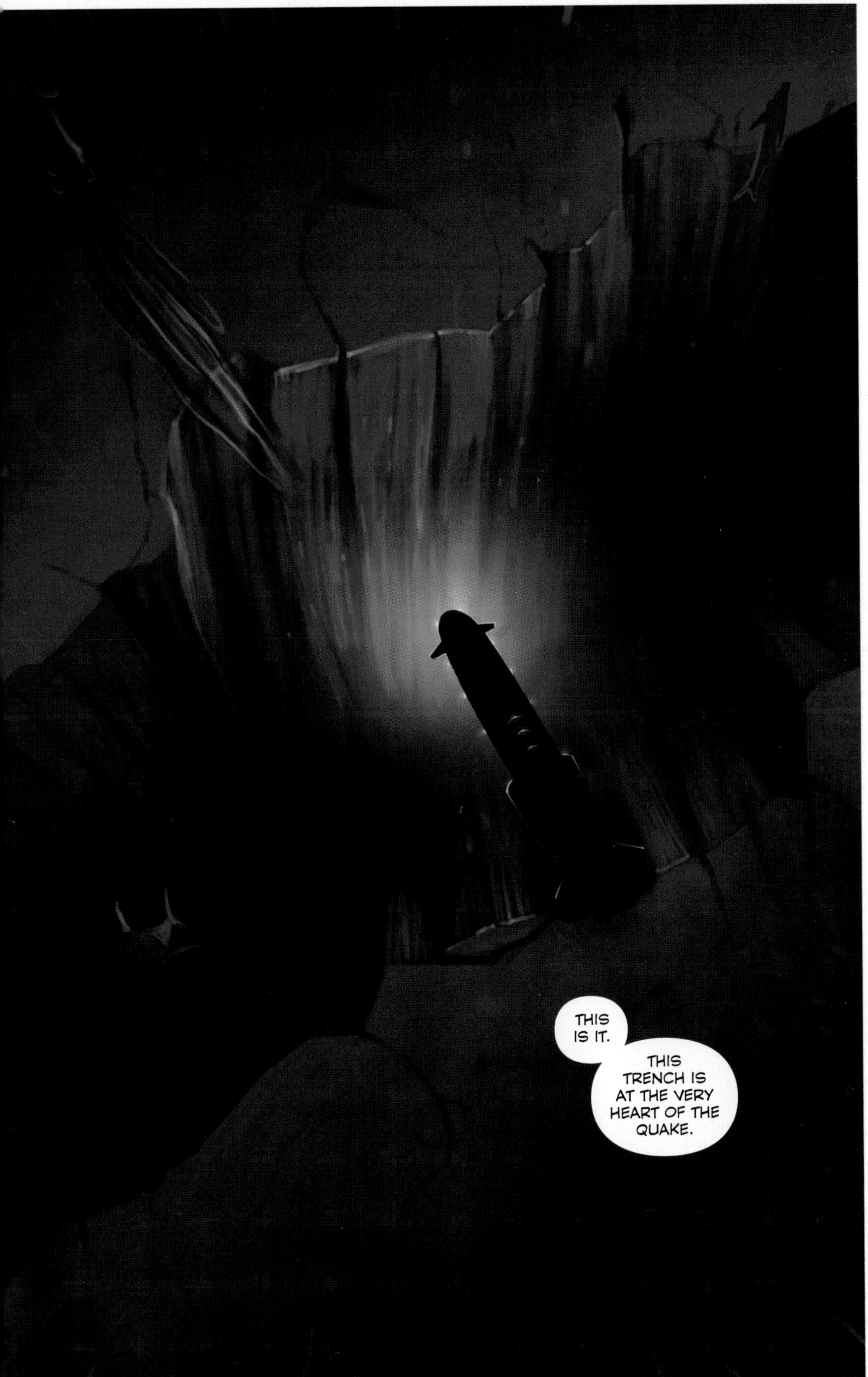
THIS IS IT.
THIS TRENCH IS AT THE VERY HEART OF THE QUAKE.

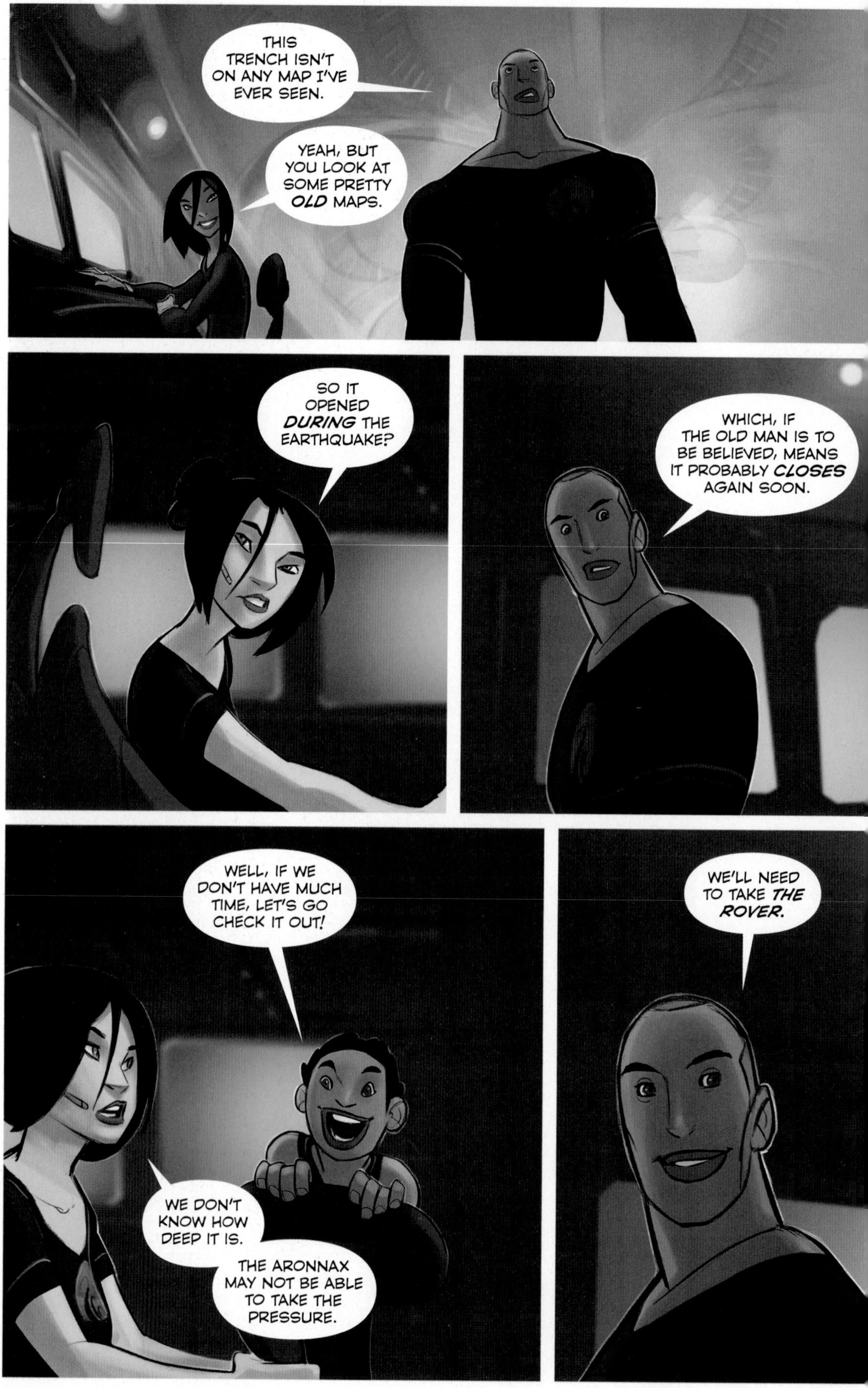
THIS TRENCH ISN'T ON ANY MAP I'VE EVER SEEN.
YEAH, BUT YOU LOOK AT SOME PRETTY *OLD* MAPS.
SO IT OPENED *DURING* THE EARTHQUAKE?
WHICH, IF THE OLD MAN IS TO BE BELIEVED, MEANS IT PROBABLY *CLOSES* AGAIN SOON.
WELL, IF WE DON'T HAVE MUCH TIME, LET'S GO CHECK IT OUT!
WE DON'T KNOW HOW DEEP IT IS.
THE ARONNAX MAY NOT BE ABLE TO TAKE THE PRESSURE.
WE'LL NEED TO TAKE *THE ROVER*.

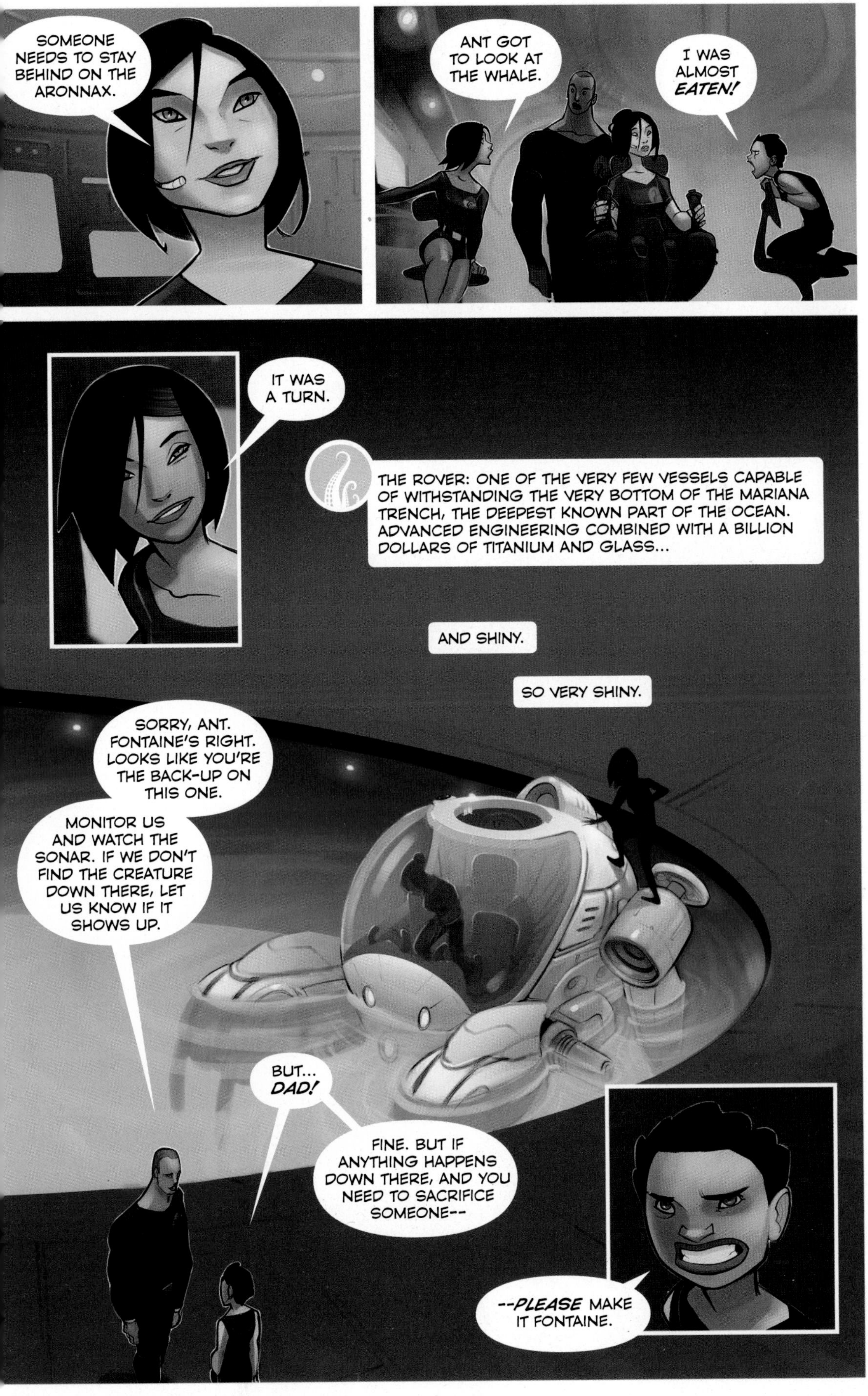
SOMEONE NEEDS TO STAY BEHIND ON THE ARONNAX.
ANT GOT TO LOOK AT THE WHALE.
I WAS ALMOST *EATEN!*
IT WAS A TURN.
THE ROVER: ONE OF THE VERY FEW VESSELS CAPABLE OF WITHSTANDING THE VERY BOTTOM OF THE MARIANA TRENCH, THE DEEPEST KNOWN PART OF THE OCEAN. ADVANCED ENGINEERING COMBINED WITH A BILLION DOLLARS OF TITANIUM AND GLASS...
AND SHINY.
SO VERY SHINY.
SORRY, ANT. FONTAINE'S RIGHT. LOOKS LIKE YOU'RE THE BACK-UP ON THIS ONE.
MONITOR US AND WATCH THE SONAR. IF WE DON'T FIND THE CREATURE DOWN THERE, LET US KNOW IF IT SHOWS UP.
BUT... *DAD!*
FINE. BUT IF ANYTHING HAPPENS DOWN THERE, AND YOU NEED TO SACRIFICE SOMEONE--
--*PLEASE* MAKE IT FONTAINE.

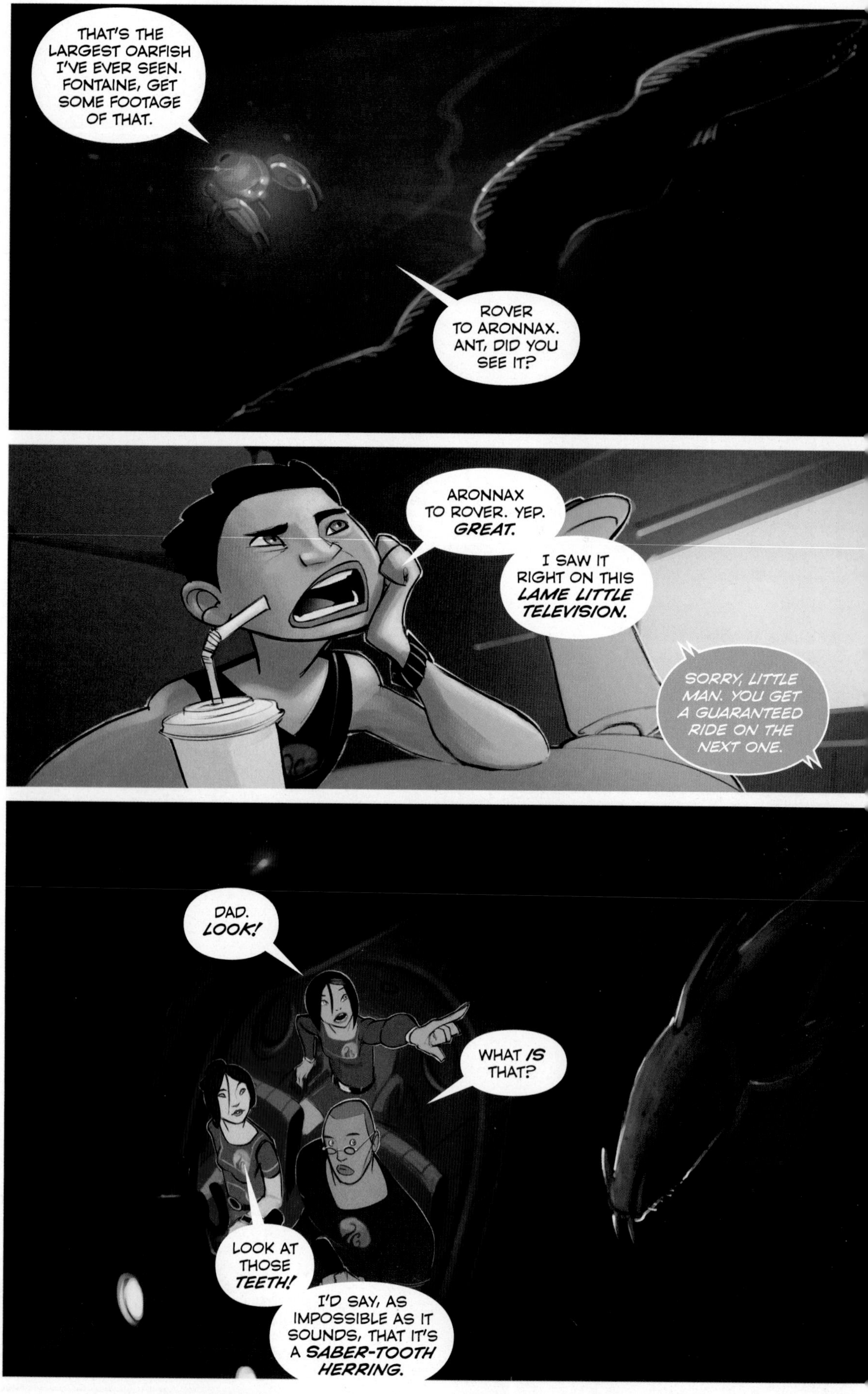

THAT'S THE LARGEST OARFISH I'VE EVER SEEN. FONTAINE, GET SOME FOOTAGE OF THAT.
ROVER TO ARONNAX. ANT, DID YOU SEE IT?
ARONNAX TO ROVER. YEP. *GREAT.*
I SAW IT RIGHT ON THIS *LAME LITTLE TELEVISION.*
*SORRY, LITTLE MAN. YOU GET A GUARANTEED RIDE ON THE NEXT ONE.*
DAD. *LOOK!*
WHAT *IS* THAT?
LOOK AT THOSE *TEETH!*
I'D SAY, AS IMPOSSIBLE AS IT SOUNDS, THAT IT'S A *SABER-TOOTH HERRING.*

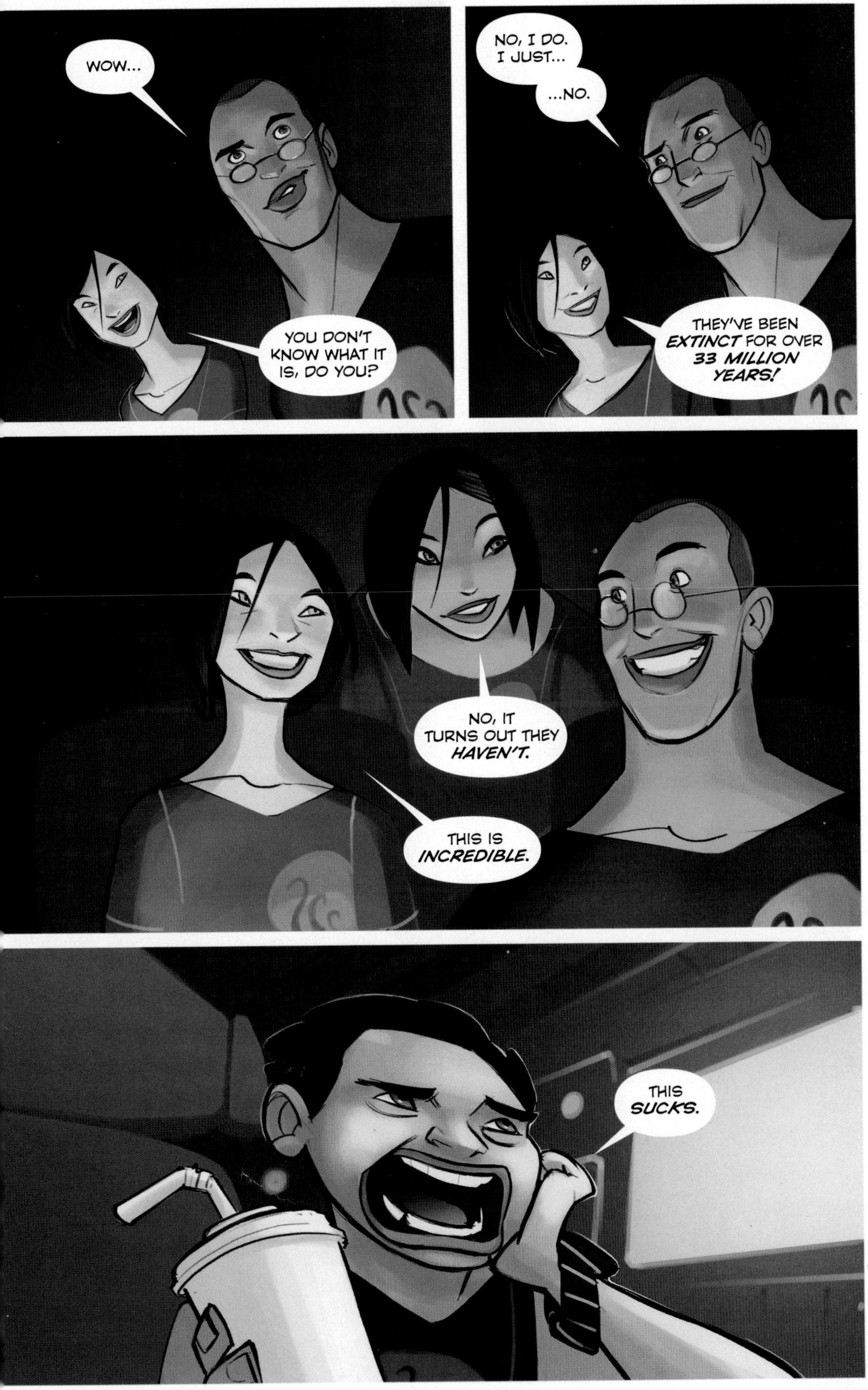
WOW...
YOU DON'T KNOW WHAT IT IS, DO YOU?
NO, I DO. I JUST...
...NO.
THEY'VE BEEN *EXTINCT* FOR OVER *33 MILLION YEARS!*
NO, IT TURNS OUT THEY *HAVEN'T.*
THIS IS *INCREDIBLE.*
THIS *SUCKS.*

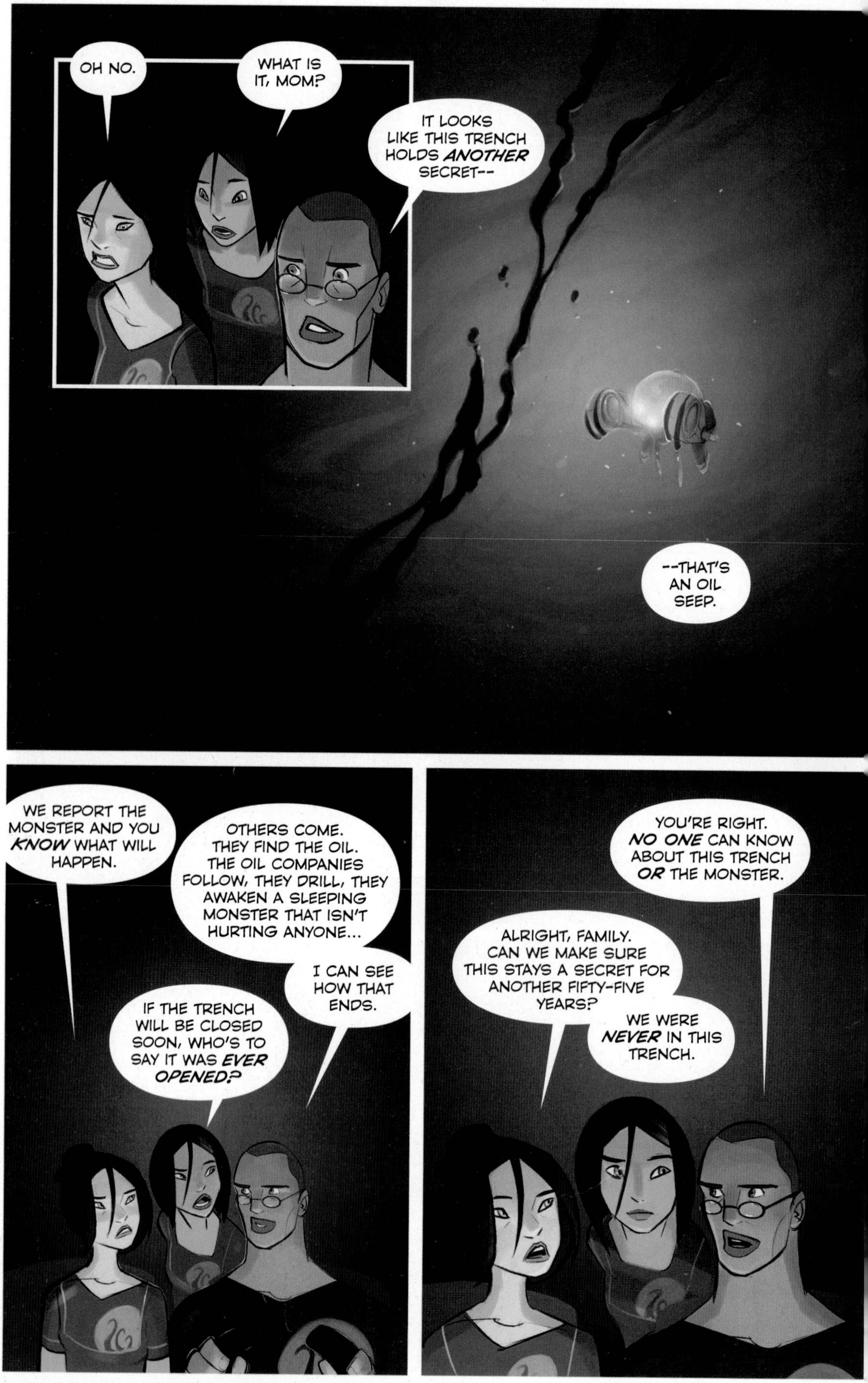

OH NO.
WHAT IS IT, MOM?
IT LOOKS LIKE THIS TRENCH HOLDS ANOTHER SECRET--
--THAT'S AN OIL SEEP.
WE REPORT THE MONSTER AND YOU KNOW WHAT WILL HAPPEN.
OTHERS COME. THEY FIND THE OIL. THE OIL COMPANIES FOLLOW, THEY DRILL, THEY AWAKEN A SLEEPING MONSTER THAT ISN'T HURTING ANYONE...
I CAN SEE HOW THAT ENDS.
IF THE TRENCH WILL BE CLOSED SOON, WHO'S TO SAY IT WAS EVER OPENED?
YOU'RE RIGHT. NO ONE CAN KNOW ABOUT THIS TRENCH OR THE MONSTER.
ALRIGHT, FAMILY. CAN WE MAKE SURE THIS STAYS A SECRET FOR ANOTHER FIFTY-FIVE YEARS?
WE WERE NEVER IN THIS TRENCH.

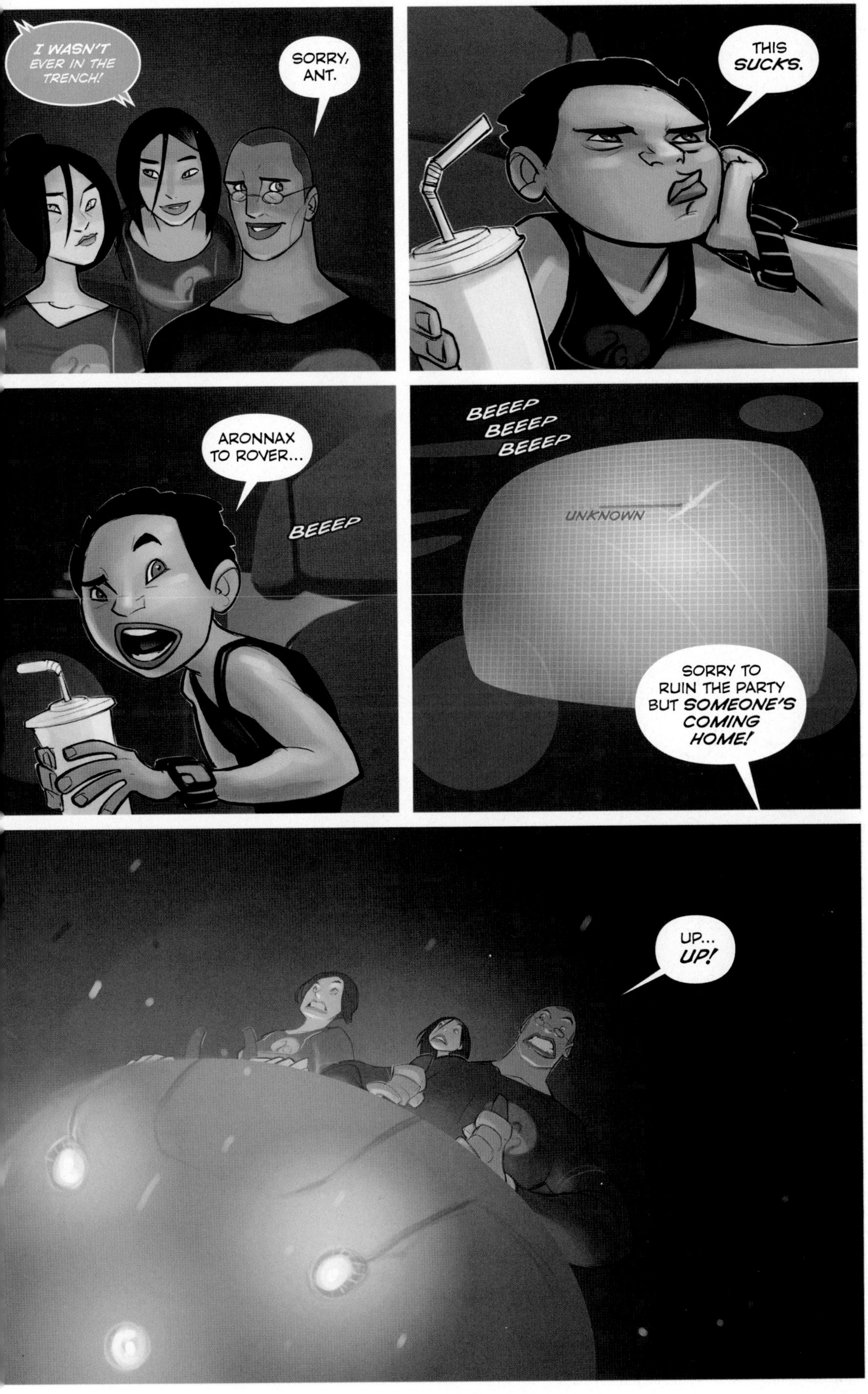
I WASN'T EVER IN THE TRENCH!
SORRY, ANT.
THIS SUCKS.
ARONNAX TO ROVER...
BEEEP
BEEEP BEEEP BEEEP
UNKNOWN
SORRY TO RUIN THE PARTY BUT SOMEONE'S COMING HOME!
UP... UP!

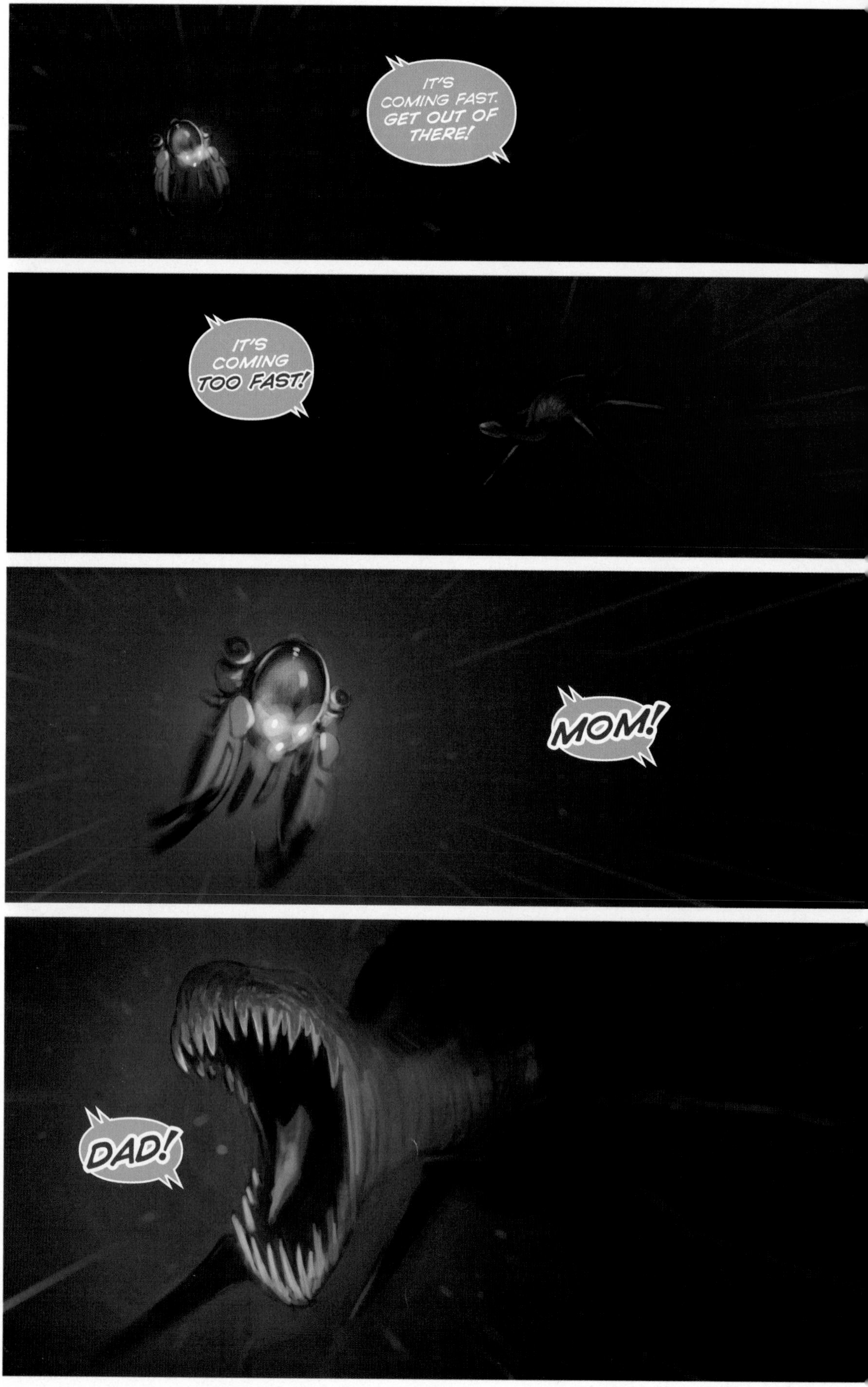
IT'S COMING FAST. GET OUT OF THERE!
IT'S COMING TOO FAST!
MOM!
DAD!

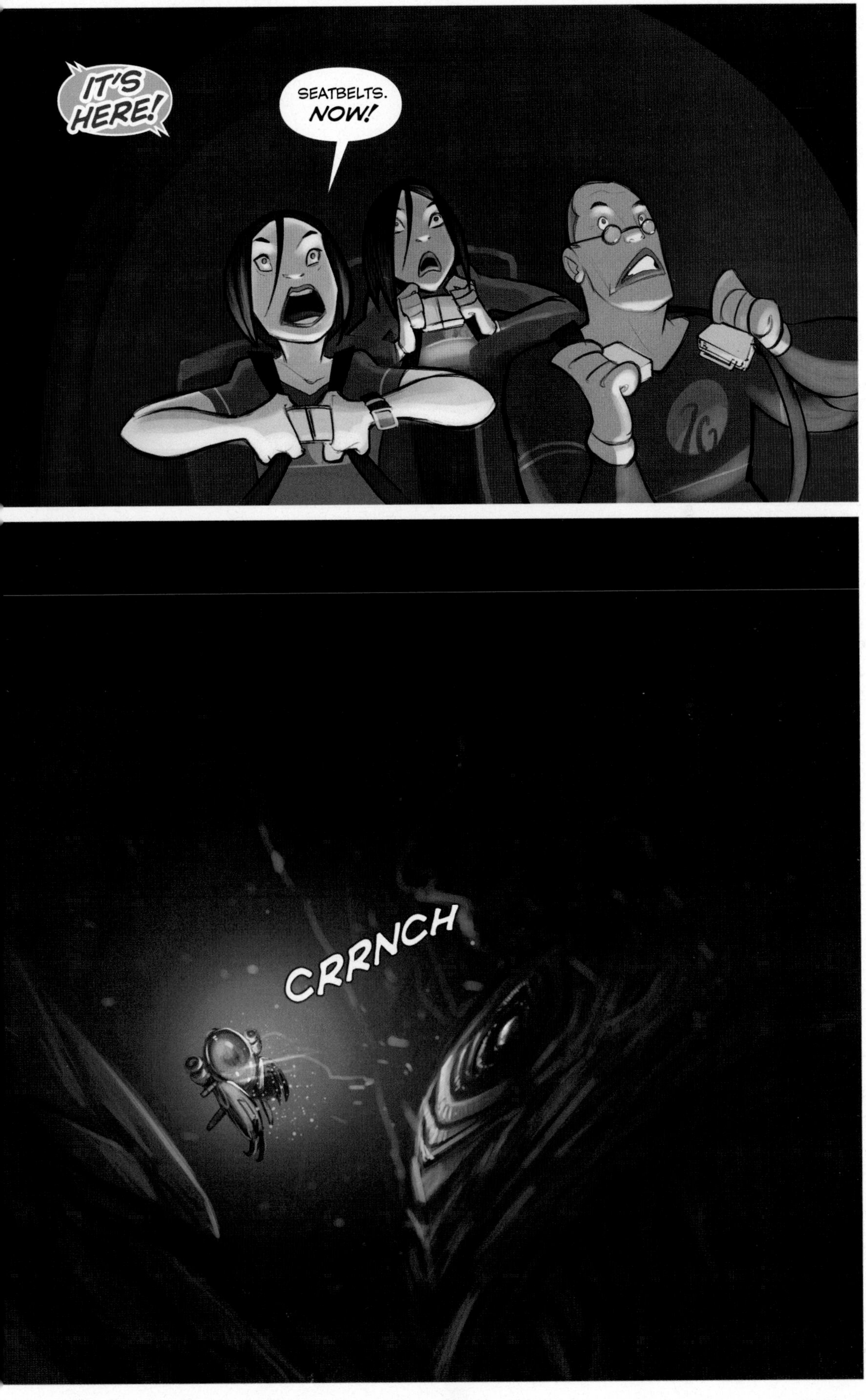
IT'S HERE!
SEATBELTS. NOW!
CRRNCH

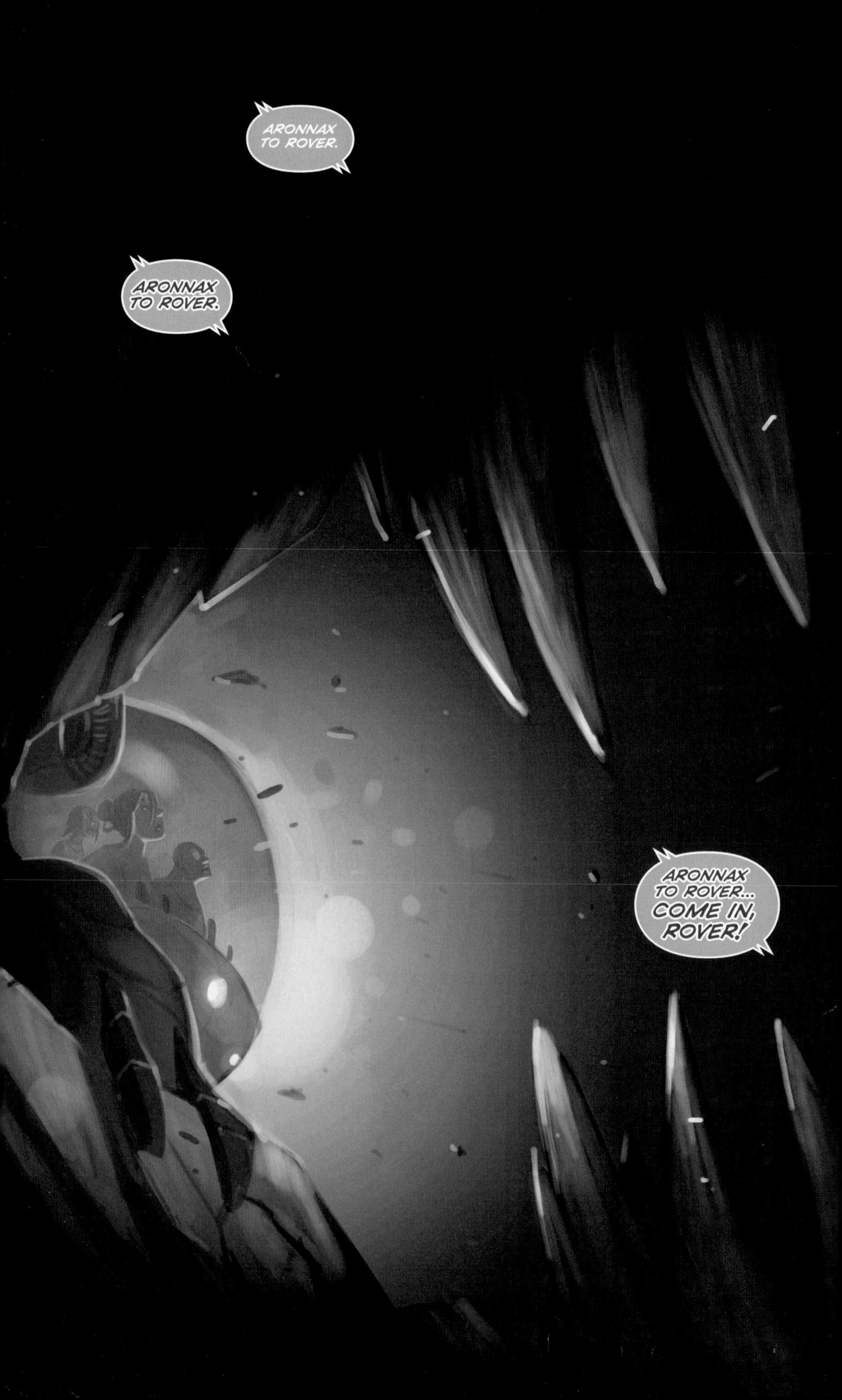
ARONNAX TO ROVER.
ARONNAX TO ROVER.
ARONNAX TO ROVER... COME IN, ROVER!

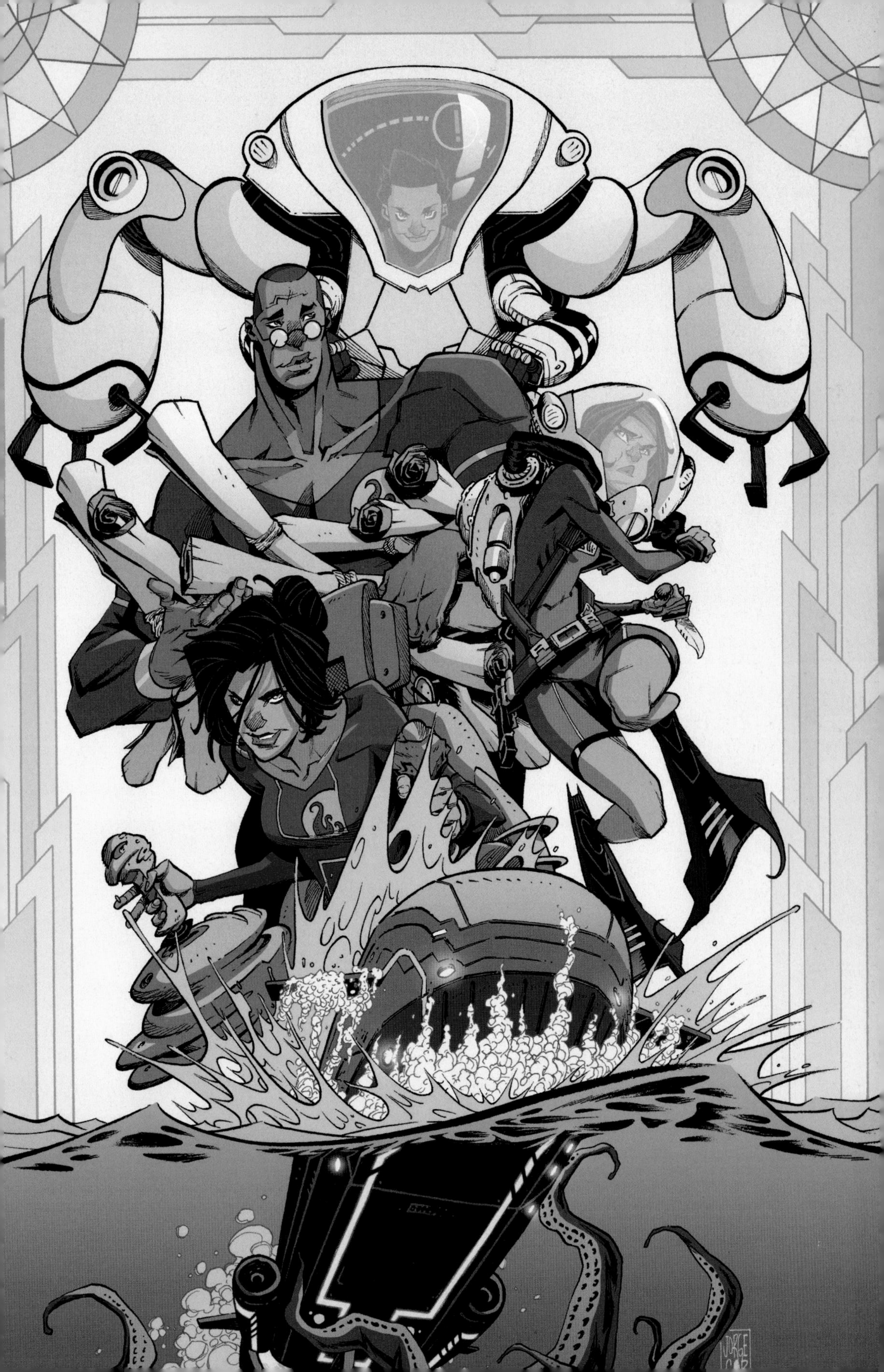

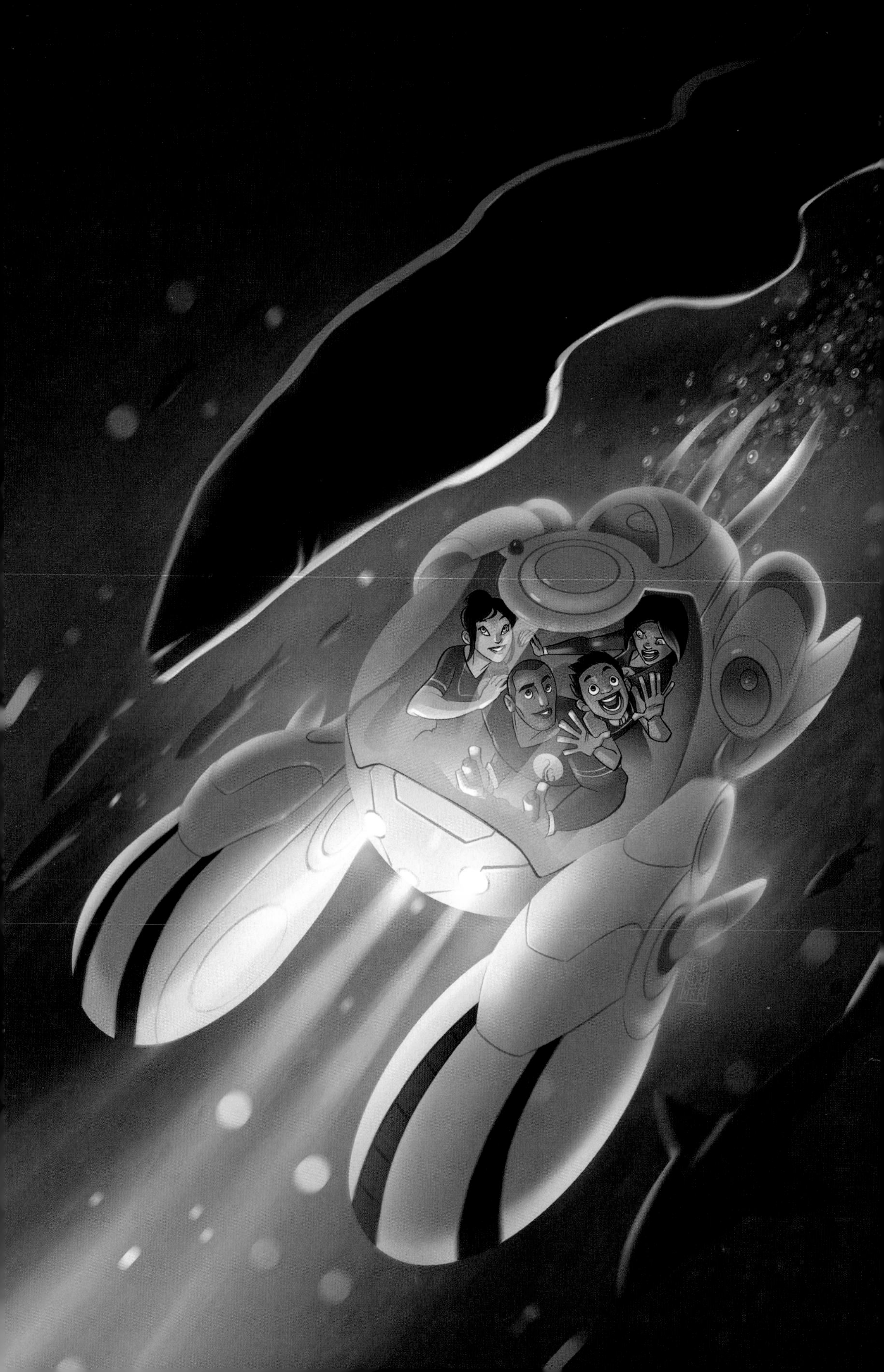

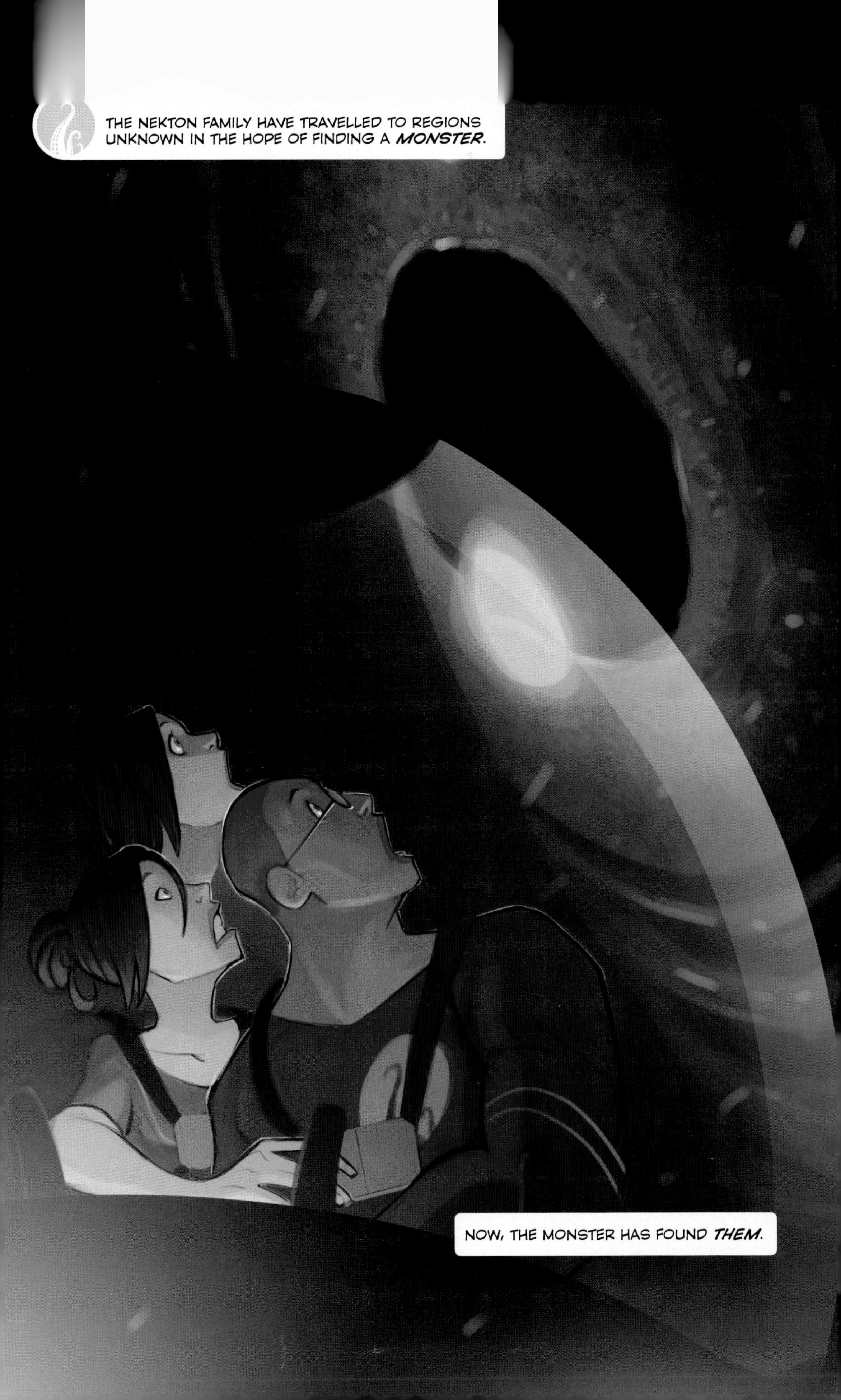
THE NEKTON FAMILY HAVE TRAVELLED TO REGIONS UNKNOWN IN THE HOPE OF FINDING A *MONSTER*.
NOW, THE MONSTER HAS FOUND *THEM*.

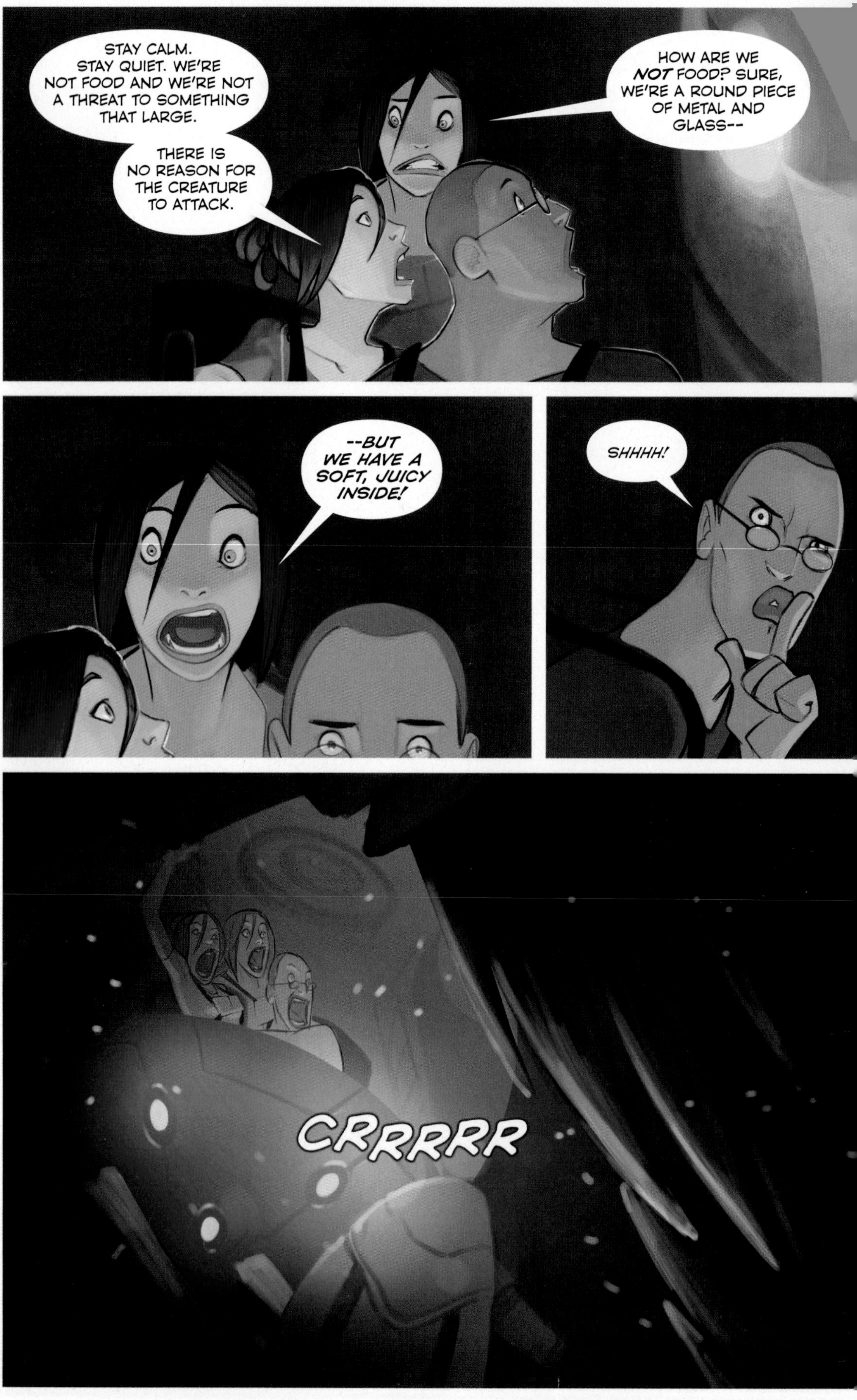
STAY CALM. STAY QUIET. WE'RE NOT FOOD AND WE'RE NOT A THREAT TO SOMETHING THAT LARGE.
THERE IS NO REASON FOR THE CREATURE TO ATTACK.
HOW ARE WE *NOT* FOOD? SURE, WE'RE A ROUND PIECE OF METAL AND GLASS--
--BUT WE HAVE A SOFT, JUICY INSIDE!
SHHHH!
CRRRRR

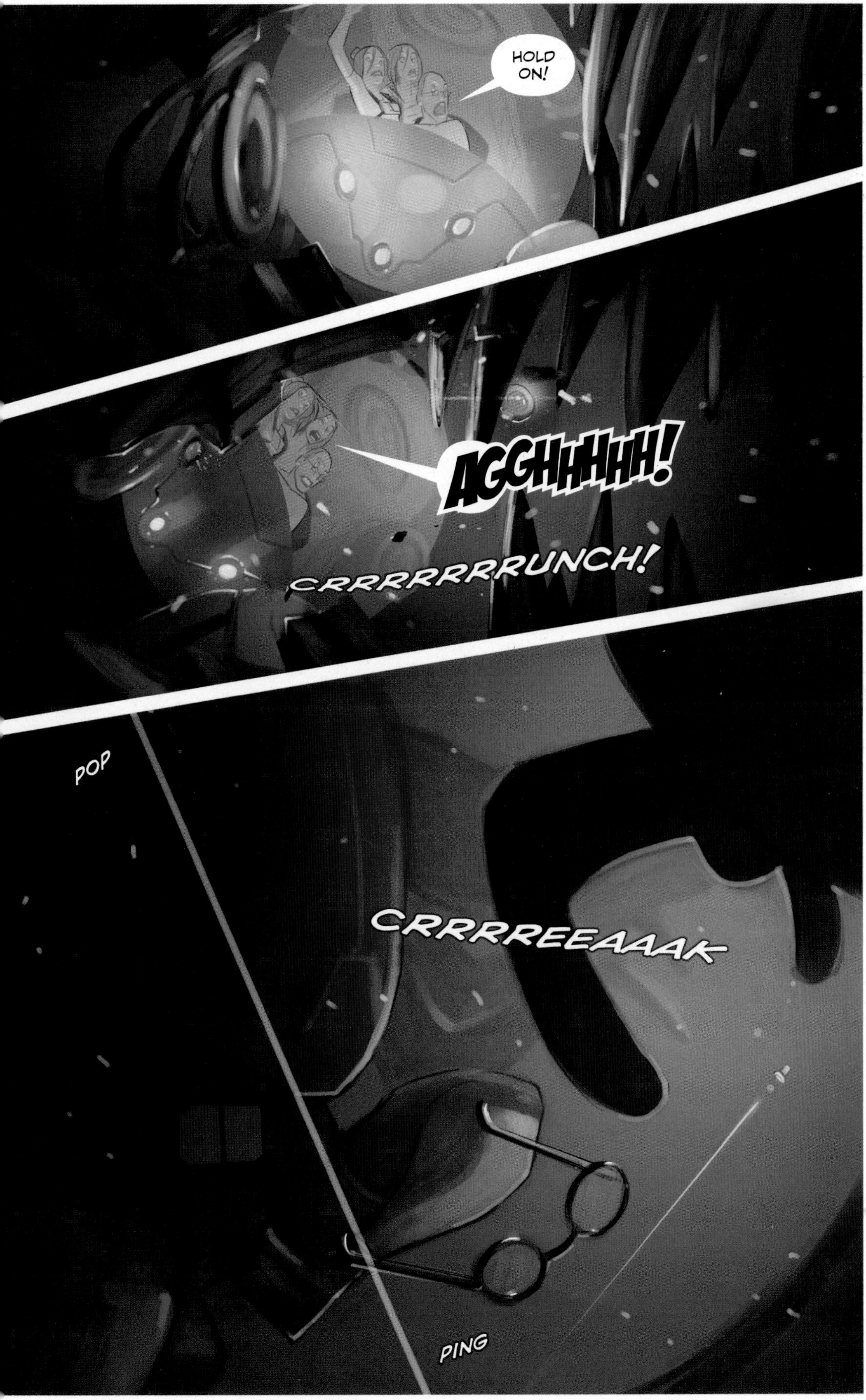
HOLD ON!
AGGHHHHH!
CRRRRRRRRUNCH!
POP
CRRRREEAAAK
PING

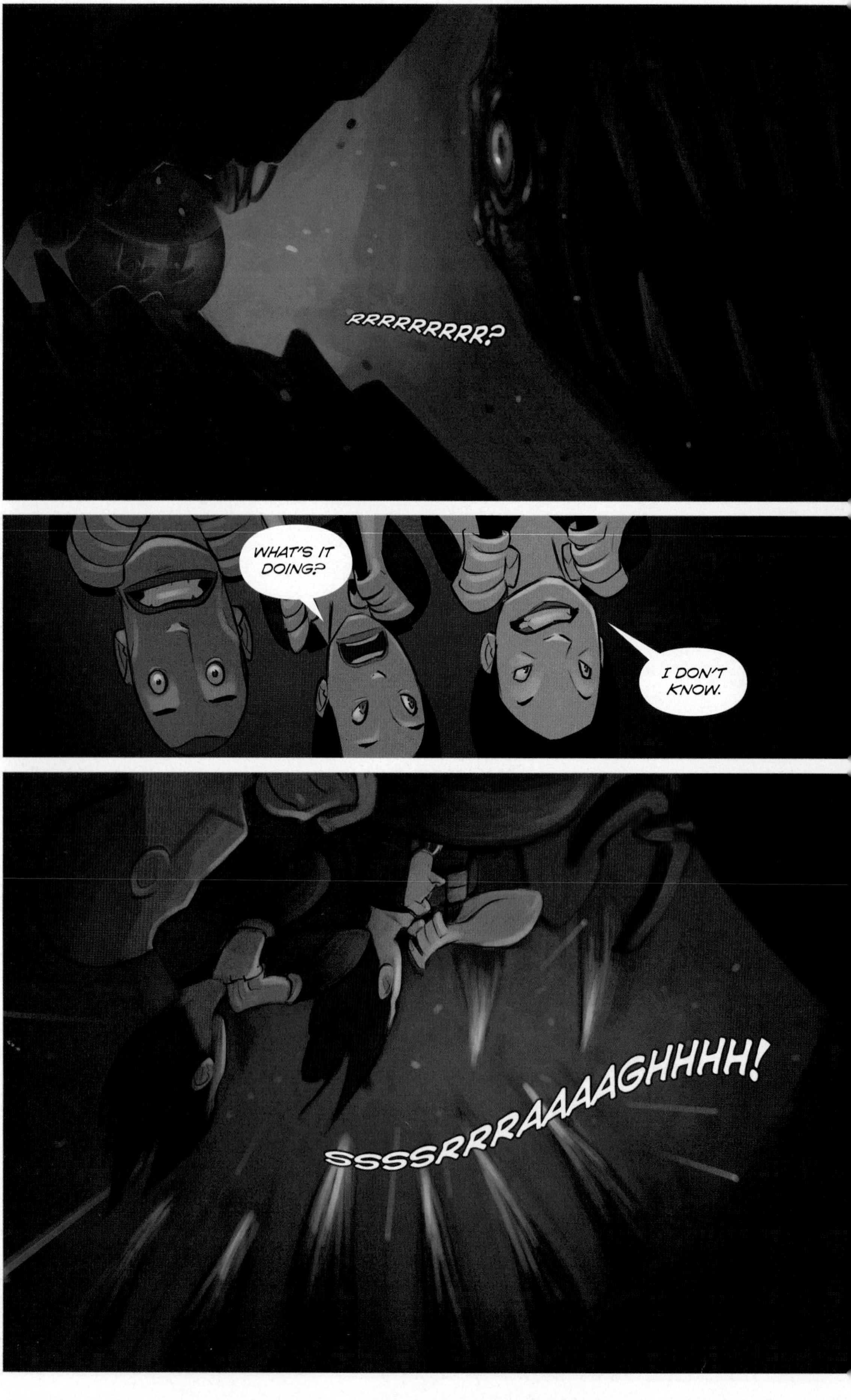
RRRRRRRRR?
WHAT'S IT DOING?
I DON'T KNOW.
SSSSRRRAAAAGHHHH!

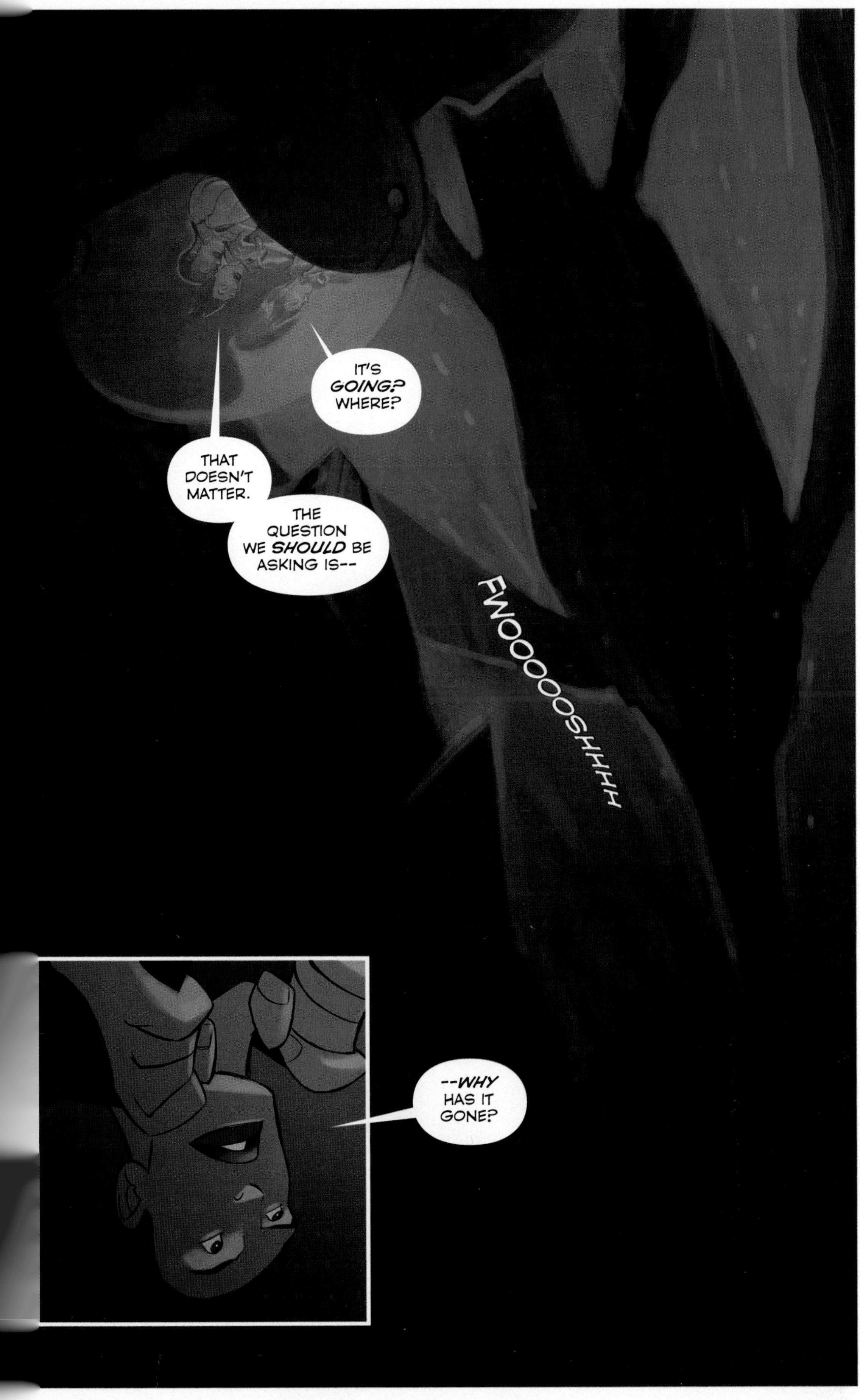

IT'S GOING? WHERE?
THAT DOESN'T MATTER.
THE QUESTION WE SHOULD BE ASKING IS--
FWOOOOOSHHHH
--WHY HAS IT GONE?

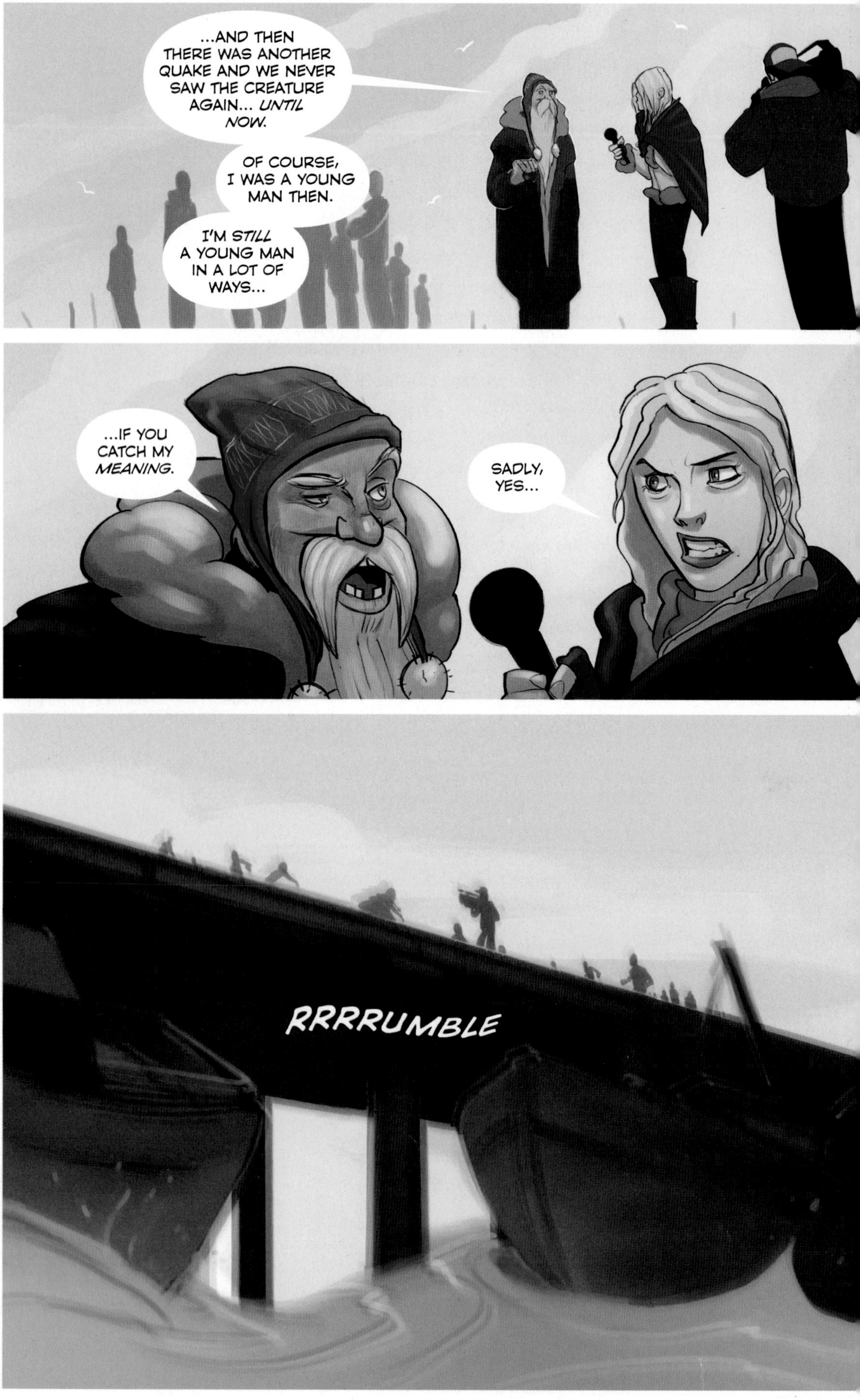

...AND THEN THERE WAS ANOTHER QUAKE AND WE NEVER SAW THE CREATURE AGAIN... *UNTIL NOW.*
OF COURSE, I WAS A YOUNG MAN THEN.
I'M *STILL* A YOUNG MAN IN A LOT OF WAYS...
...IF YOU CATCH MY *MEANING*.
SADLY, YES...
RRRRUMBLE

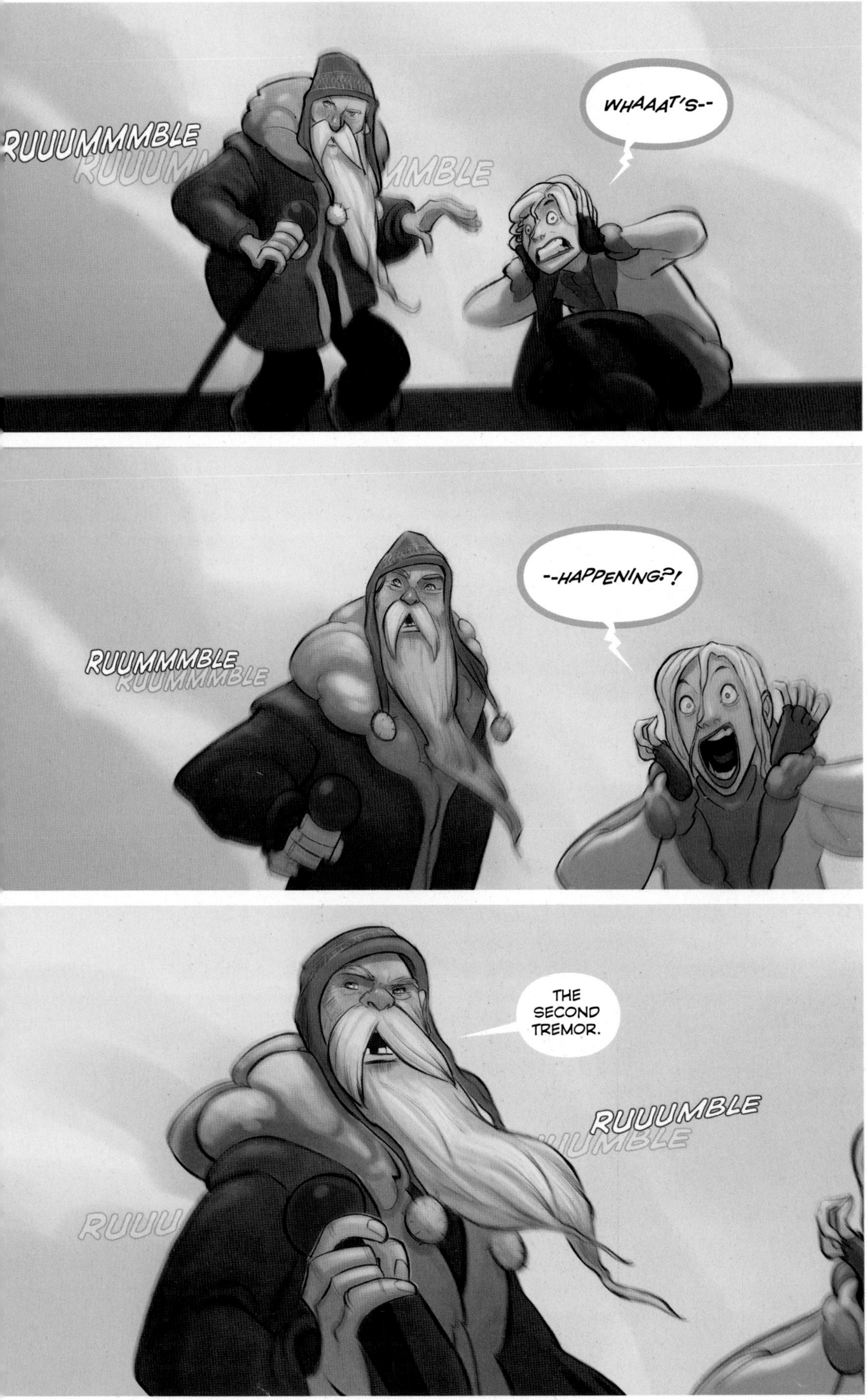
WHAAAT'S--
RUUUMMMMBLE
RUUUMMMMBLE
RUUMMMBLE
RUUMMMBLE
--HAPPENING?!
THE SECOND TREMOR.
RUUUMBLE
RUUUMBLE
RUUU

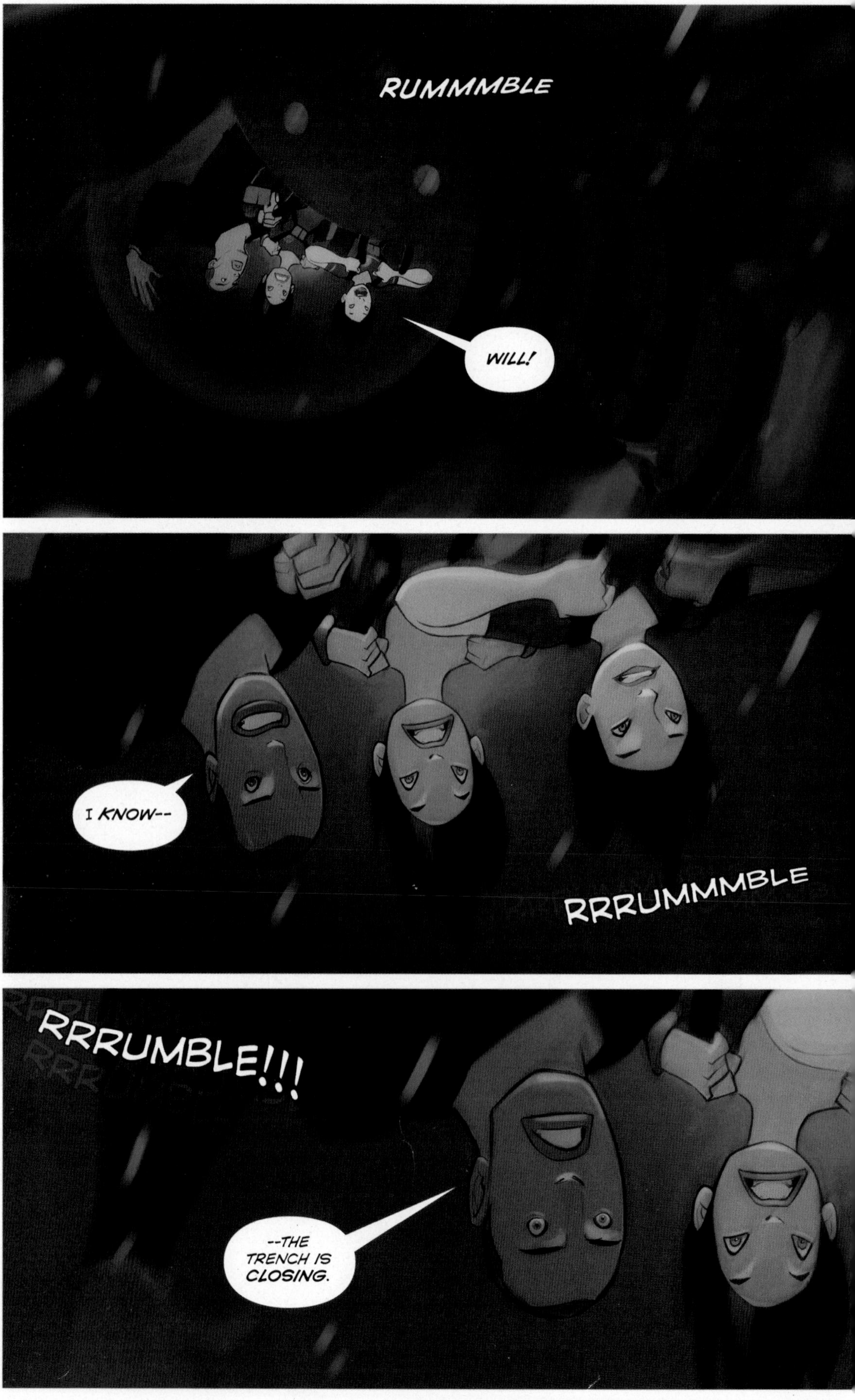
RUMMMBLE
WILL!
I KNOW--
RRRUMMMBLE
RRRUMBLE!!!
--THE TRENCH IS CLOSING.

THEN LET'S GET OUT OF HERE!

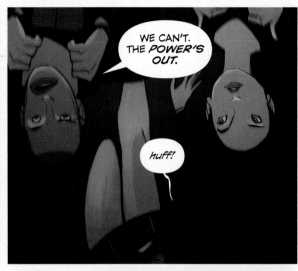

WE CAN'T. THE *POWER'S OUT.*

huff!

WHAT DO YOU MEAN 'THE POWER'S OUT'?

WHAT ABOUT THIS LIGHT?

THAT'S THE LIGHT THAT TELLS US WE'VE LOST POWER.

WHY DOES THAT *LIGHT* HAVE POWER--

--BUT NOTHING THAT COULD *PROPEL US OUT OF HERE* DOES?

WHAT ABOUT THE HOMING BEACON?

IT'S GONE! IT MUST HAVE BEEN KNOCKED OFF BY THE CREATURE.

ALL RIGHT. BREATHE *CALMLY.* WITHOUT THE POWER WE ONLY HAVE SO MUCH *AIR.*

ANT WILL GET HELP. SOMEONE WILL FIND US.

WITHOUT THE *HOMING BEACON...?*

SOMEONE.
WILL.

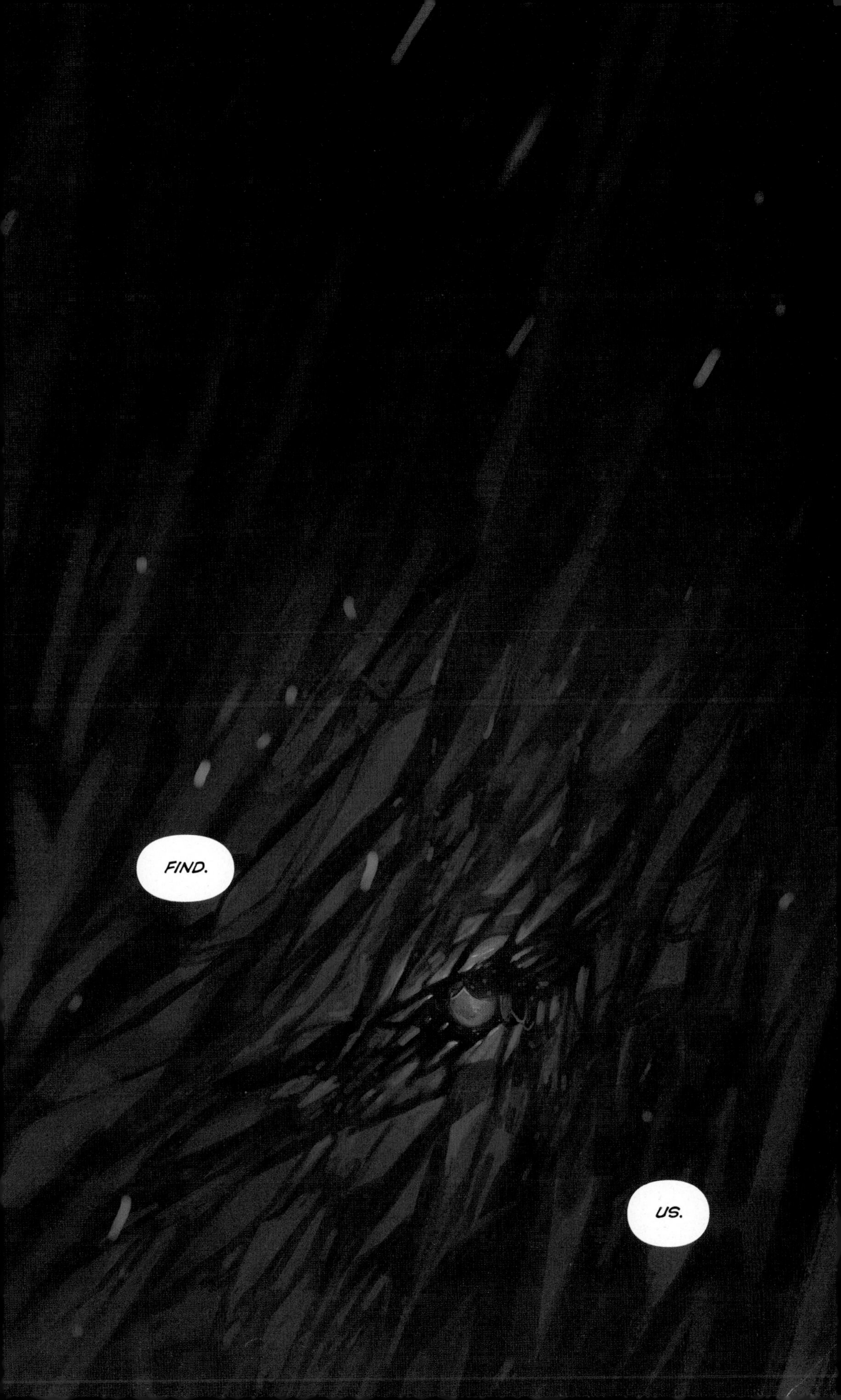
FIND.
US.

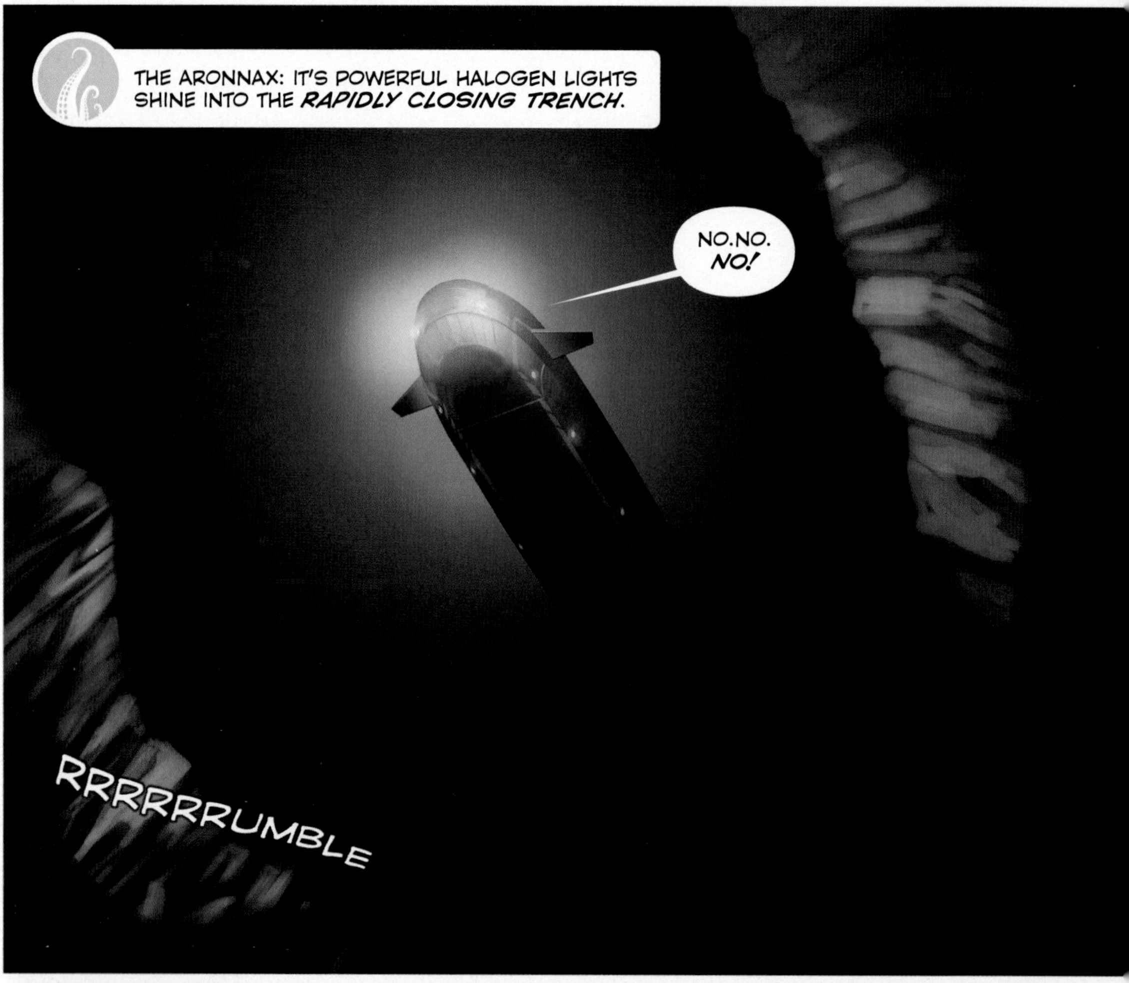
THE ARONNAX: IT'S POWERFUL HALOGEN LIGHTS SHINE INTO THE RAPIDLY CLOSING TRENCH.
NO.NO. NO!
RRRRRRRUMBLE

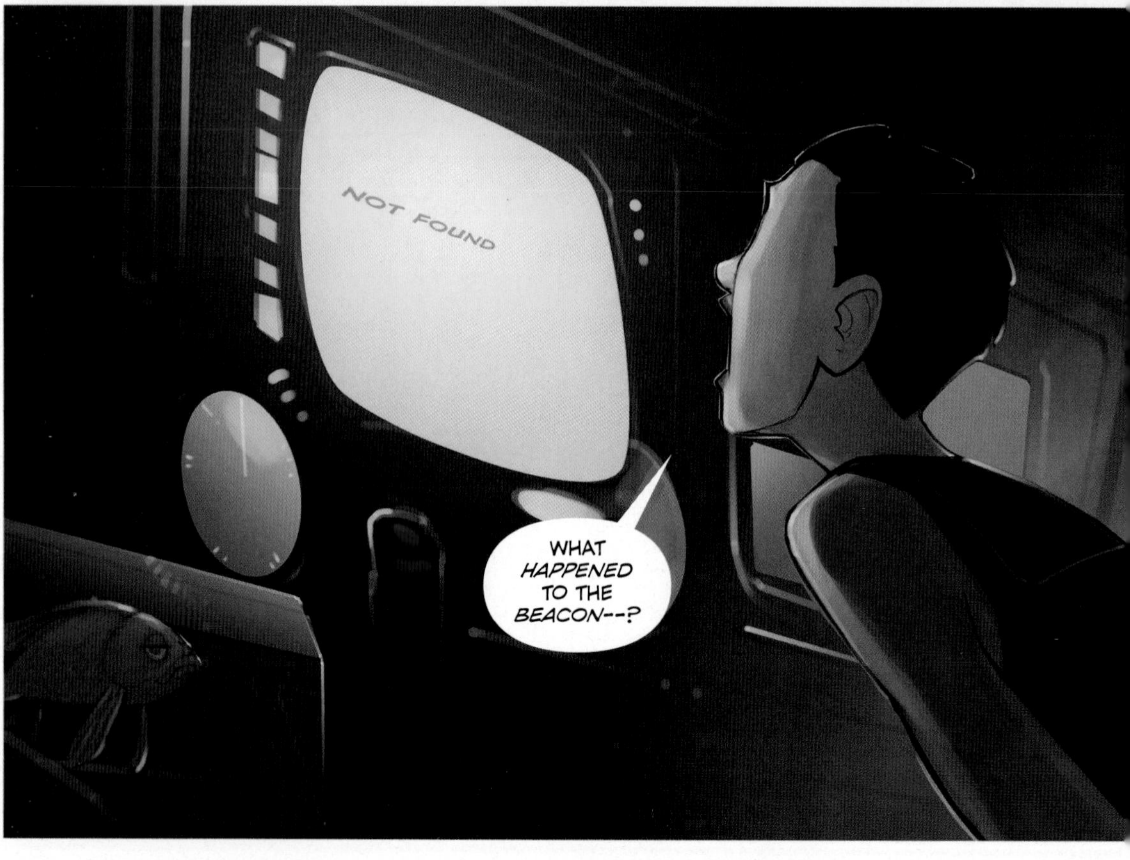
NOT FOUND
WHAT HAPPENED TO THE BEACON--?

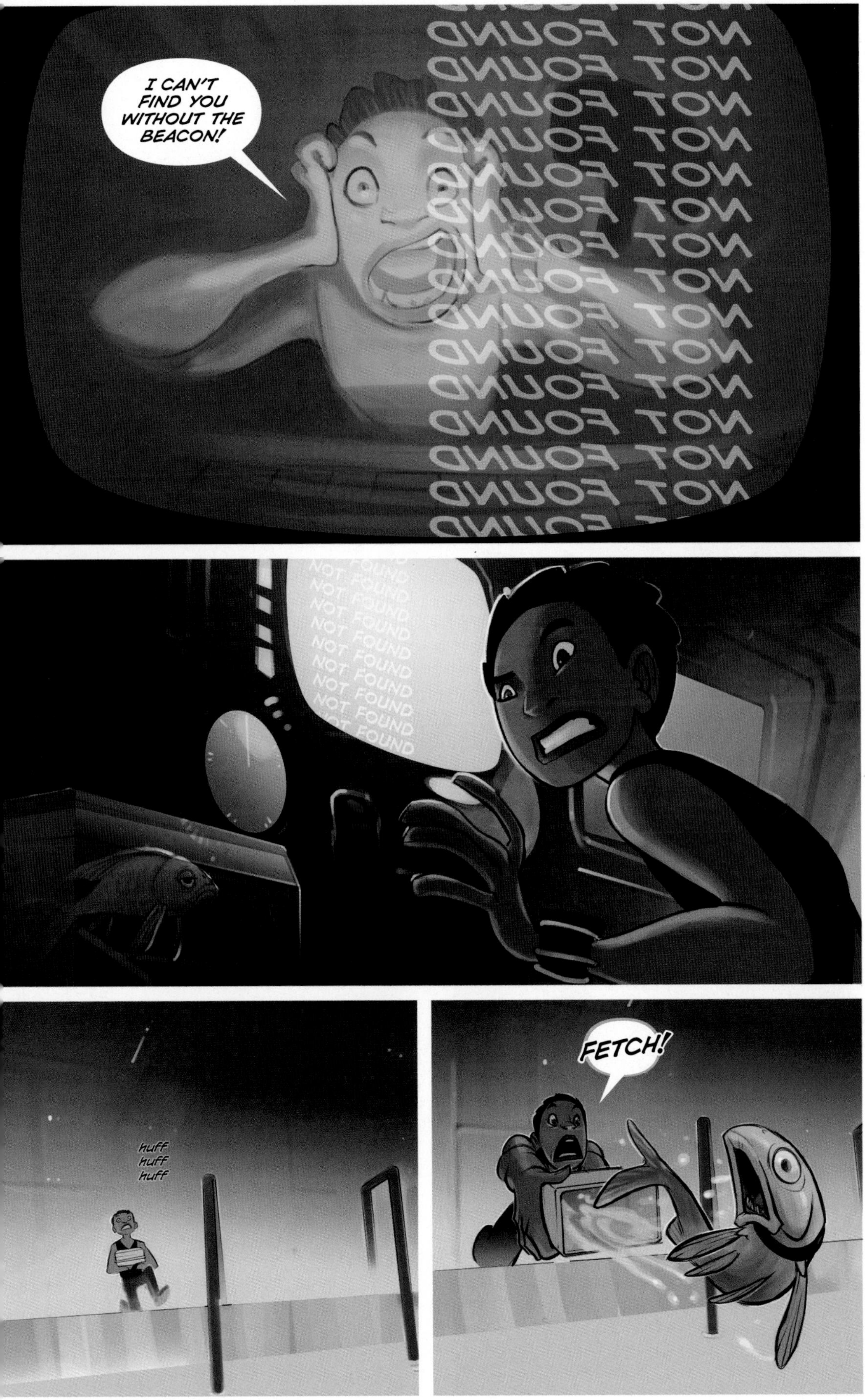
I CAN'T FIND YOU WITHOUT THE BEACON!
NOT FOUND
huff huff huff
FETCH!

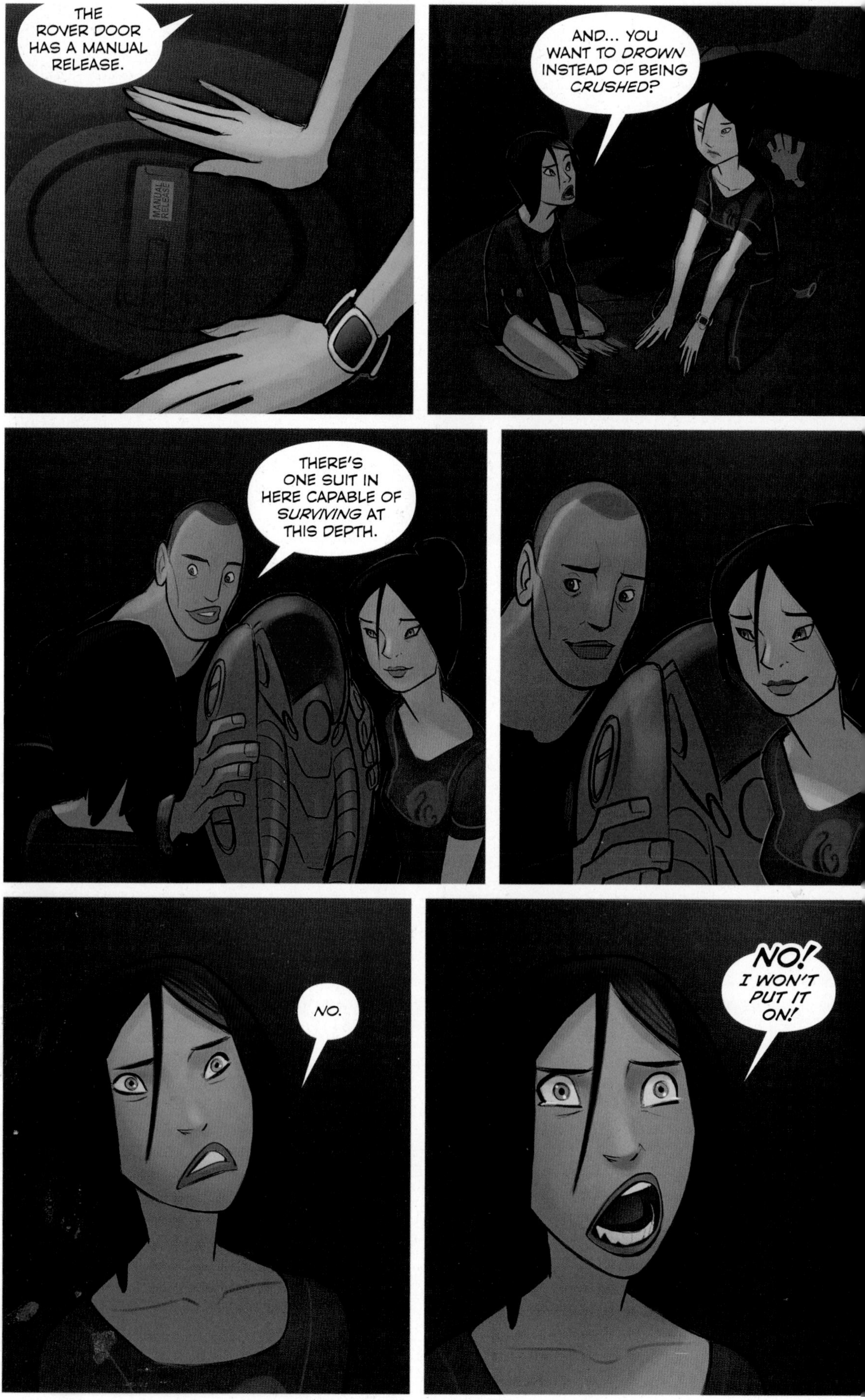
THE ROVER DOOR HAS A MANUAL RELEASE.
MANUAL RELEASE
AND... YOU WANT TO *DROWN* INSTEAD OF BEING *CRUSHED*?
THERE'S ONE SUIT IN HERE CAPABLE OF *SURVIVING* AT THIS DEPTH.
NO.
NO! I WON'T PUT IT ON!

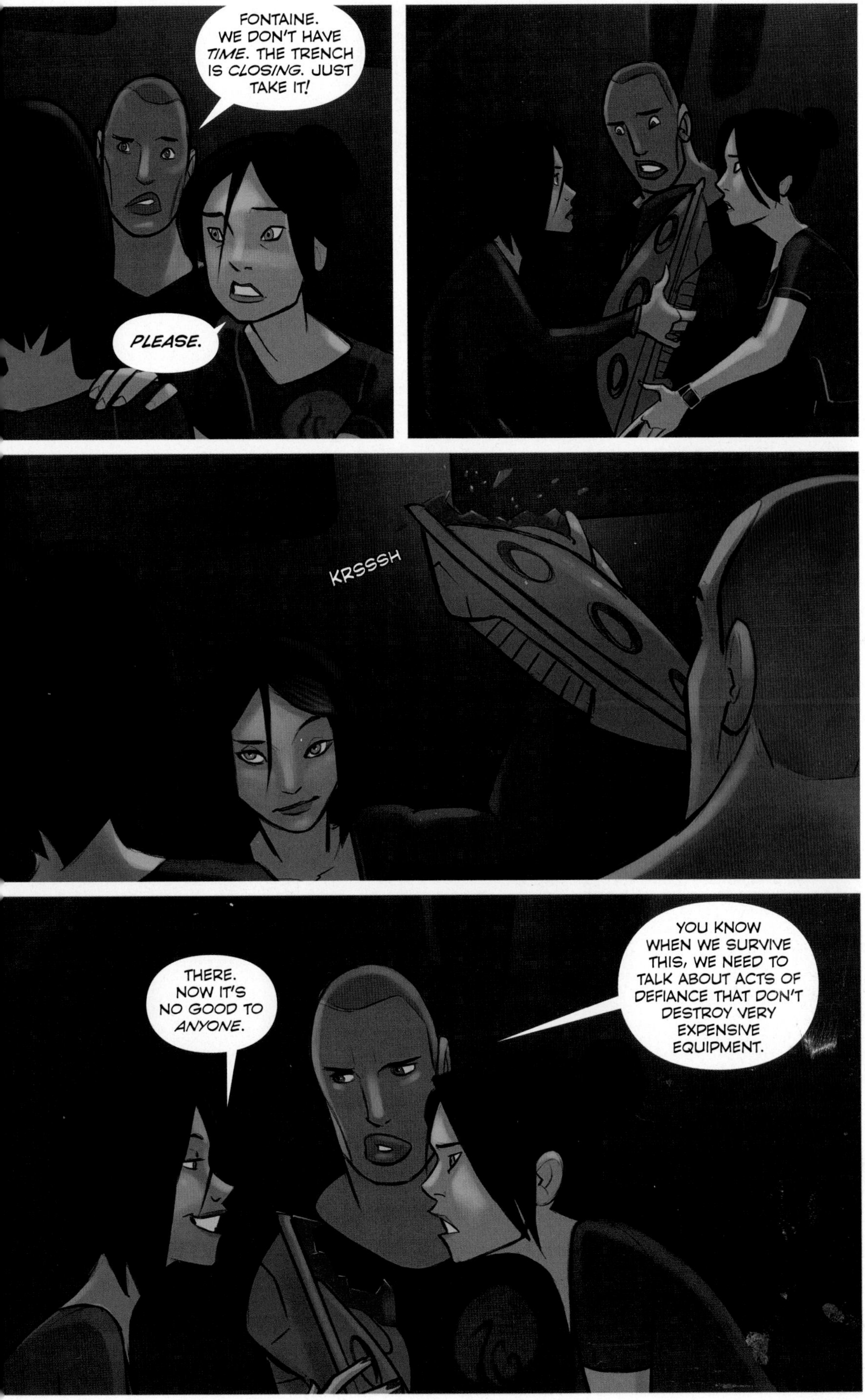
FONTAINE. WE DON'T HAVE *TIME*. THE TRENCH IS *CLOSING*. JUST TAKE IT!
*PLEASE.*
KRSSSH
THERE. NOW IT'S NO GOOD TO *ANYONE*.
YOU KNOW WHEN WE SURVIVE THIS, WE NEED TO TALK ABOUT ACTS OF DEFIANCE THAT DON'T DESTROY VERY EXPENSIVE EQUIPMENT.

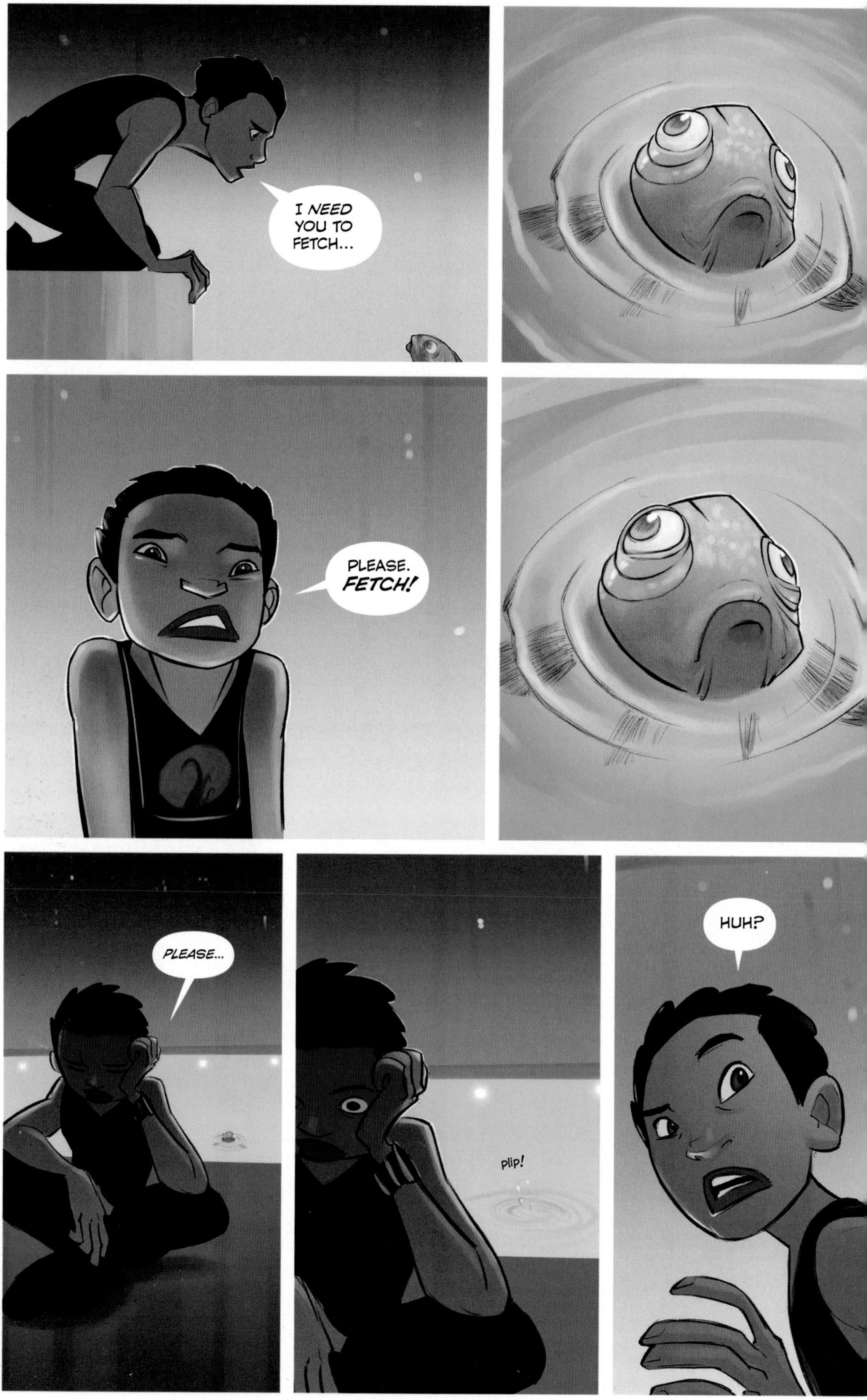
I NEED YOU TO FETCH...
PLEASE. FETCH!
PLEASE...
plip!
HUH?

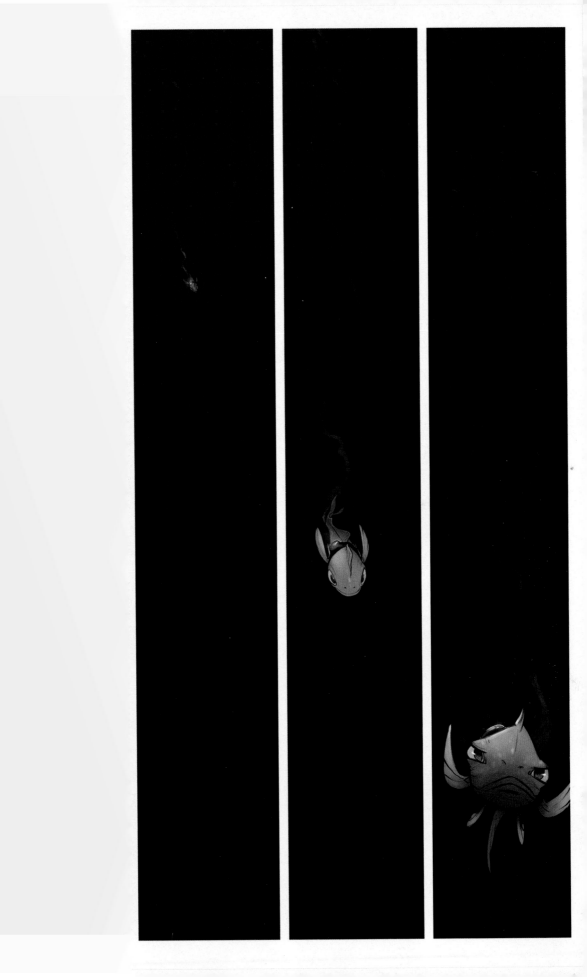

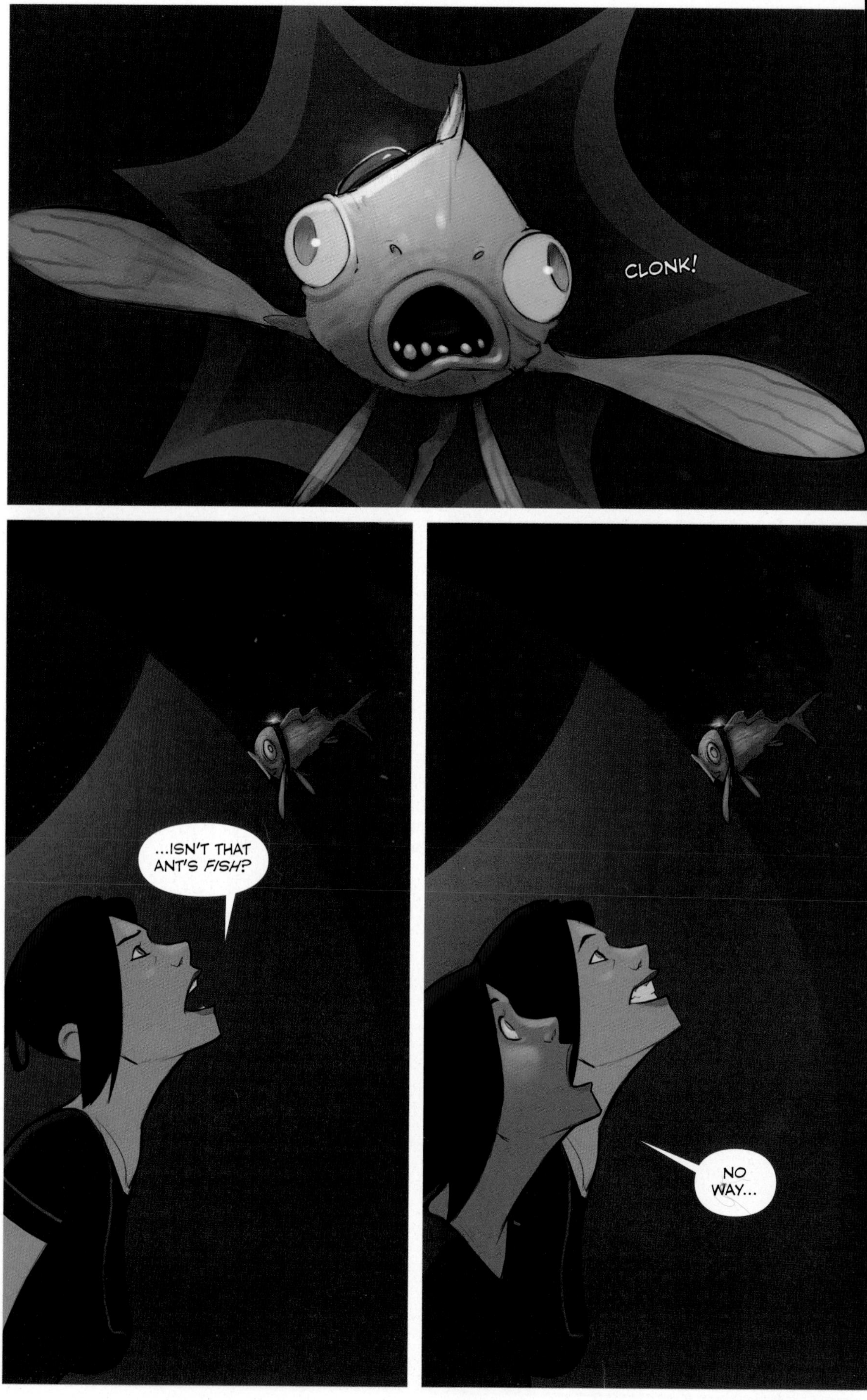
CLONK!
...ISN'T THAT ANT'S *FISH*?
NO WAY...

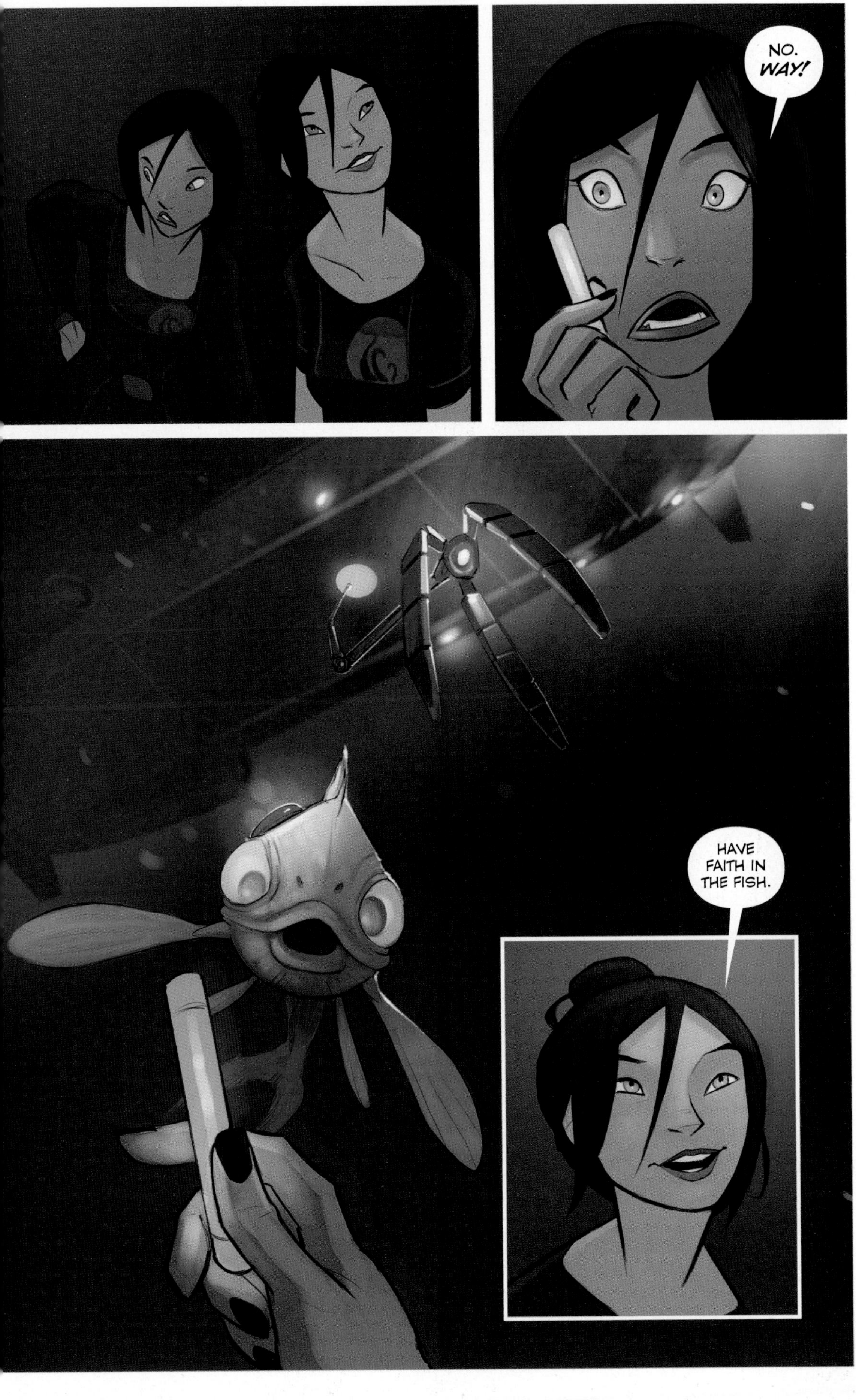
NO. WAY!
HAVE FAITH IN THE FISH.

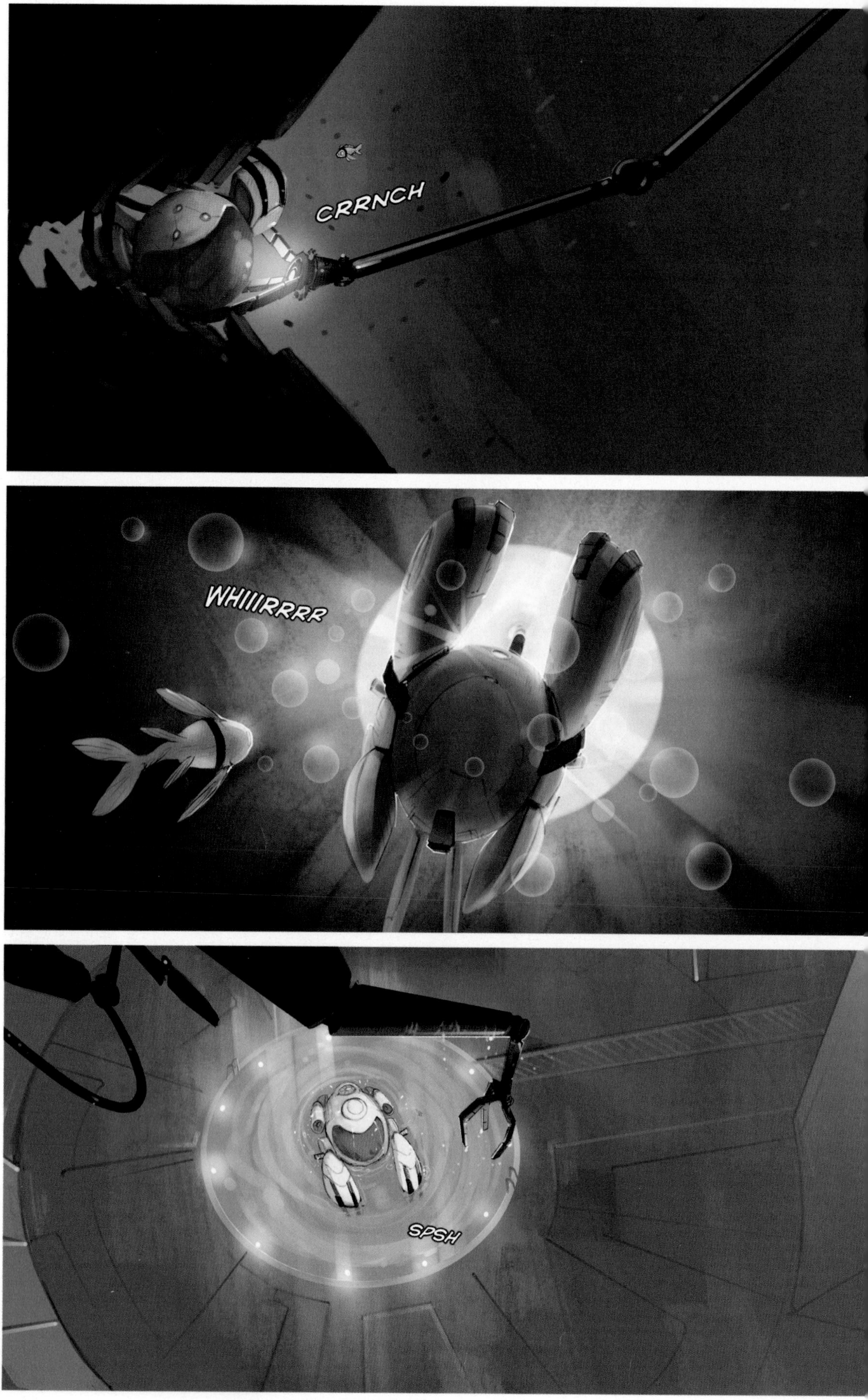
CRRNCH
WHIIIRRRR
SPSH

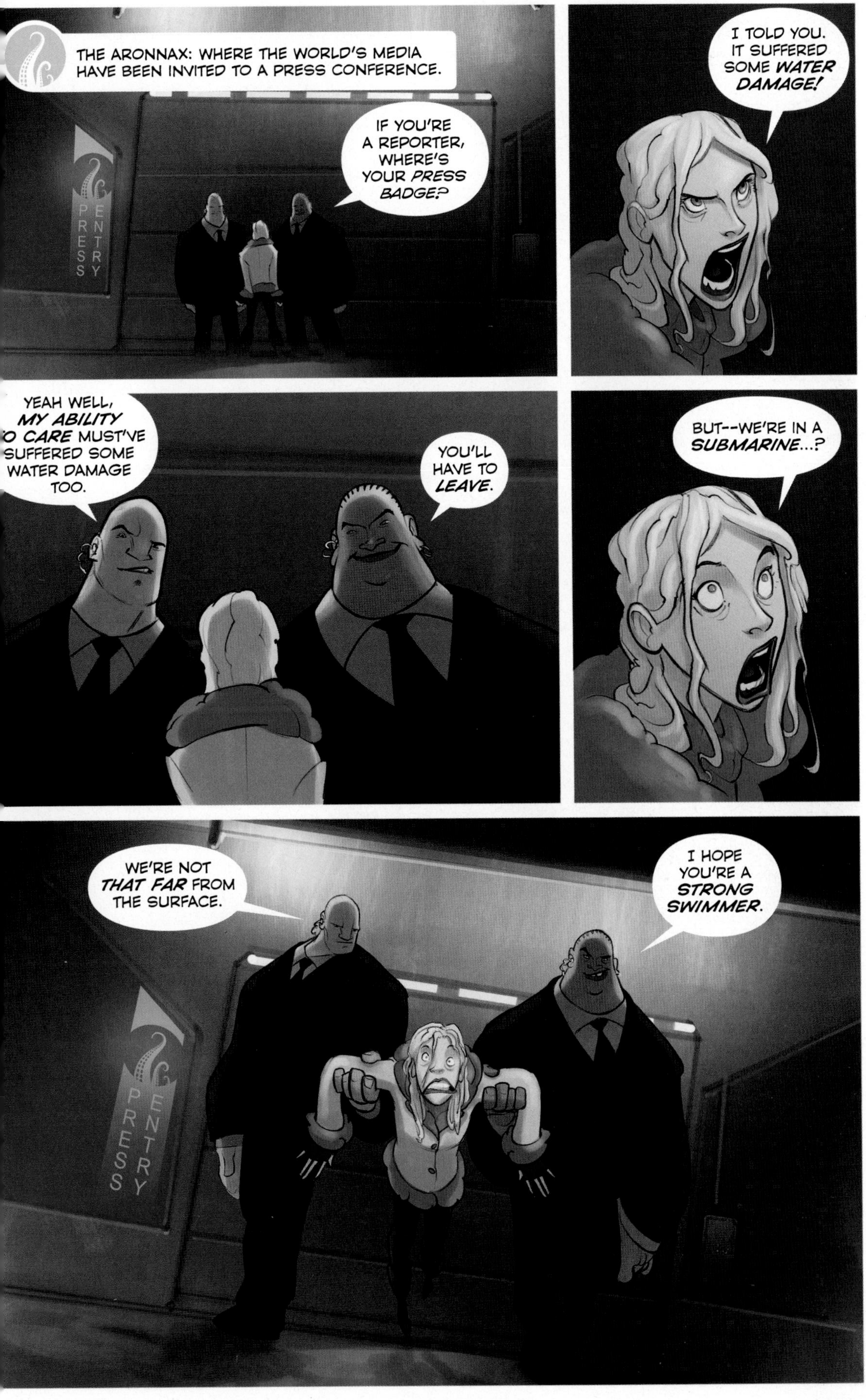
THE ARONNAX: WHERE THE WORLD'S MEDIA HAVE BEEN INVITED TO A PRESS CONFERENCE.
PRESS ENTRY
IF YOU'RE A REPORTER, WHERE'S YOUR PRESS BADGE?
I TOLD YOU. IT SUFFERED SOME WATER DAMAGE!
YEAH WELL, MY ABILITY TO CARE MUST'VE SUFFERED SOME WATER DAMAGE TOO.
YOU'LL HAVE TO LEAVE.
BUT--WE'RE IN A SUBMARINE...?
WE'RE NOT THAT FAR FROM THE SURFACE.
I HOPE YOU'RE A STRONG SWIMMER.
PRESS ENTRY

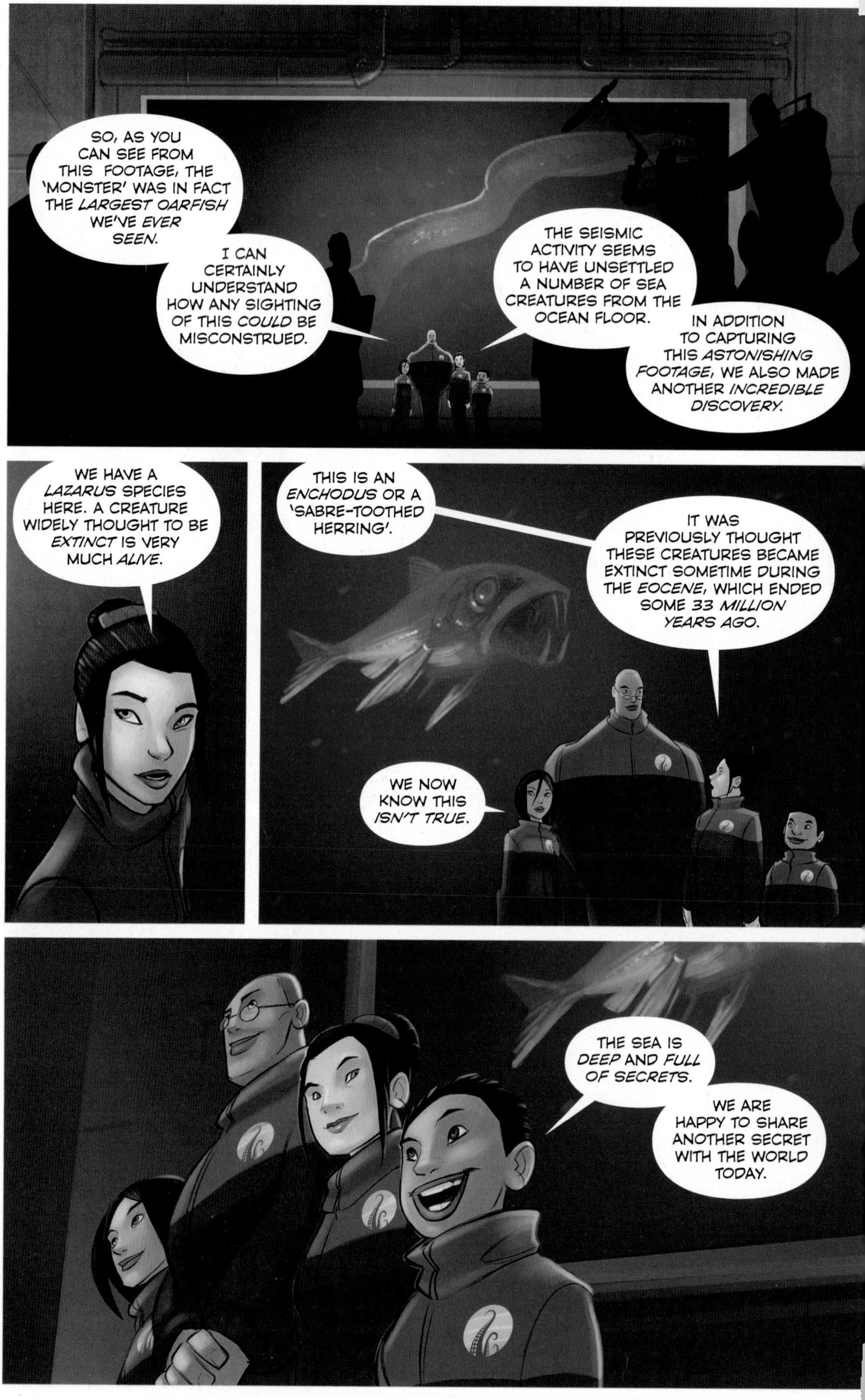
SO, AS YOU CAN SEE FROM THIS FOOTAGE, THE 'MONSTER' WAS IN FACT THE *LARGEST OARFISH* WE'VE *EVER* SEEN.
I CAN CERTAINLY UNDERSTAND HOW ANY SIGHTING OF THIS *COULD* BE MISCONSTRUED.
THE SEISMIC ACTIVITY SEEMS TO HAVE UNSETTLED A NUMBER OF SEA CREATURES FROM THE OCEAN FLOOR.
IN ADDITION TO CAPTURING THIS *ASTONISHING FOOTAGE*, WE ALSO MADE ANOTHER *INCREDIBLE DISCOVERY*.
WE HAVE A *LAZARUS* SPECIES HERE. A CREATURE WIDELY THOUGHT TO BE *EXTINCT* IS VERY MUCH *ALIVE*.
THIS IS AN *ENCHODUS* OR A 'SABRE-TOOTHED HERRING'.
IT WAS PREVIOUSLY THOUGHT THESE CREATURES BECAME EXTINCT SOMETIME DURING THE *EOCENE*, WHICH ENDED SOME *33 MILLION YEARS AGO*.
WE NOW KNOW THIS *ISN'T TRUE*.
THE SEA IS *DEEP* AND *FULL OF SECRETS*.
WE ARE HAPPY TO SHARE ANOTHER SECRET WITH THE WORLD TODAY.

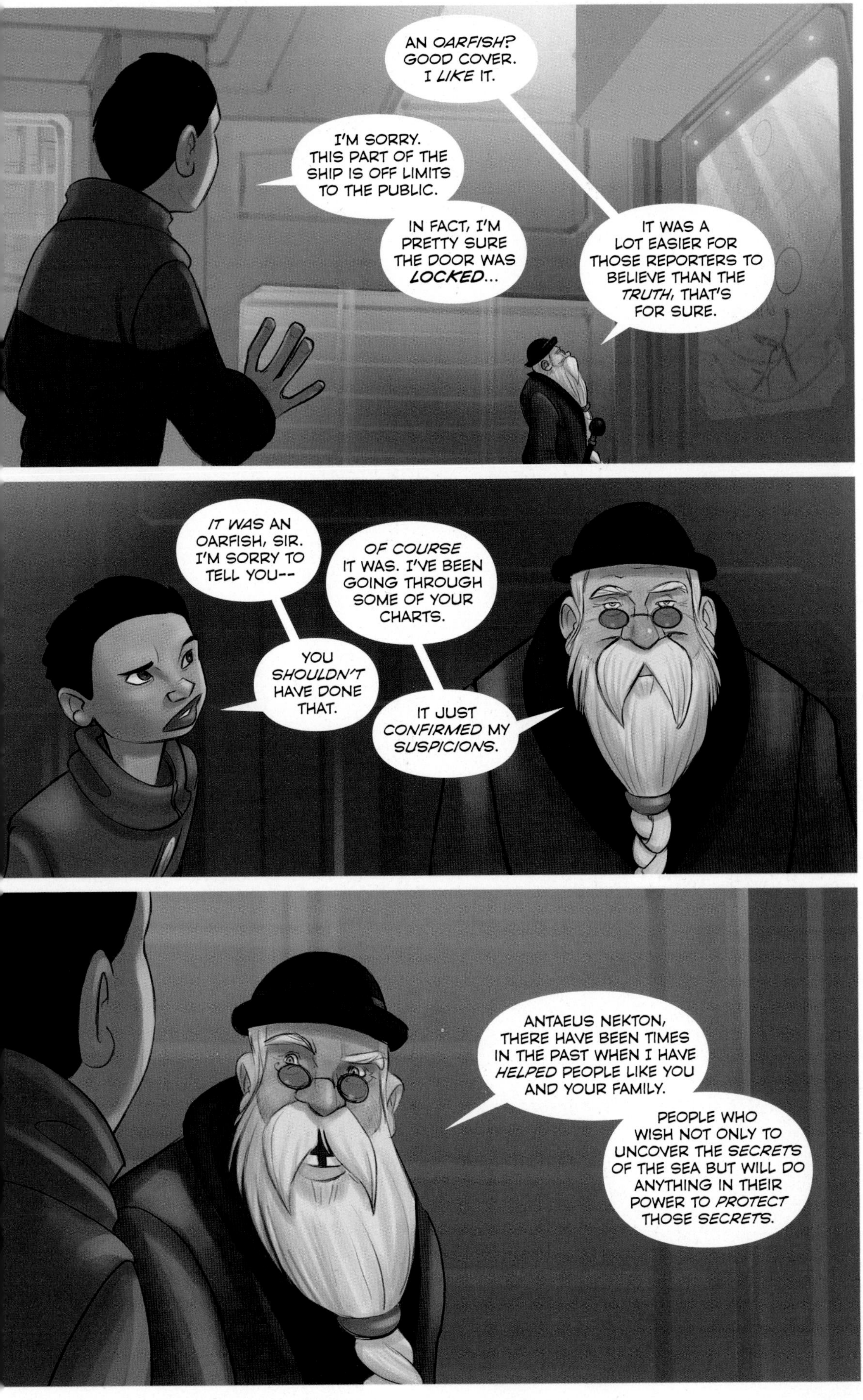
AN OARFISH? GOOD COVER. I LIKE IT.
I'M SORRY. THIS PART OF THE SHIP IS OFF LIMITS TO THE PUBLIC.
IN FACT, I'M PRETTY SURE THE DOOR WAS LOCKED...
IT WAS A LOT EASIER FOR THOSE REPORTERS TO BELIEVE THAN THE TRUTH, THAT'S FOR SURE.
IT WAS AN OARFISH, SIR. I'M SORRY TO TELL YOU--
OF COURSE IT WAS. I'VE BEEN GOING THROUGH SOME OF YOUR CHARTS.
YOU SHOULDN'T HAVE DONE THAT.
IT JUST CONFIRMED MY SUSPICIONS.
ANTAEUS NEKTON, THERE HAVE BEEN TIMES IN THE PAST WHEN I HAVE HELPED PEOPLE LIKE YOU AND YOUR FAMILY.
PEOPLE WHO WISH NOT ONLY TO UNCOVER THE SECRETS OF THE SEA BUT WILL DO ANYTHING IN THEIR POWER TO PROTECT THOSE SECRETS.

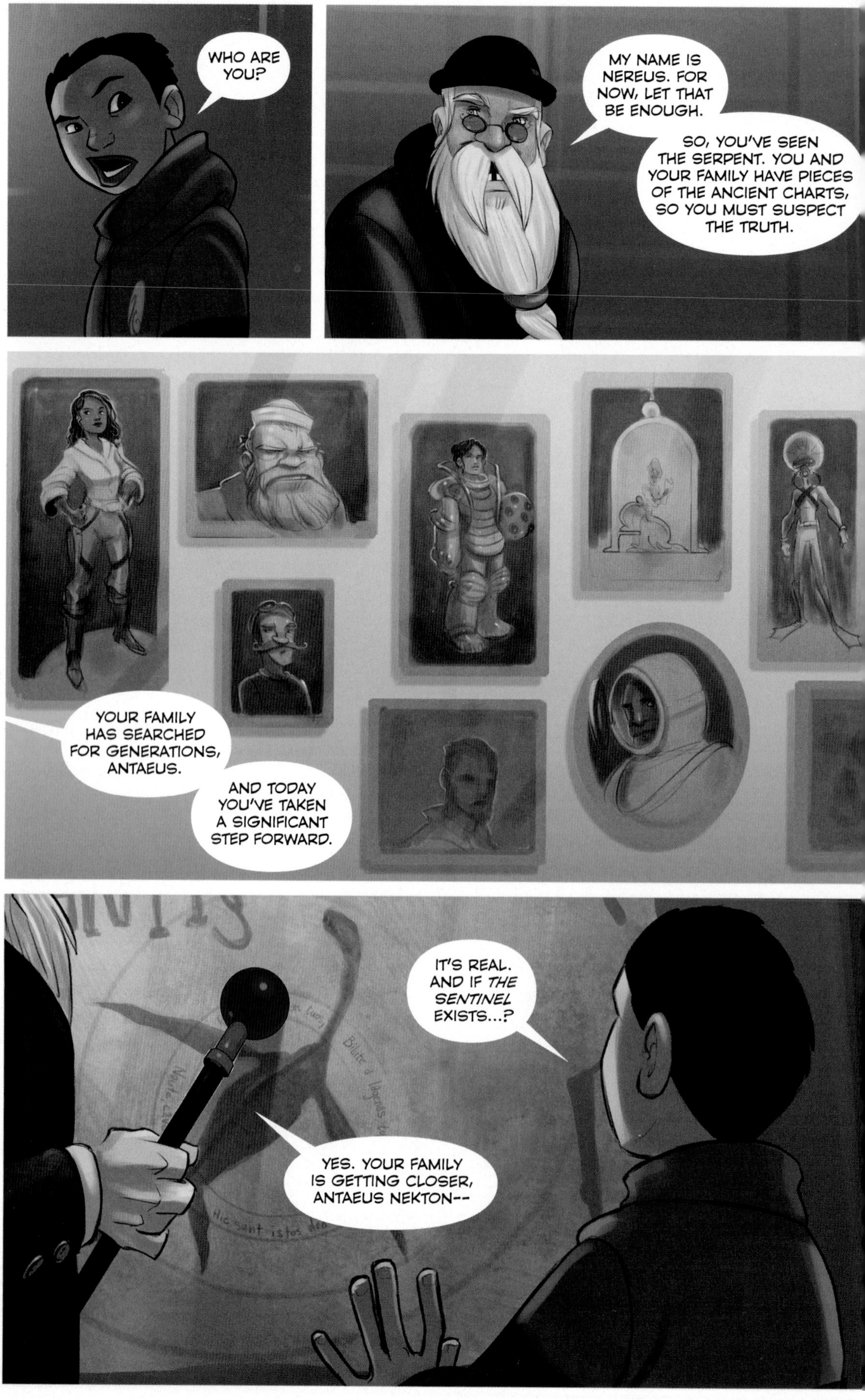
WHO ARE YOU?
MY NAME IS NEREUS. FOR NOW, LET THAT BE ENOUGH.
SO, YOU'VE SEEN THE SERPENT. YOU AND YOUR FAMILY HAVE PIECES OF THE ANCIENT CHARTS, SO YOU MUST SUSPECT THE TRUTH.
YOUR FAMILY HAS SEARCHED FOR GENERATIONS, ANTAEUS.
AND TODAY YOU'VE TAKEN A SIGNIFICANT STEP FORWARD.
IT'S REAL. AND IF *THE SENTINEL* EXISTS...?
YES. YOUR FAMILY IS GETTING CLOSER, ANTAEUS NEKTON--

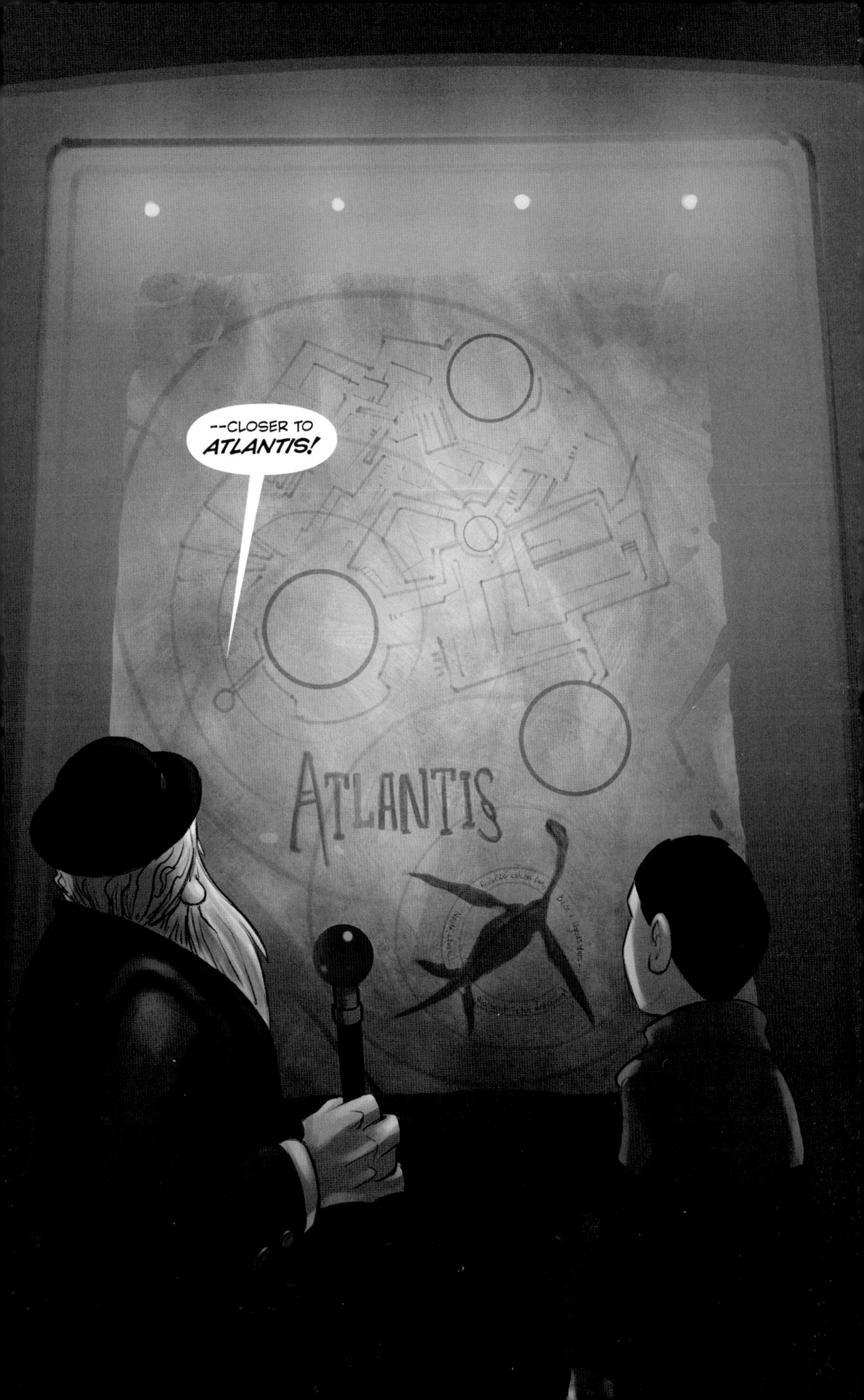
--CLOSER TO ATLANTIS!
ATLANTIS

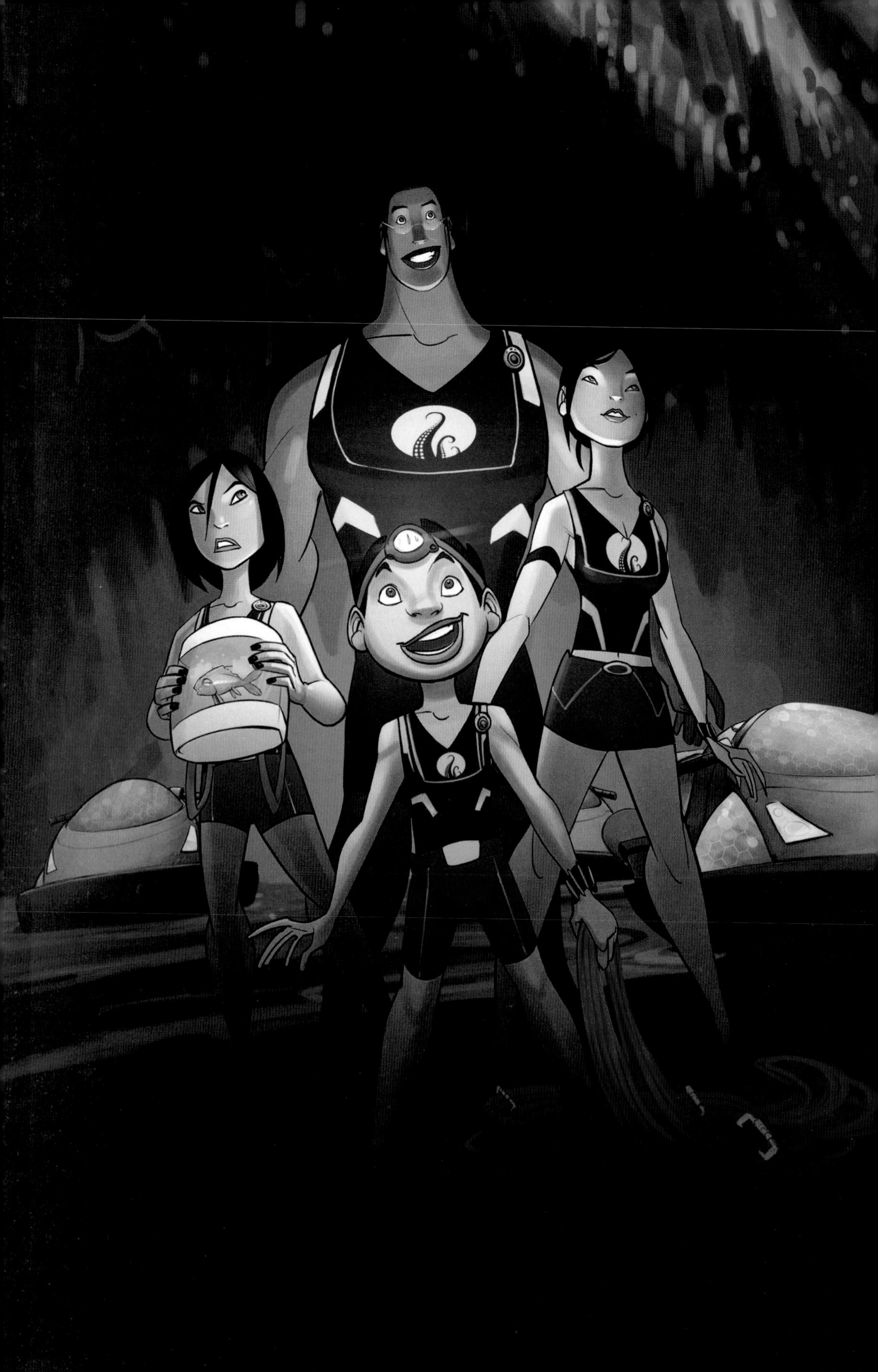

# CHAPTER **FOUR**

Issue 04 cover by

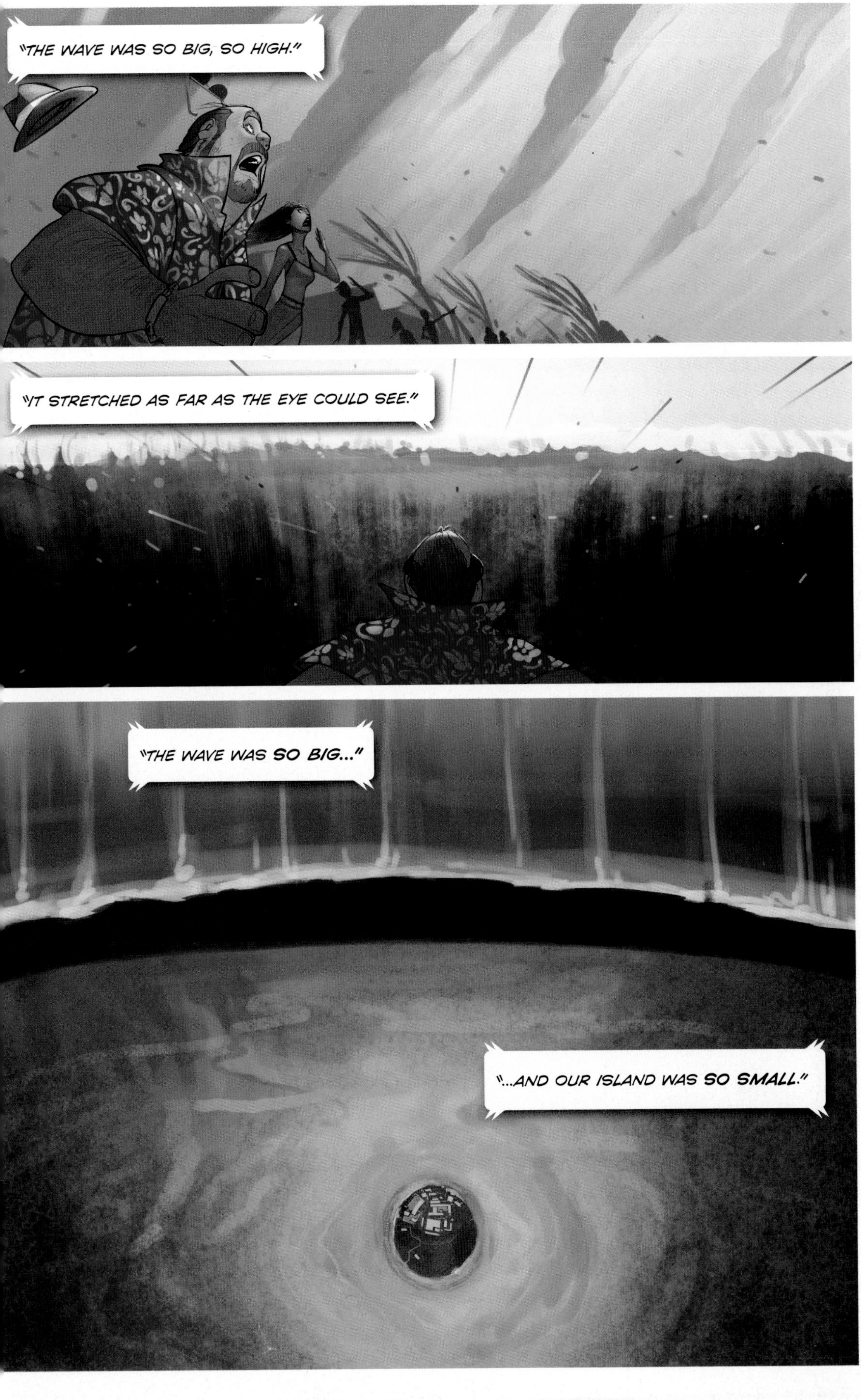
"THE WAVE WAS SO BIG, SO HIGH."
"IT STRETCHED AS FAR AS THE EYE COULD SEE."
"THE WAVE WAS **SO BIG**..."
"...AND OUR ISLAND WAS **SO SMALL**."

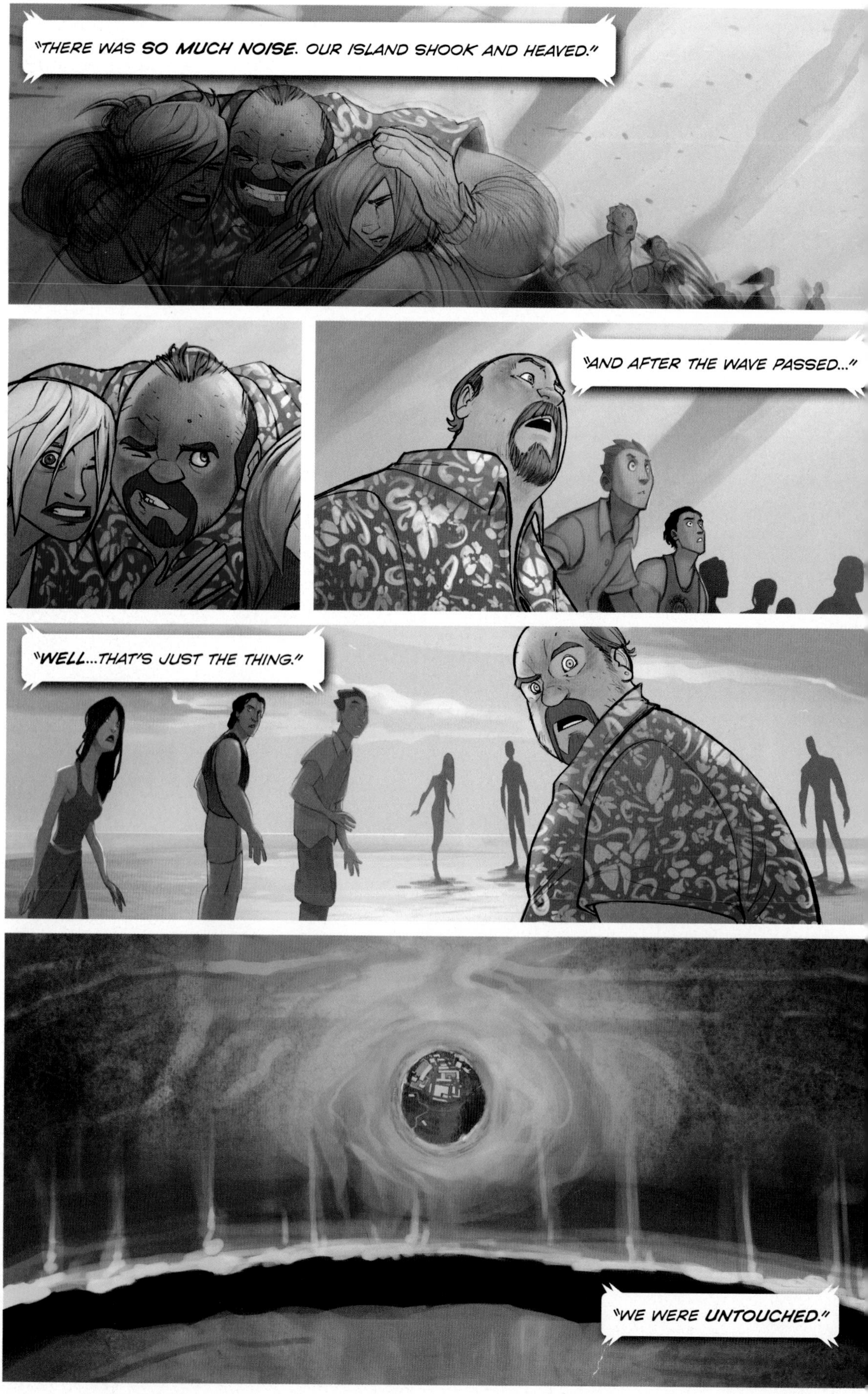
"THERE WAS **SO MUCH NOISE**. OUR ISLAND SHOOK AND HEAVED."
"AND AFTER THE WAVE PASSED..."
"**WELL**...THAT'S JUST THE THING."
"WE WERE **UNTOUCHED**."

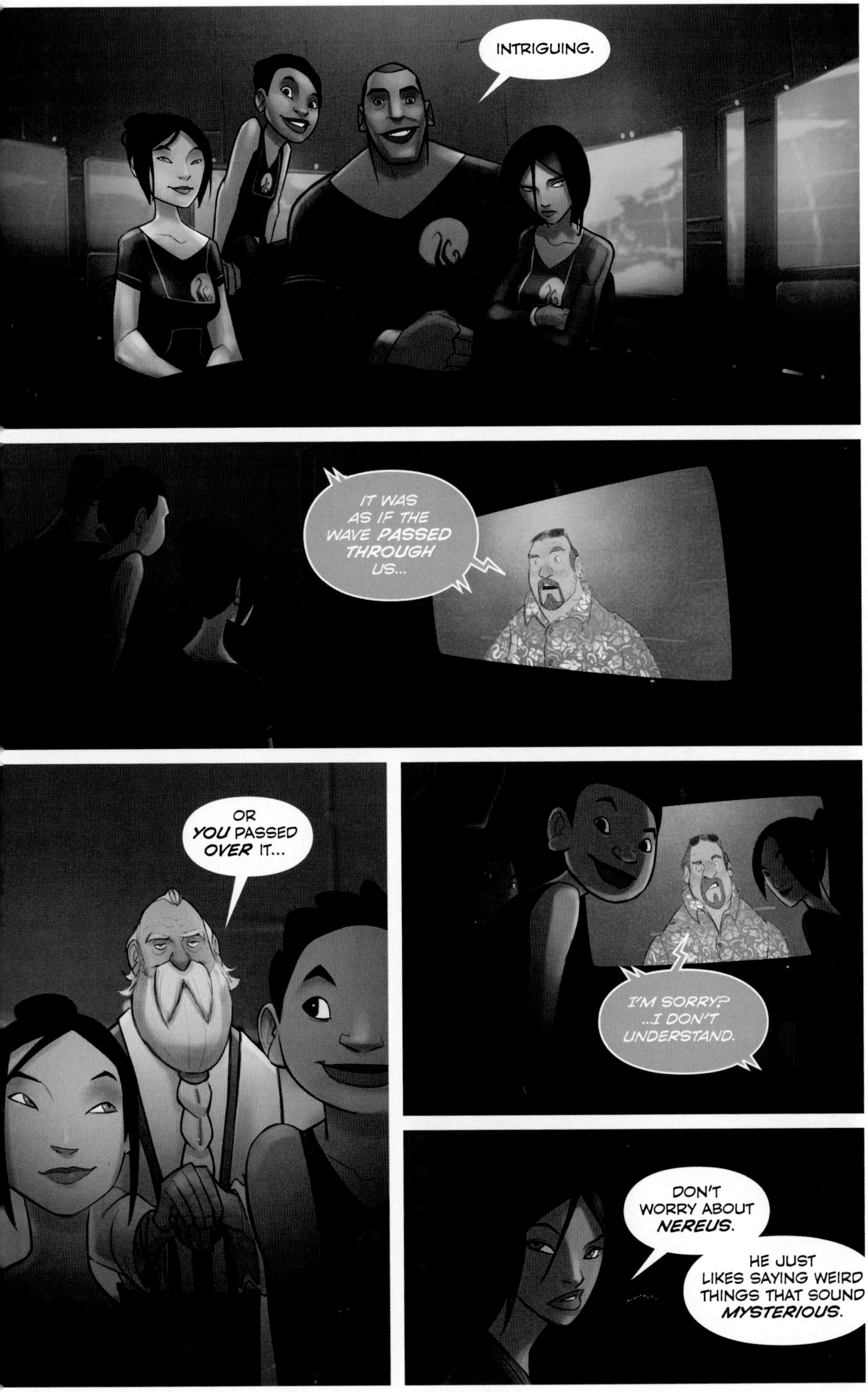
INTRIGUING.
IT WAS AS IF THE WAVE PASSED THROUGH US...
OR YOU PASSED OVER IT...
I'M SORRY? ...I DON'T UNDERSTAND.
DON'T WORRY ABOUT NEREUS.
HE JUST LIKES SAYING WEIRD THINGS THAT SOUND MYSTERIOUS.

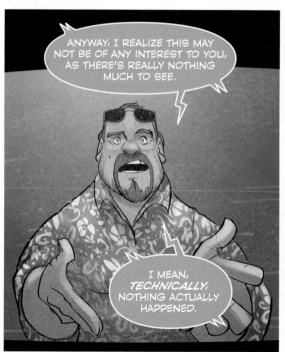

ANYWAY, I REALIZE THIS MAY NOT BE OF ANY INTEREST TO YOU, AS THERE'S REALLY NOTHING MUCH TO SEE.

I MEAN, *TECHNICALLY*, NOTHING ACTUALLY HAPPENED.

ARE YOU KIDDING? YOUR *ENTIRE ISLAND* WAS COMPLETELY *NOT* HIT BY A TSUNAMI.

THAT'S *TOTALLY* WORT INVESTIGATING

NEKTON FAMILY--

--SET *SAIL!*

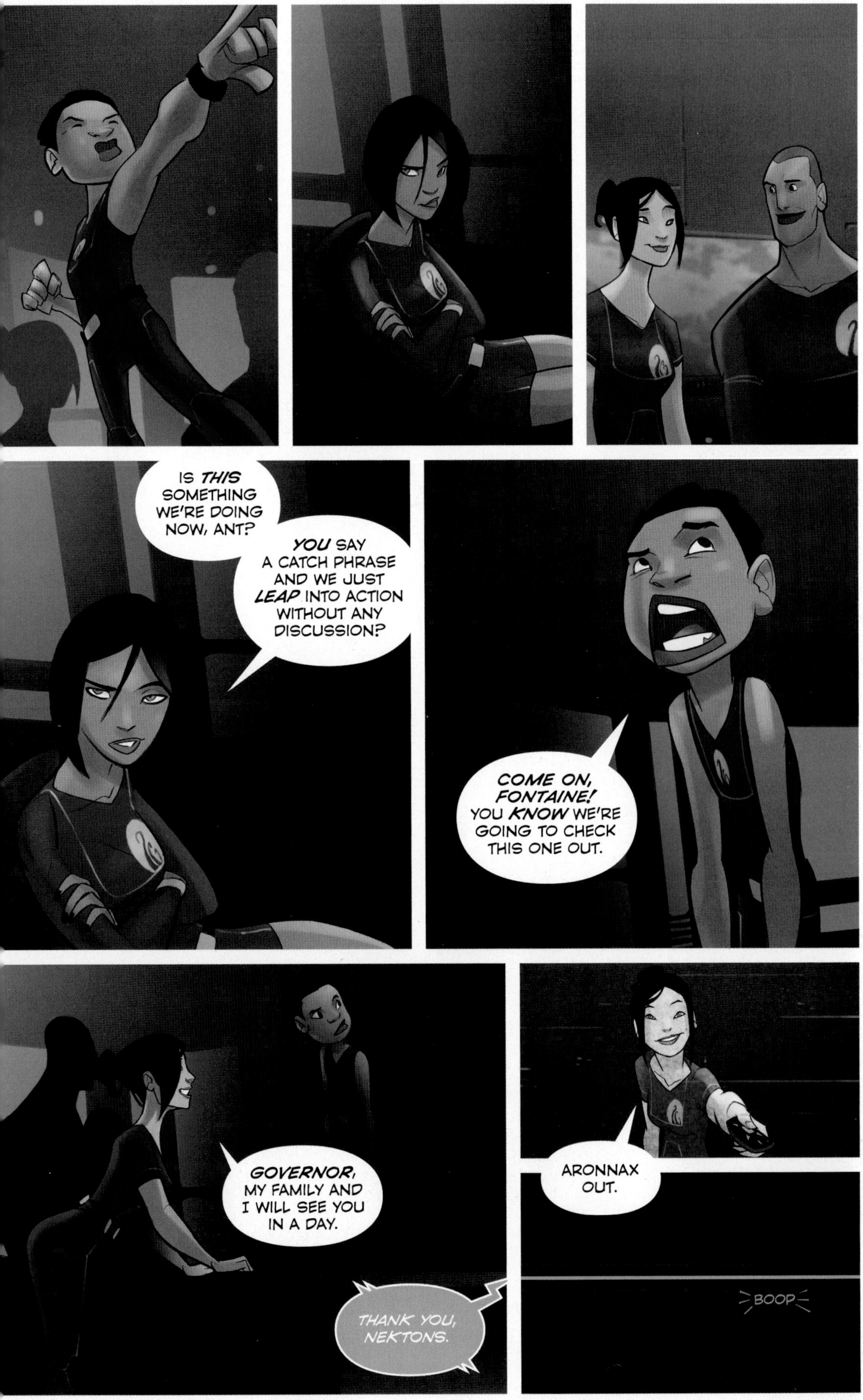
IS THIS SOMETHING WE'RE DOING NOW, ANT?
YOU SAY A CATCH PHRASE AND WE JUST LEAP INTO ACTION WITHOUT ANY DISCUSSION?
COME ON, FONTAINE! YOU KNOW WE'RE GOING TO CHECK THIS ONE OUT.
GOVERNOR, MY FAMILY AND I WILL SEE YOU IN A DAY.
ARONNAX OUT.
THANK YOU, NEKTONS.
BOOP

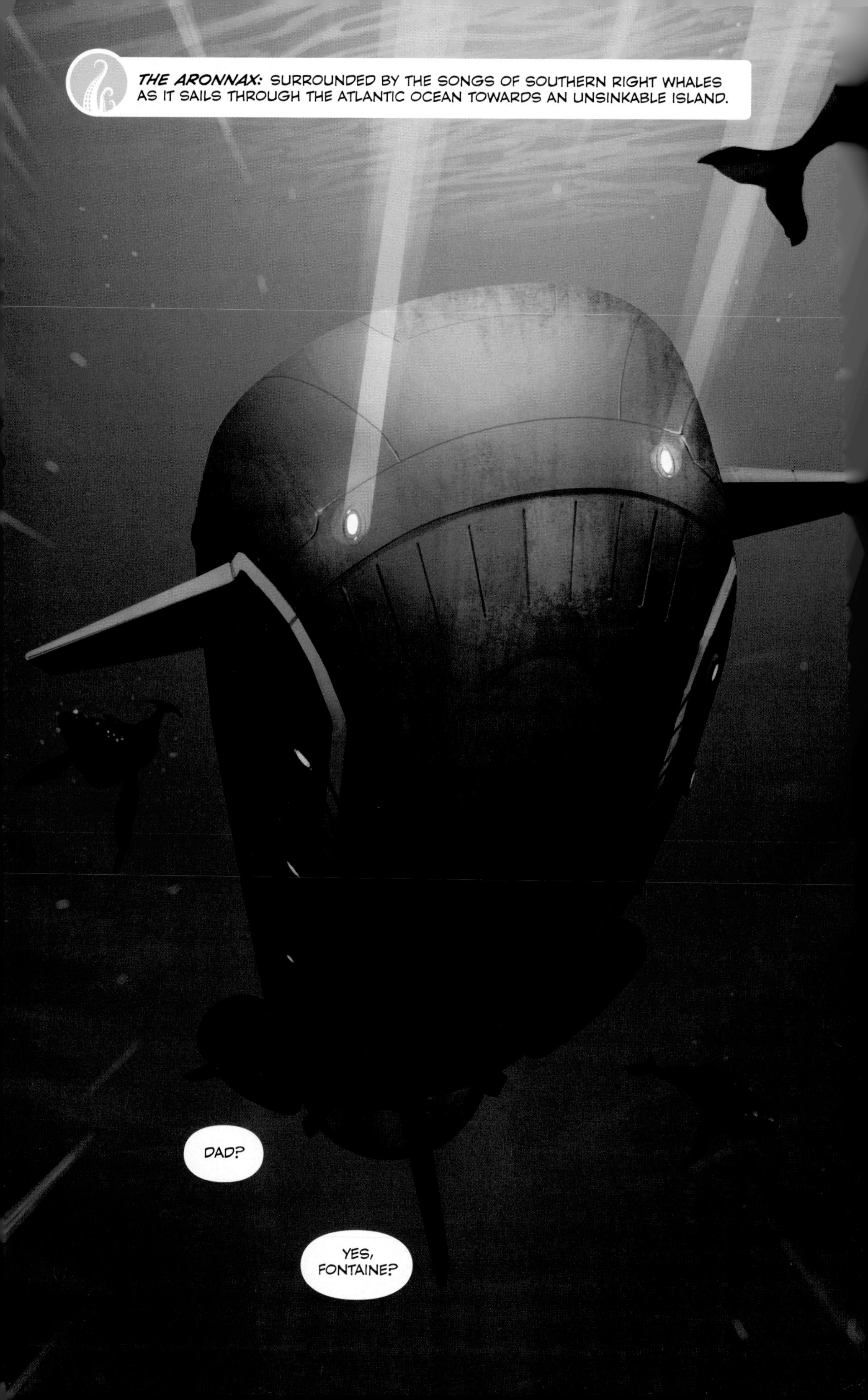
THE ARONNAX: SURROUNDED BY THE SONGS OF SOUTHERN RIGHT WHALES AS IT SAILS THROUGH THE ATLANTIC OCEAN TOWARDS AN UNSINKABLE ISLAND.
DAD?
YES, FONTAINE?

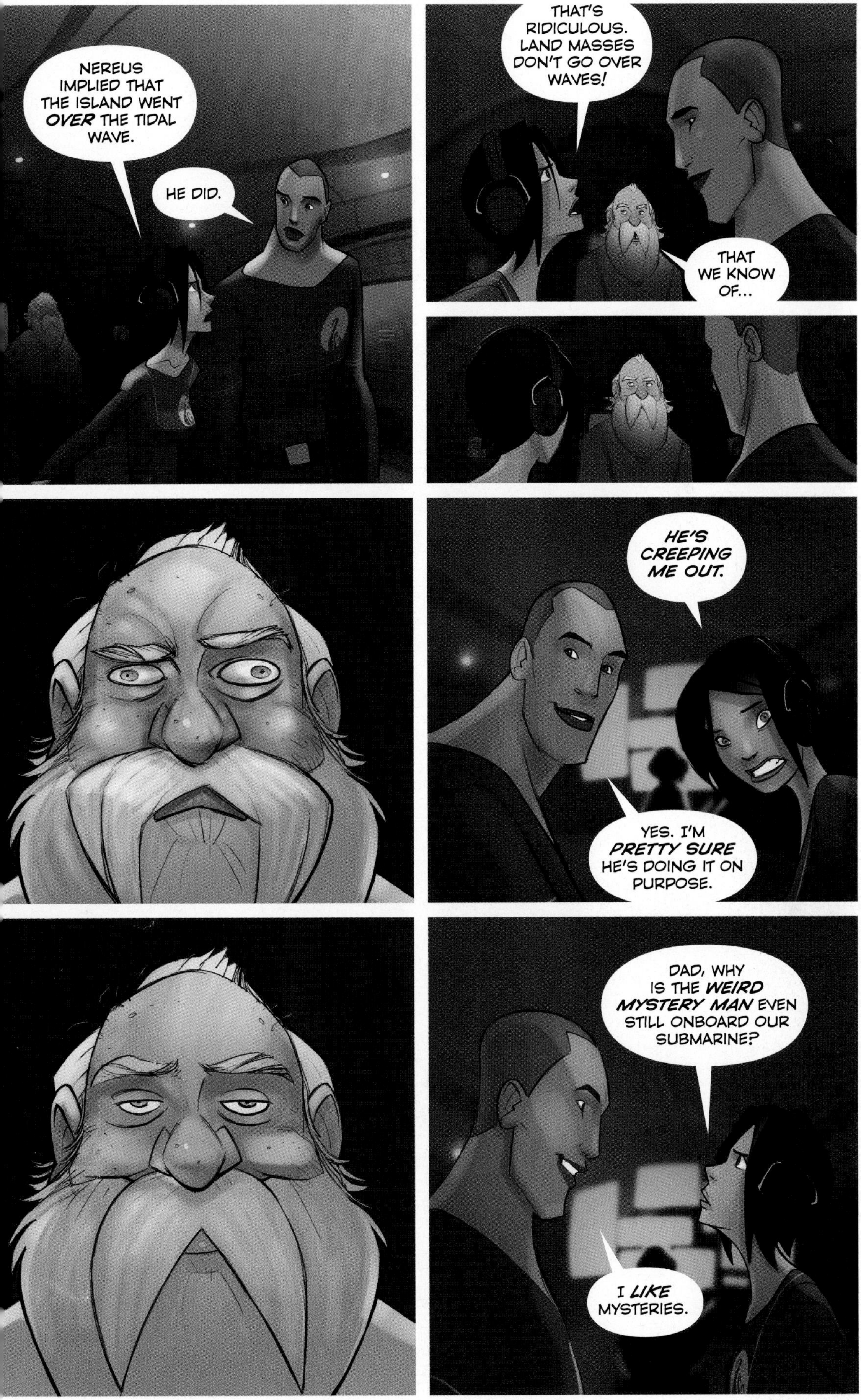
NEREUS IMPLIED THAT THE ISLAND WENT *OVER* THE TIDAL WAVE.
HE DID.
THAT'S RIDICULOUS. LAND MASSES DON'T GO OVER WAVES!
THAT WE KNOW OF...
*HE'S CREEPING ME OUT.*
YES. I'M *PRETTY SURE* HE'S DOING IT ON PURPOSE.
DAD, WHY IS THE *WEIRD MYSTERY MAN* EVEN STILL ONBOARD OUR SUBMARINE?
I *LIKE* MYSTERIES.

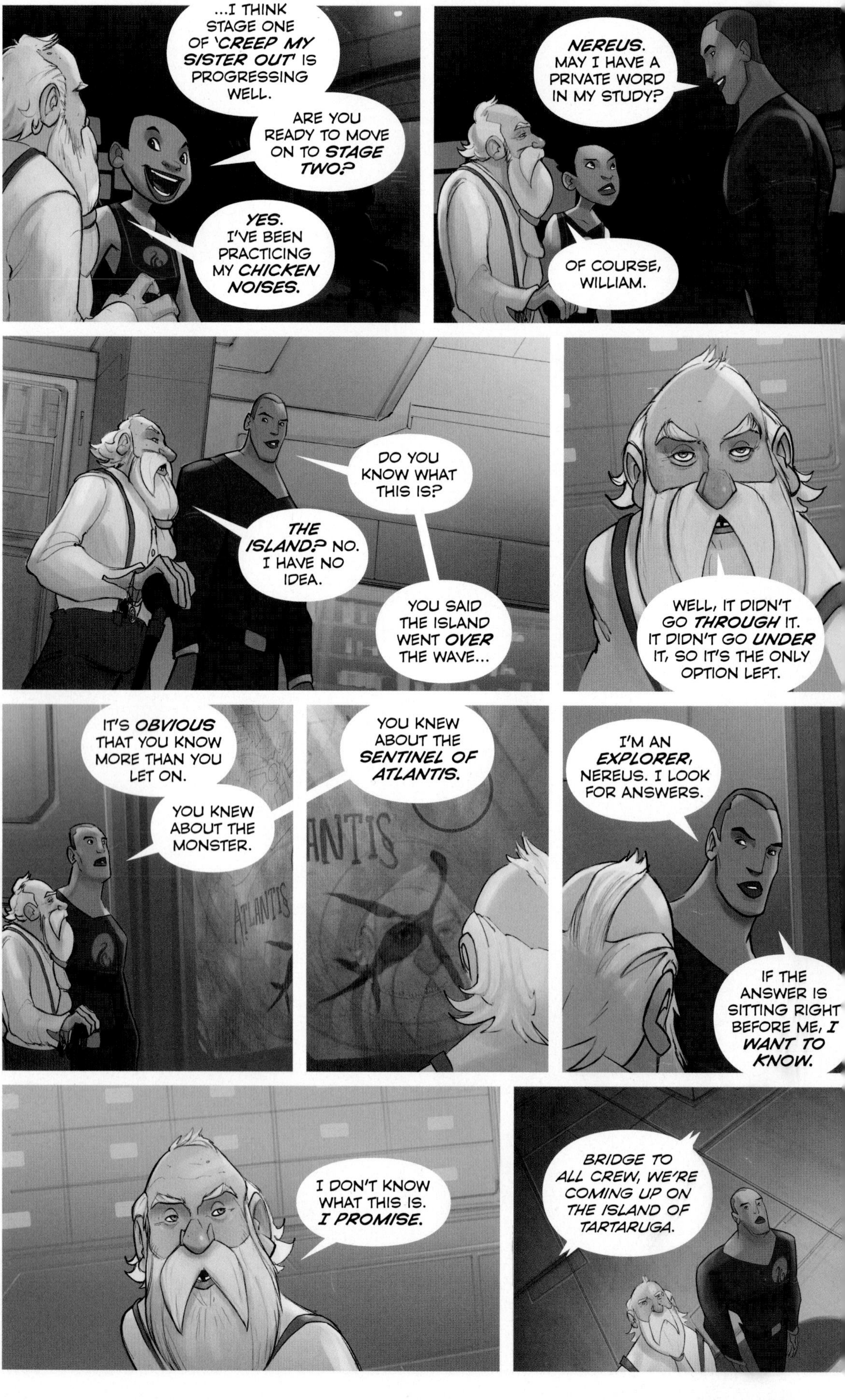
...I THINK STAGE ONE OF 'CREEP MY SISTER OUT' IS PROGRESSING WELL.
ARE YOU READY TO MOVE ON TO STAGE TWO?
YES. I'VE BEEN PRACTICING MY CHICKEN NOISES.
NEREUS. MAY I HAVE A PRIVATE WORD IN MY STUDY?
OF COURSE, WILLIAM.
DO YOU KNOW WHAT THIS IS?
THE ISLAND? NO. I HAVE NO IDEA.
YOU SAID THE ISLAND WENT OVER THE WAVE...
WELL, IT DIDN'T GO THROUGH IT. IT DIDN'T GO UNDER IT, SO IT'S THE ONLY OPTION LEFT.
IT'S OBVIOUS THAT YOU KNOW MORE THAN YOU LET ON.
YOU KNEW ABOUT THE MONSTER.
YOU KNEW ABOUT THE SENTINEL OF ATLANTIS.
ATLANTIS
ANTIS
I'M AN EXPLORER, NEREUS. I LOOK FOR ANSWERS.
IF THE ANSWER IS SITTING RIGHT BEFORE ME, I WANT TO KNOW.
I DON'T KNOW WHAT THIS IS. I PROMISE.
BRIDGE TO ALL CREW, WE'RE COMING UP ON THE ISLAND OF TARTARUGA.

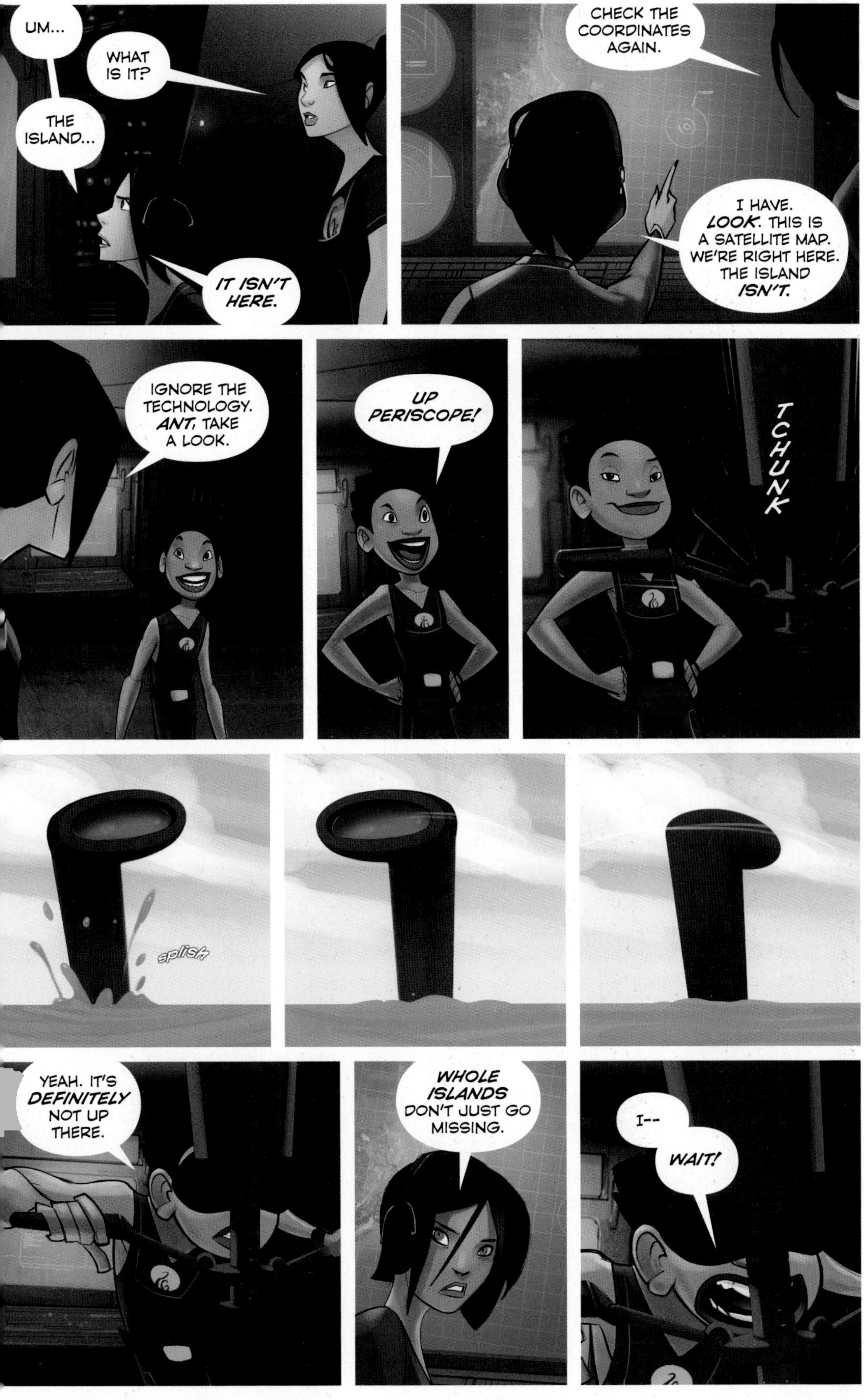
UM...
WHAT IS IT?
THE ISLAND...
IT ISN'T HERE.
CHECK THE COORDINATES AGAIN.
I HAVE. LOOK. THIS IS A SATELLITE MAP. WE'RE RIGHT HERE. THE ISLAND ISN'T.
IGNORE THE TECHNOLOGY. ANT, TAKE A LOOK.
UP PERISCOPE!
TCHUNK
splish
YEAH. IT'S DEFINITELY NOT UP THERE.
WHOLE ISLANDS DON'T JUST GO MISSING.
I--
WAIT!

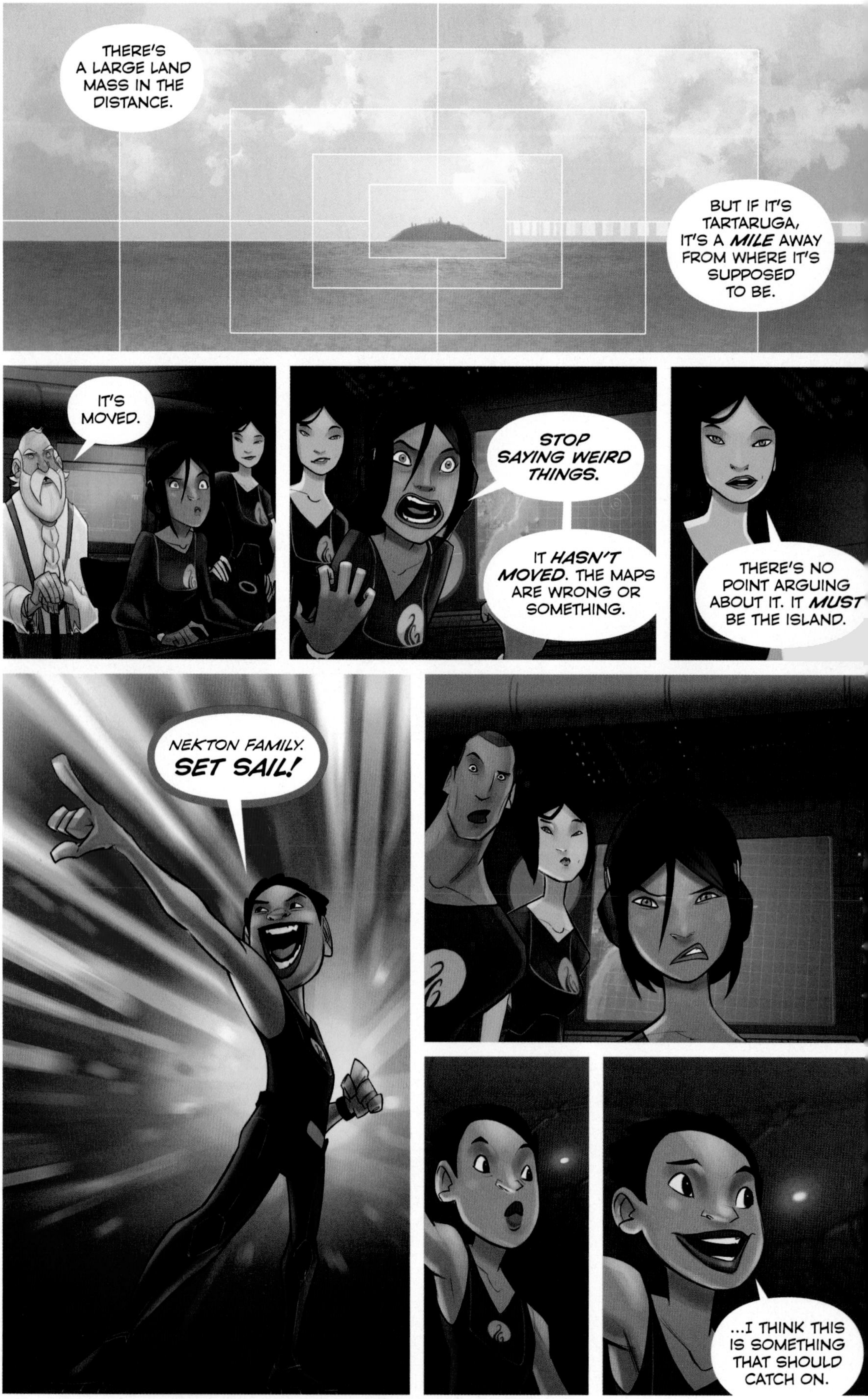
THERE'S A LARGE LAND MASS IN THE DISTANCE.
BUT IF IT'S TARTARUGA, IT'S A MILE AWAY FROM WHERE IT'S SUPPOSED TO BE.
IT'S MOVED.
STOP SAYING WEIRD THINGS.
IT HASN'T MOVED. THE MAPS ARE WRONG OR SOMETHING.
THERE'S NO POINT ARGUING ABOUT IT. IT MUST BE THE ISLAND.
NEKTON FAMILY. SET SAIL!
...I THINK THIS IS SOMETHING THAT SHOULD CATCH ON.

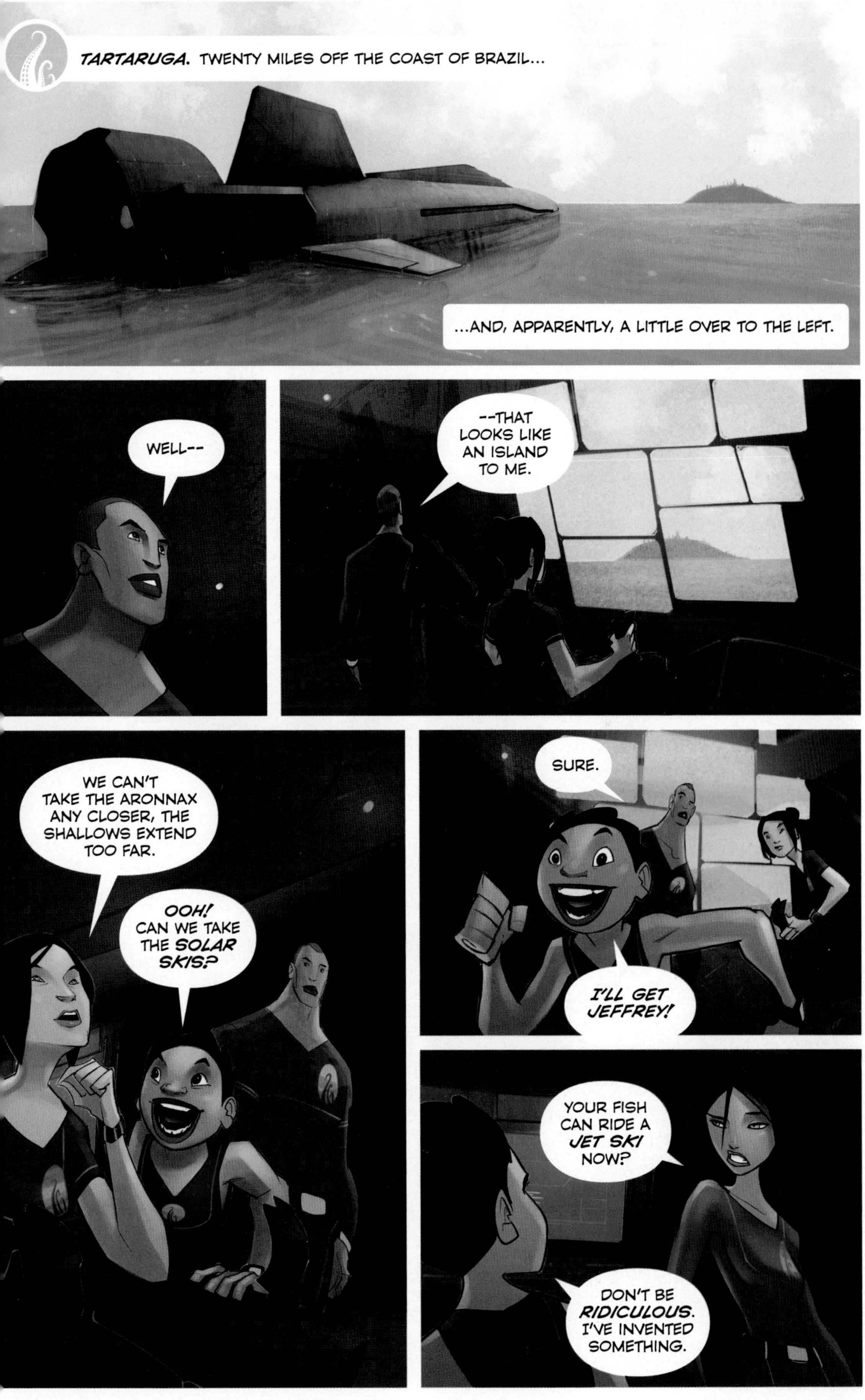
TARTARUGA. TWENTY MILES OFF THE COAST OF BRAZIL...
...AND, APPARENTLY, A LITTLE OVER TO THE LEFT.
WELL--
--THAT LOOKS LIKE AN ISLAND TO ME.
WE CAN'T TAKE THE ARONNAX ANY CLOSER, THE SHALLOWS EXTEND TOO FAR.
OOH! CAN WE TAKE THE SOLAR SKIS?
SURE.
I'LL GET JEFFREY!
YOUR FISH CAN RIDE A JET SKI NOW?
DON'T BE RIDICULOUS. I'VE INVENTED SOMETHING.

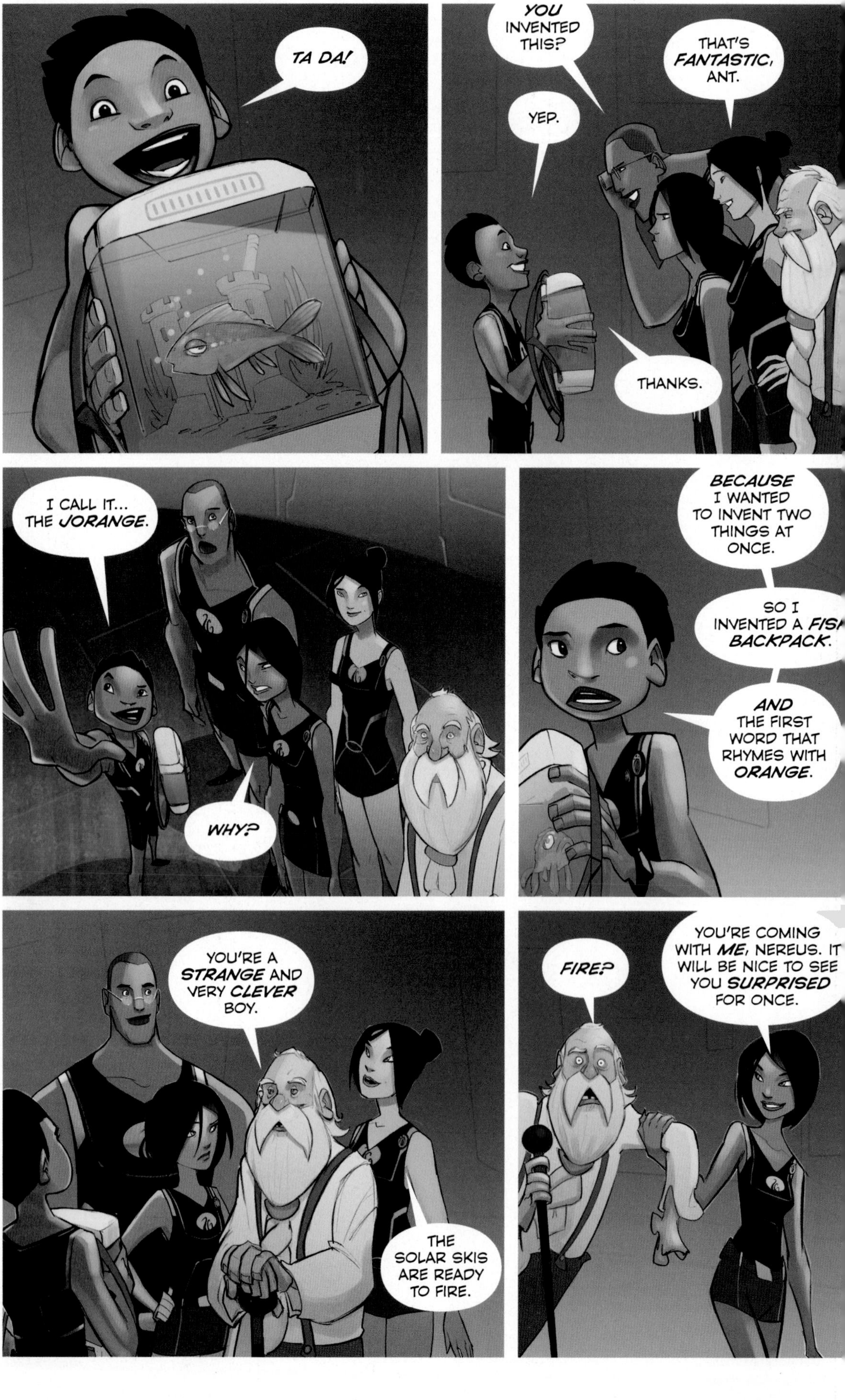

TA DA!
YOU INVENTED THIS?
YEP.
THAT'S FANTASTIC, ANT.
THANKS.
I CALL IT... THE JORANGE.
WHY?
BECAUSE I WANTED TO INVENT TWO THINGS AT ONCE.
SO I INVENTED A FISH BACKPACK.
AND THE FIRST WORD THAT RHYMES WITH ORANGE.
YOU'RE A STRANGE AND VERY CLEVER BOY.
THE SOLAR SKIS ARE READY TO FIRE.
FIRE?
YOU'RE COMING WITH ME, NEREUS. IT WILL BE NICE TO SEE YOU SURPRISED FOR ONCE.

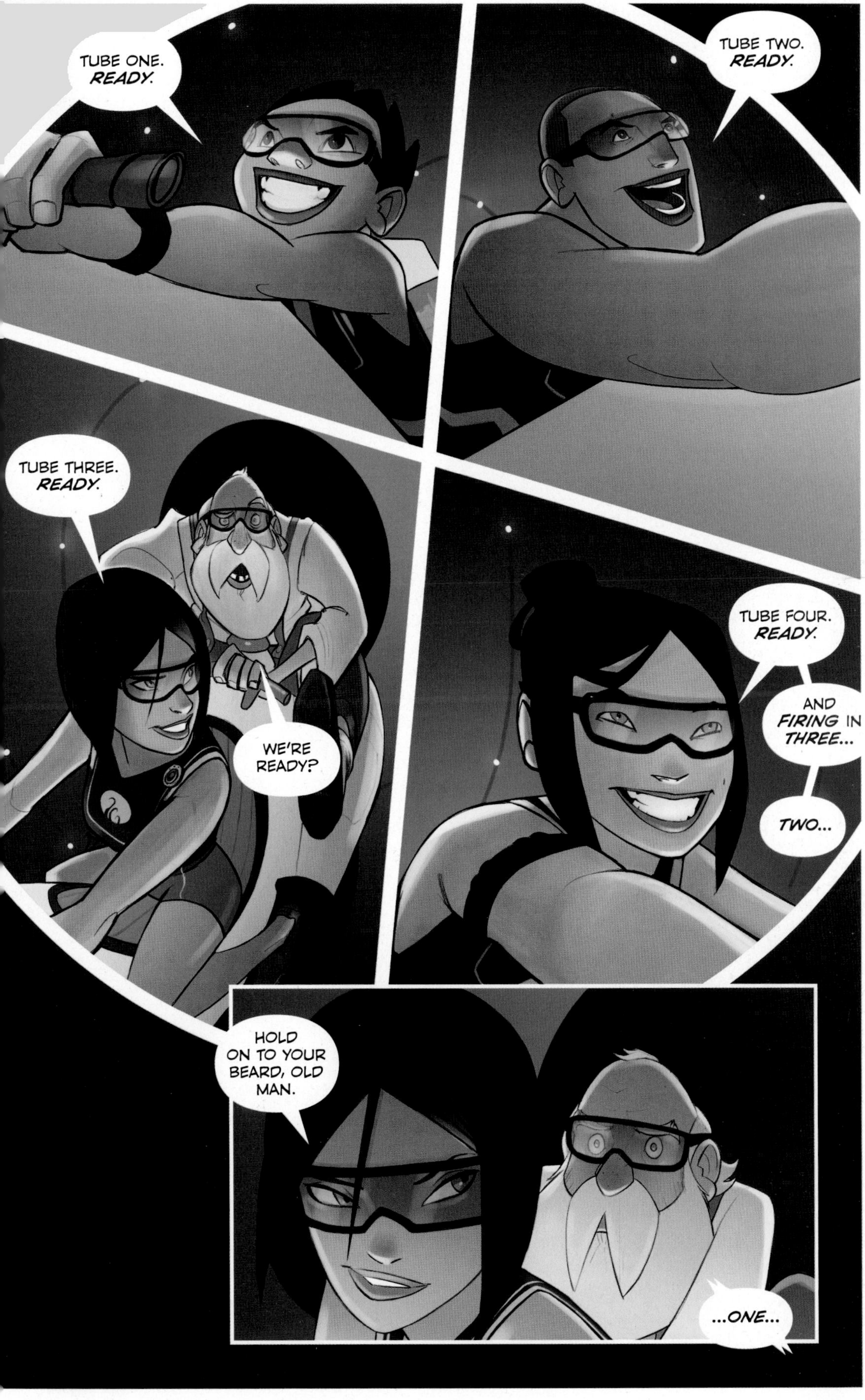
TUBE ONE. READY.
TUBE TWO. READY.
TUBE THREE. READY.
WE'RE READY?
TUBE FOUR. READY.
AND FIRING IN THREE...
TWO...
HOLD ON TO YOUR BEARD, OLD MAN.
...ONE...

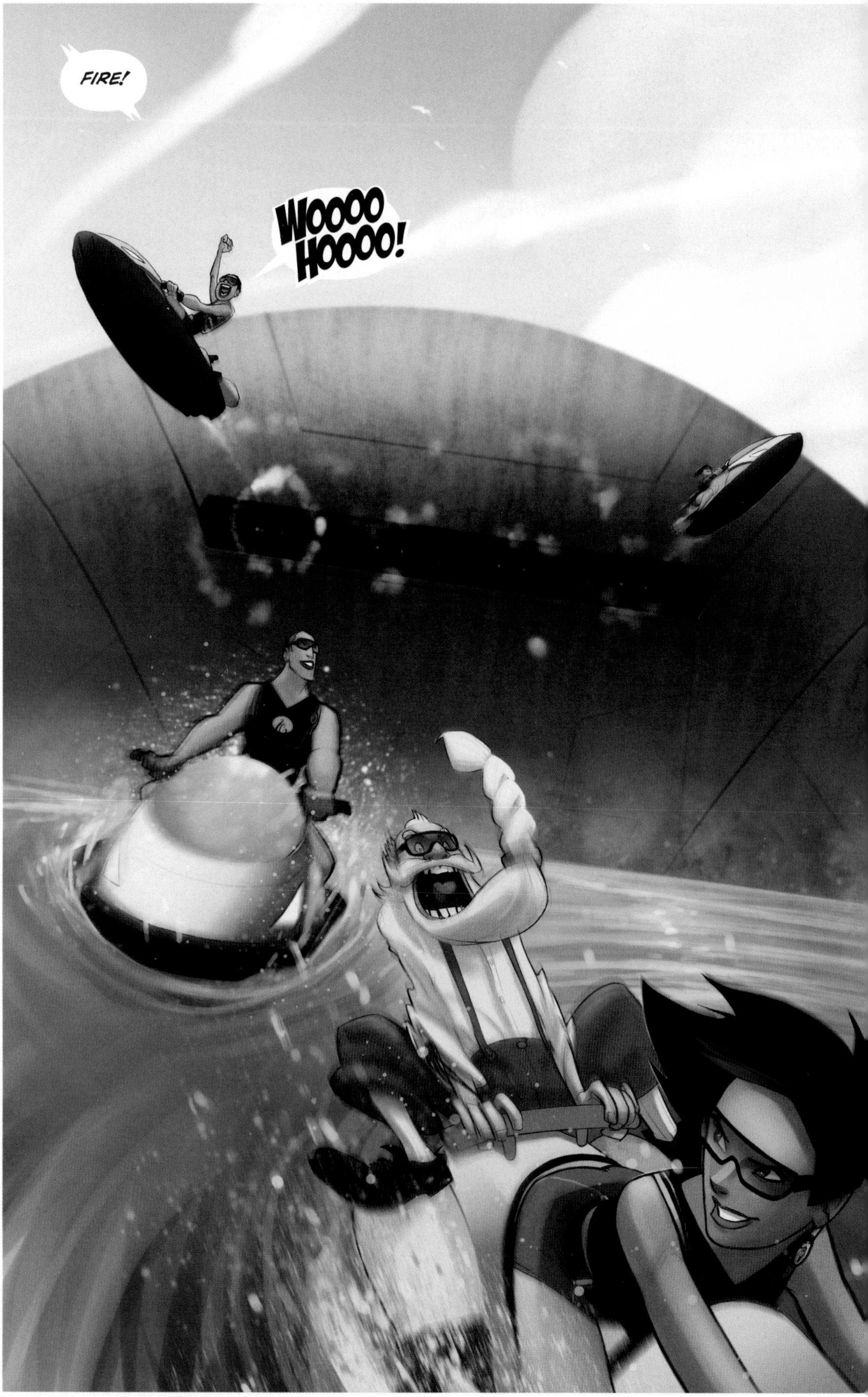
FIRE!
WOOOO HOOOO!

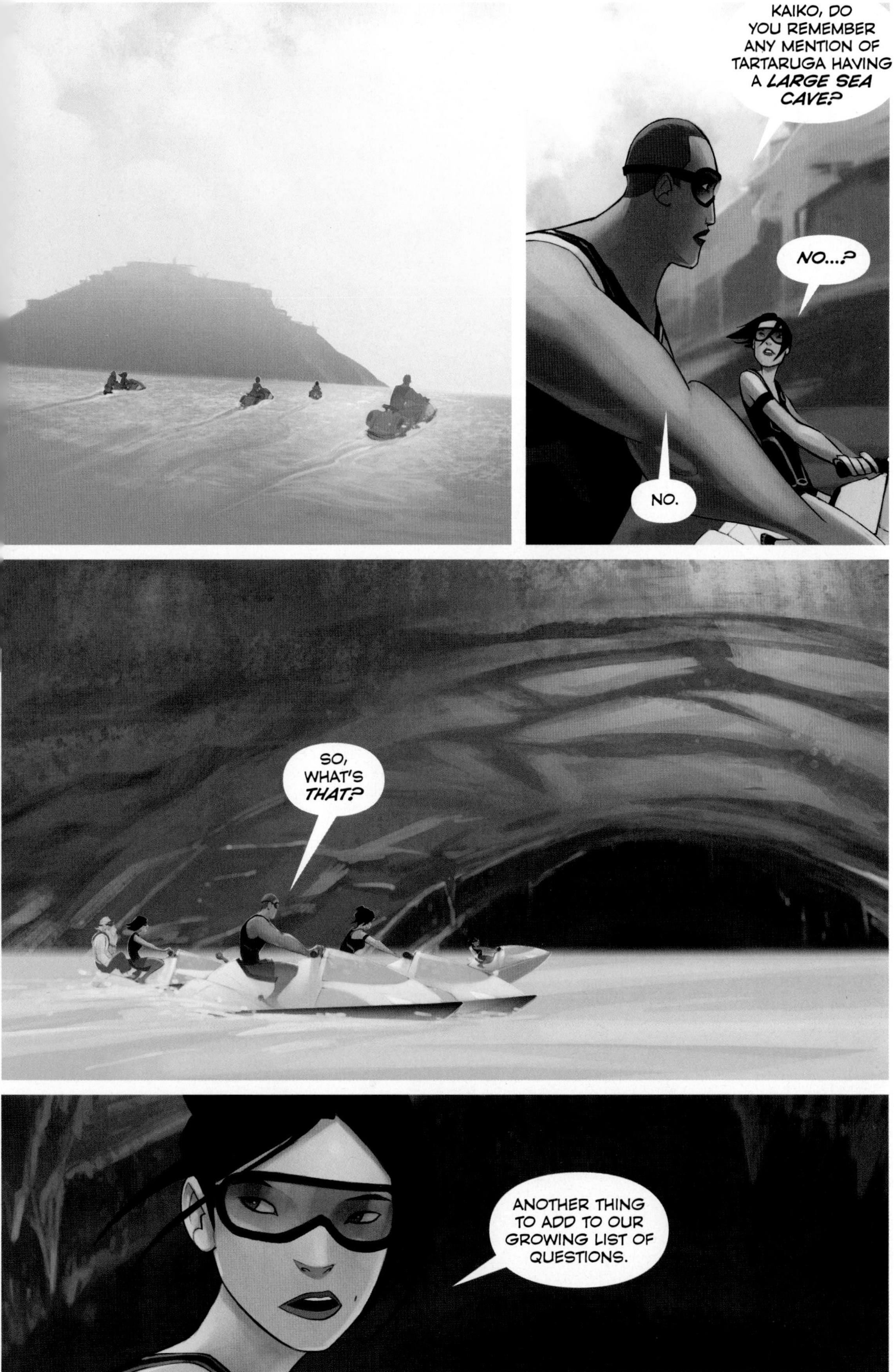
KAIKO, DO YOU REMEMBER ANY MENTION OF TARTARUGA HAVING A *LARGE SEA CAVE?*
*NO...?*
NO.
SO, WHAT'S *THAT?*
ANOTHER THING TO ADD TO OUR GROWING LIST OF QUESTIONS.

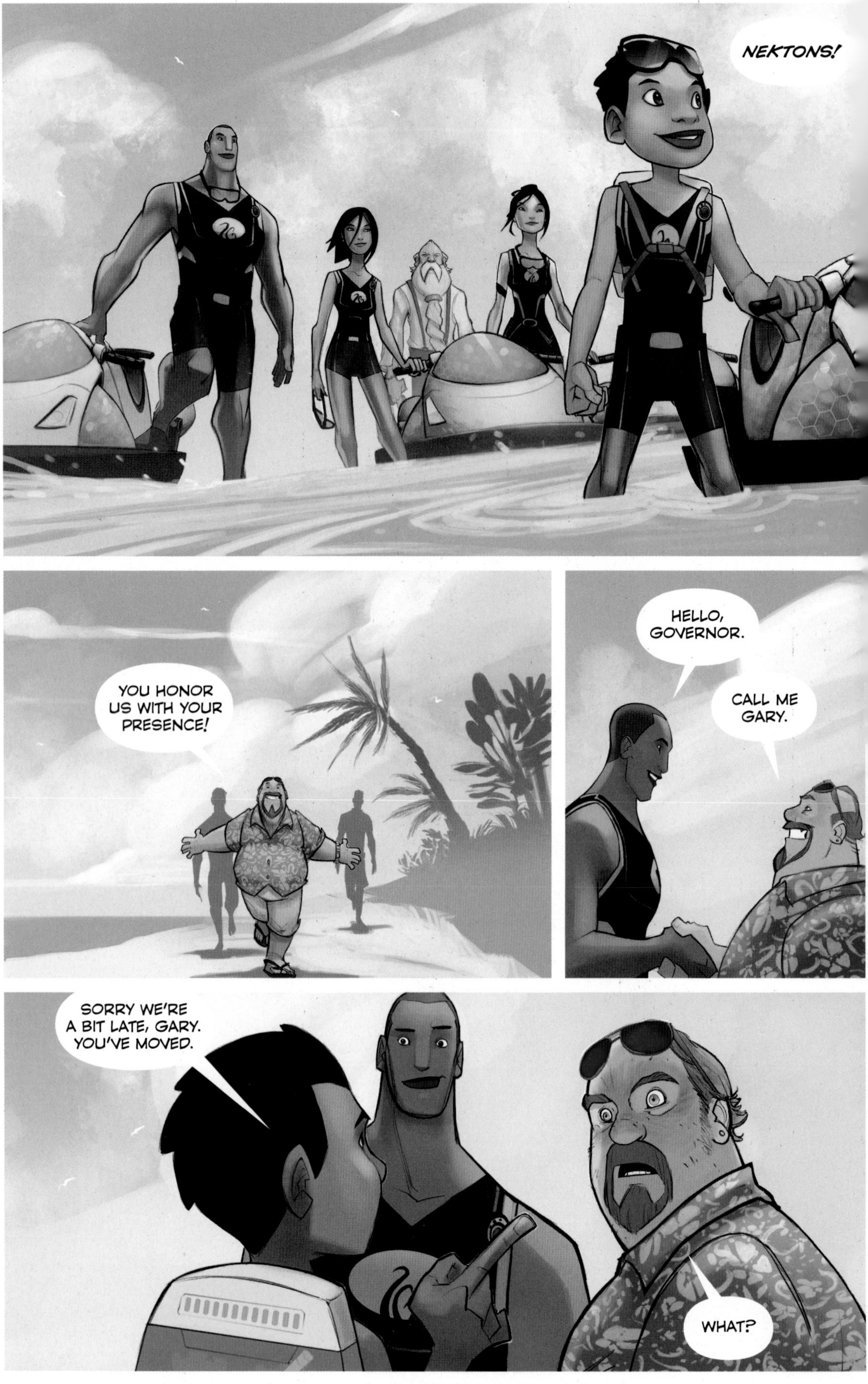
NEKTONS!
YOU HONOR US WITH YOUR PRESENCE!
HELLO, GOVERNOR.
CALL ME GARY.
SORRY WE'RE A BIT LATE, GARY. YOU'VE MOVED.
WHAT?

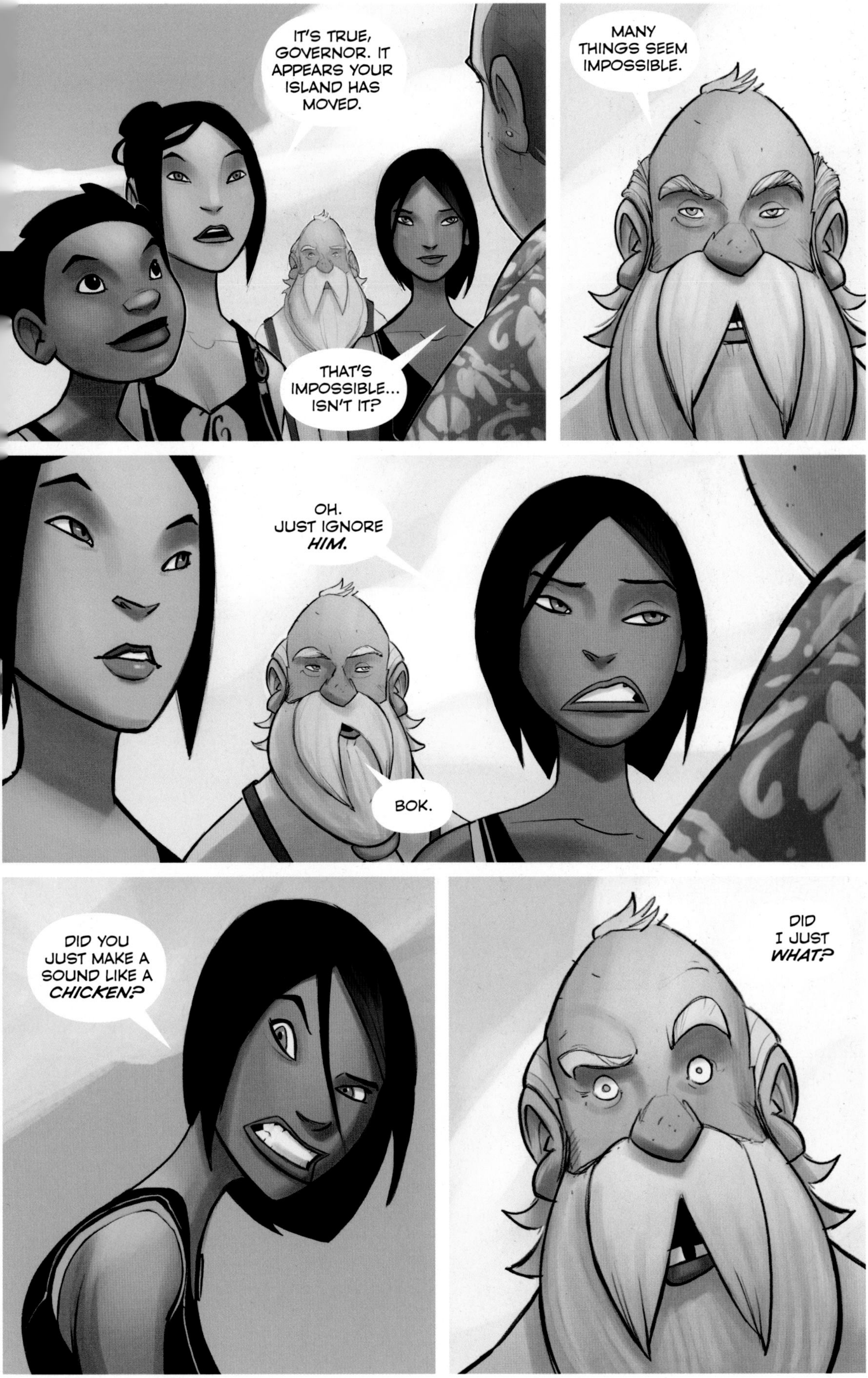
IT'S TRUE, GOVERNOR. IT APPEARS YOUR ISLAND HAS MOVED.
THAT'S IMPOSSIBLE... ISN'T IT?
MANY THINGS SEEM IMPOSSIBLE.
OH. JUST IGNORE *HIM.*
BOK.
DID YOU JUST MAKE A SOUND LIKE A *CHICKEN?*
DID I JUST *WHAT?*

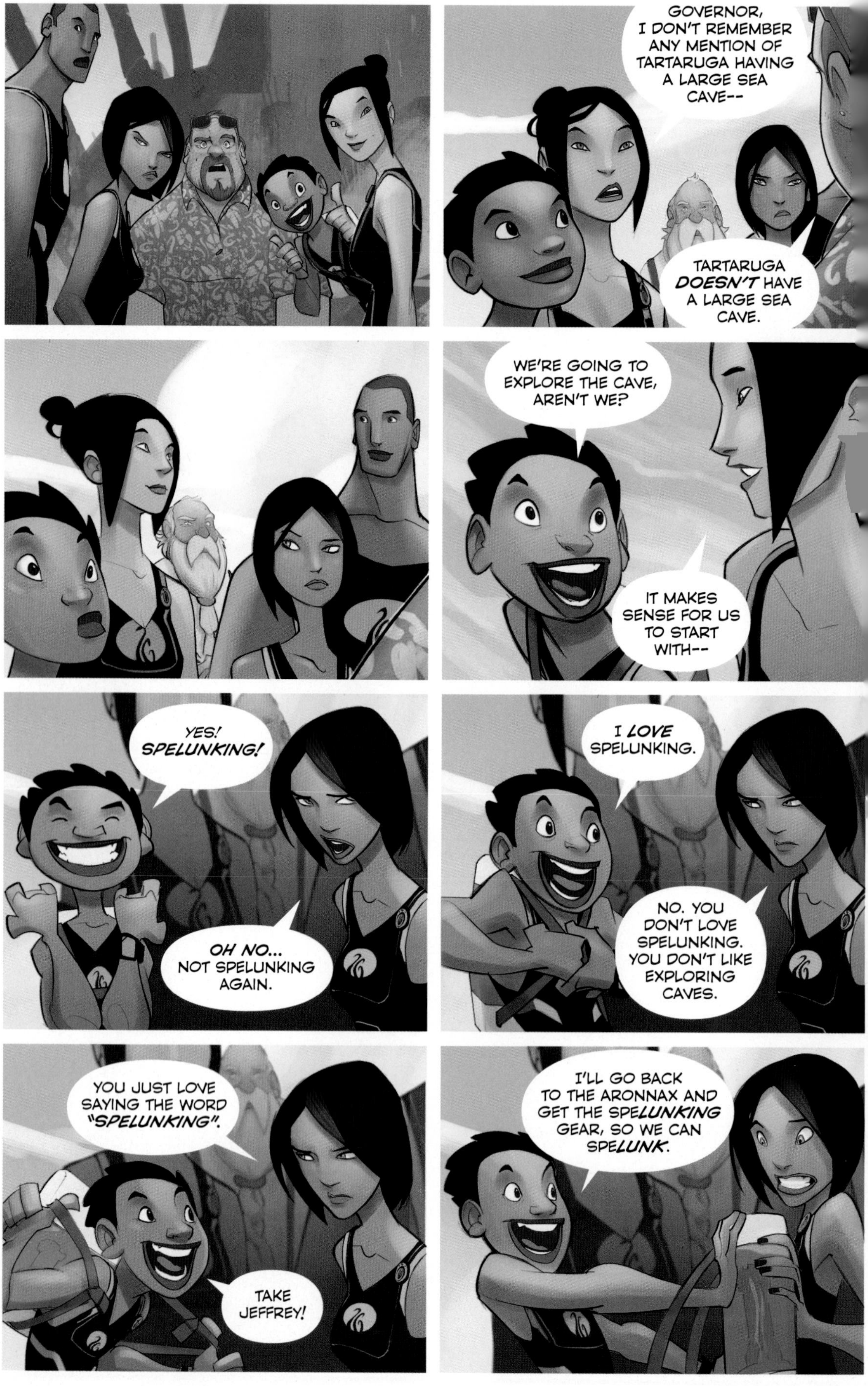
GOVERNOR, I DON'T REMEMBER ANY MENTION OF TARTARUGA HAVING A LARGE SEA CAVE--
TARTARUGA *DOESN'T* HAVE A LARGE SEA CAVE.
WE'RE GOING TO EXPLORE THE CAVE, AREN'T WE?
IT MAKES SENSE FOR US TO START WITH--
*YES! SPELUNKING!*
*OH NO...* NOT SPELUNKING AGAIN.
I *LOVE* SPELUNKING.
NO. YOU DON'T LOVE SPELUNKING. YOU DON'T LIKE EXPLORING CAVES.
YOU JUST LOVE SAYING THE WORD *"SPELUNKING"*.
TAKE JEFFREY!
I'LL GO BACK TO THE ARONNAX AND GET THE SPE*LUNKING* GEAR, SO WE CAN SPE*LUNK*.

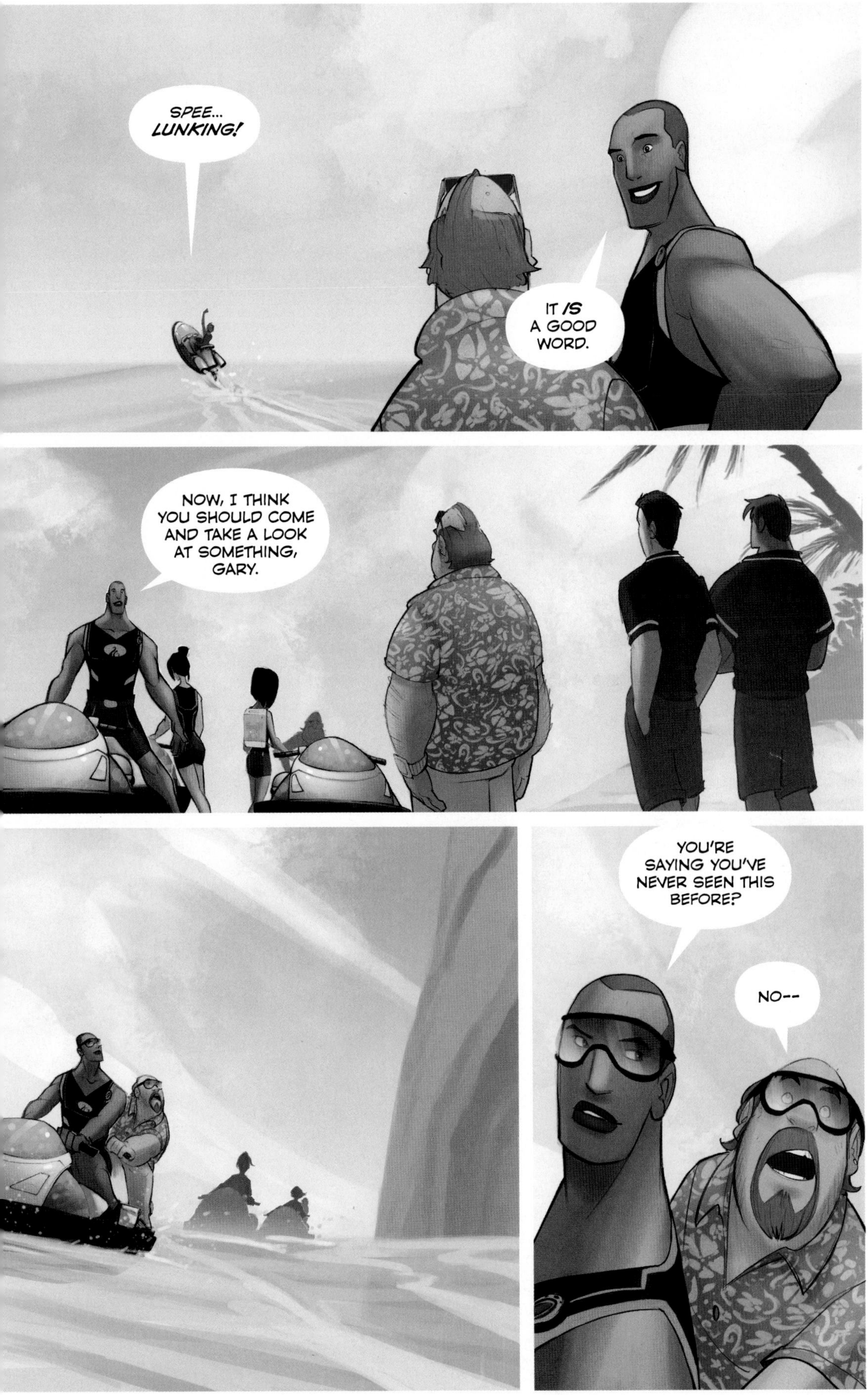
SPEE...
LUNKING!
IT IS A GOOD WORD.
NOW, I THINK YOU SHOULD COME AND TAKE A LOOK AT SOMETHING, GARY.
YOU'RE SAYING YOU'VE NEVER SEEN THIS BEFORE?
NO--

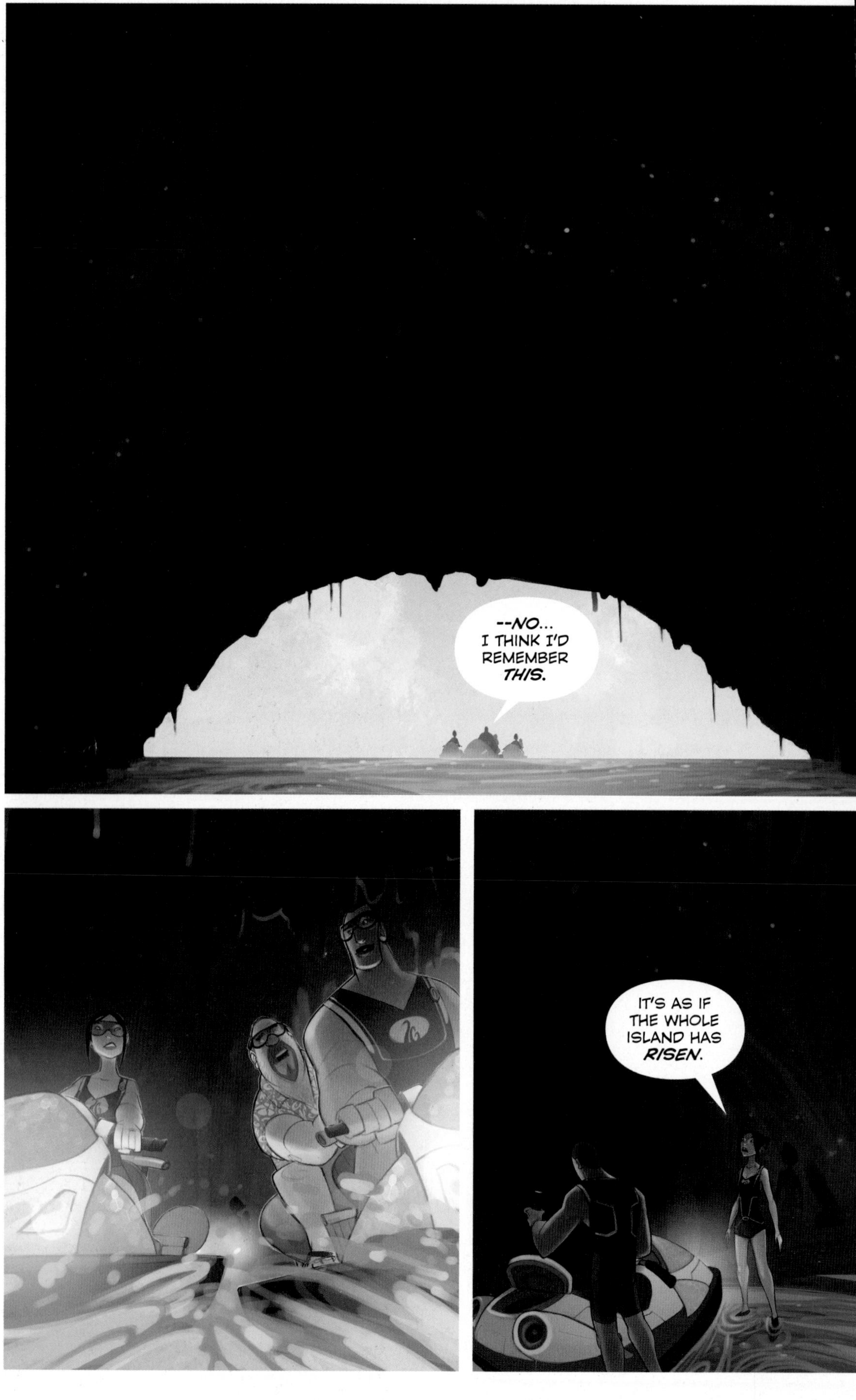
--NO... I THINK I'D REMEMBER THIS.
IT'S AS IF THE WHOLE ISLAND HAS RISEN.

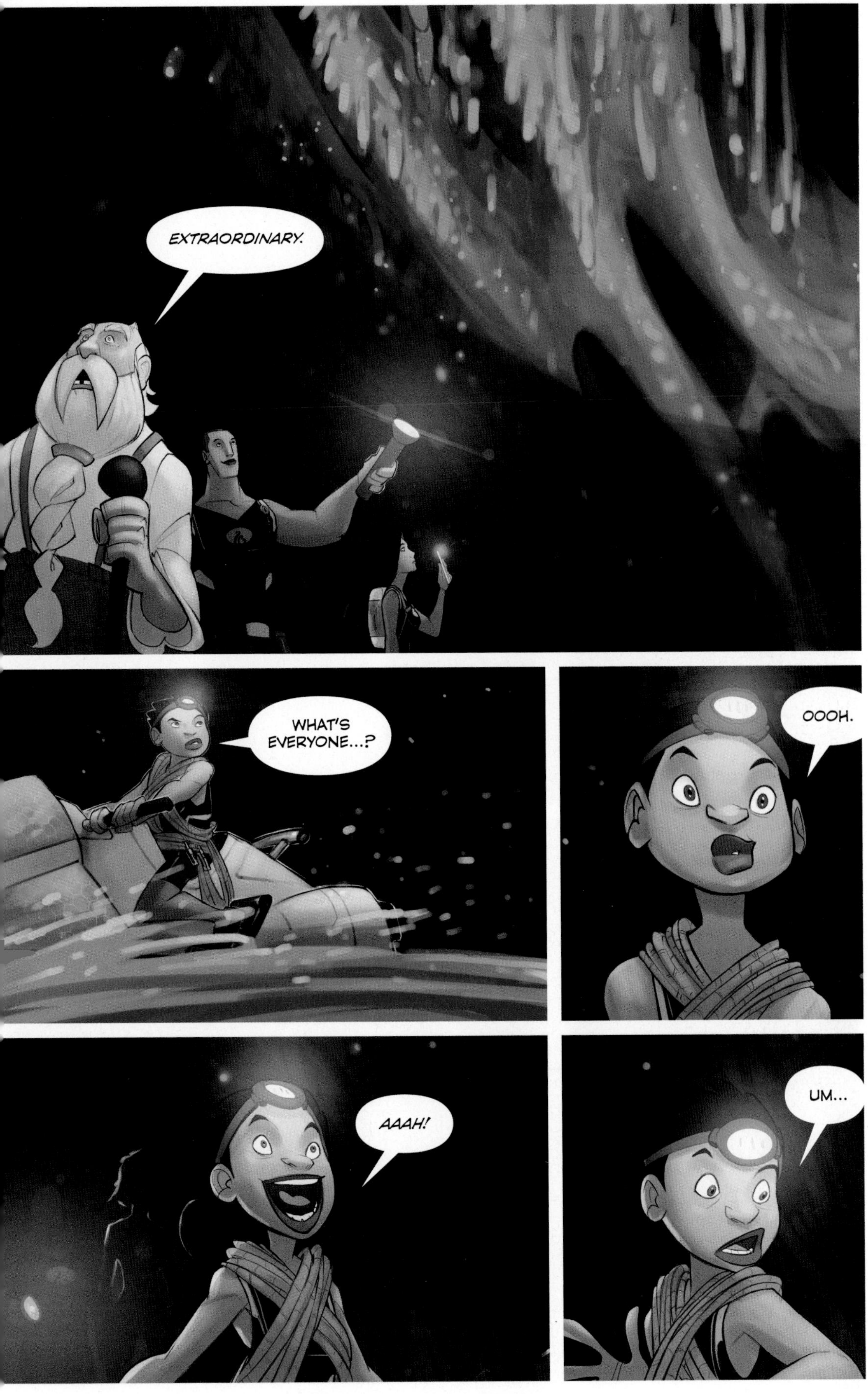
EXTRAORDINARY.
WHAT'S EVERYONE...?
OOOH.
AAAH!
UM...

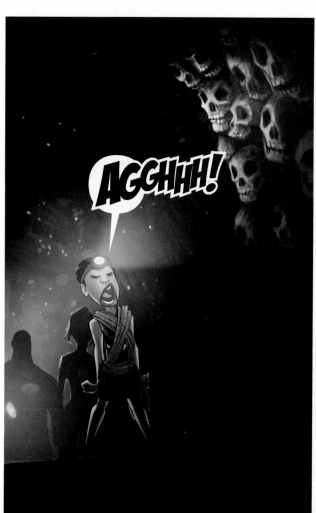

AGGHHH!

WHAT'S WRONG, ANT? YOU'VE SEEN SKELETONS BEFORE.

GET IT OFF! *GET IT OFF!*

YOU HAPPILY SWIM WITH SHARKS BUT YOU'RE *SCARED* OF A *LITTLE SPIDER?*

SHARKS ARE DIFFERENT.

*HOW?*

SHARKS AREN'T *ICKY.*

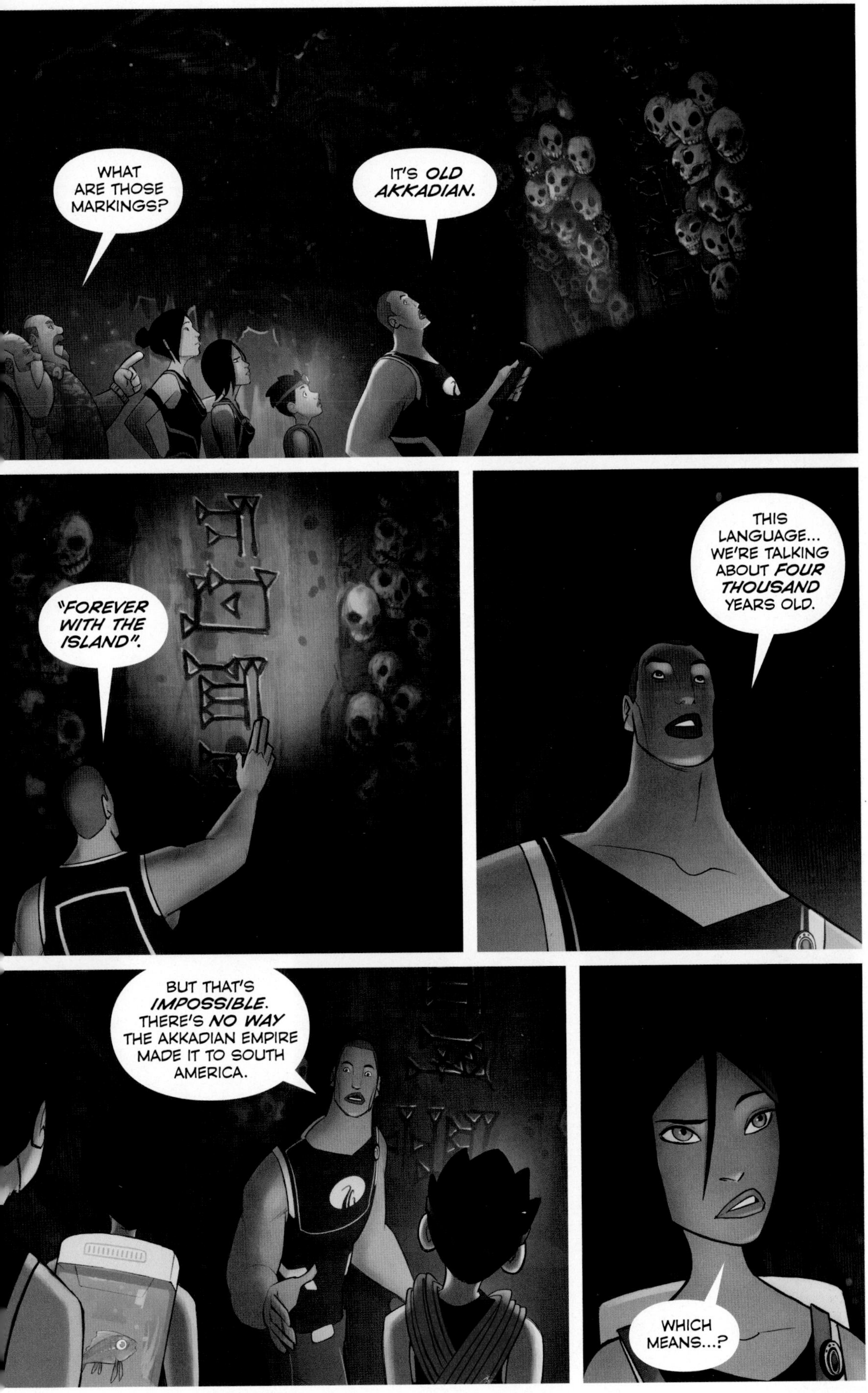
WHAT ARE THOSE MARKINGS?
IT'S *OLD AKKADIAN.*
*"FOREVER WITH THE ISLAND".*
THIS LANGUAGE... WE'RE TALKING ABOUT *FOUR THOUSAND* YEARS OLD.
BUT THAT'S *IMPOSSIBLE.* THERE'S *NO WAY* THE AKKADIAN EMPIRE MADE IT TO SOUTH AMERICA.
WHICH MEANS...?

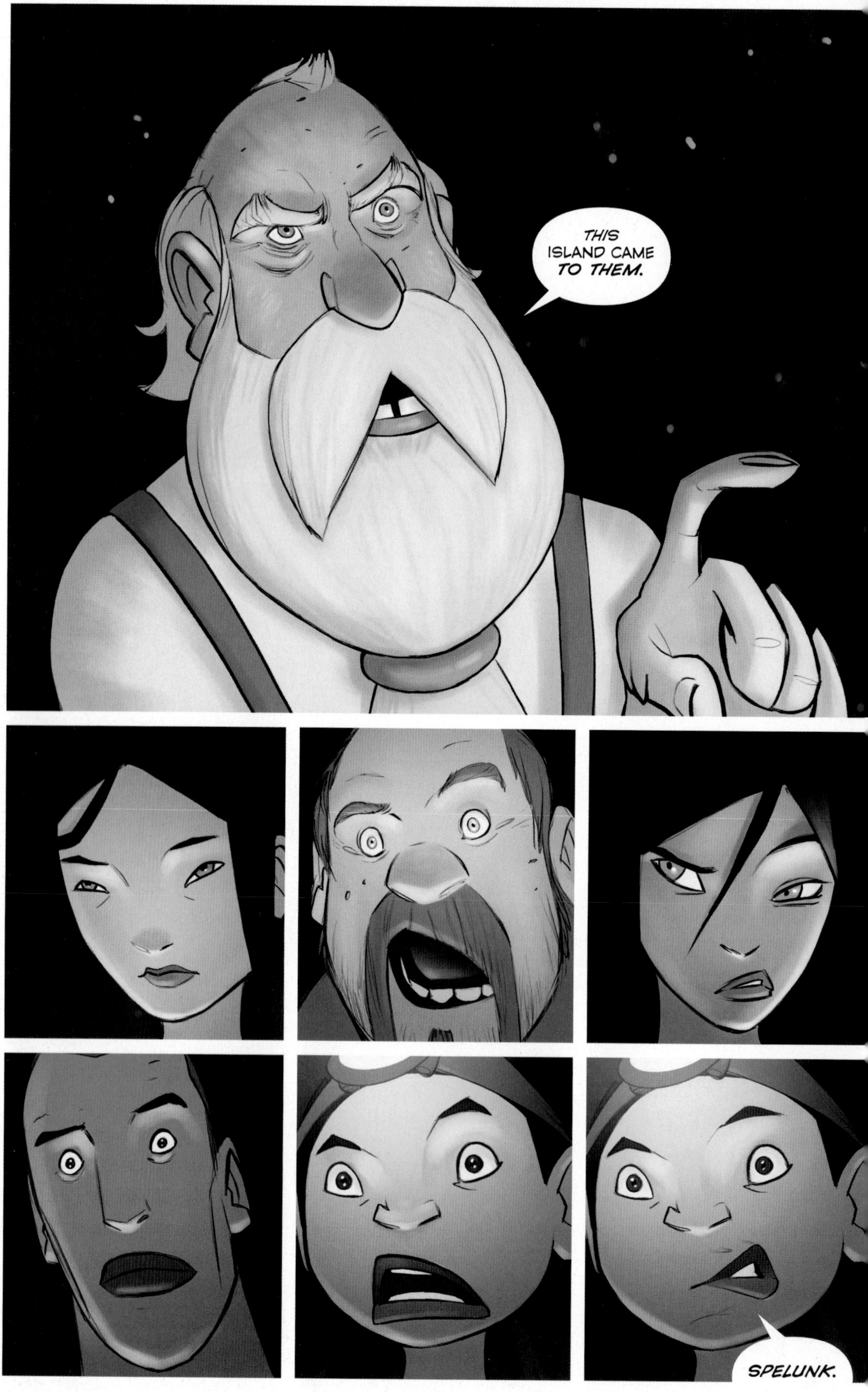
THIS ISLAND CAME TO THEM.
SPELUNK.

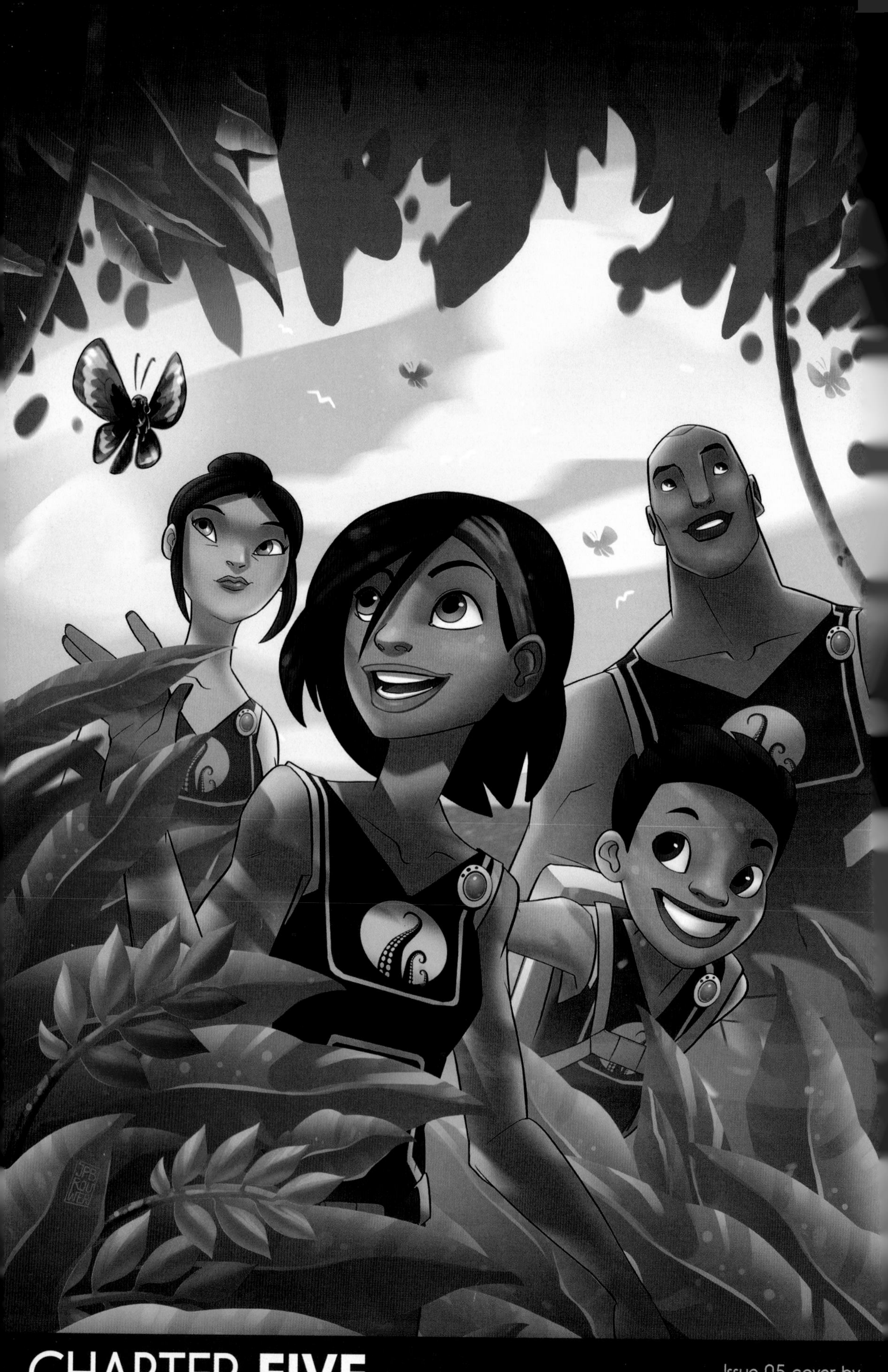

# CHAPTER **FIVE**

Issue 05 cover by
**James Brouwer**

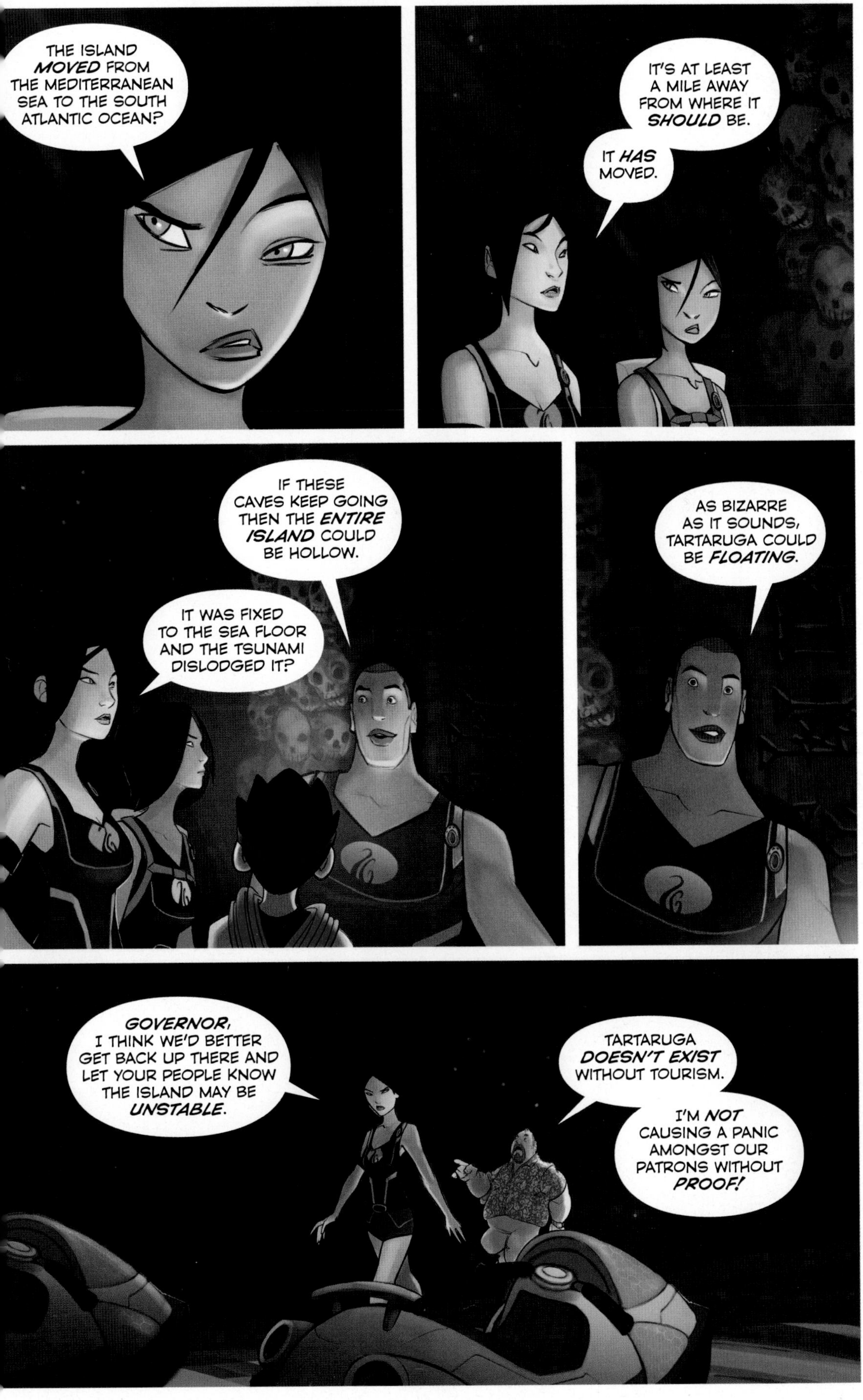

THE ISLAND MOVED FROM THE MEDITERRANEAN SEA TO THE SOUTH ATLANTIC OCEAN?
IT'S AT LEAST A MILE AWAY FROM WHERE IT SHOULD BE.
IT HAS MOVED.
IF THESE CAVES KEEP GOING THEN THE ENTIRE ISLAND COULD BE HOLLOW.
IT WAS FIXED TO THE SEA FLOOR AND THE TSUNAMI DISLODGED IT?
AS BIZARRE AS IT SOUNDS, TARTARUGA COULD BE FLOATING.
GOVERNOR, I THINK WE'D BETTER GET BACK UP THERE AND LET YOUR PEOPLE KNOW THE ISLAND MAY BE UNSTABLE.
TARTARUGA DOESN'T EXIST WITHOUT TOURISM.
I'M NOT CAUSING A PANIC AMONGST OUR PATRONS WITHOUT PROOF!

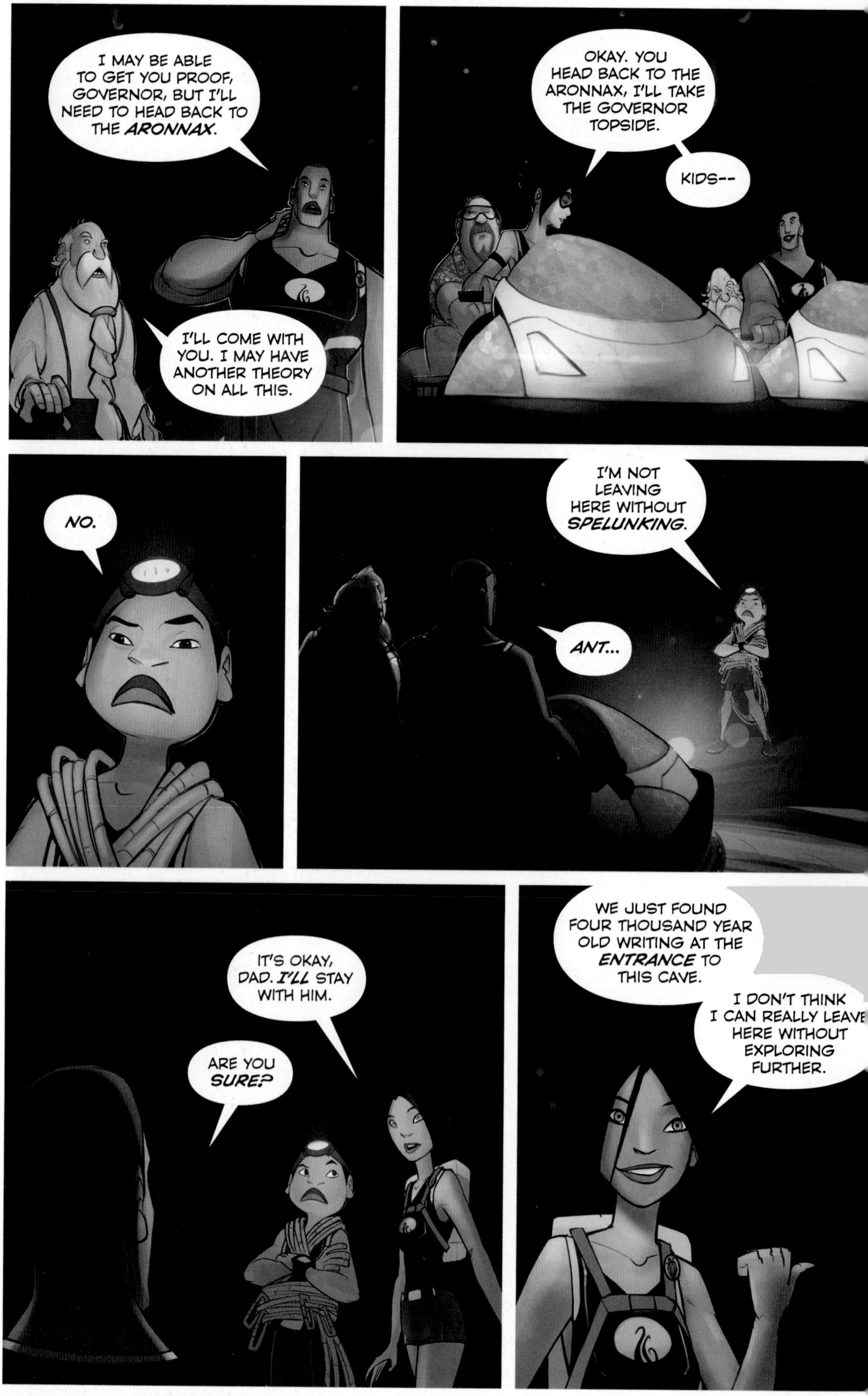
I MAY BE ABLE TO GET YOU PROOF, GOVERNOR, BUT I'LL NEED TO HEAD BACK TO THE *ARONNAX*.
I'LL COME WITH YOU. I MAY HAVE ANOTHER THEORY ON ALL THIS.
OKAY. YOU HEAD BACK TO THE ARONNAX, I'LL TAKE THE GOVERNOR TOPSIDE.
KIDS--
*NO.*
I'M NOT LEAVING HERE WITHOUT *SPELUNKING*.
*ANT...*
IT'S OKAY, DAD. *I'LL* STAY WITH HIM.
ARE YOU *SURE?*
WE JUST FOUND FOUR THOUSAND YEAR OLD WRITING AT THE *ENTRANCE* TO THIS CAVE.
I DON'T THINK I CAN REALLY LEAVE HERE WITHOUT EXPLORING FURTHER.

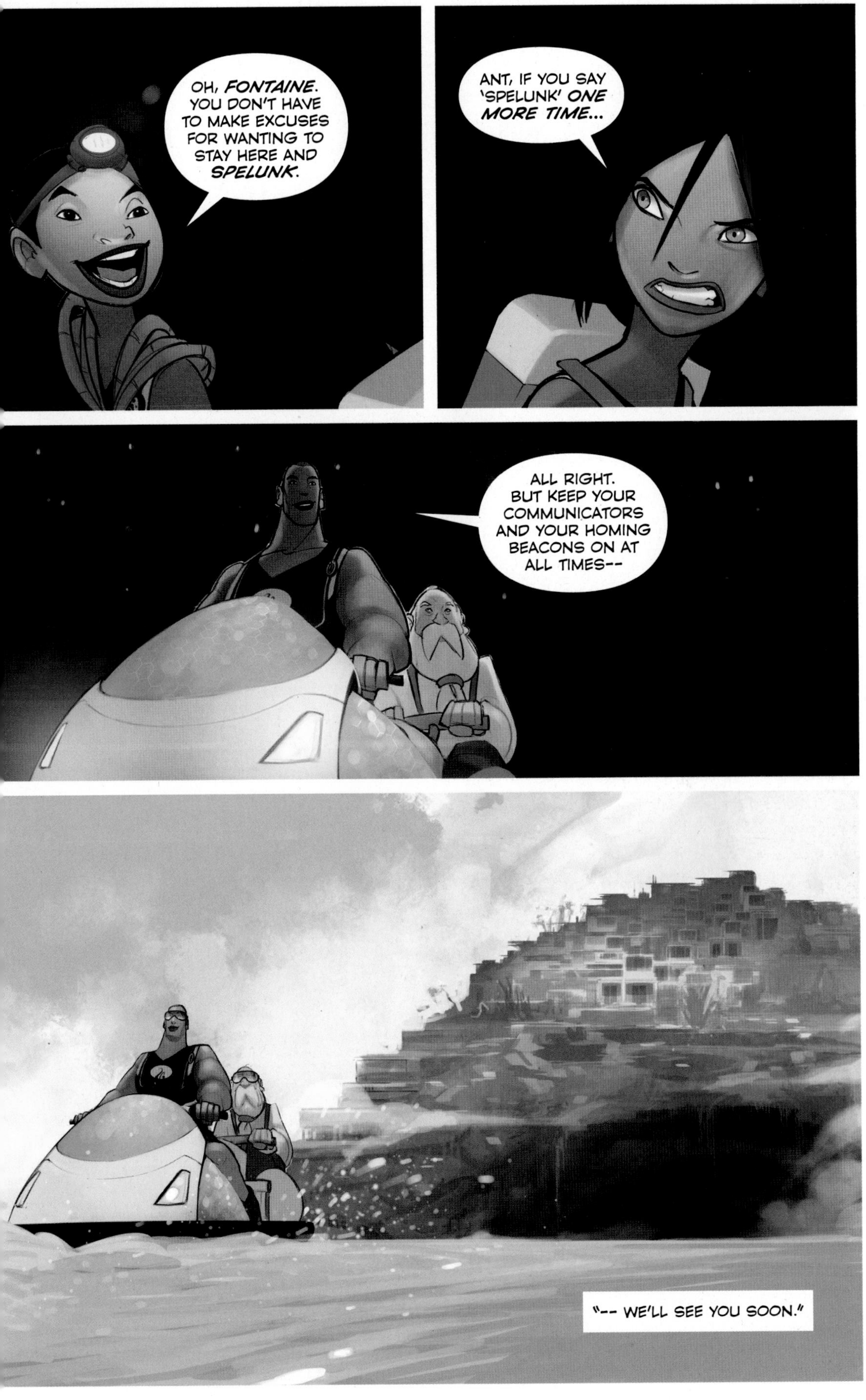
OH, FONTAINE. YOU DON'T HAVE TO MAKE EXCUSES FOR WANTING TO STAY HERE AND SPELUNK.
ANT, IF YOU SAY 'SPELUNK' ONE MORE TIME...
ALL RIGHT. BUT KEEP YOUR COMMUNICATORS AND YOUR HOMING BEACONS ON AT ALL TIMES--
"-- WE'LL SEE YOU SOON."

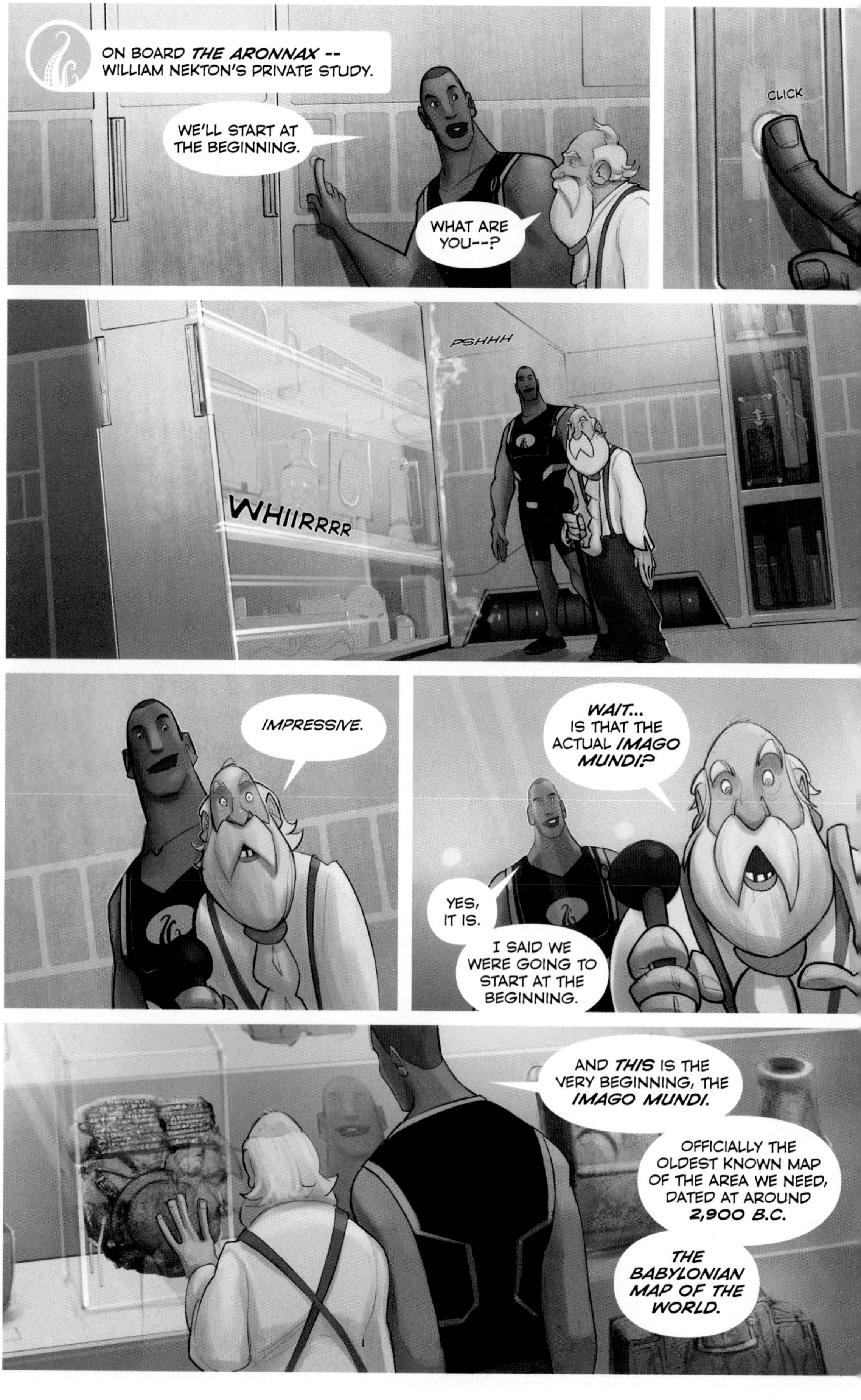
ON BOARD *THE ARONNAX* -- WILLIAM NEKTON'S PRIVATE STUDY.
WE'LL START AT THE BEGINNING.
WHAT ARE YOU--?
CLICK
PSHHH
WHIIRRRR
*IMPRESSIVE.*
*WAIT...* IS THAT THE ACTUAL *IMAGO MUNDI?*
YES, IT IS.
I SAID WE WERE GOING TO START AT THE BEGINNING.
AND *THIS* IS THE VERY BEGINNING, THE *IMAGO MUNDI.*
OFFICIALLY THE OLDEST KNOWN MAP OF THE AREA WE NEED, DATED AT AROUND **2,900 B.C.**
*THE BABYLONIAN MAP OF THE WORLD.*

AND YOU *JUST HAPPEN* TO HAVE THE *OLDEST KNOWN* MAP OF THE WORLD IN YOUR *PRIVATE STUDY?*

IT'S ONLY THE *OLDEST* AS FAR AS THE PUBLIC KNOW. I KNOW OF *SEVEN* THAT ARE OLDER AND I'VE SEEN *THREE* *FIRST-HAND.*

I THOUGHT THIS WAS ON DISPLAY IN THE *BRITISH MUSEUM.*

THEY HAVE A NICE REPLICA BUT I WOULDN'T TRUST THEM WITH THIS AND, FRANKLY, THEY DON'T TRUST THEMSELVES WITH IT EITHER.

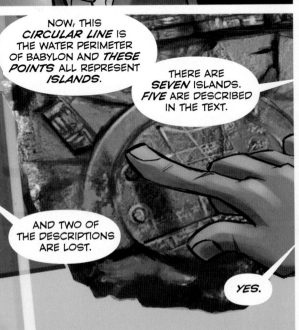

NOW, THIS *CIRCULAR LINE* IS THE WATER PERIMETER OF BABYLON AND *THESE POINTS* ALL REPRESENT *ISLANDS.*

THERE ARE *SEVEN* ISLANDS. *FIVE* ARE DESCRIBED IN THE TEXT.

AND TWO OF THE DESCRIPTIONS ARE LOST.

YES.

YOU BELIEVE ONE OF THE LOST TEXTS MAY HAVE DESCRIBED *TARTARUGA?*

I BELIEVE *YOU AND I* ARE GOING TO GET TO THE BOTTOM OF THIS.

THE *VERY* BOTTOM.

IT'S TIME TO SEE WHAT LIES BENEATH TARTARUGA.

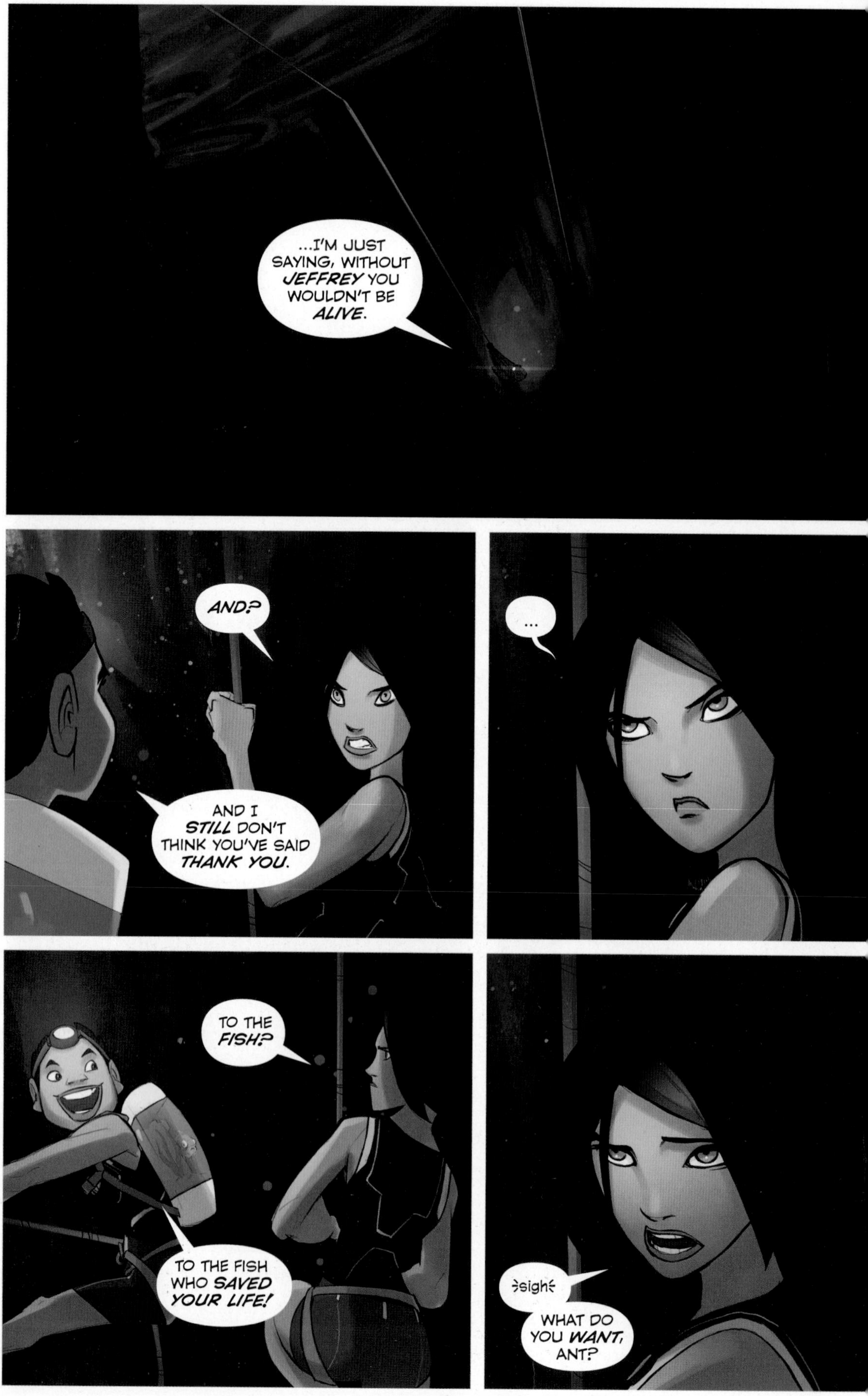
...I'M JUST SAYING, WITHOUT JEFFREY YOU WOULDN'T BE ALIVE.
AND?
AND I STILL DON'T THINK YOU'VE SAID THANK YOU.
...
TO THE FISH?
TO THE FISH WHO SAVED YOUR LIFE!
sigh
WHAT DO YOU WANT, ANT?

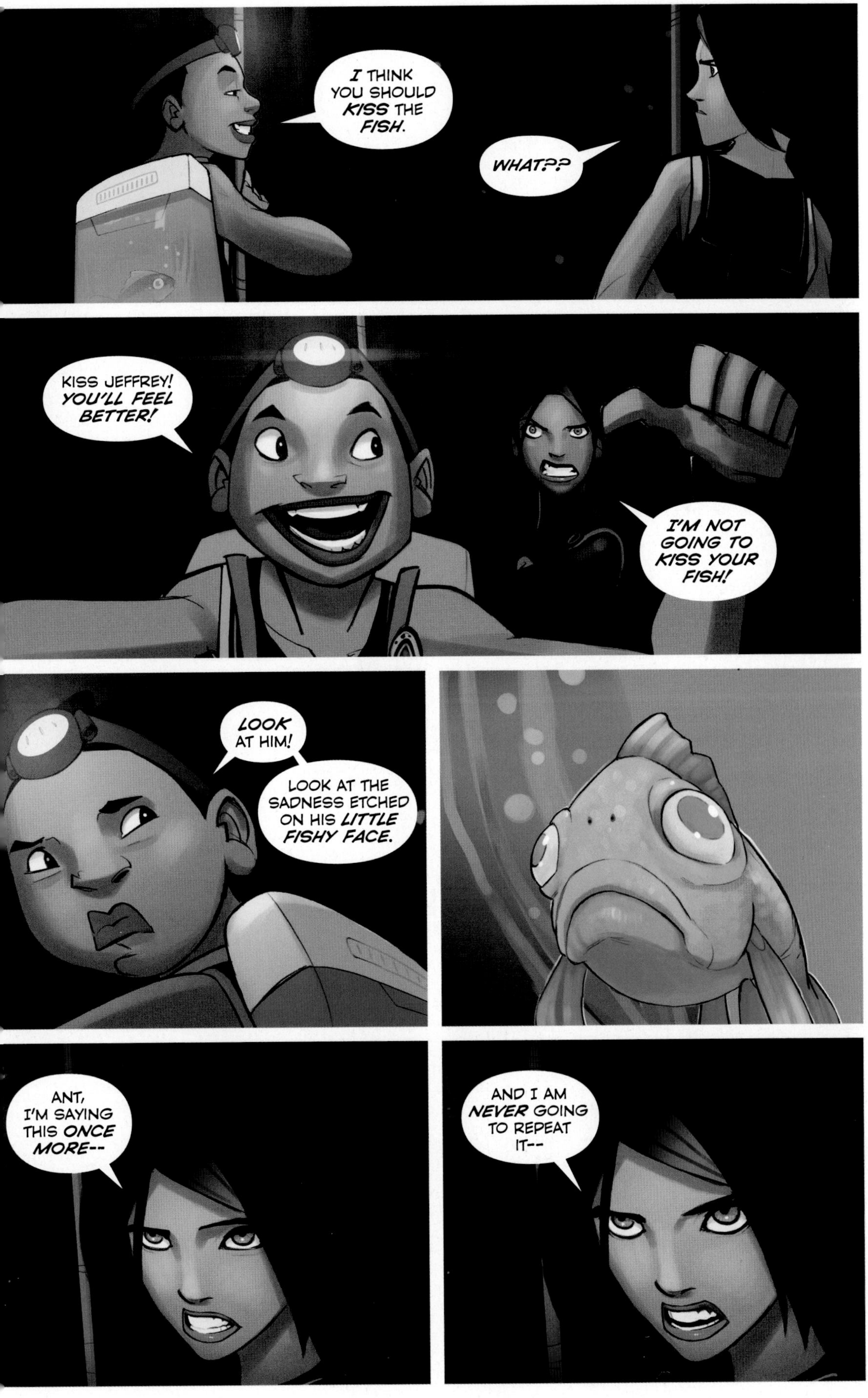
I THINK YOU SHOULD KISS THE FISH.
WHAT??
KISS JEFFREY! YOU'LL FEEL BETTER!
I'M NOT GOING TO KISS YOUR FISH!
LOOK AT HIM!
LOOK AT THE SADNESS ETCHED ON HIS LITTLE FISHY FACE.
ANT, I'M SAYING THIS ONCE MORE--
AND I AM NEVER GOING TO REPEAT IT--

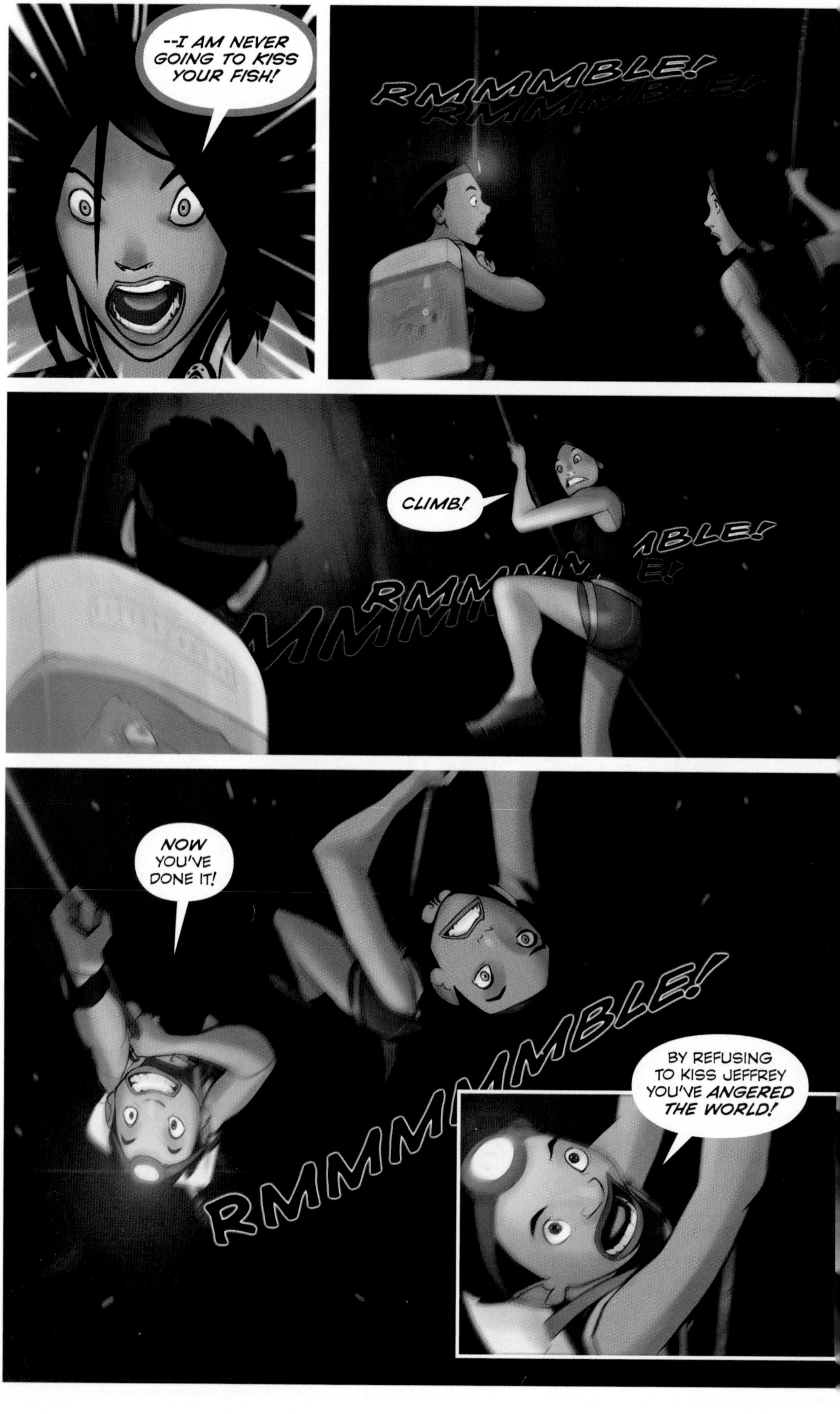
--I AM NEVER GOING TO KISS YOUR FISH!
RMMMMBLE! RMMMMBLE!
CLIMB!
RMMMMMMBLE!
NOW YOU'VE DONE IT!
RMMMMMMBLE!
BY REFUSING TO KISS JEFFREY YOU'VE ANGERED THE WORLD!

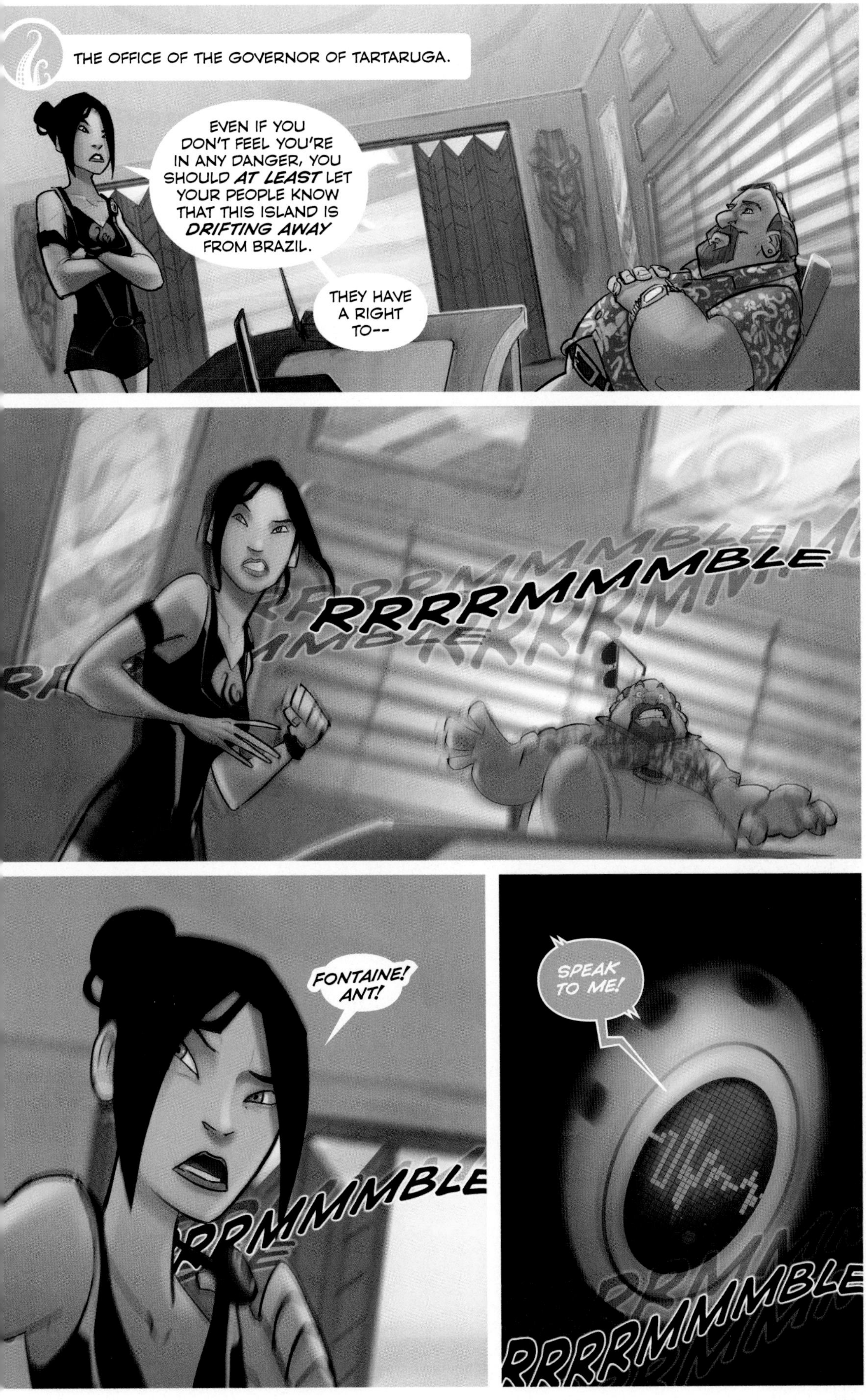
THE OFFICE OF THE GOVERNOR OF TARTARUGA.
EVEN IF YOU DON'T FEEL YOU'RE IN ANY DANGER, YOU SHOULD *AT LEAST* LET YOUR PEOPLE KNOW THAT THIS ISLAND IS *DRIFTING AWAY* FROM BRAZIL.
THEY HAVE A RIGHT TO--
RRRRMMMMBLE
FONTAINE! ANT!
RRMMMBLE
SPEAK TO ME!
RRRRMMMMBLE

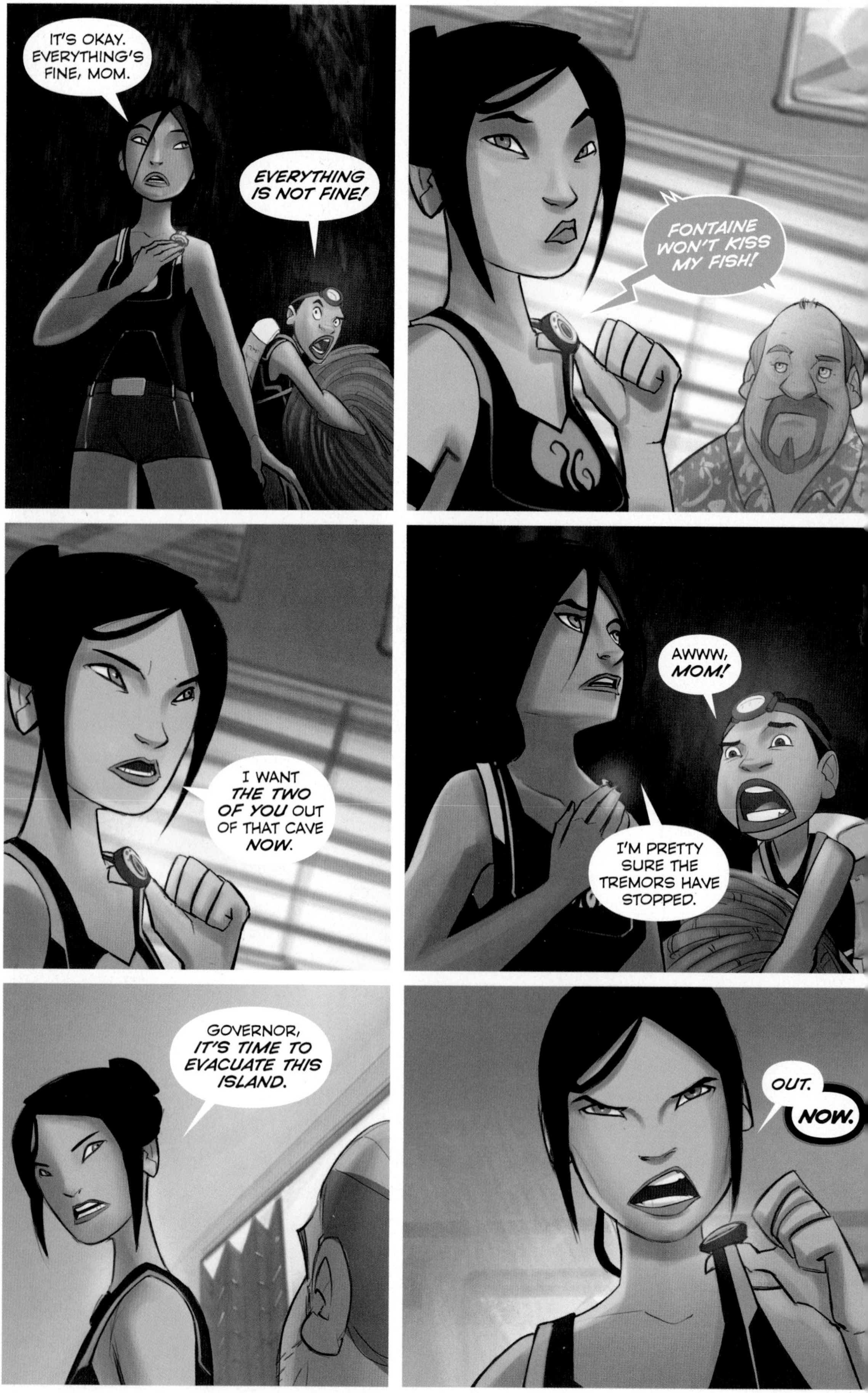
IT'S OKAY. EVERYTHING'S FINE, MOM.
EVERYTHING IS NOT FINE!
FONTAINE WON'T KISS MY FISH!
I WANT THE TWO OF YOU OUT OF THAT CAVE NOW.
AWWW, MOM!
I'M PRETTY SURE THE TREMORS HAVE STOPPED.
GOVERNOR, IT'S TIME TO EVACUATE THIS ISLAND.
OUT.
NOW.

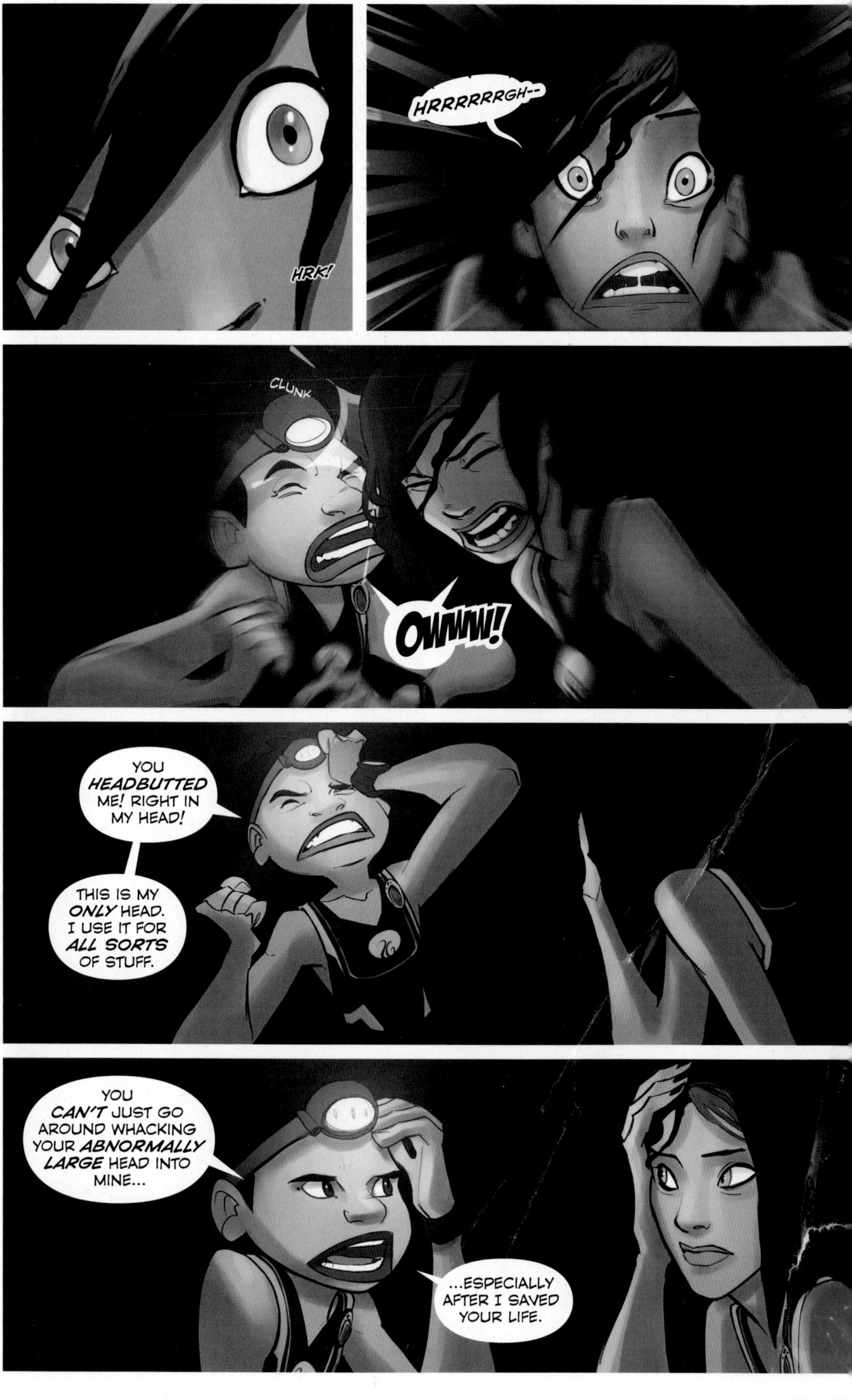

HRK!
HRRRRRRGH--
CLUNK
OWWW!
YOU HEADBUTTED ME! RIGHT IN MY HEAD!
THIS IS MY ONLY HEAD. I USE IT FOR ALL SORTS OF STUFF.
YOU CAN'T JUST GO AROUND WHACKING YOUR ABNORMALLY LARGE HEAD INTO MINE...
...ESPECIALLY AFTER I SAVED YOUR LIFE.

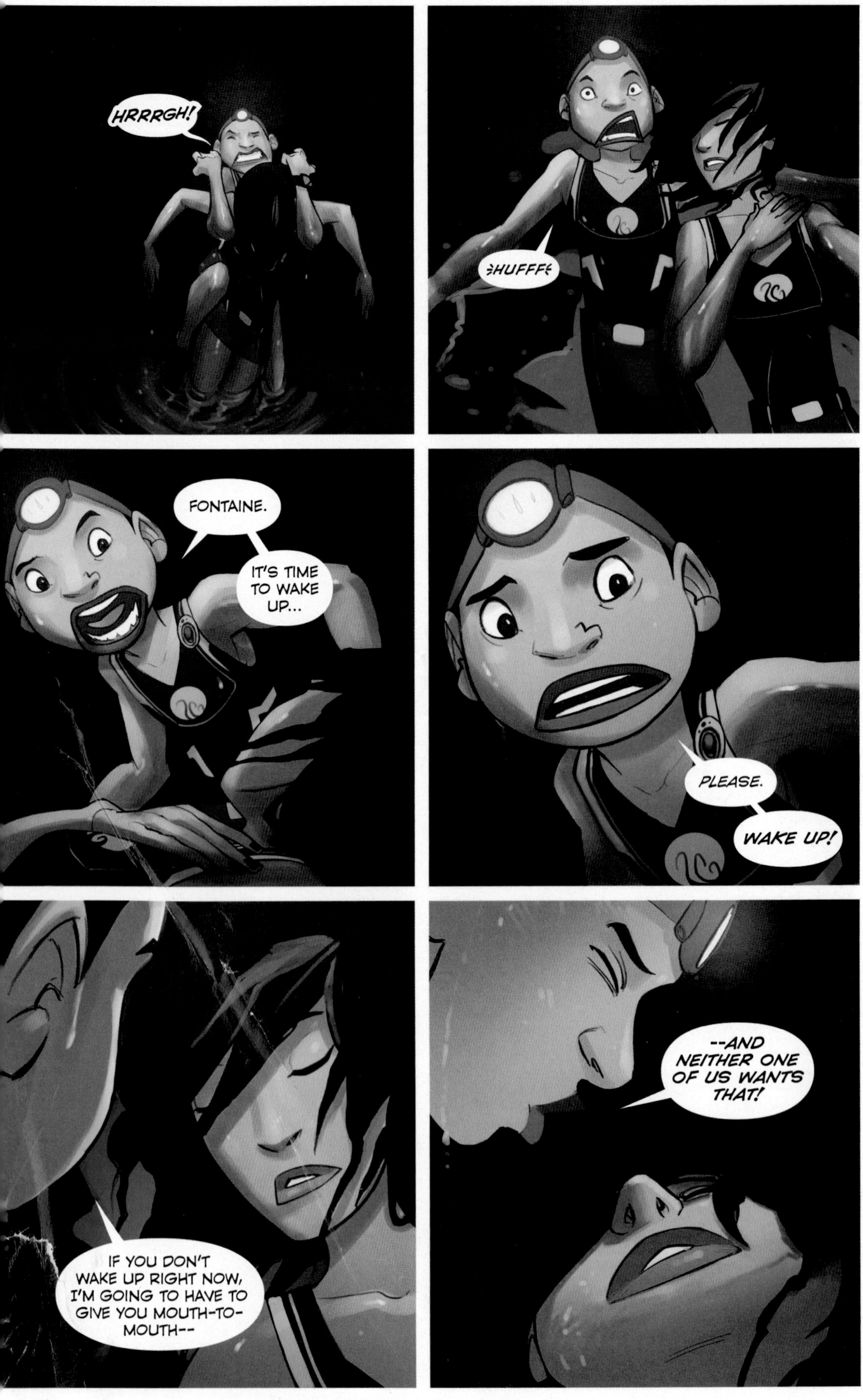
HRRRGH!
HUFFF
FONTAINE.
IT'S TIME TO WAKE UP...
PLEASE.
WAKE UP!
IF YOU DON'T WAKE UP RIGHT NOW, I'M GOING TO HAVE TO GIVE YOU MOUTH-TO-MOUTH--
--AND NEITHER ONE OF US WANTS THAT!

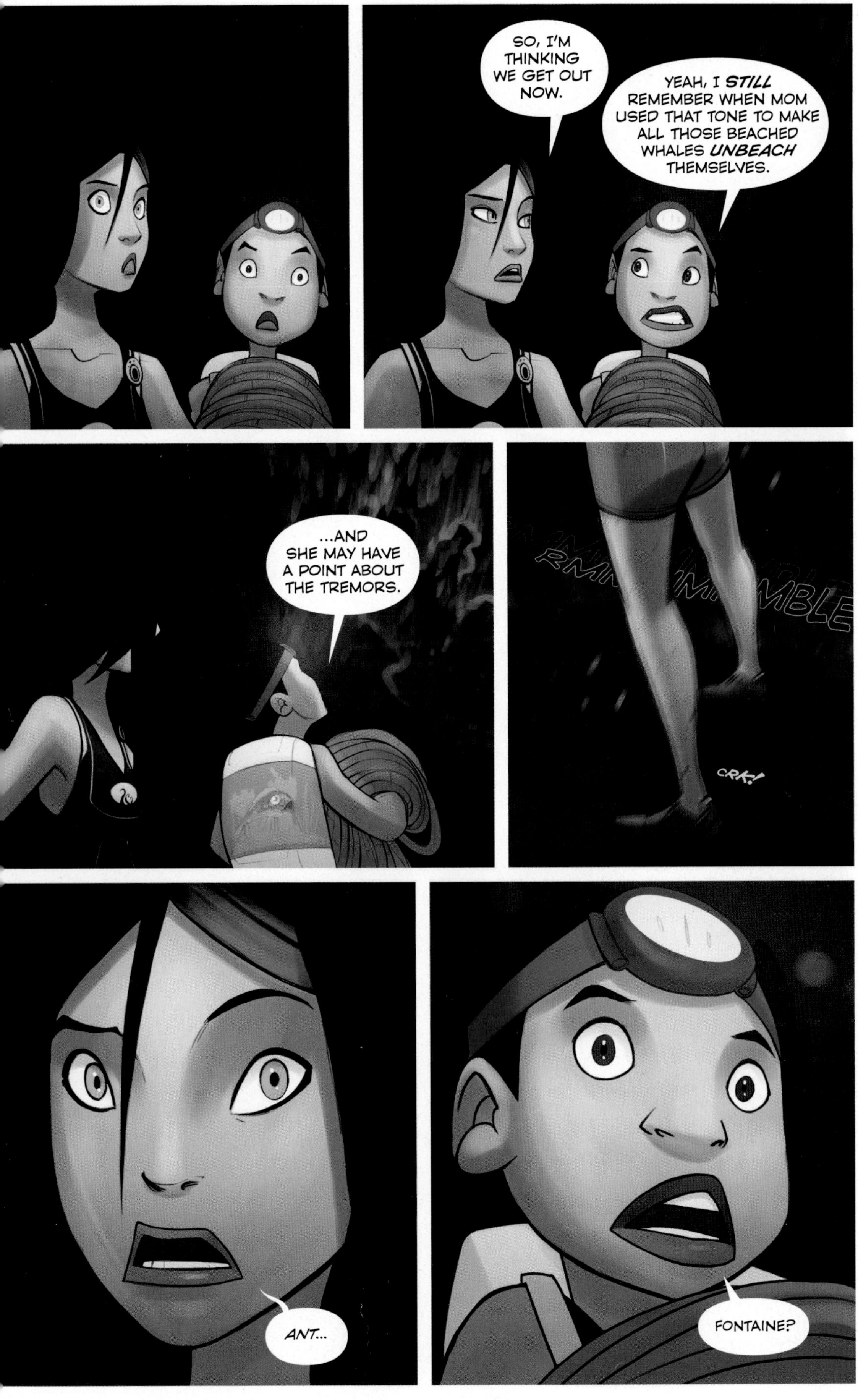
SO, I'M THINKING WE GET OUT NOW.
YEAH, I STILL REMEMBER WHEN MOM USED THAT TONE TO MAKE ALL THOSE BEACHED WHALES UNBEACH THEMSELVES.
...AND SHE MAY HAVE A POINT ABOUT THE TREMORS.
RMMMMMMBLE
CRK!
ANT...
FONTAINE?

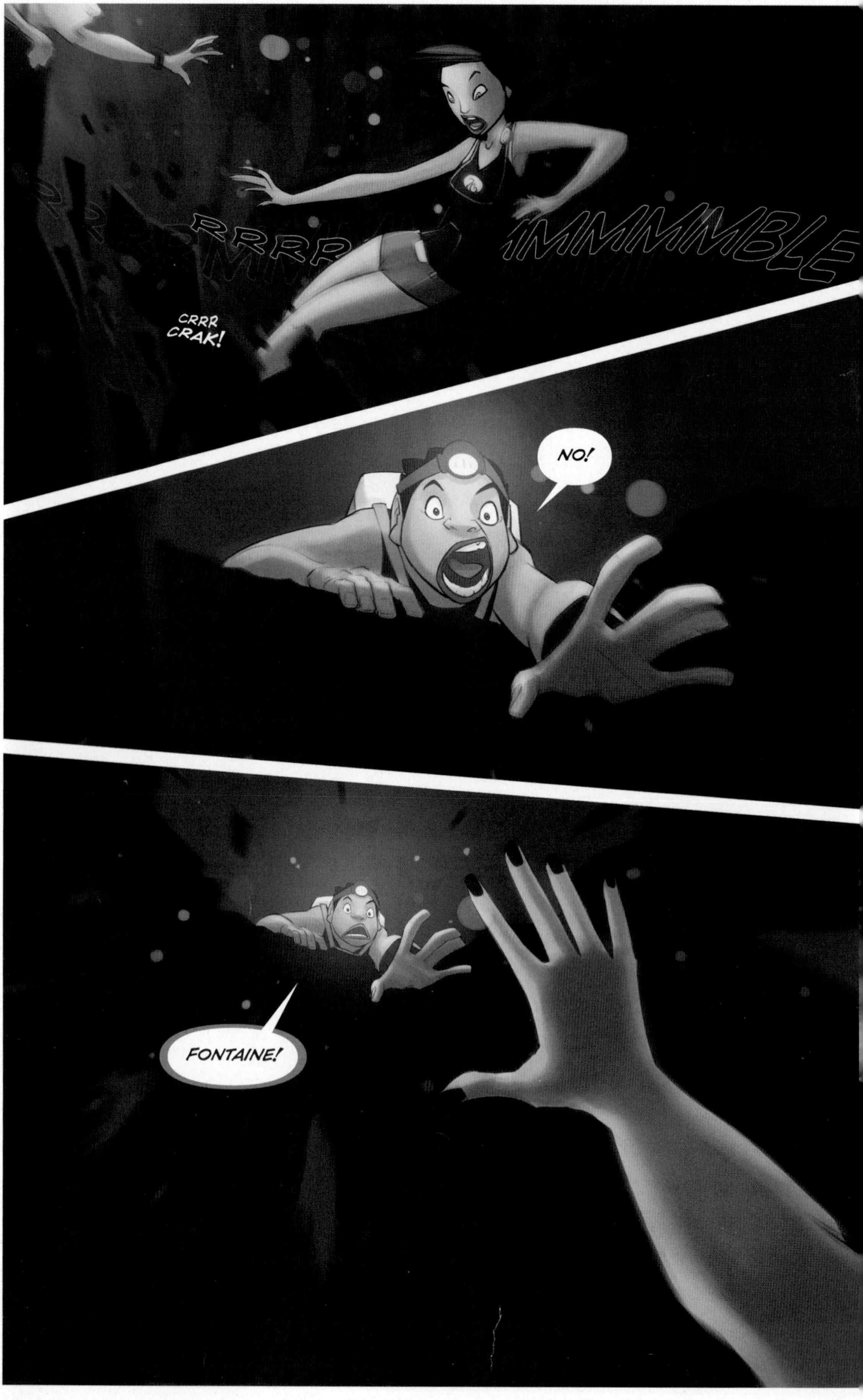
RRRRRUMMMMMMMBLE
CRRR
CRAK!
NO!
FONTAINE!

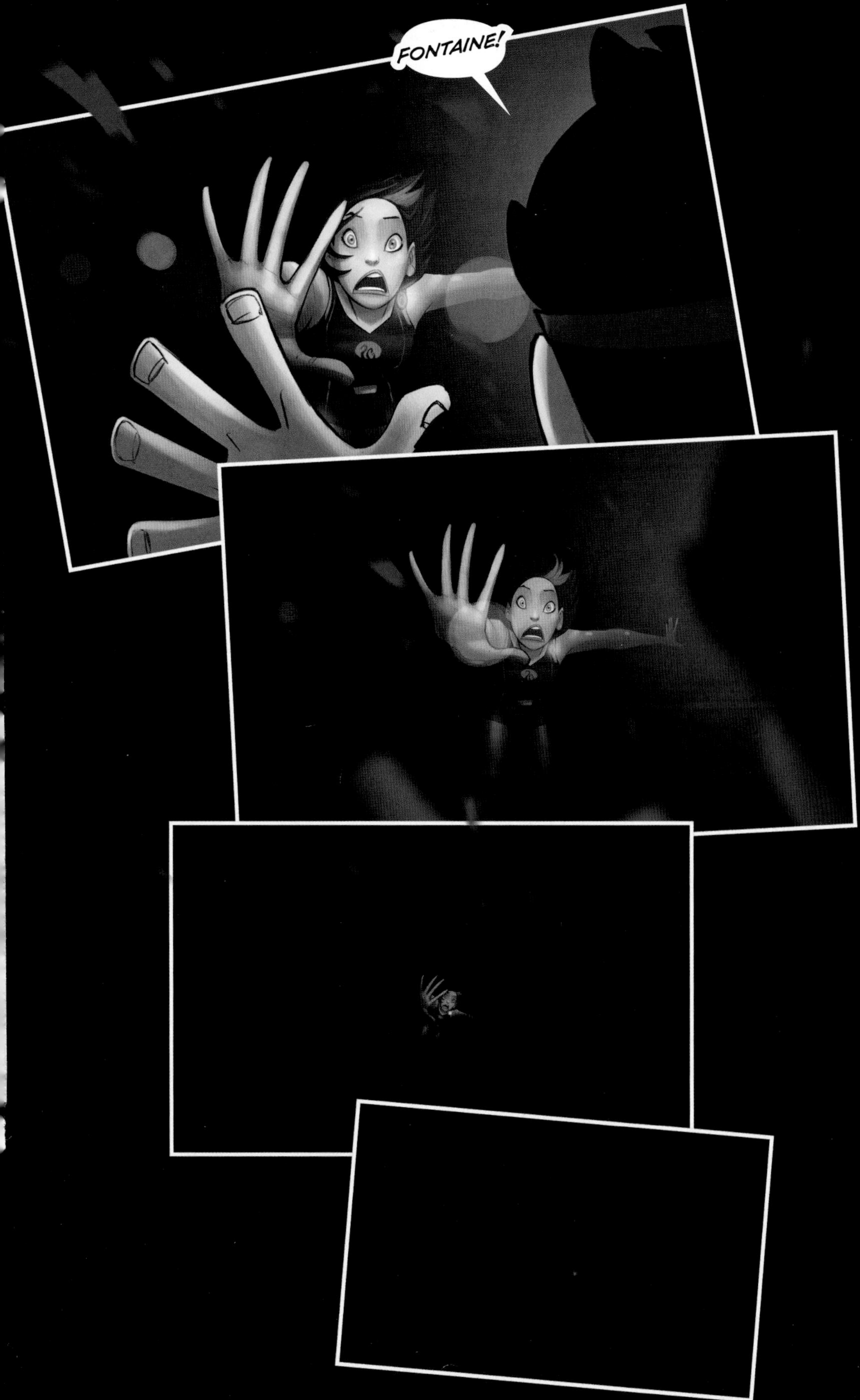
FONTAINE!

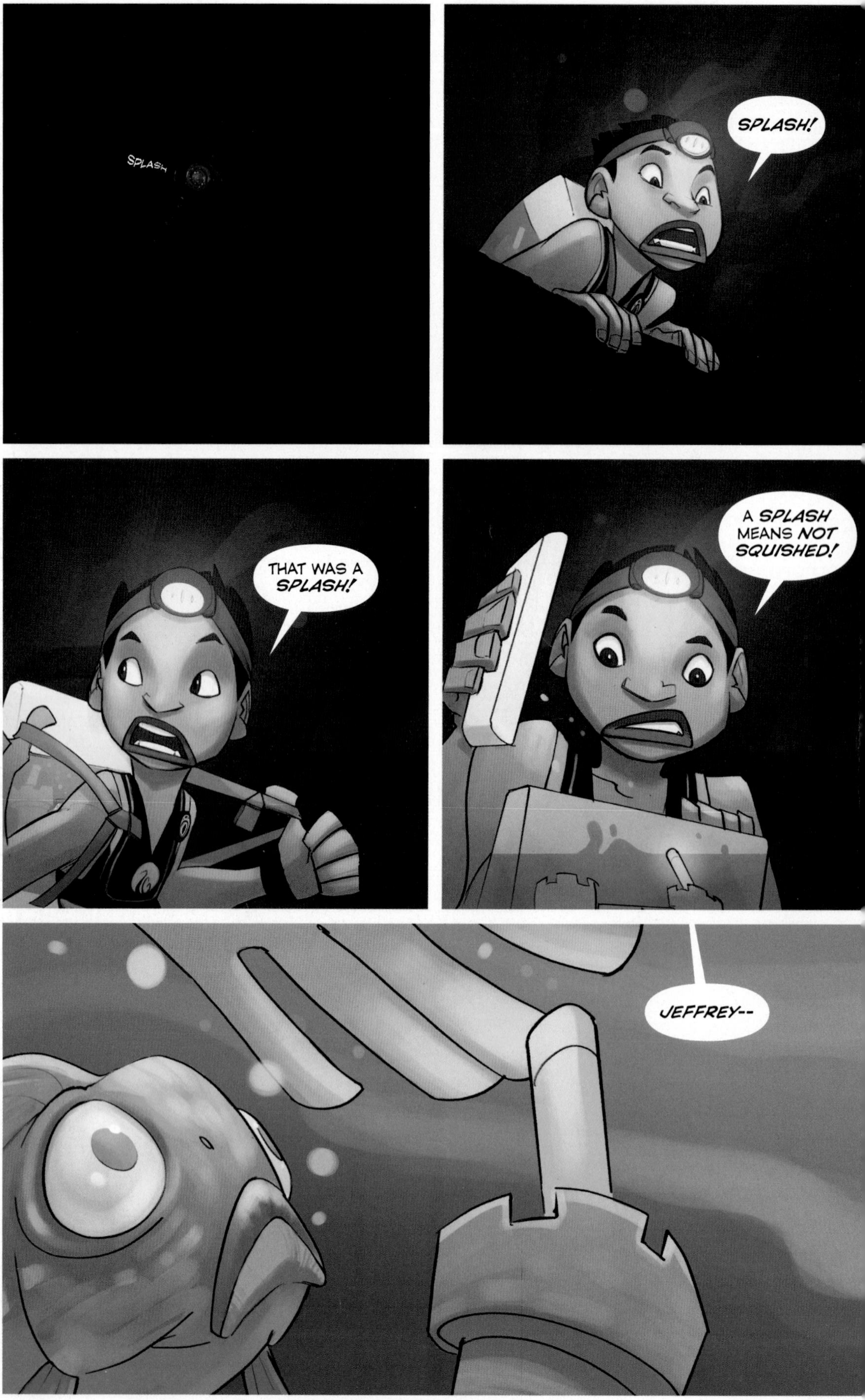
SPLASH
SPLASH!
THAT WAS A SPLASH!
A SPLASH MEANS NOT SQUISHED!
JEFFREY--

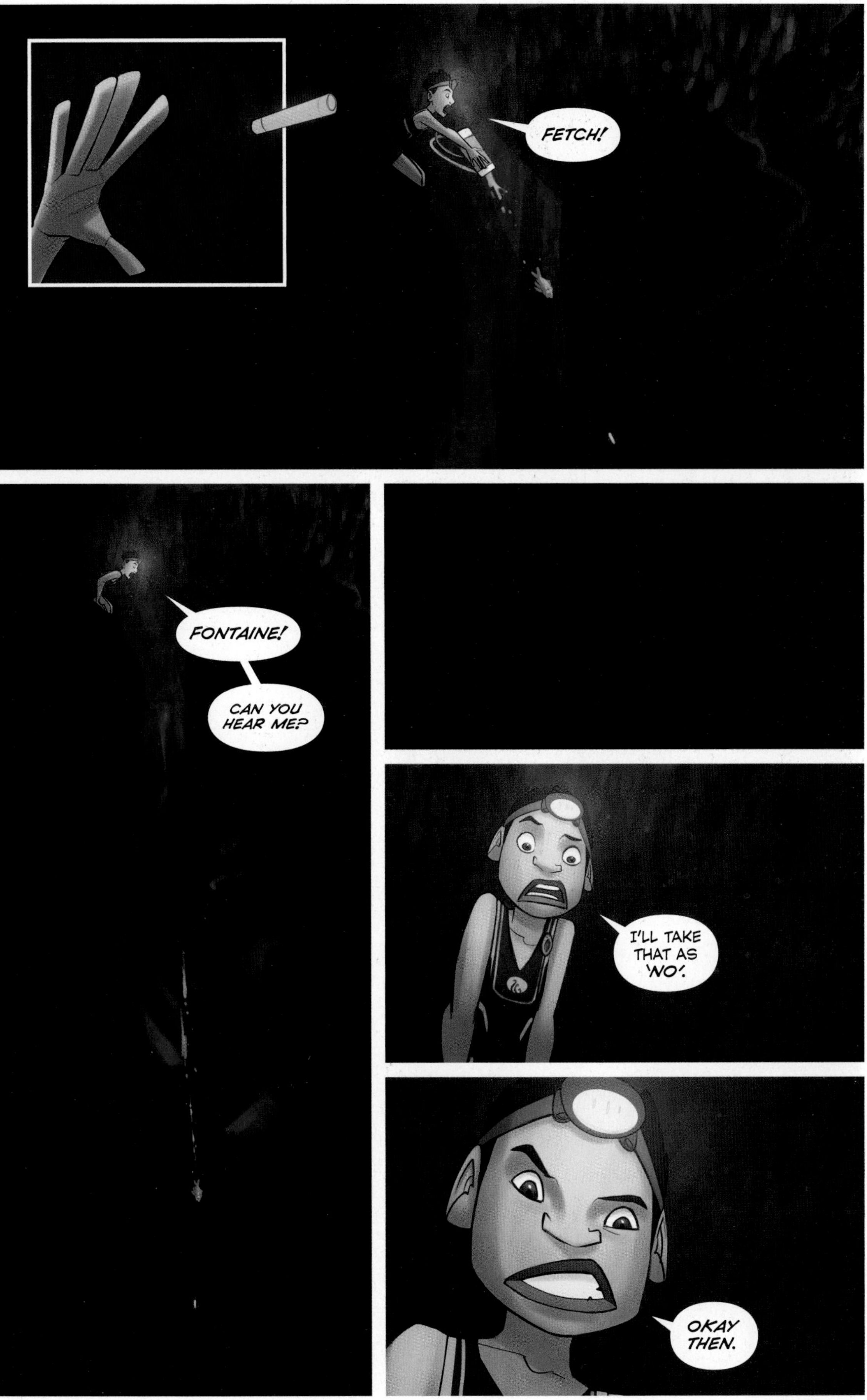
FETCH!
FONTAINE!
CAN YOU HEAR ME?
I'LL TAKE THAT AS 'NO'.
OKAY THEN.

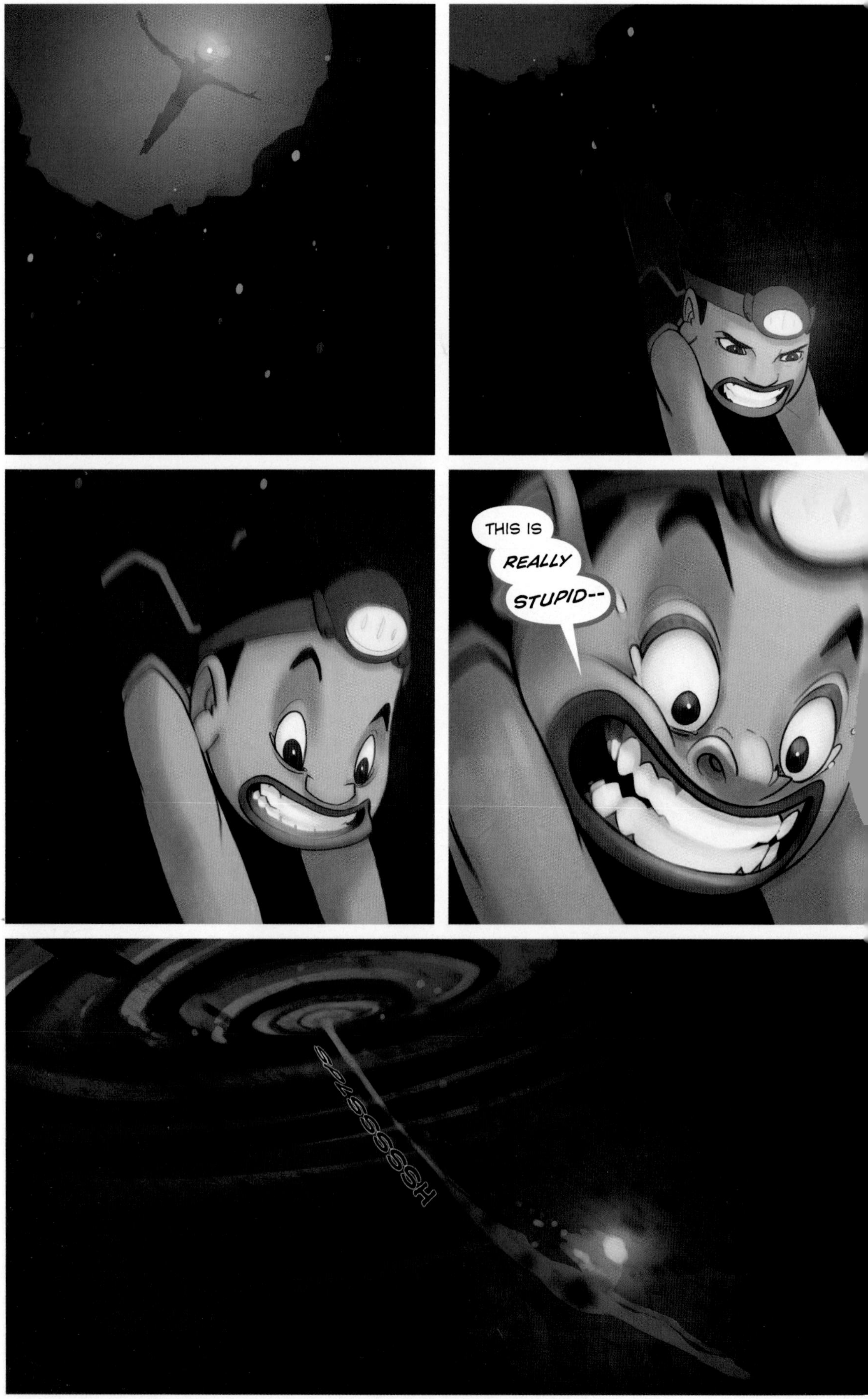

THIS IS REALLY STUPID--
SPLSSSSSH

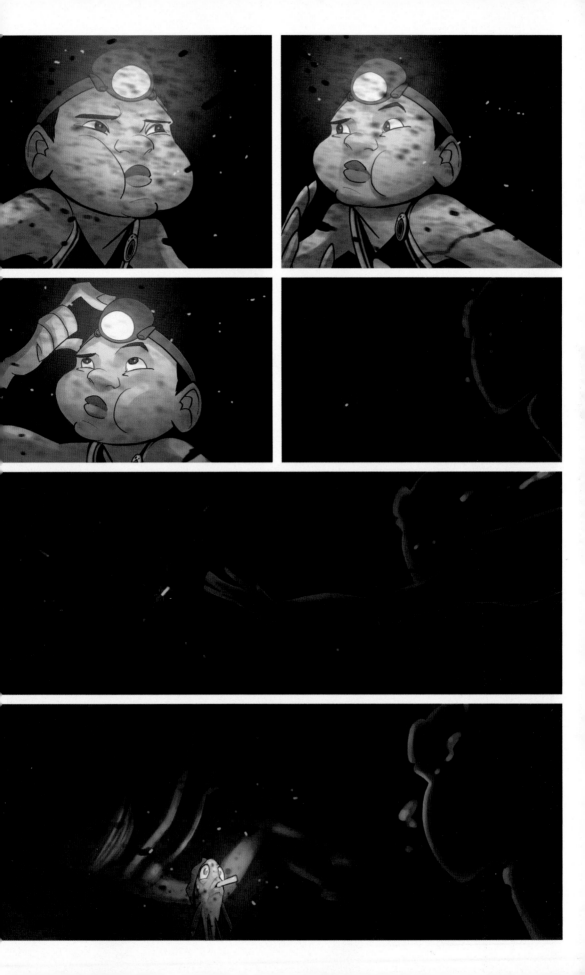

THIS IS INCREDIBLE.
I MEAN, IT WAS THE *ONLY* THING THAT MADE SENSE, BUT STILL--
*THE ENTIRE ISLAND TRULY IS FLOATING!*

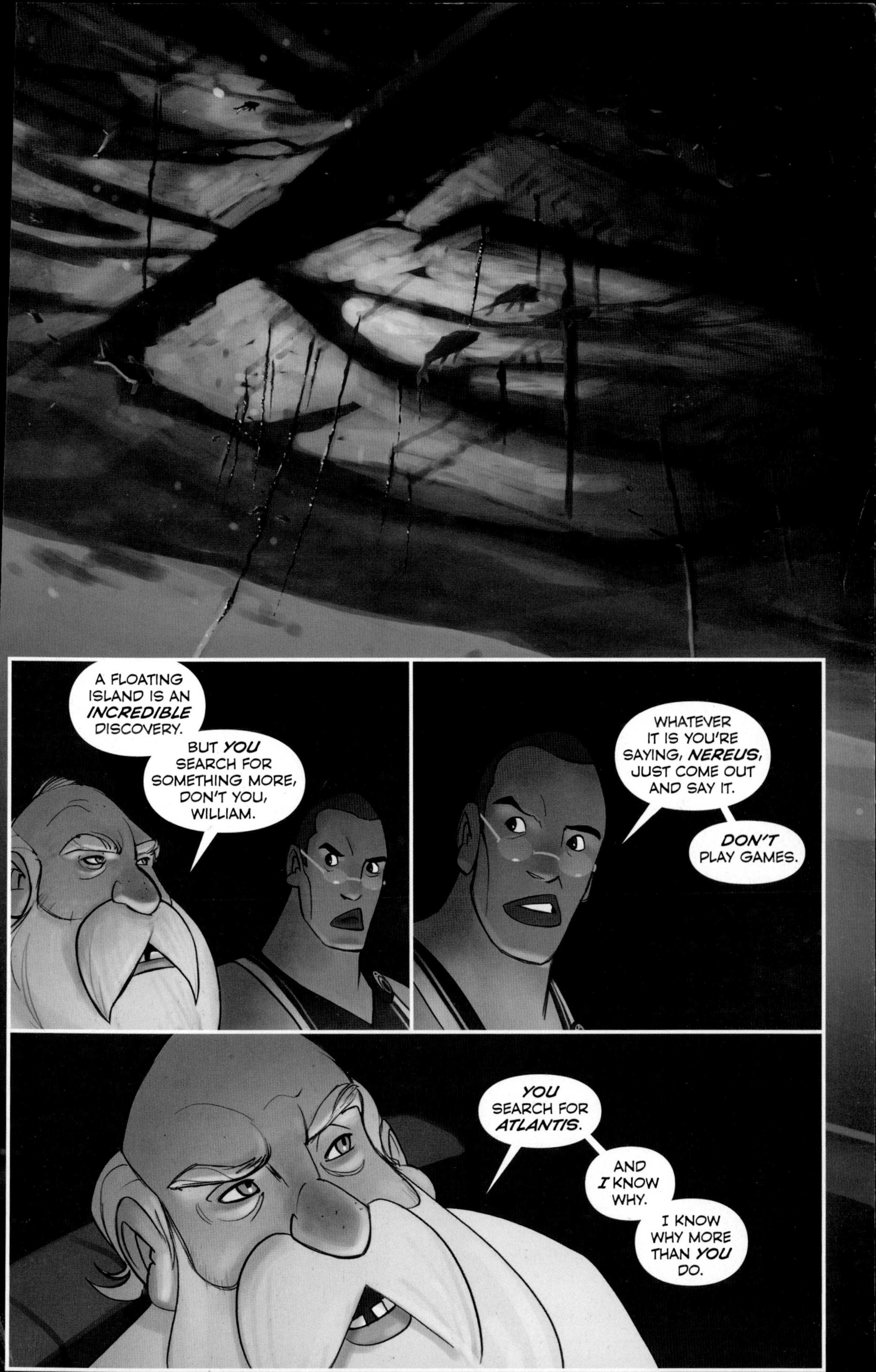
A FLOATING ISLAND IS AN INCREDIBLE DISCOVERY.
BUT YOU SEARCH FOR SOMETHING MORE, DON'T YOU, WILLIAM.
WHATEVER IT IS YOU'RE SAYING, NEREUS, JUST COME OUT AND SAY IT.
DON'T PLAY GAMES.
YOU SEARCH FOR ATLANTIS.
AND I KNOW WHY.
I KNOW WHY MORE THAN YOU DO.

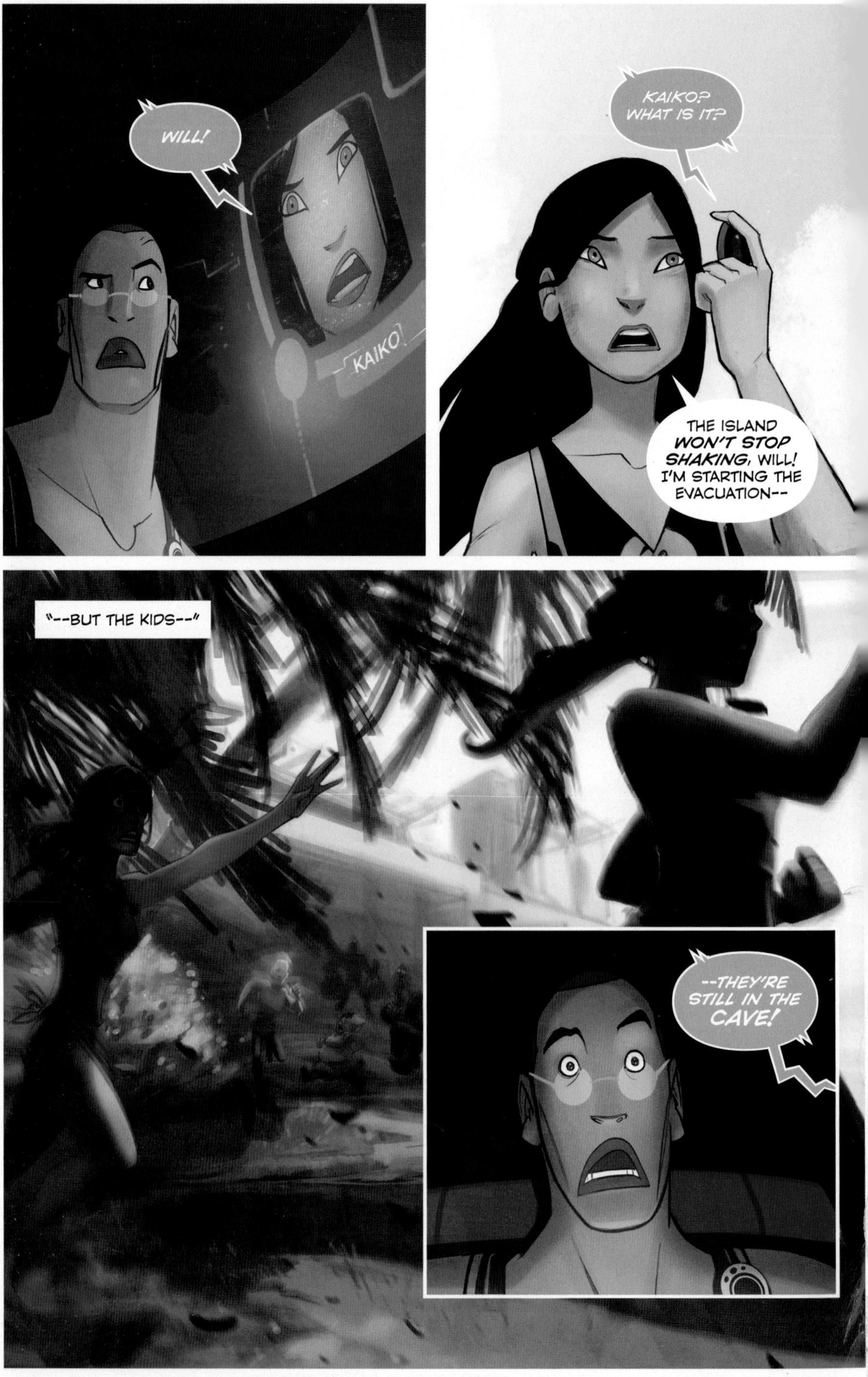
WILL!
KAIKO
KAIKO? WHAT IS IT?
THE ISLAND WON'T STOP SHAKING, WILL! I'M STARTING THE EVACUATION--
"--BUT THE KIDS--"
--THEY'RE STILL IN THE CAVE!

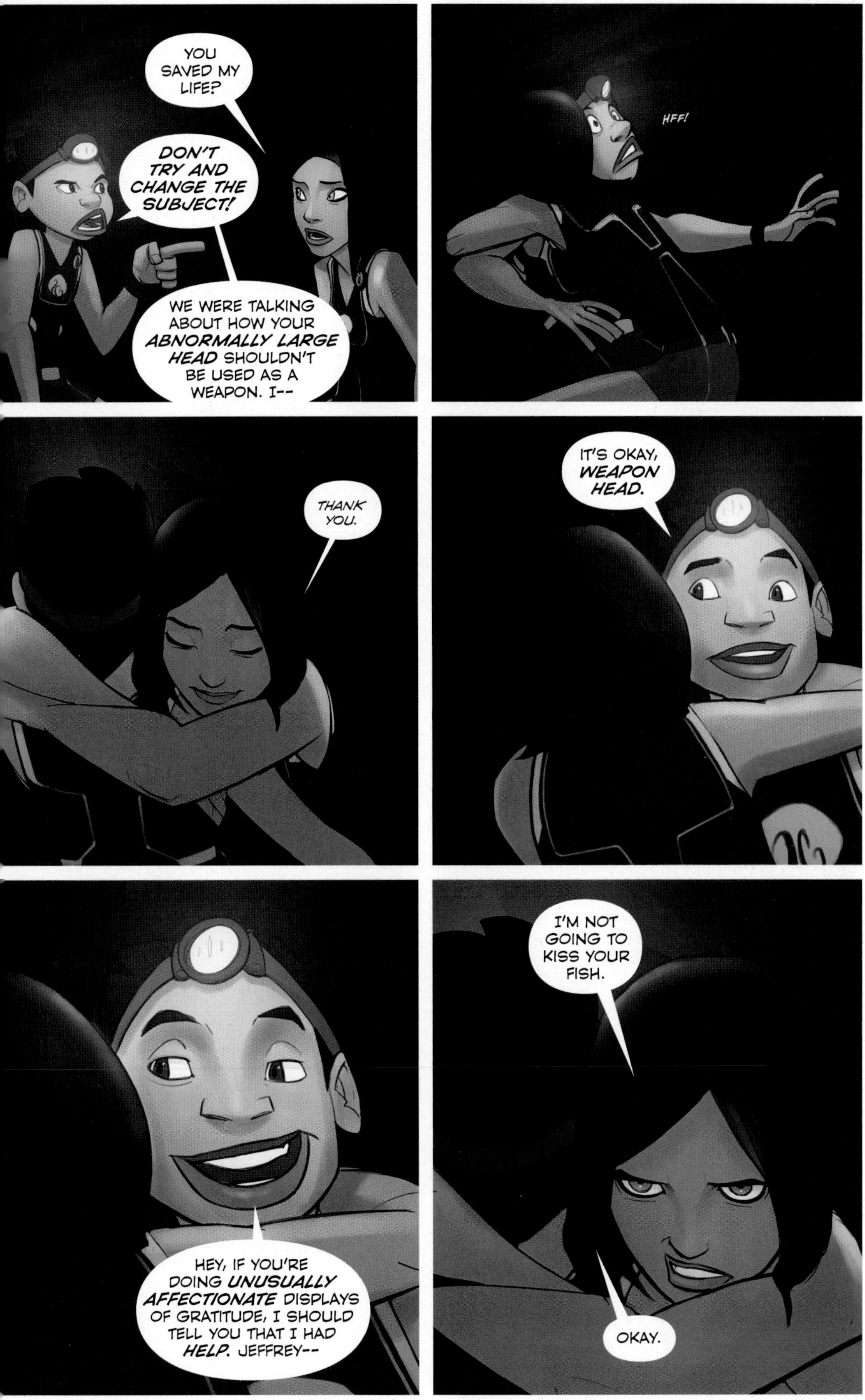
YOU SAVED MY LIFE?
DON'T TRY AND CHANGE THE SUBJECT!
WE WERE TALKING ABOUT HOW YOUR ABNORMALLY LARGE HEAD SHOULDN'T BE USED AS A WEAPON. I--
HFF!
THANK YOU.
IT'S OKAY, WEAPON HEAD.
HEY, IF YOU'RE DOING UNUSUALLY AFFECTIONATE DISPLAYS OF GRATITUDE, I SHOULD TELL YOU THAT I HAD HELP. JEFFREY--
I'M NOT GOING TO KISS YOUR FISH.
OKAY.

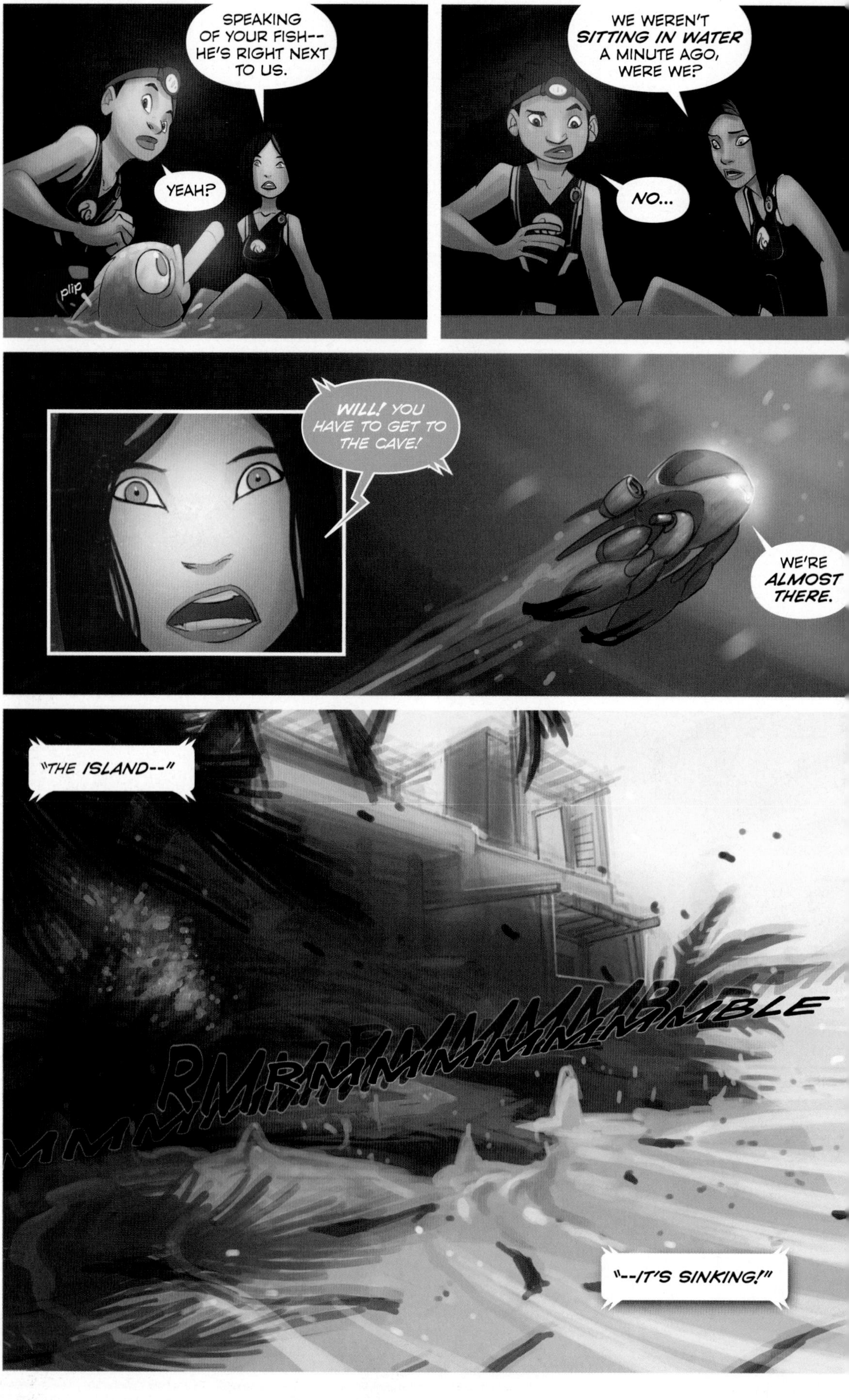
SPEAKING OF YOUR FISH-- HE'S RIGHT NEXT TO US.
YEAH?
plip
WE WEREN'T SITTING IN WATER A MINUTE AGO, WERE WE?
NO...
WILL! YOU HAVE TO GET TO THE CAVE!
WE'RE ALMOST THERE.
"THE ISLAND--"
RMMMRMMMMMMMMMMBLE
"--IT'S SINKING!"

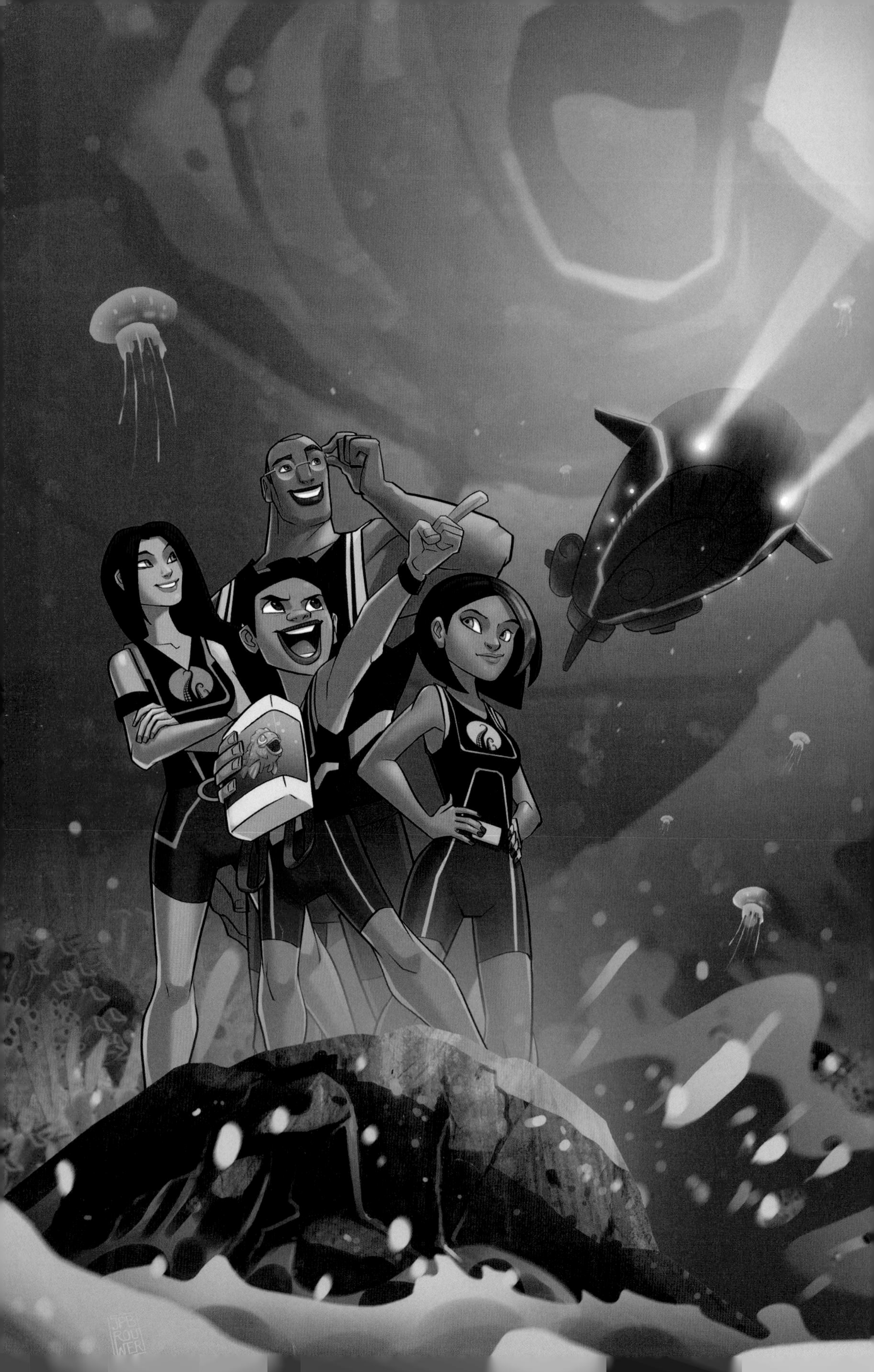

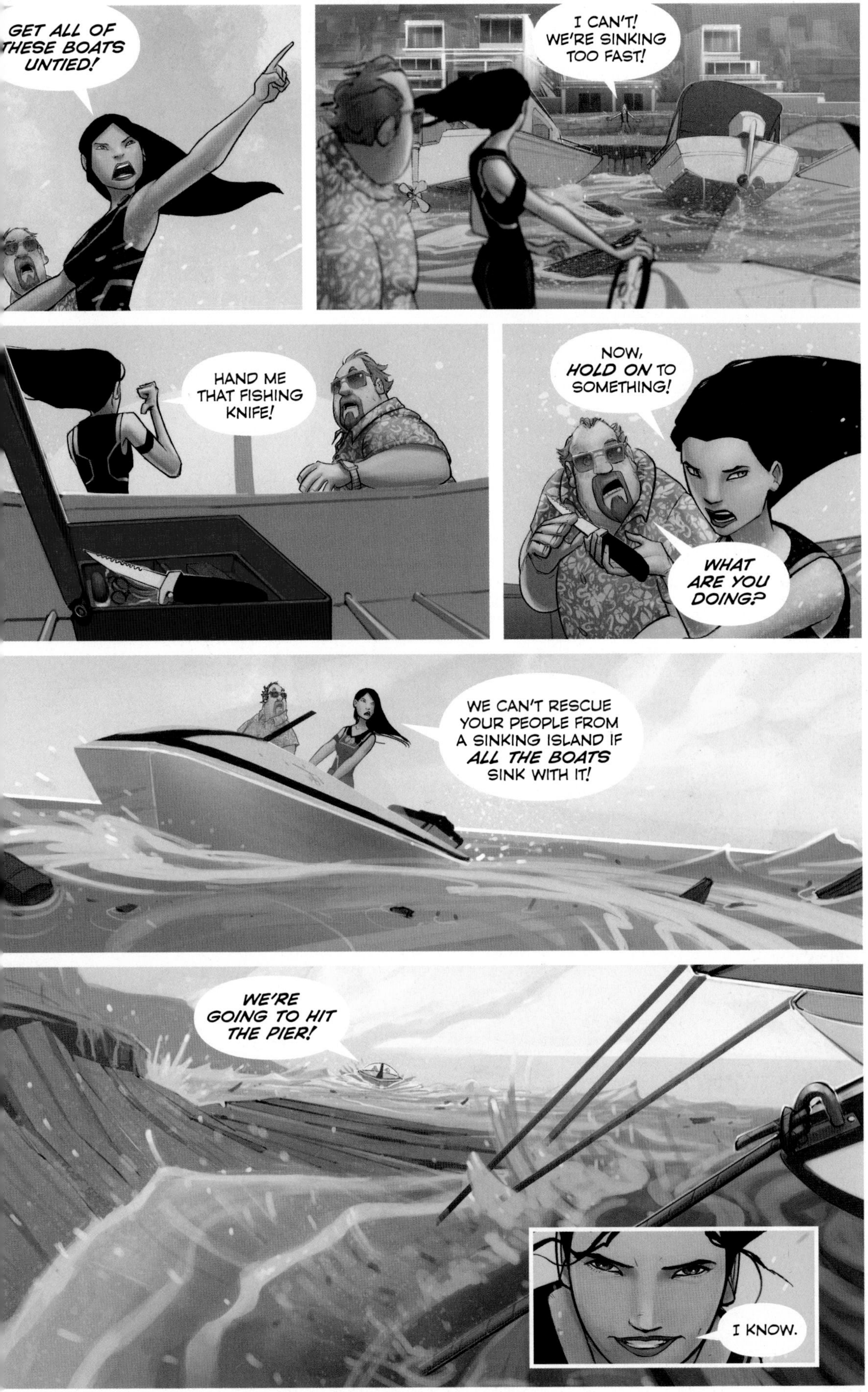

GET ALL OF THESE BOATS UNTIED!
I CAN'T! WE'RE SINKING TOO FAST!
HAND ME THAT FISHING KNIFE!
NOW, HOLD ON TO SOMETHING!
WHAT ARE YOU DOING?
WE CAN'T RESCUE YOUR PEOPLE FROM A SINKING ISLAND IF ALL THE BOATS SINK WITH IT!
WE'RE GOING TO HIT THE PIER!
I KNOW.

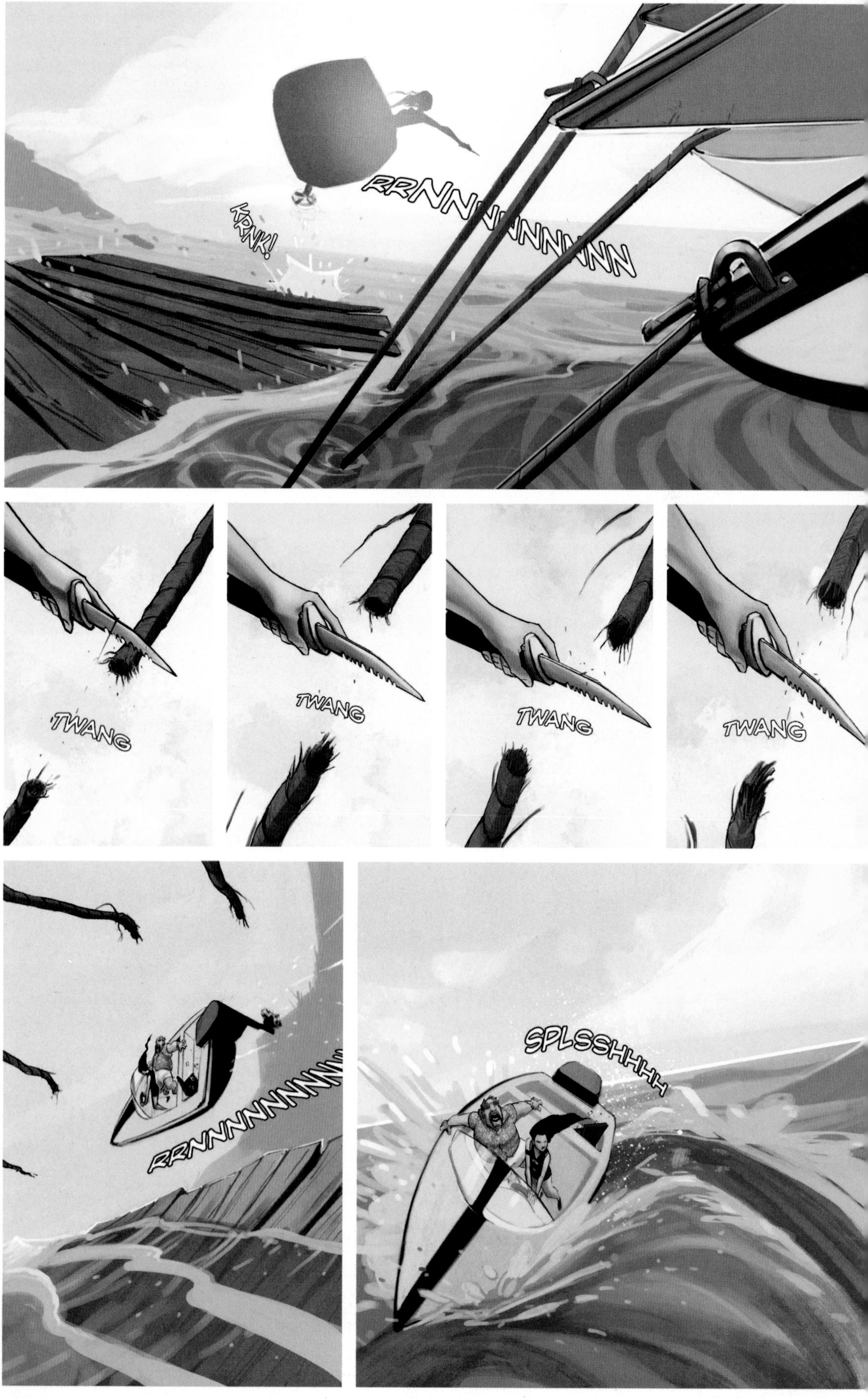
KRNK!
RRNNNNNNNNNNN
TWANG
TWANG
TWANG
TWANG
RRNNNNNNNNNN
SPLSSHHHH

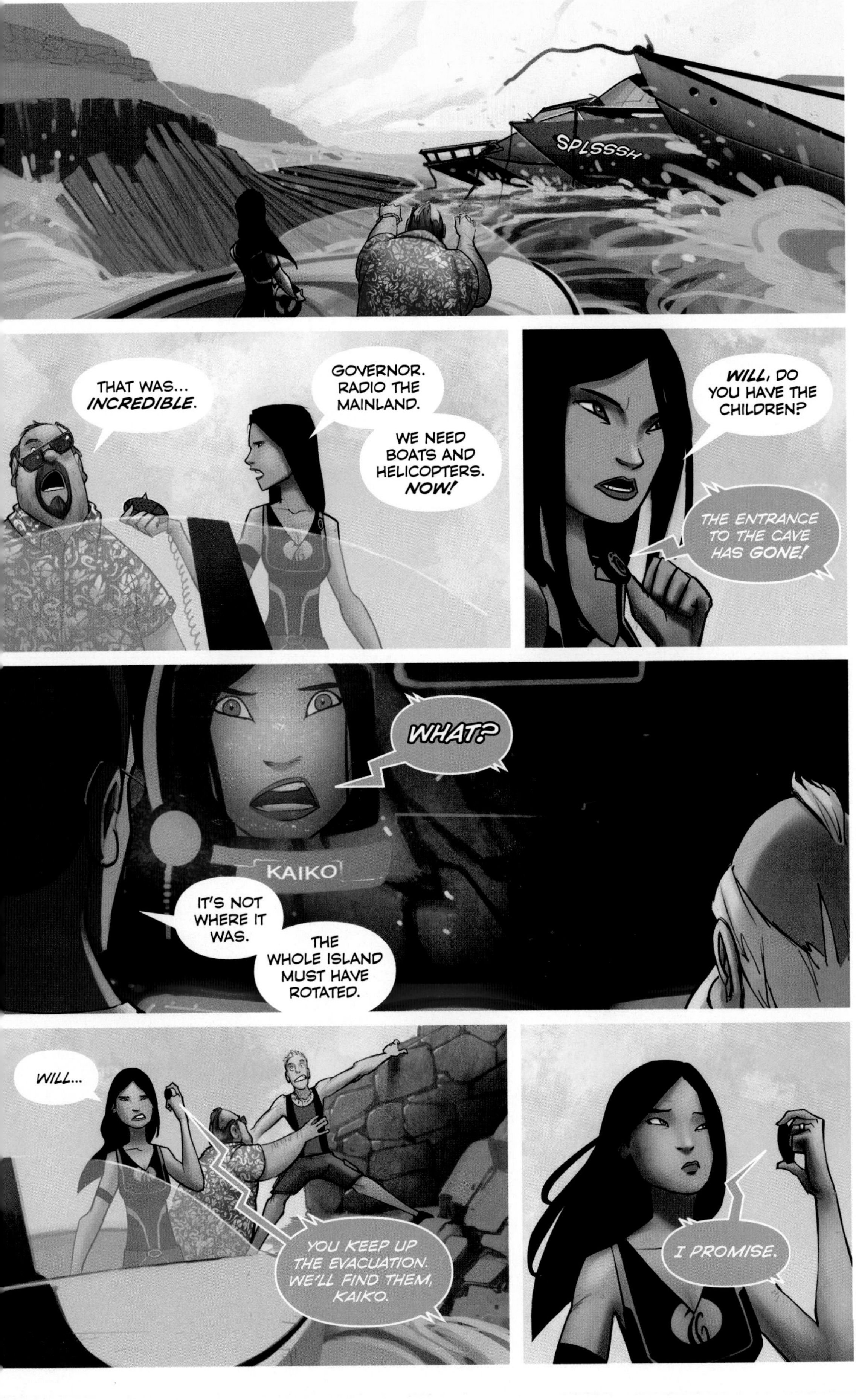
SPLSSSH
THAT WAS... *INCREDIBLE*.
GOVERNOR. RADIO THE MAINLAND.
WE NEED BOATS AND HELICOPTERS. *NOW!*
*WILL*, DO YOU HAVE THE CHILDREN?
*THE ENTRANCE TO THE CAVE HAS GONE!*
*WHAT?*
KAIKO
IT'S NOT WHERE IT WAS.
THE WHOLE ISLAND MUST HAVE ROTATED.
*WILL...*
*YOU KEEP UP THE EVACUATION. WE'LL FIND THEM, KAIKO.*
*I PROMISE.*

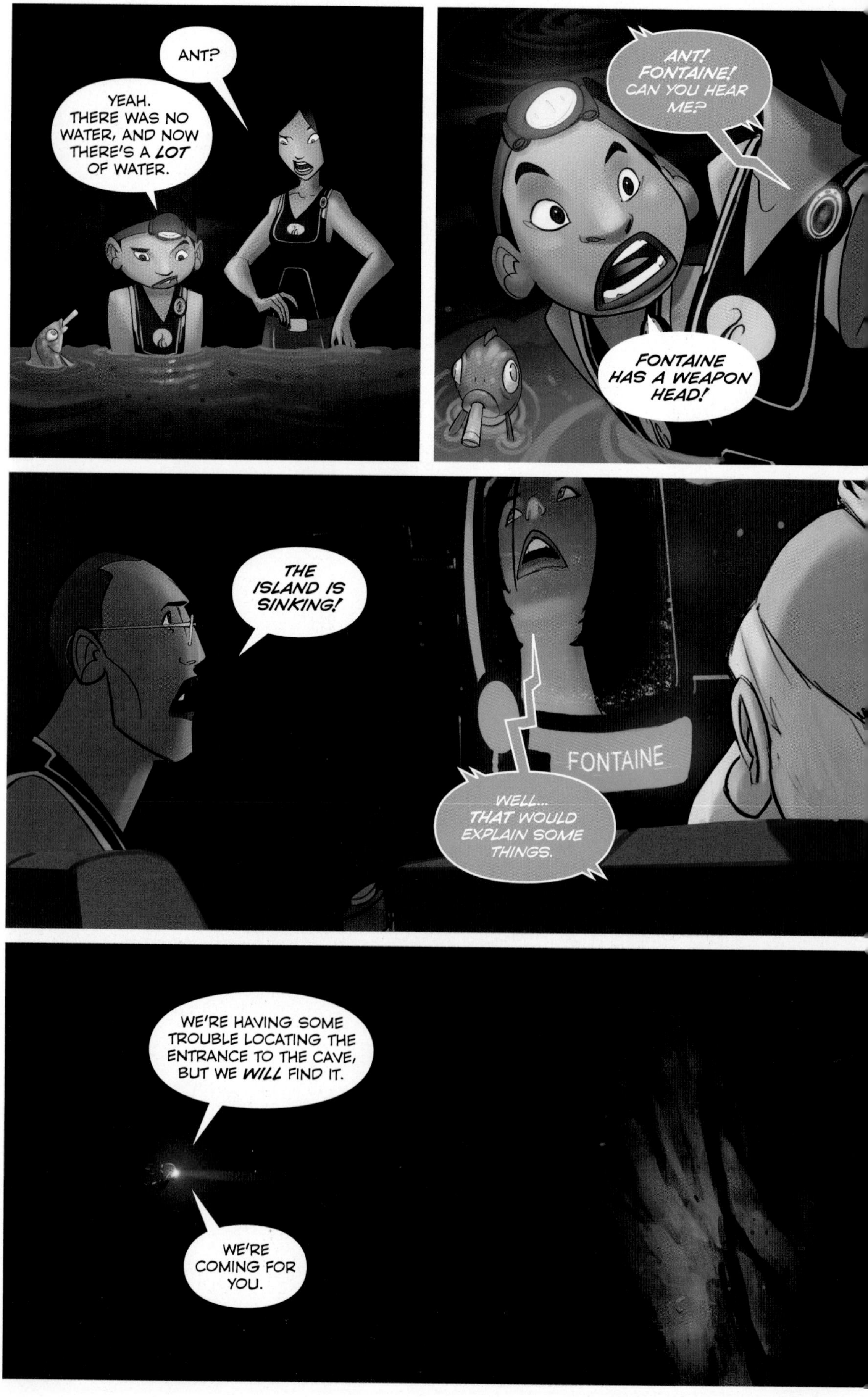
ANT?
YEAH. THERE WAS NO WATER, AND NOW THERE'S A *LOT* OF WATER.
ANT! FONTAINE! CAN YOU HEAR ME?
FONTAINE HAS A WEAPON HEAD!
THE ISLAND IS SINKING!
FONTAINE
WELL... *THAT* WOULD EXPLAIN SOME THINGS.
WE'RE HAVING SOME TROUBLE LOCATING THE ENTRANCE TO THE CAVE, BUT WE *WILL* FIND IT.
WE'RE COMING FOR YOU.

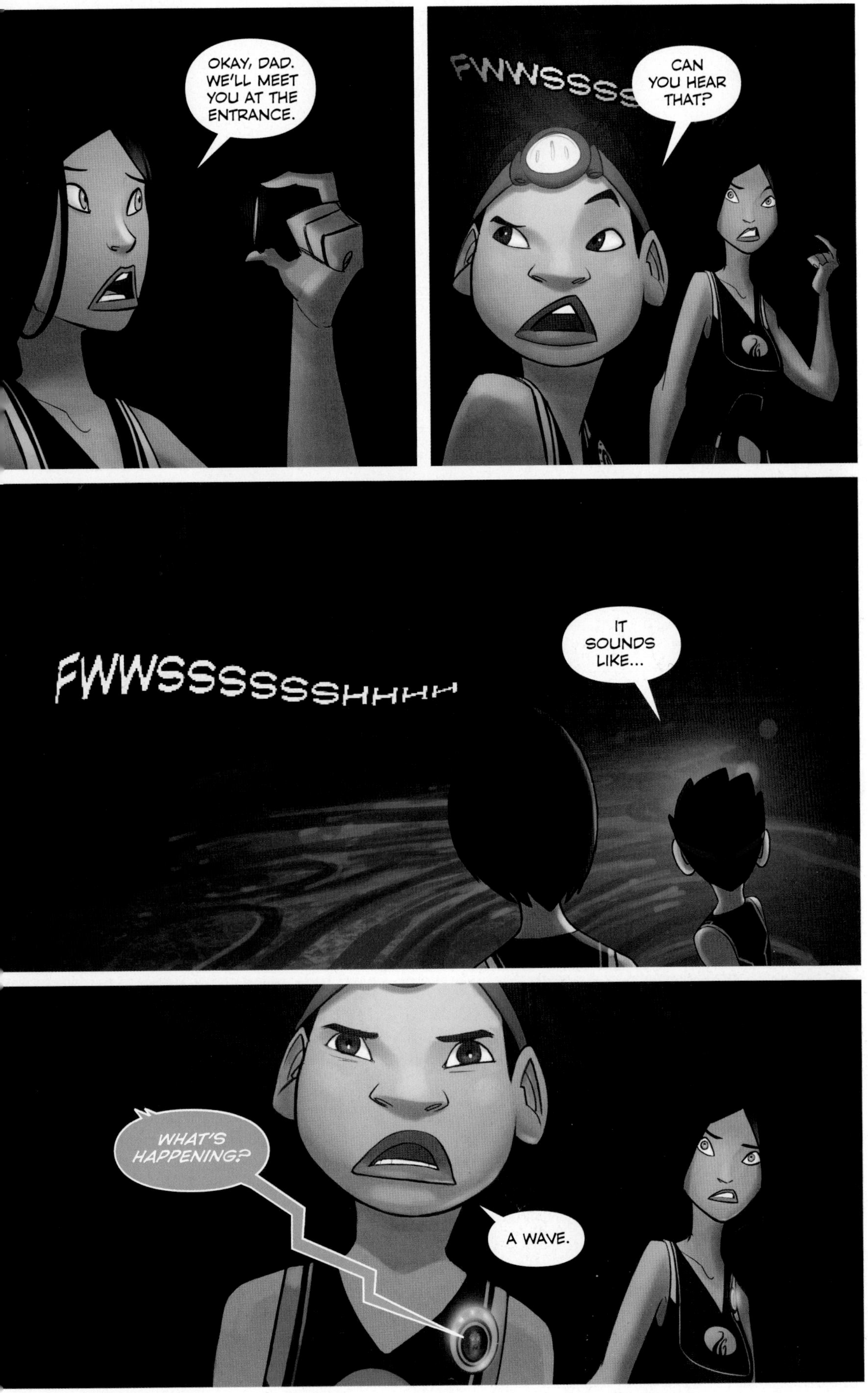
OKAY, DAD. WE'LL MEET YOU AT THE ENTRANCE.
FWWSSSS
CAN YOU HEAR THAT?
FWWSSSSSSSHHHH
IT SOUNDS LIKE...
WHAT'S HAPPENING?
A WAVE.

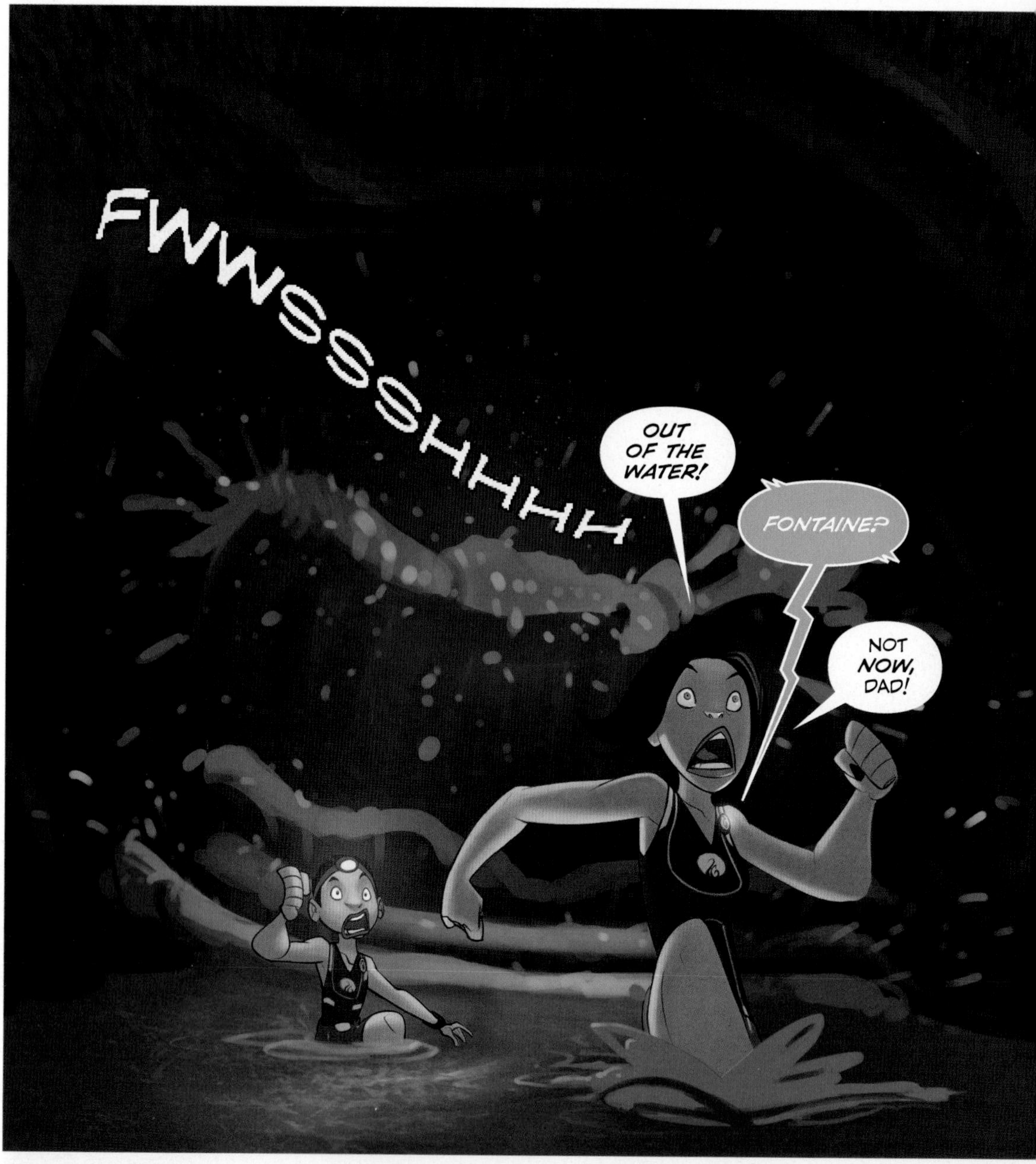
FWWSSSHHHHH
OUT OF THE WATER!
FONTAINE?
NOT NOW, DAD!
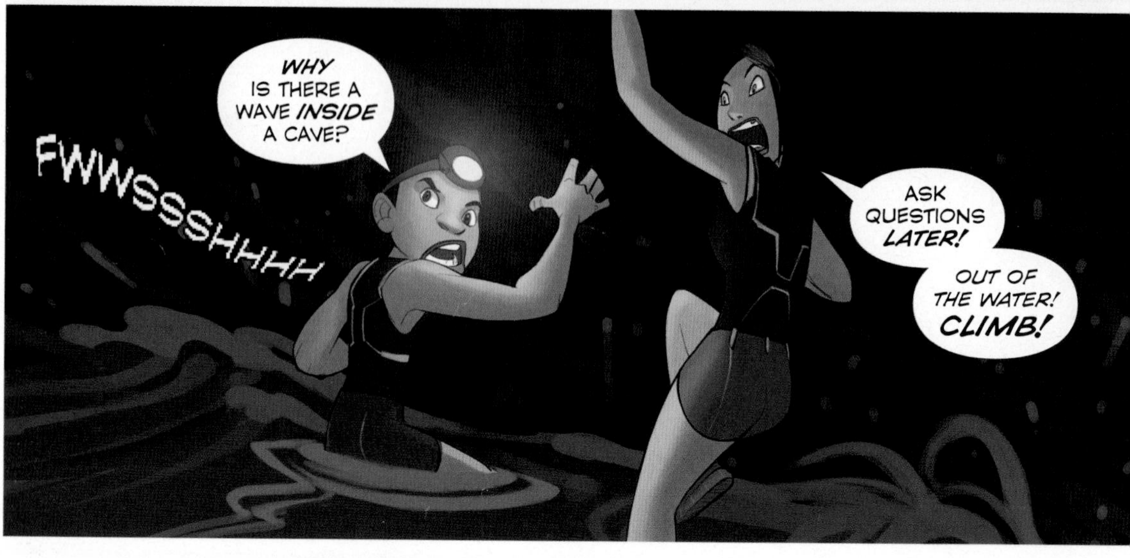
WHY IS THERE A WAVE INSIDE A CAVE?
FWWSSSHHHH
ASK QUESTIONS LATER!
OUT OF THE WATER! CLIMB!

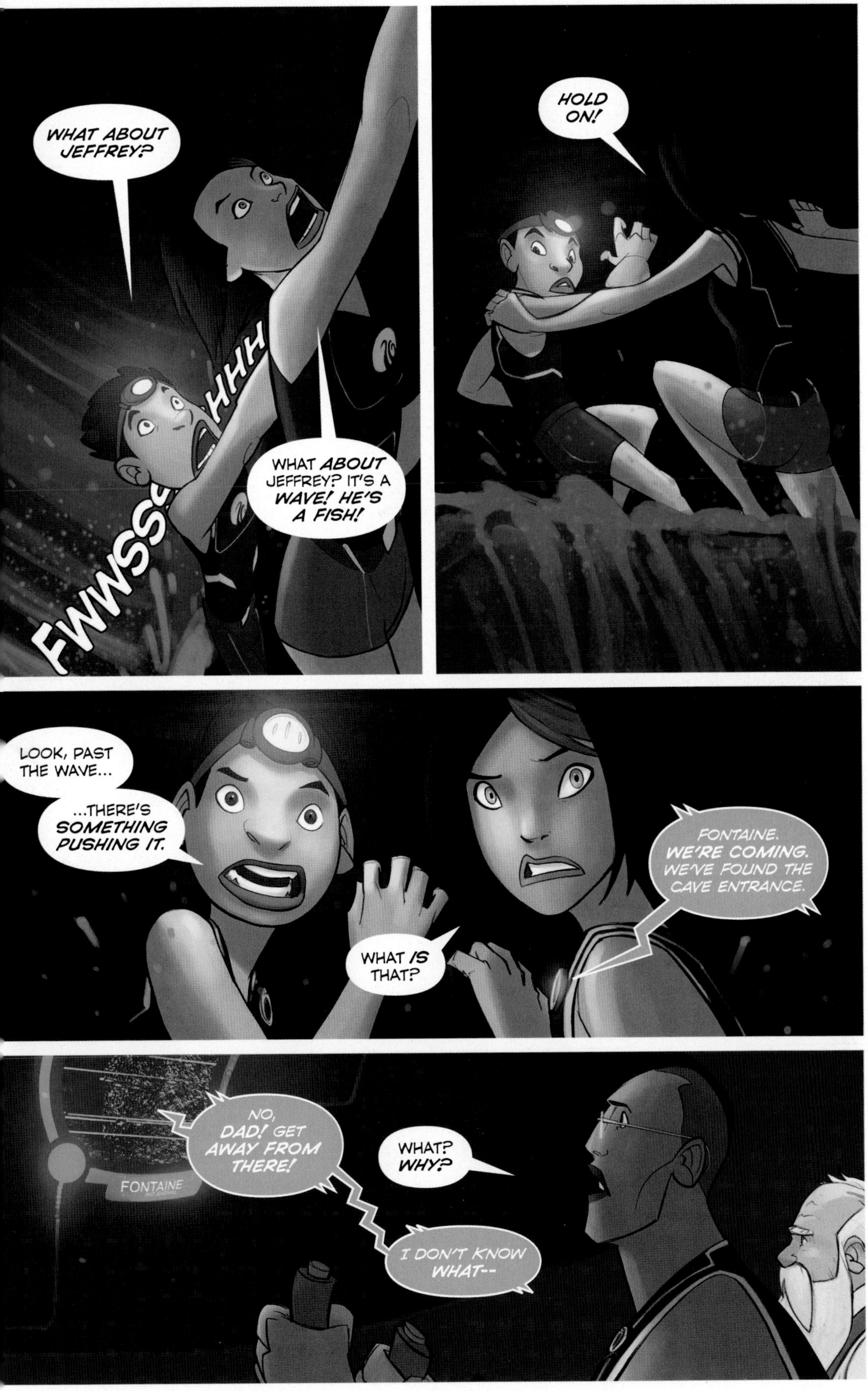
WHAT ABOUT JEFFREY?
FWWSSHHH
WHAT ABOUT JEFFREY? IT'S A WAVE! HE'S A FISH!
HOLD ON!
LOOK, PAST THE WAVE...
...THERE'S SOMETHING PUSHING IT.
WHAT IS THAT?
FONTAINE. WE'RE COMING. WE'VE FOUND THE CAVE ENTRANCE.
FONTAINE
NO, DAD! GET AWAY FROM THERE!
WHAT? WHY?
I DON'T KNOW WHAT--

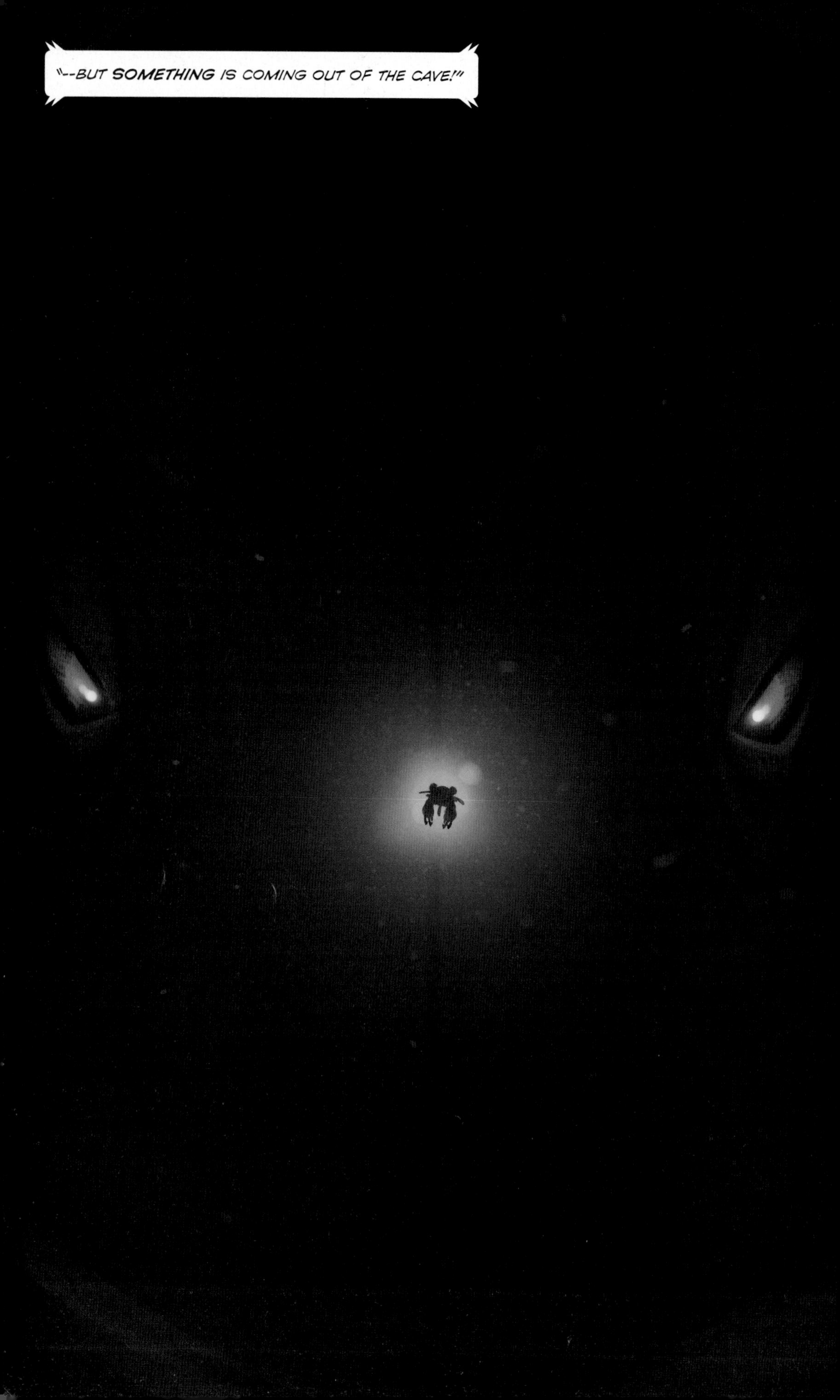
"--BUT SOMETHING IS COMING OUT OF THE CAVE!"

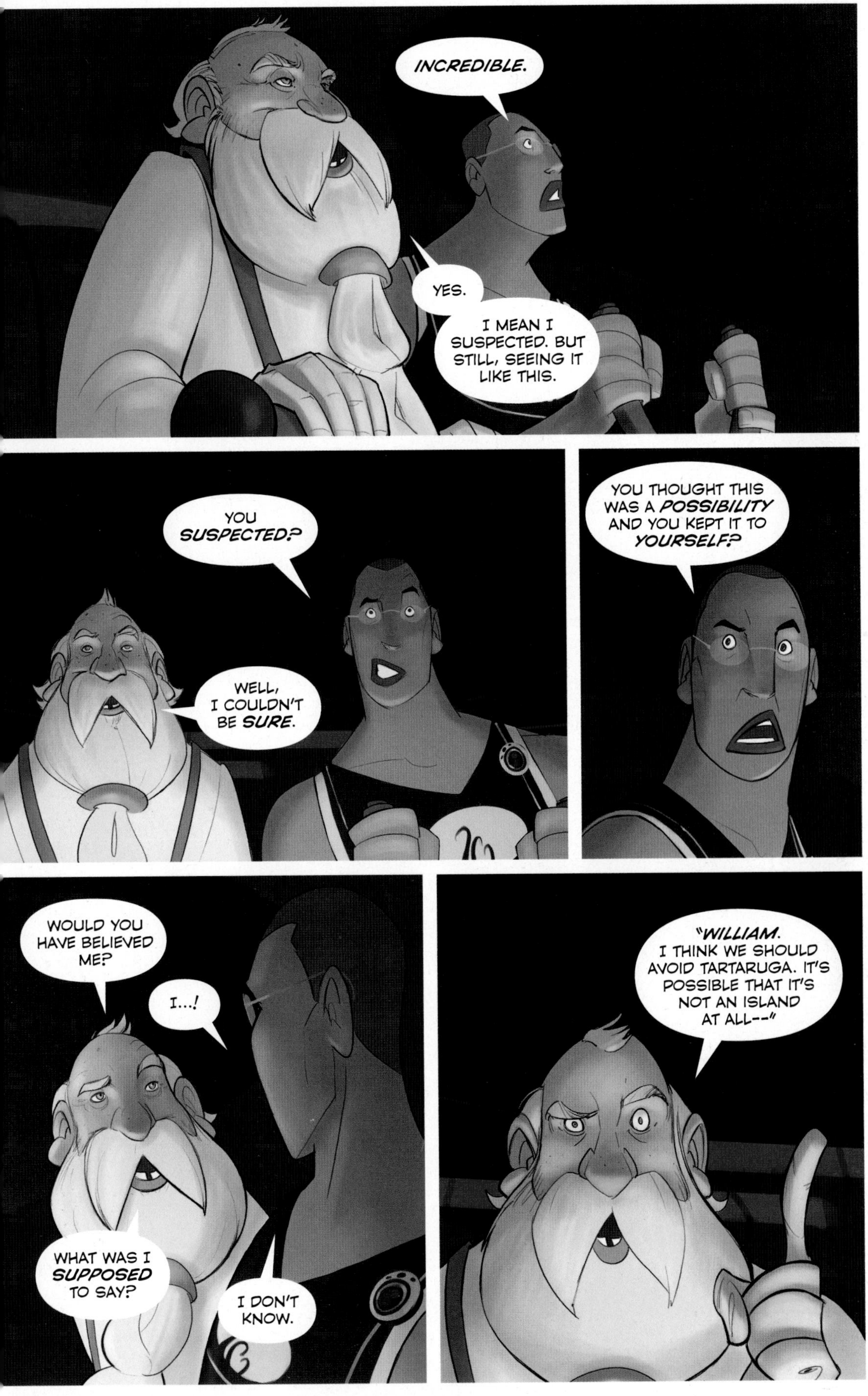

INCREDIBLE.
YES.
I MEAN I SUSPECTED. BUT STILL, SEEING IT LIKE THIS.
YOU SUSPECTED?
WELL, I COULDN'T BE SURE.
YOU THOUGHT THIS WAS A POSSIBILITY AND YOU KEPT IT TO YOURSELF?
WOULD YOU HAVE BELIEVED ME?
I...!
WHAT WAS I SUPPOSED TO SAY?
I DON'T KNOW.
"WILLIAM. I THINK WE SHOULD AVOID TARTARUGA. IT'S POSSIBLE THAT IT'S NOT AN ISLAND AT ALL--"

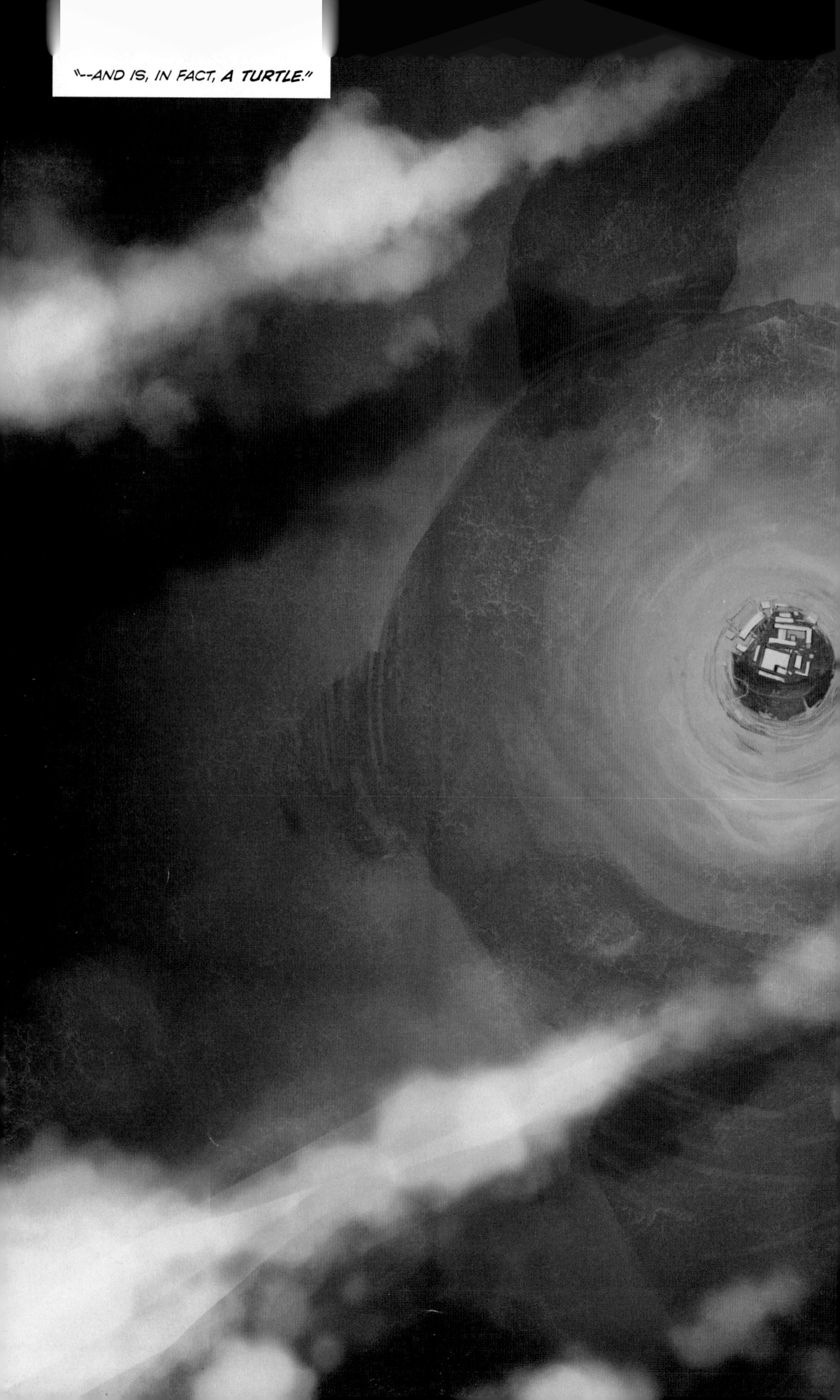
"--AND IS, IN FACT, A TURTLE."

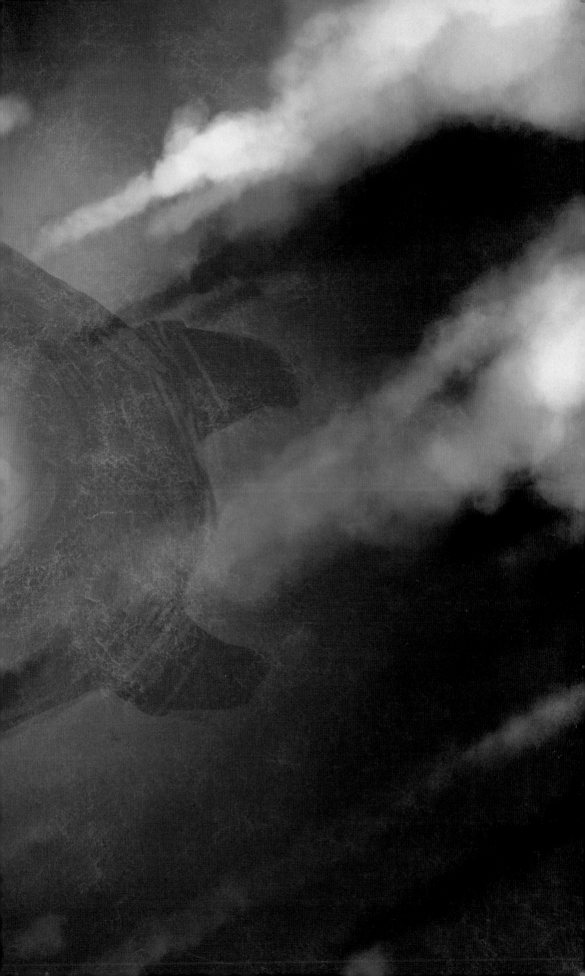

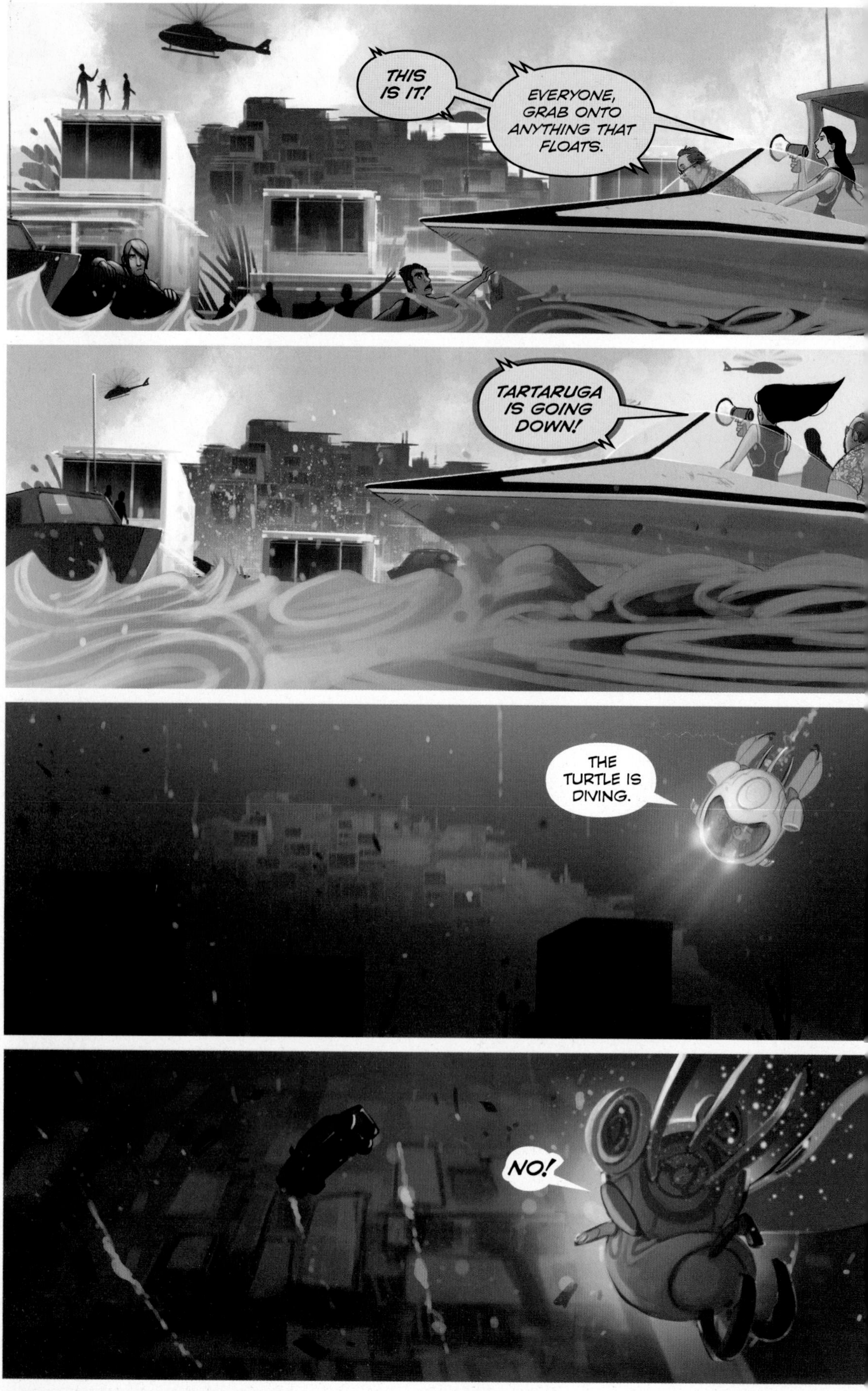
THIS IS IT!
EVERYONE, GRAB ONTO ANYTHING THAT FLOATS.
TARTARUGA IS GOING DOWN!
THE TURTLE IS DIVING.
NO!

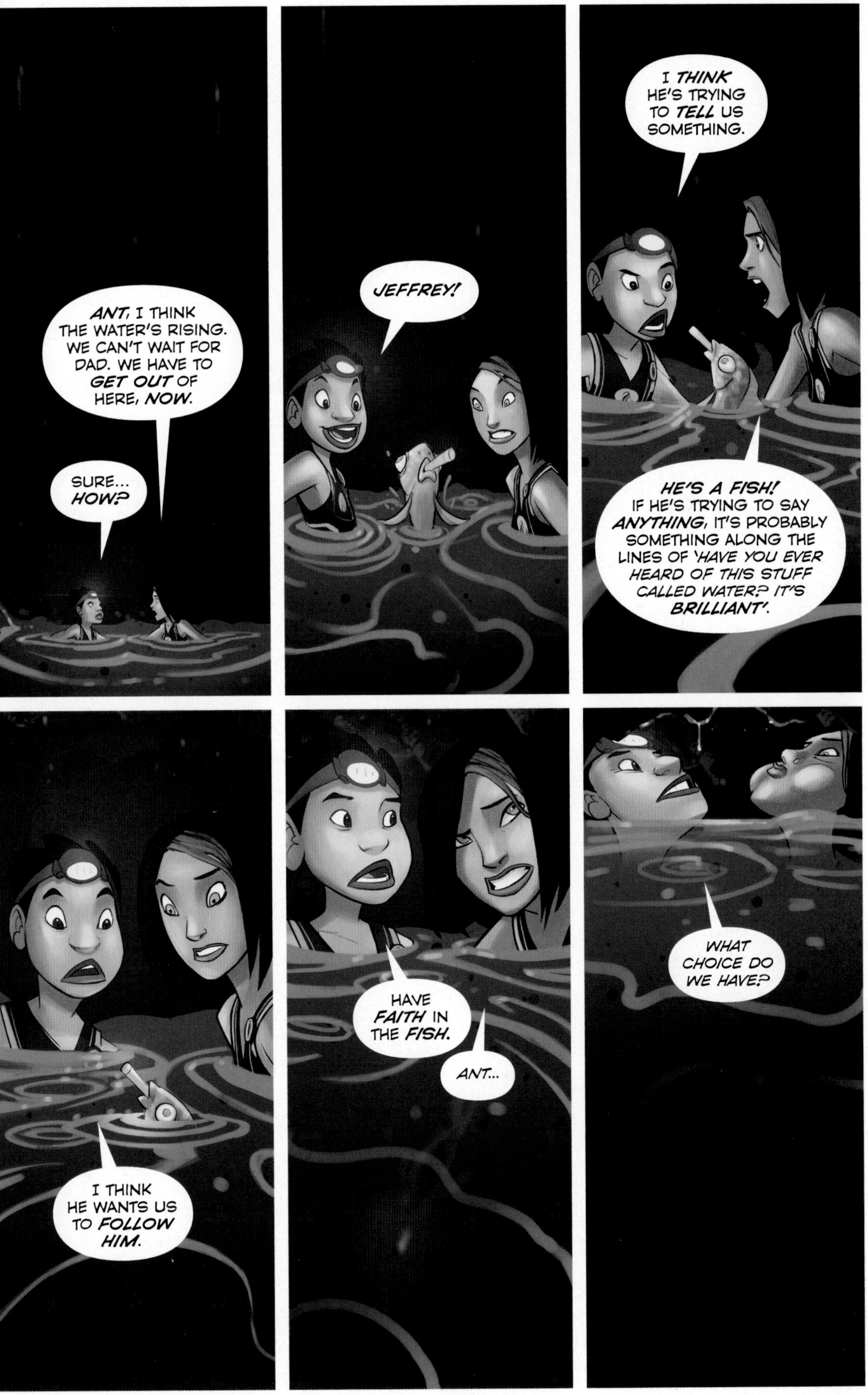
ANT, I THINK THE WATER'S RISING. WE CAN'T WAIT FOR DAD. WE HAVE TO GET OUT OF HERE, NOW.
SURE... HOW?
JEFFREY!
I THINK HE'S TRYING TO TELL US SOMETHING.
HE'S A FISH! IF HE'S TRYING TO SAY ANYTHING, IT'S PROBABLY SOMETHING ALONG THE LINES OF 'HAVE YOU EVER HEARD OF THIS STUFF CALLED WATER? IT'S BRILLIANT'.
I THINK HE WANTS US TO FOLLOW HIM.
HAVE FAITH IN THE FISH.
ANT...
WHAT CHOICE DO WE HAVE?

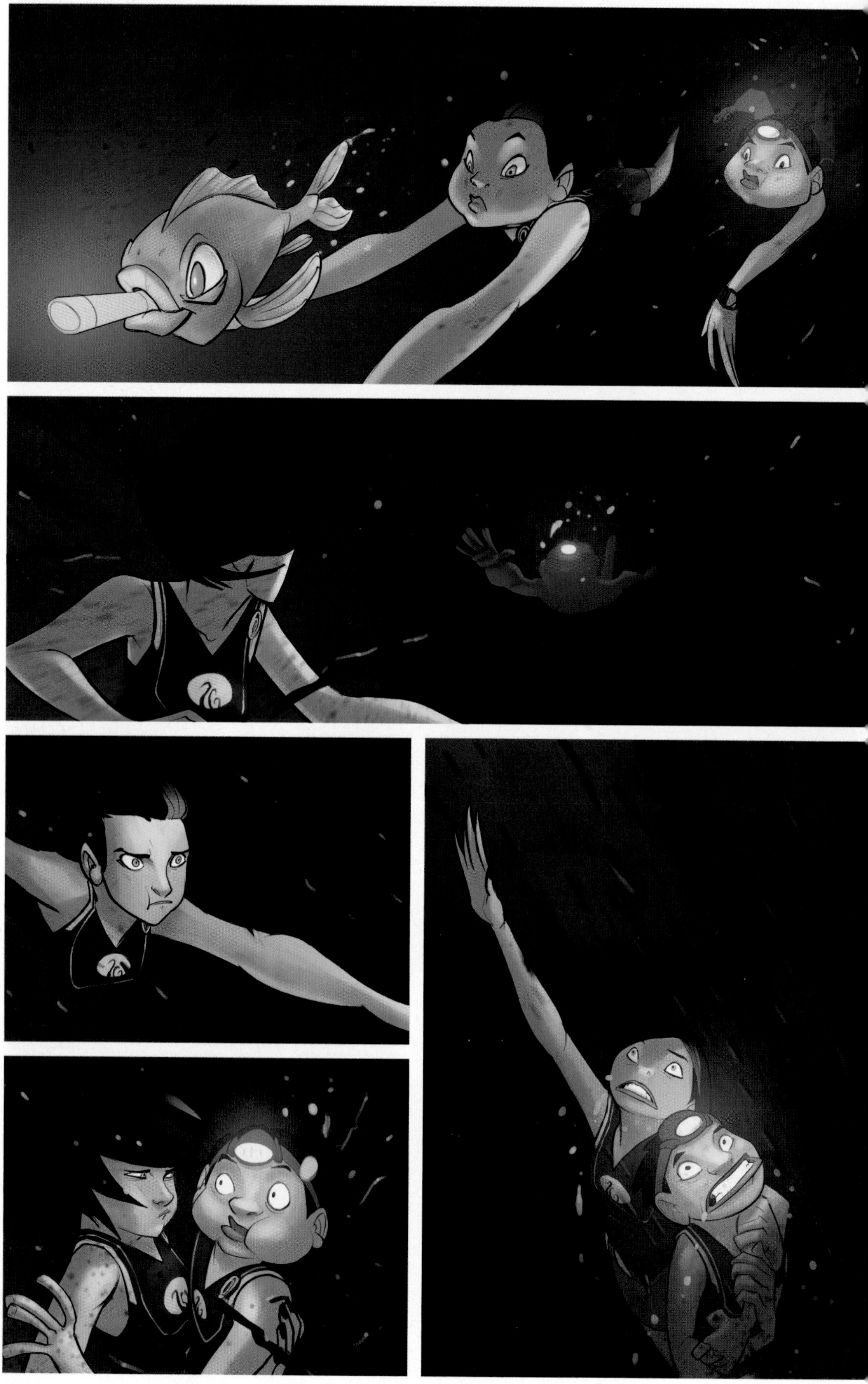

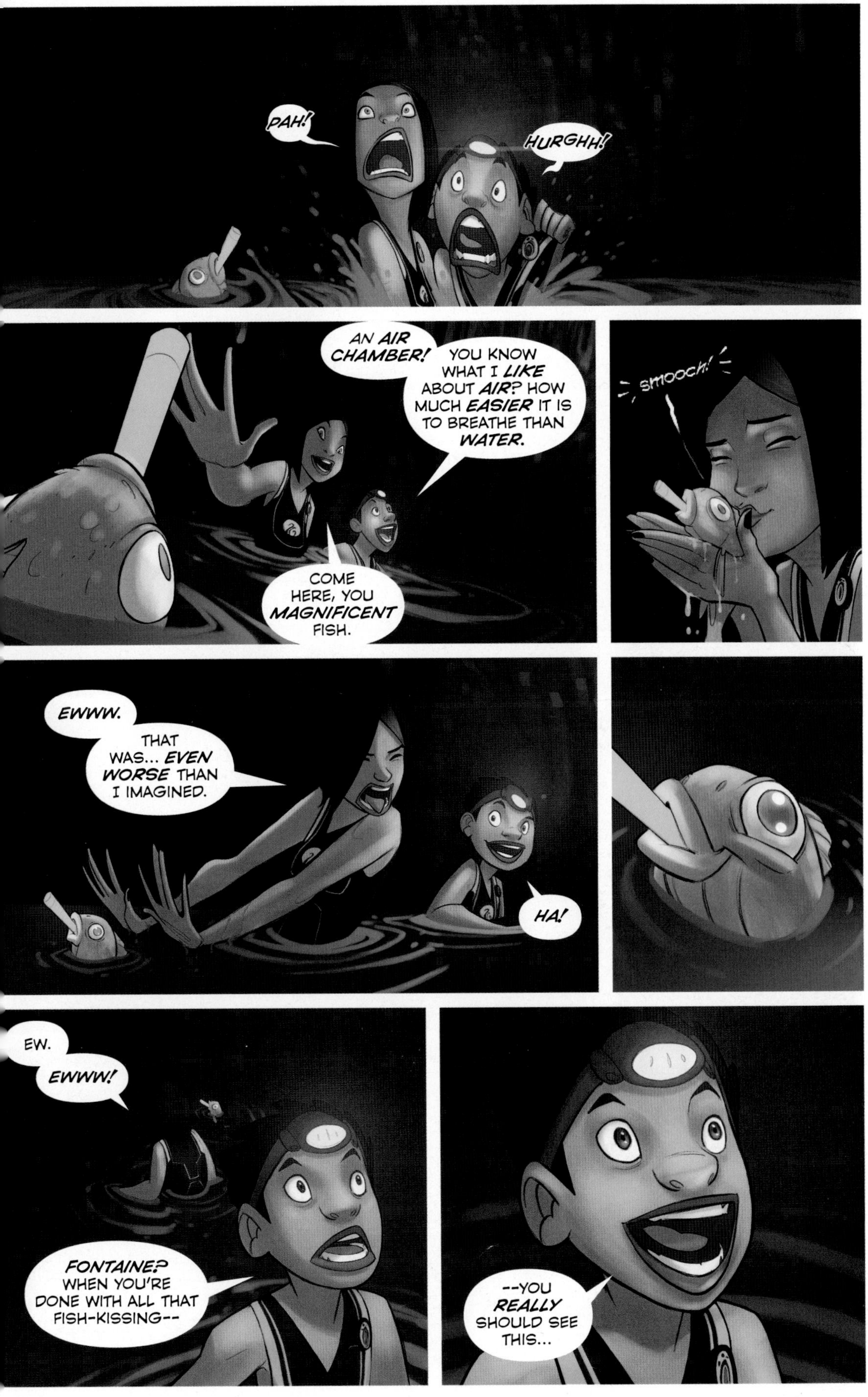
PAH!
HURGHH!
AN AIR CHAMBER!
YOU KNOW WHAT I LIKE ABOUT AIR? HOW MUCH EASIER IT IS TO BREATHE THAN WATER.
COME HERE, YOU MAGNIFICENT FISH.
SMOOCH!
EWWW.
THAT WAS... EVEN WORSE THAN I IMAGINED.
HA!
EW.
EWWW!
FONTAINE? WHEN YOU'RE DONE WITH ALL THAT FISH-KISSING--
--YOU REALLY SHOULD SEE THIS...

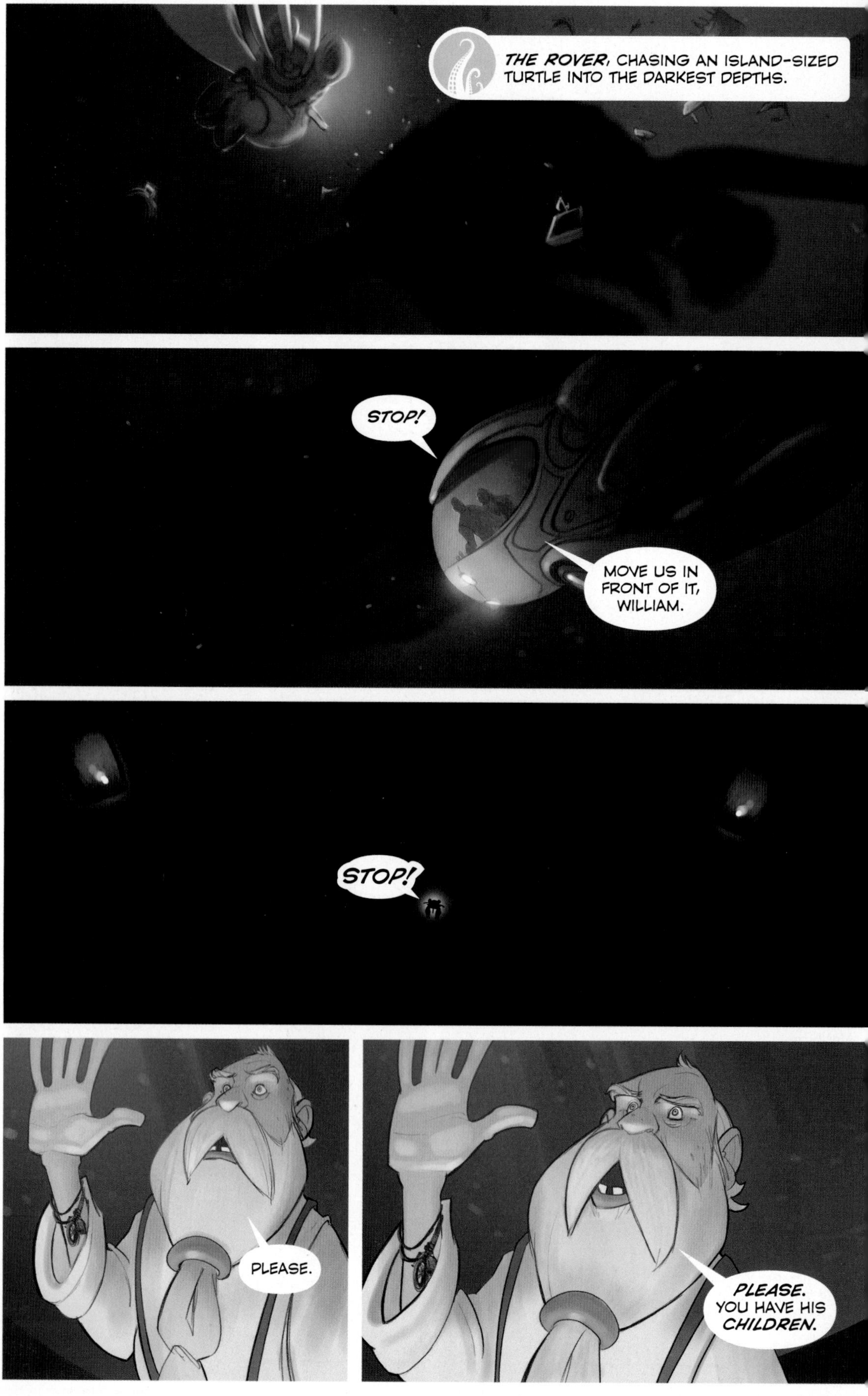
THE ROVER, CHASING AN ISLAND-SIZED TURTLE INTO THE DARKEST DEPTHS.
STOP!
MOVE US IN FRONT OF IT, WILLIAM.
STOP!
PLEASE.
PLEASE. YOU HAVE HIS CHILDREN.

JUST LET US RETRIEVE THEM AND YOU CAN BE ON YOUR WAY.

ROOOOOOOOOOOOON!

"IT'S PULLING ITS HEAD IN!"

"IT'S LETTING US BACK IN THE SHELL..."

...AND YOU JUST *SPOKE* TO A *TURTLE.*

I DID.

DID YOU *KNOW* YOU COULD DO THAT?

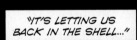

OF COURSE. *ANYONE* CAN TALK TO A TURTLE.

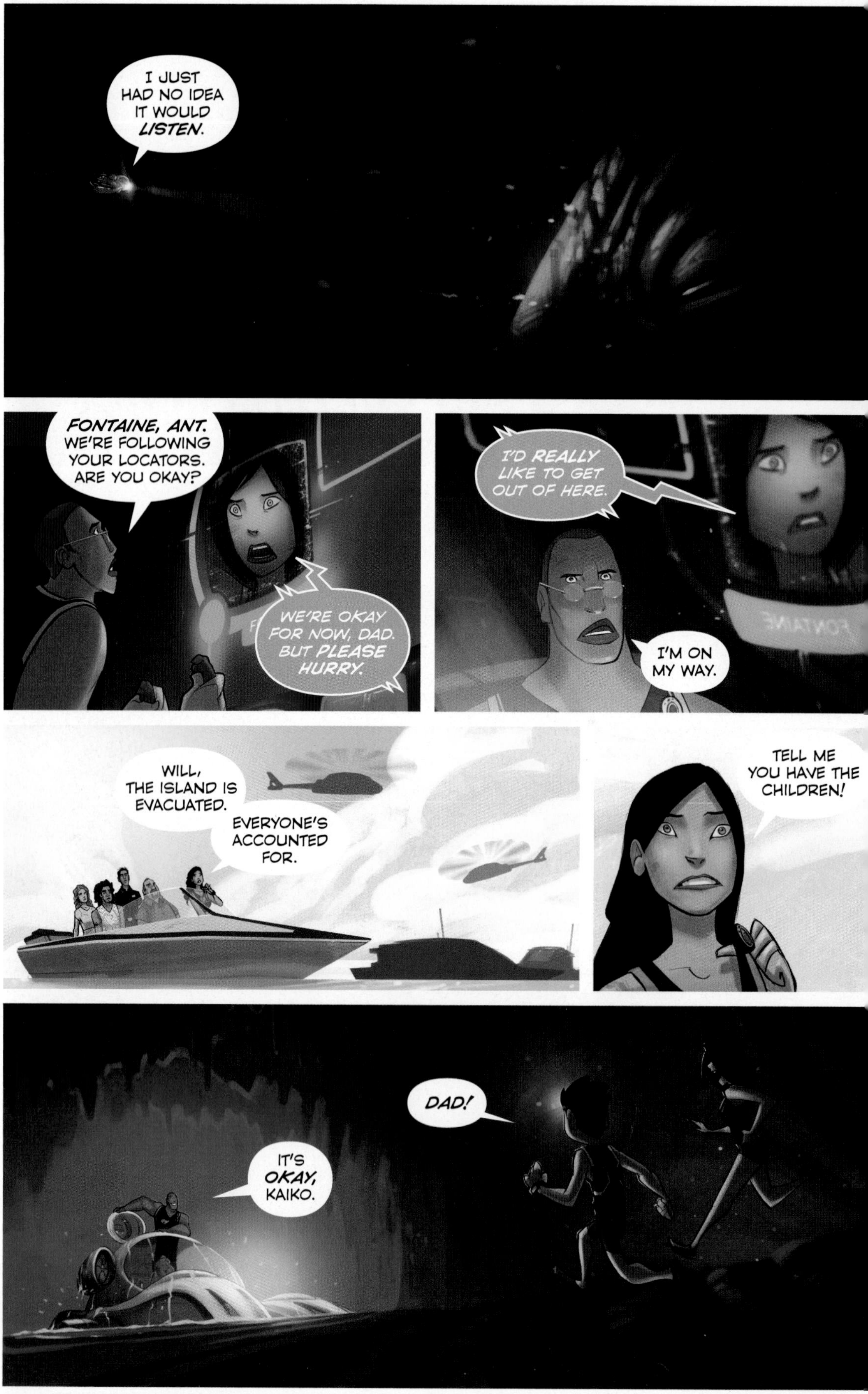

I JUST HAD NO IDEA IT WOULD LISTEN.
FONTAINE, ANT. WE'RE FOLLOWING YOUR LOCATORS. ARE YOU OKAY?
WE'RE OKAY FOR NOW, DAD. BUT PLEASE HURRY.
I'D REALLY LIKE TO GET OUT OF HERE.
FONTAINE
I'M ON MY WAY.
WILL, THE ISLAND IS EVACUATED.
EVERYONE'S ACCOUNTED FOR.
TELL ME YOU HAVE THE CHILDREN!
DAD!
IT'S OKAY, KAIKO.

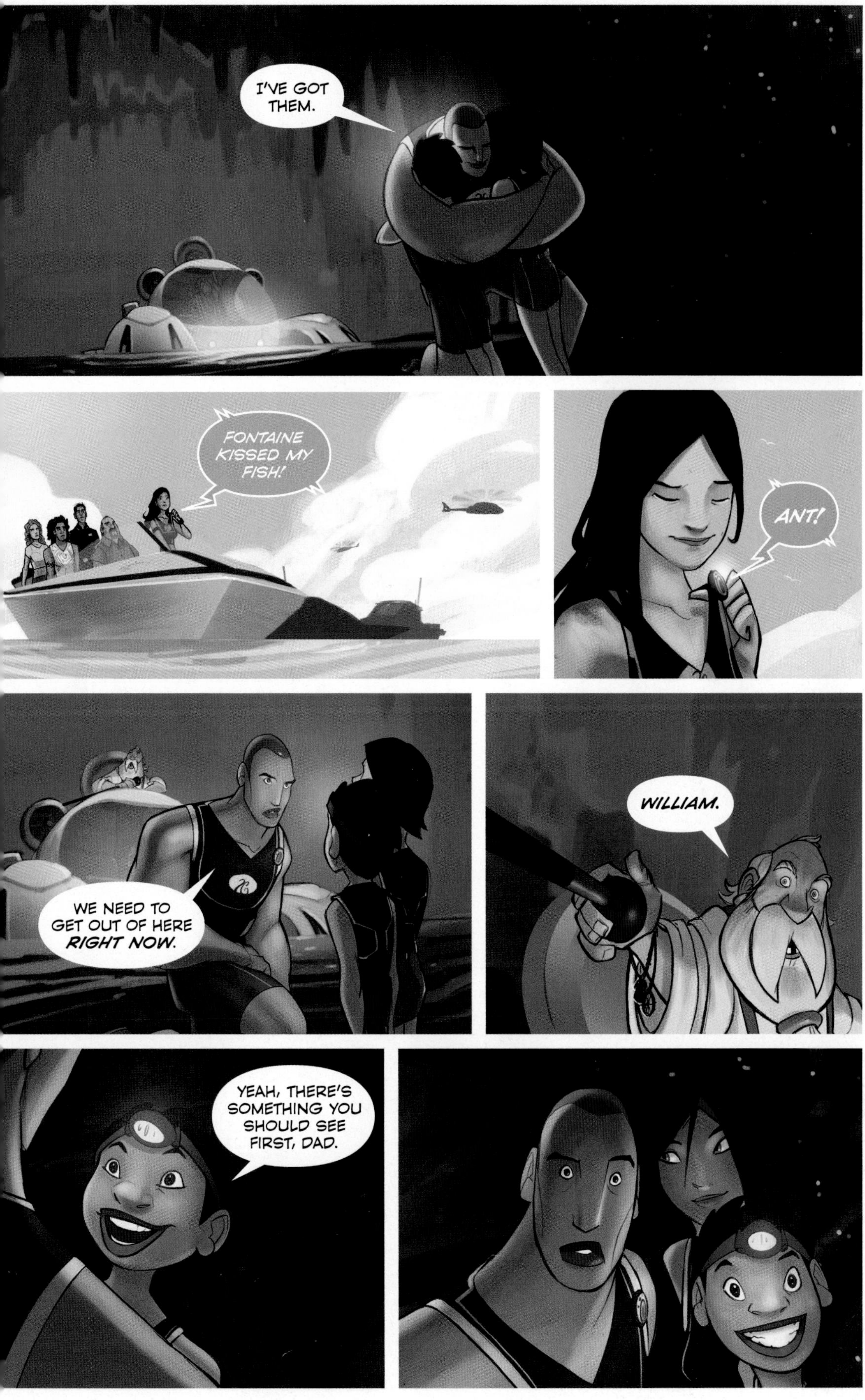
I'VE GOT THEM.
FONTAINE KISSED MY FISH!
ANT!
WE NEED TO GET OUT OF HERE *RIGHT NOW*.
WILLIAM.
YEAH, THERE'S SOMETHING YOU SHOULD SEE FIRST, DAD.

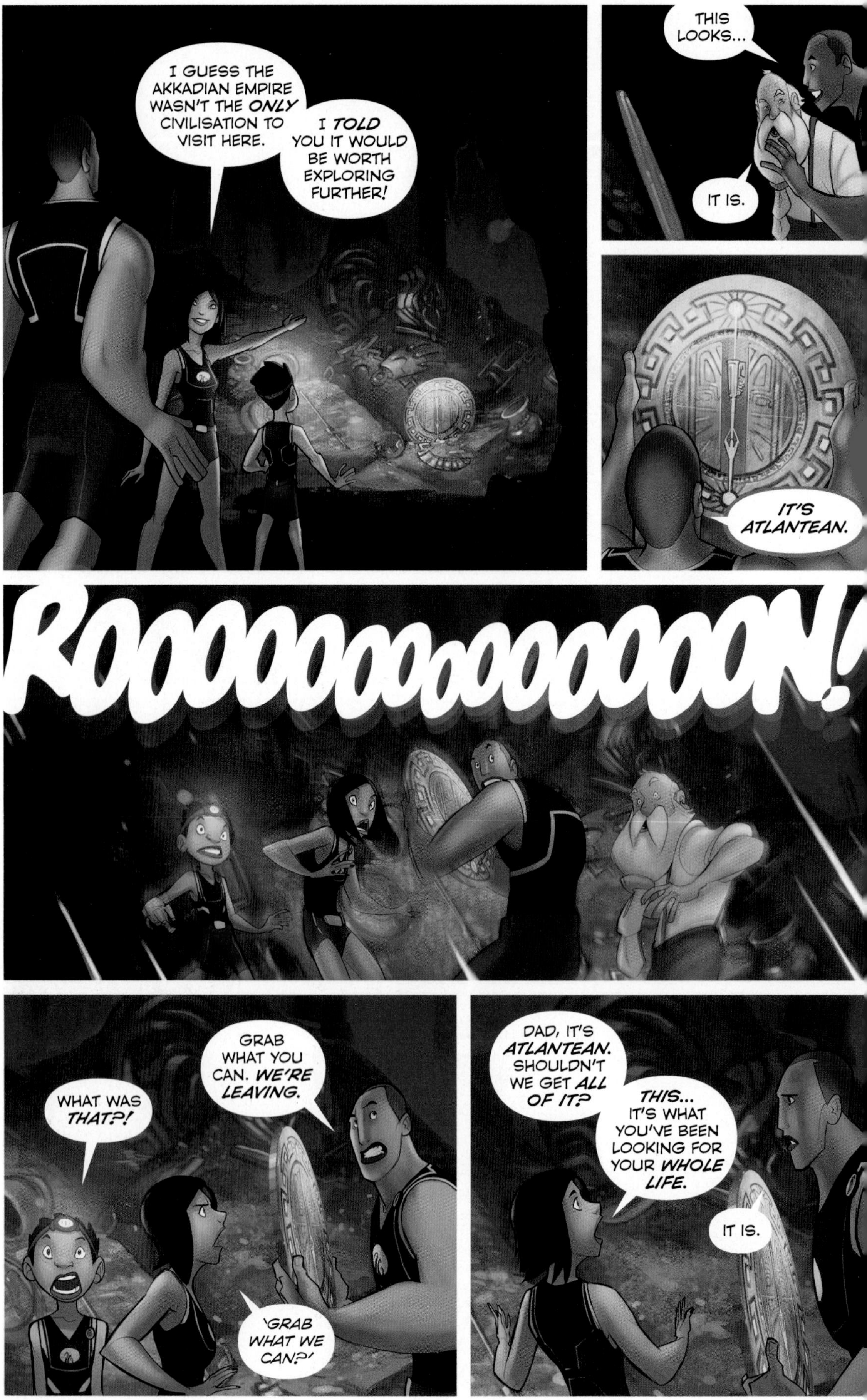
I GUESS THE AKKADIAN EMPIRE WASN'T THE *ONLY* CIVILISATION TO VISIT HERE.
I *TOLD* YOU IT WOULD BE WORTH EXPLORING FURTHER!
THIS LOOKS...
IT IS.
*IT'S ATLANTEAN.*
ROOOOOOOOOOOOON!
WHAT WAS *THAT?!*
GRAB WHAT YOU CAN. *WE'RE LEAVING.*
*'GRAB WHAT WE CAN?'*
DAD, IT'S *ATLANTEAN.* SHOULDN'T WE GET *ALL OF IT?*
*THIS...* IT'S WHAT YOU'VE BEEN LOOKING FOR YOUR *WHOLE LIFE.*
IT IS.

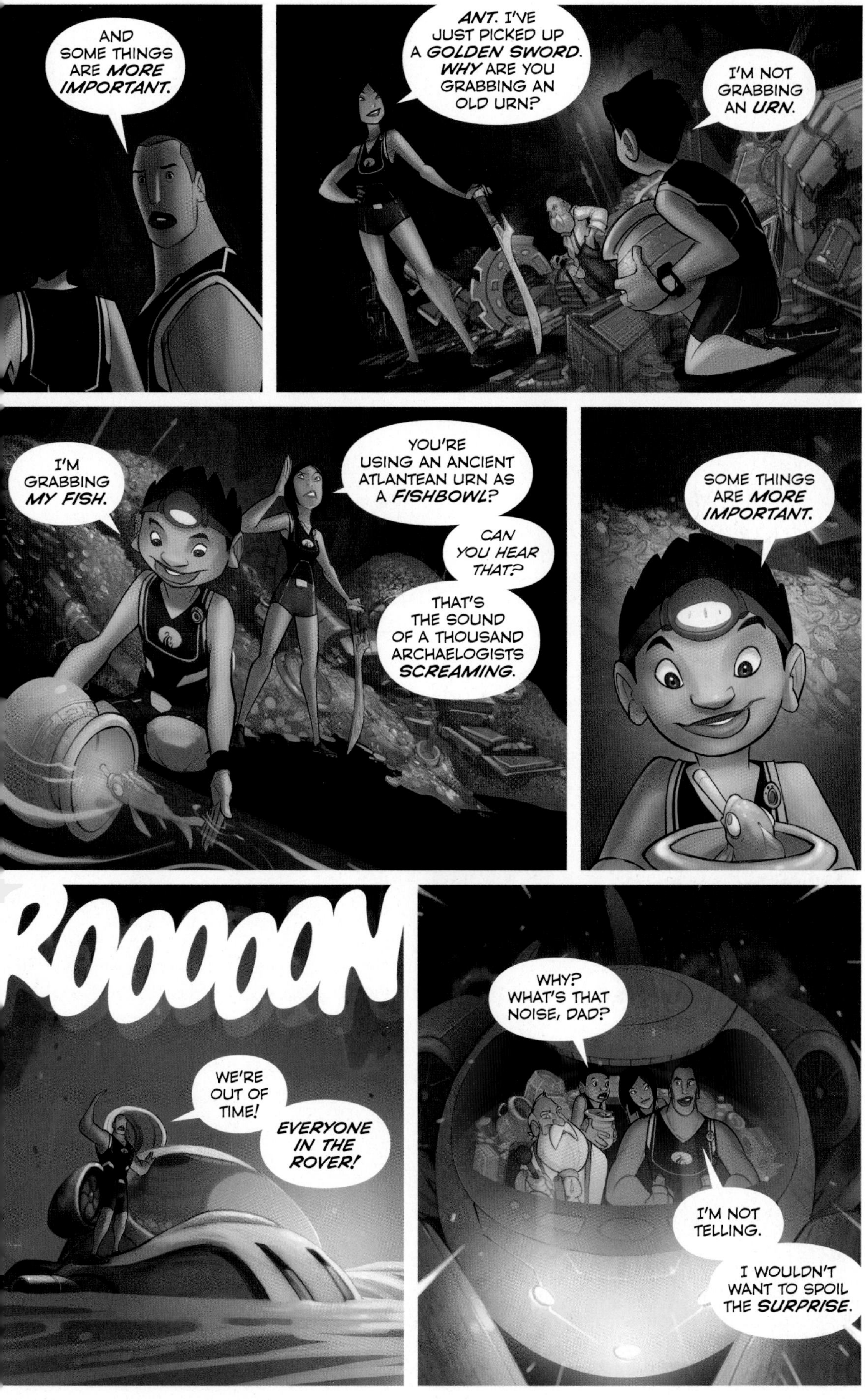
AND SOME THINGS ARE MORE IMPORTANT.
ANT. I'VE JUST PICKED UP A GOLDEN SWORD. WHY ARE YOU GRABBING AN OLD URN?
I'M NOT GRABBING AN URN.
I'M GRABBING MY FISH.
YOU'RE USING AN ANCIENT ATLANTEAN URN AS A FISHBOWL?
CAN YOU HEAR THAT?
THAT'S THE SOUND OF A THOUSAND ARCHAELOGISTS SCREAMING.
SOME THINGS ARE MORE IMPORTANT.
ROOOOON
WE'RE OUT OF TIME!
EVERYONE IN THE ROVER!
WHY? WHAT'S THAT NOISE, DAD?
I'M NOT TELLING.
I WOULDN'T WANT TO SPOIL THE SURPRISE.

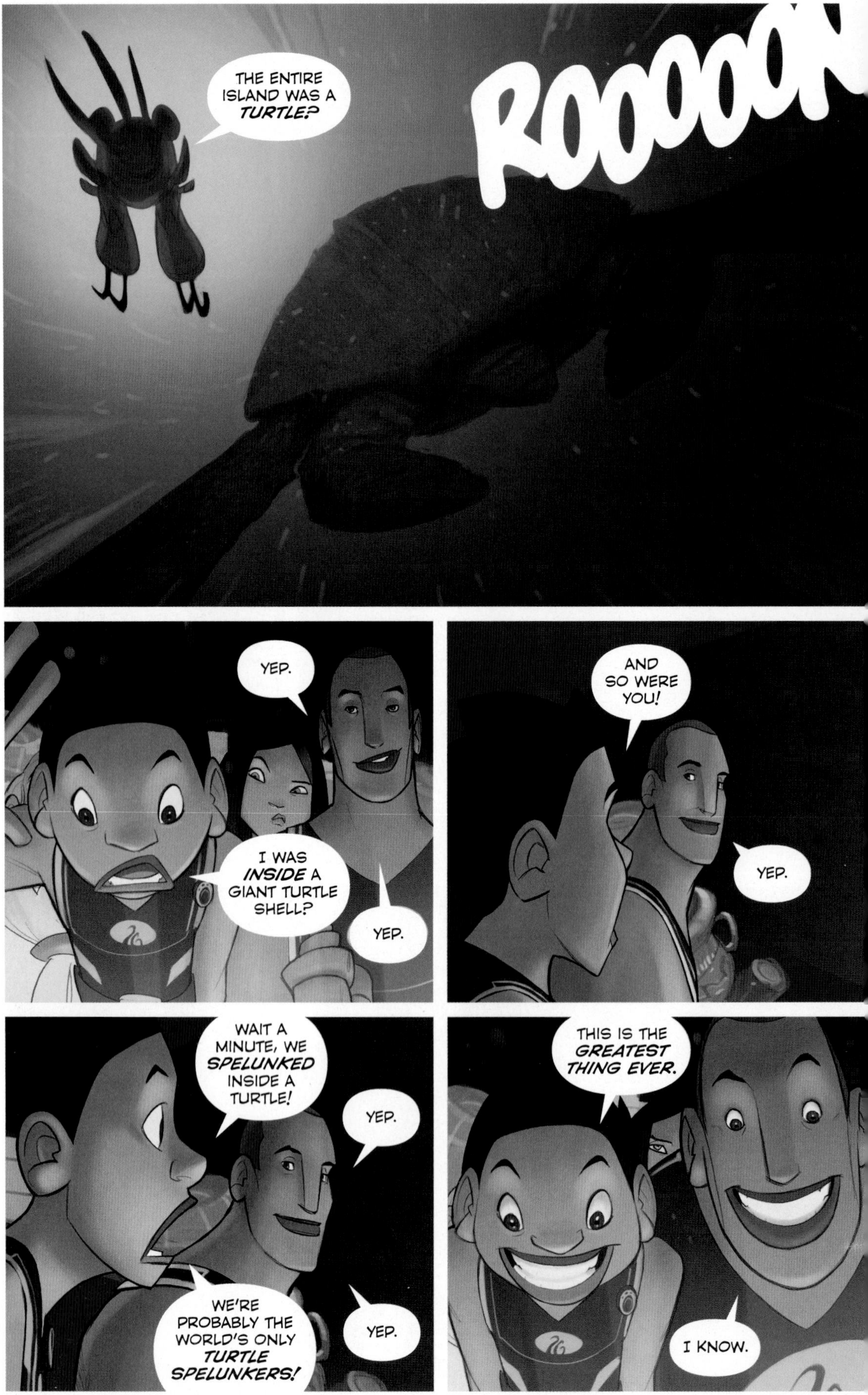
THE ENTIRE ISLAND WAS A TURTLE?
ROOOOON
YEP.
I WAS INSIDE A GIANT TURTLE SHELL?
YEP.
AND SO WERE YOU!
YEP.
WAIT A MINUTE, WE SPELUNKED INSIDE A TURTLE!
YEP.
WE'RE PROBABLY THE WORLD'S ONLY TURTLE SPELUNKERS!
YEP.
THIS IS THE GREATEST THING EVER.
I KNOW.

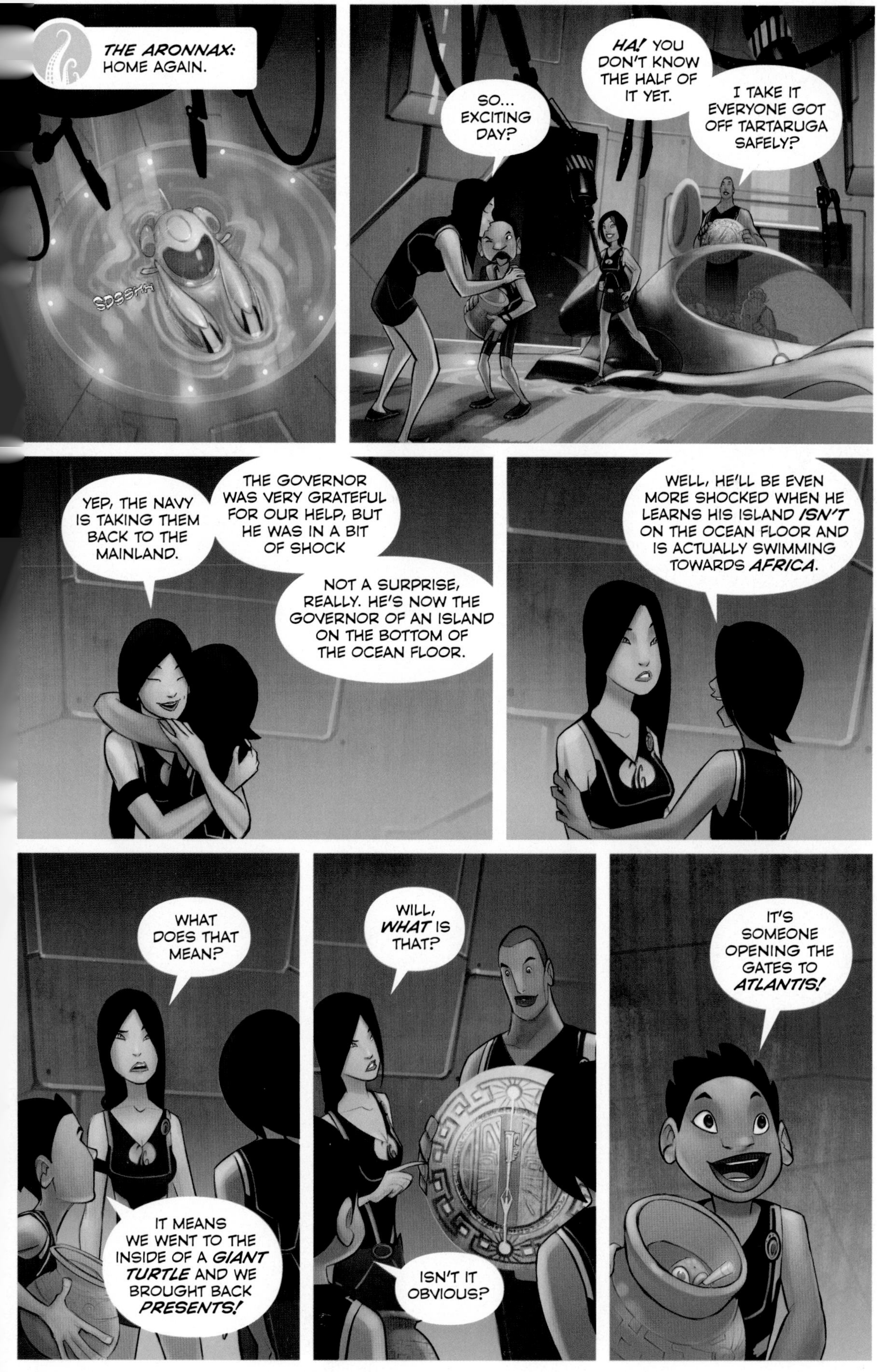
THE ARONNAX: HOME AGAIN.
SDSSHH
SO... EXCITING DAY?
HA! YOU DON'T KNOW THE HALF OF IT YET.
I TAKE IT EVERYONE GOT OFF TARTARUGA SAFELY?
YEP, THE NAVY IS TAKING THEM BACK TO THE MAINLAND.
THE GOVERNOR WAS VERY GRATEFUL FOR OUR HELP, BUT HE WAS IN A BIT OF SHOCK
NOT A SURPRISE, REALLY. HE'S NOW THE GOVERNOR OF AN ISLAND ON THE BOTTOM OF THE OCEAN FLOOR.
WELL, HE'LL BE EVEN MORE SHOCKED WHEN HE LEARNS HIS ISLAND ISN'T ON THE OCEAN FLOOR AND IS ACTUALLY SWIMMING TOWARDS AFRICA.
WHAT DOES THAT MEAN?
IT MEANS WE WENT TO THE INSIDE OF A GIANT TURTLE AND WE BROUGHT BACK PRESENTS!
WILL, WHAT IS THAT?
ISN'T IT OBVIOUS?
IT'S SOMEONE OPENING THE GATES TO ATLANTIS!

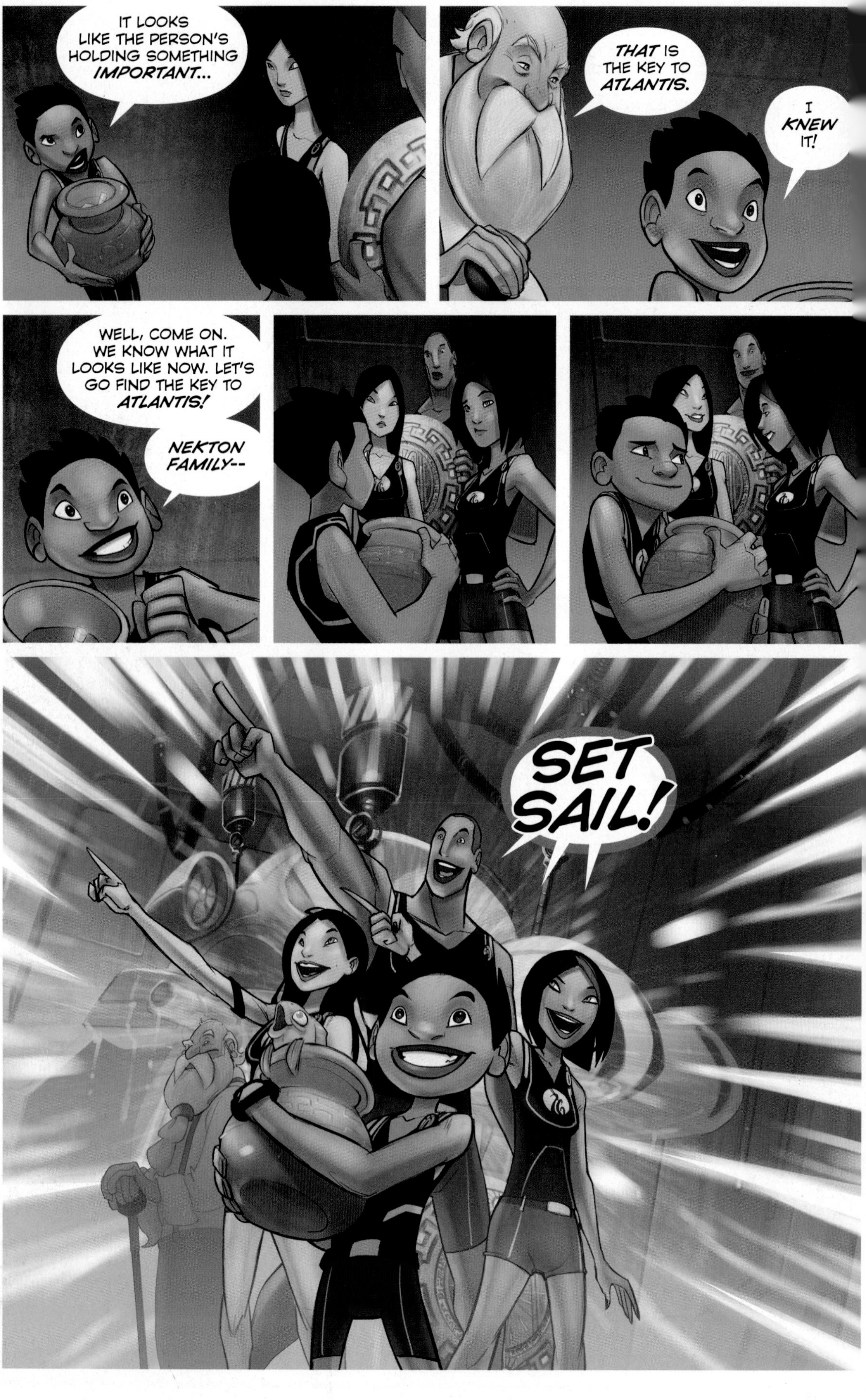

IT LOOKS LIKE THE PERSON'S HOLDING SOMETHING *IMPORTANT...*
*THAT* IS THE KEY TO *ATLANTIS.*
I *KNEW* IT!
WELL, COME ON. WE KNOW WHAT IT LOOKS LIKE NOW. LET'S GO FIND THE KEY TO *ATLANTIS!*
*NEKTON FAMILY--*
SET SAIL!

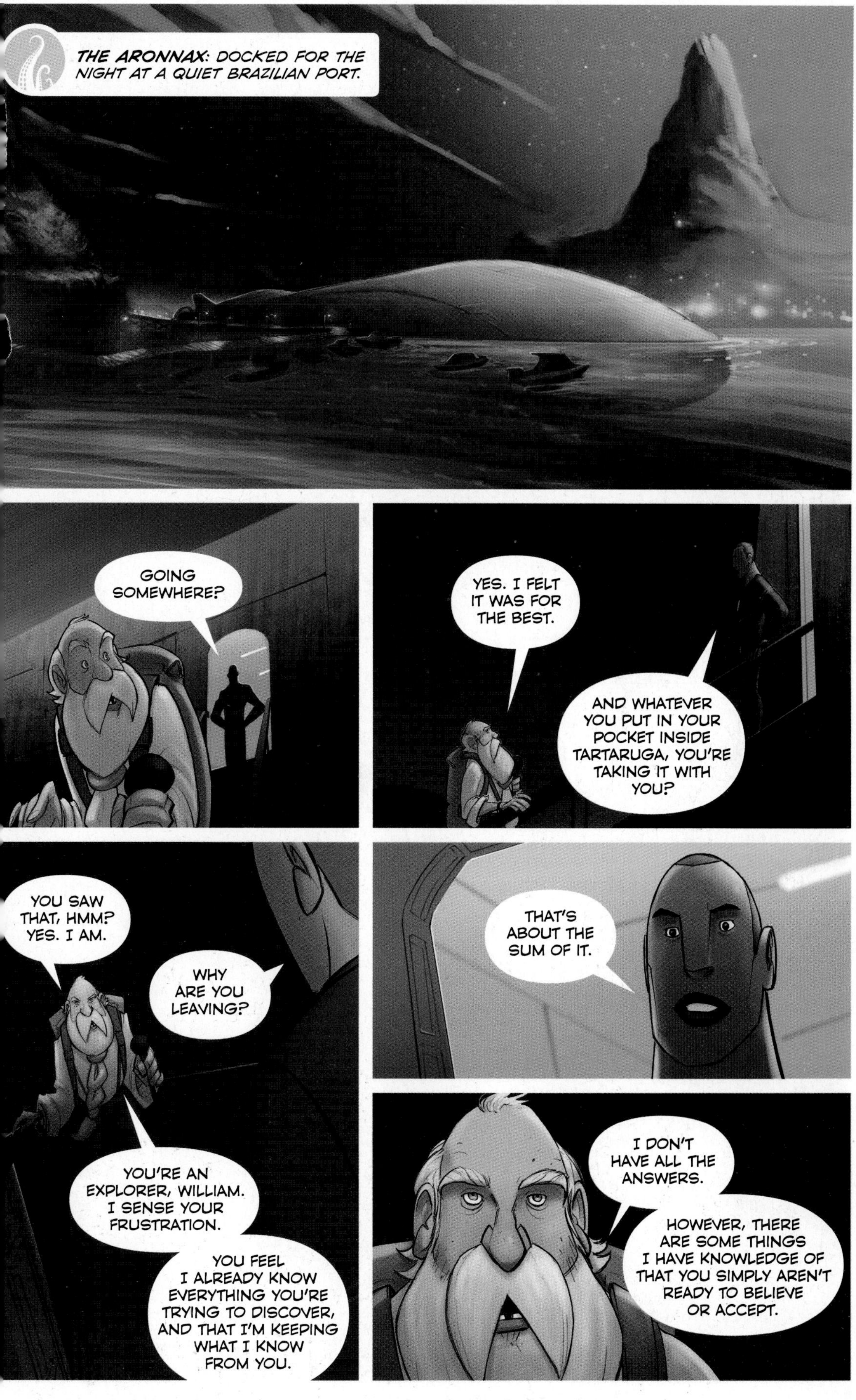
THE ARONNAX: DOCKED FOR THE NIGHT AT A QUIET BRAZILIAN PORT.
GOING SOMEWHERE?
YES. I FELT IT WAS FOR THE BEST.
AND WHATEVER YOU PUT IN YOUR POCKET INSIDE TARTARUGA, YOU'RE TAKING IT WITH YOU?
YOU SAW THAT, HMM? YES. I AM.
WHY ARE YOU LEAVING?
YOU'RE AN EXPLORER, WILLIAM. I SENSE YOUR FRUSTRATION.
YOU FEEL I ALREADY KNOW EVERYTHING YOU'RE TRYING TO DISCOVER, AND THAT I'M KEEPING WHAT I KNOW FROM YOU.
THAT'S ABOUT THE SUM OF IT.
I DON'T HAVE ALL THE ANSWERS.
HOWEVER, THERE ARE SOME THINGS I HAVE KNOWLEDGE OF THAT YOU SIMPLY AREN'T READY TO BELIEVE OR ACCEPT.

WHY DON'T YOU TRY ME? I WAS JUST INSIDE A *GIANT TURTLE*. I'M PRETTY OPEN TO THE BIZARRE.

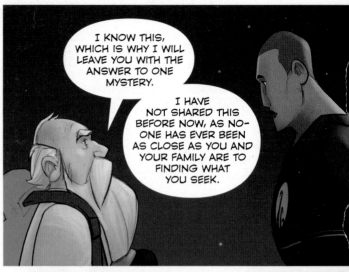

I KNOW THIS, WHICH IS WHY I WILL LEAVE YOU WITH THE ANSWER TO ONE MYSTERY.

I HAVE NOT SHARED THIS BEFORE NOW, AS NO-ONE HAS EVER BEEN AS CLOSE AS YOU AND YOUR FAMILY ARE TO FINDING WHAT YOU SEEK.

DO YOU KNOW WHY YOUR FAMILY HAS ALWAYS BEEN PULLED TOWARDS THE OCEAN?

WHY EVERY GENERATION OF NEKTONS HAVE EXPLORED THE SEAS?

DO YOU KNOW WHY YOU SEARCH FOR ATLANTIS SO TENACIOUSLY?

BECAUSE YOU ARE *FROM* THERE. YOUR ANCESTORS WERE *ATLANTEAN*.

WILLIAM NEKTON.

YOU ARE SEARCHING FOR HOME.

END.